Critics Agree:

JUST ONE LIFE

is the funniest book you'll read this year!

A 2022 ERIC HOFFER FICTION AWARD FINALIST!

"A great pick for fans of John Kennedy Toole's Pulitzer Prize winning, *A Confederacy of Dunces.*" *--Booklife*

"A wild blast of humor, wit, and heartbreak, beautifully written. Ernest Cohen's *JUST ONE LIFE* is a must-read novel." (Highest Rating) *--Anthony Avina, Hollywood Book Review*

"Ernest Cohen, a master at mixing genres, writes with finesse delivering a complex novel that skillfully interweaves heady doses of satire, black comedy, fantasy, family saga, social commentary, and even a touch of magic realism. (It's a) rollicking tale, seeded with profound insights throughout."
--BlueInk Reviews

"Cohen's debut novel is, in a word, brilliant. He weaves a tale of life and love so mesmerizing one finds it hard to put down. Protagonist Geoffrey's witty one-liners are truly laugh-out-loud funny. The writing is crisp, the plot is imaginative, and the characters are memorable. The novel's three parts —*"The Art of*

Coincidence," "Season of the Witch," and "The Silver Shoes"—are contained in 450 pages of pure, must-read genius. Cohen is an author to watch. His work is certain to stand the test of time. And if the Governors of the Given have a say, it will become a classic." (Highest Rating)   --Kat Kennedy, *US Review*

"*JUST ONE LIFE* is stunning to the core. It is so incredibly fun and complex; I cannot stop talking about it. Ernest Cohen is a master in the making. Highly recommended for any reader seeking something totally original. You will not be disappointed." (Highest Rating)

--Anelynde Smit, *ReadersFavorite.com*

Ernest Cohen succeeds in spinning a hilarious and thought-provoking yarn. *JUST ONE LIFE* is a captivating reflection on life's ironies and challenges. Its lively observations and unexpected twists will keep readers involved to the end. (Highest Rating)

--D. Donovan, Senior Reviewer, *Midwest Book Review*

"Set in a sprawling satire of Los Angeles and filled with strong comic scenes, *JUST ONE LIFE* inspires full-throated LOLs."

--*Booklife*

"Cohen's multilayered debut knits together elaborately written, comical scenes. Readers will find his tale of Geoffrey's zany existence worth the trip."   --*Kirkus Reviews*

Cohen leaves readers with a real sense of satisfaction after a raucous, often hilarious ride. (Highest Rating)

-- Barbara B. Scott, *Pacific Book Review*

ABOUT
JUST ONE LIFE

Meet Geoffrey Zukor, a bumbler of superhero proportions whose daily calamities have him waltzing through life with all the grace of a one-legged unicyclist. But then, something happens, something quite extraordinary — *everything changes*. Did he finally catch a lucky break or was it actually the consequence of an intervention by none other than a Grand Master in the *Art of Coincidence?*

Full of humor and heartbreak, *JUST ONE LIFE* is an exploration of a very special father/daughter relationship, finding the courage to change your life, and the sustaining power of friendship.

ABOUT
THE AUTHOR

Showing promise at an early age, ERNEST COHEN was accepted straight from high school into an elite graduate school program at New York University School of the Arts. This is his debut novel, over 20 years in the making.

JUST ONE LIFE

Cover, Book Design, and Graphics by Ernest Cohen
Cover typeset in Arial
Text set in Minion Pro

Book Two "Season of the Witch" tower graphic constructed of elements from a drawing by J. C. Ohio.

Print Date: October 17, 2022

The author welcomes comments at:
www.ECintheOC.com
ec@ecintheoc.com

JUST ONE LIFE

PART ONE

THE ART OF COINCIDENCE

THE ART OF COINCIDENCE

By changing
JUST ONE LIFE
you can change the world

—The Governors of The Given

A darkness reached for him, a darkness that would not be denied. He stood there, trembling. His mind raced…

Who, who, who's there?

He searched for an answer, but no; the night refused him her secrets. Still, he could sense something, something close, something that terrified him. His eyes jittered, chest tight. He couldn't breathe.

Is there something behind me? Who is it? Who?

He had to run, escape, but carefully, silently. The slightest sound could—

Shhh…

Geoffrey Zukor inched his right foot forward, his back hunched, expecting a beating. He froze. It took a moment to sink in.

Nothing…? Nothing happened? Really?

Ever so cautiously, Geoffrey brought his left foot up alongside his right and then even a bit further. Again, he waited, so very, very afraid. But…

Still nothing?

And so, he dared scoot himself forward a bit more. And then a bit more. And then even a bit more.

Nothing! Nothing happened!

He couldn't believe it. His chest loosened. A fragile flame of optimism dared flicker within.

Maybe… Maybe it'll be okay?

As if on cue, the black, weather-beaten planks beneath his feet splintered, crackling like embers of a midnight fire, and then they gave way all together.

Geoffrey screamed. His arms shot out, his hands searching for something, anything to latch onto, anything that might save his fall. But no — no, no, no — it was not to be, not on an occasion as momentous as this. Geoffrey's screams filled the sky as he tumbled head over heels into a dark, death-smeared chasm of certain doom.

THE ART OF COINCIDENCE

Rather dramatic, that whole tumbling into the chasm of doom bit, wasn't it? Surprisingly though, drama was not the objective here. What the man behind the curtain was going for was memorable. That's what you need in a situation like this; you need m-e-m-o-r-a-b-l-e. For Geoffrey's impending high-speed head butt with the cold, blood-stained rocks of the canyon floor wasn't just some run-of-the-mill neural oscillation run amuck. No, this snippet of dream was something else entirely.

But to understand all that is transpiring, all that is hidden from view, we must travel, *mi compadre,* across both distance and dimension to a laboratory dug deep into the core of a distant planet — a world that moves, unnamed, hidden in a nebula of embryonic stars.

The main floor area of the lab was vast by any standard, and yet remained empty save for a most peculiar thing: a 6.3333-square inch black cube floating 6.3333-inches above the stone floor, this without any apparent means of propulsion. Neither were there wires nor antennae protruding from its surface except for when things were moving along better than expected. Then The Cube would sprout a pair of Mickey Mouse legs and do a jaunty little jig for the amusement of all. But sadly, those times were few and far between for The Cube didn't really care much for its work, the endless computation of probabilities, environmental dynamics, sociological influences, personal histories and inclinations, space/time confluences, astral underpinnings, and the quantification of sexual proclivities. Its calculations were based on a theory developed by the brightest minds in the galaxy, a collective known as The Governors of The Given. Their charge was to help Earthlings avoid the fate that had befallen similar creatures on other worlds as they struggled to evolve from lower life forms (aka Republicans) into elevated beings and therefore take their place as a positive force in the universe. Their name reflected the focal point of their research — data — a word derived from a Latin noun meaning, *"something given."* After thousands of years of scientific analysis, The Governors proved that with a full and complete understanding of factors influencing the present, it was simply a matter of applied mathematics to ascertain how, with careful manipulation, one could arrive at a specifically re-tailored future. And once every possible future was identified, each could be analyzed and the one that provided for the greatest good was implemented for the benefit of all. It was as simple as that. At least it should have been...

THE ART of COINCIDENCE

Above an elevated platform in the far corner of the facility, multi-angle, high-def images of Geoffrey's downward spiral were being projected onto an array of shimmering screens. Below them stood a bespectacled old man of great renown known by everyone within five moons as The Giver, The Giver of the Given.

Dressed in black tuxedo pants, a pleated black cummerbund, and a ruffled lavender shirt cut with a black lace garter across his right bicep, he studied a glass wall of pulsing meters, gauges, and graphs. He checked his watch. The countdown began.

In three, two, one… Right on schedule, a small white ball arrived via a pneumatic tube that protruded from the floor on the left side of his workstation, stopping with a pronounced *"Thup!"* On its heels, another ball arrived, it too with a *"Thup!"* And then came the third and final ball, also stopping with a — nothing.

Nothing?? The old man blinked in disbelief. *Where's the third ball?* He gave the tube an aggravated little wiggle, but still, nothing.

His eyes darted back to his watch and then up at Geoffrey on the screens behind him. Clearly exasperated by this unexpected turn of events, the old man sprang into action. He raced down a dozen or so steps and took off in the direction of The Cube, his black patent leather shoes slapping the stone floor like a Gene Krupa drum solo. Moving faster than humanly possible, it was only seconds before he skid to a stop.

The Cube tilted toward him and smirked, "I'm so happy to see you — said no one — *ever!*"

"We don't have time for this!" the old man scolded.

The Cube shrugged. "I told you not to install Windows, but did you listen? *Nooooo!*"

"We don't have time for this!" the old man repeated, even more urgently.

"You're reminding me what time it is? That's a good one!"

"Ball, now!"

"Is there a vent open somewhere? It's terribly drafty in here."

"NOW!"

"Sorry but I refused to work in these conditions. It's simply beneath my station." A brown derby materialized on top of The Cube along with a Sherlock Holmes pipe that bobbed beneath his suddenly sprouted handlebar mustache. "So be a good boy, won't you, and run grab me a spot of tea? Go on. Ta-ta." He then broke into a rather spirited version of *Rule, Britannia.*

With two fingers, the old man double-tapped the top of his unadorned left wrist and said, "Jules, bring Duke down to the lab, please."

A voice from no particular direction replied, "Yes, sir. Right away, sir."

To the cube, The Giver added, "Sorry to interrupt, but you remember Duke, don't you? Such a good doggie."

"You wouldn't dare! If I ever see that mutt again, I swear I'll—"

"BALL NOW OR YOU'LL BE SWIMMING IN IT!"

The Cube stewed for a moment.

The old man hollered, "Here, boy. You remember Cubie, don't you? Let's make sure everyone knows this is your favorite spot, okay?"

"Fine! It's done! It's done!"

With that, the old man was gone.

"And just so you know, you call me Cubie again, I'll short every circuit this side of the Suns of Galatar, got it? And would it kill you to bring me a cheese and pickle sandwich every once in a while? And have them hold the cheese. Cheese gives me the gassies!"

When the old man returned to his desk, three balls were indeed waiting. Taking nary a second to compose himself, he removed the first ball from its plastic enclosure, reached for the gold-sputtered diaphragm of a Western Electric Model 600 Microphone dangling from above, and with all the solemnity the Queen's English could afford, announced, "Number 5." His words filled the vast facility and beyond. He removed the second ball. "Number 9." And then the last, "Number 4." The old man's pale eyes shifted back to his watch. He had made it, but just barely — probably not in time to do much good.

The numbers 5, 9, 4 swirled around Geoffrey, but by then he was in no mood for omens. For all the while, he had been falling, shrinking, down, down, with only seconds remaining before he was devoured by the darkness of death.

THE ART OF COINCIDENCE

"No!" Geoffrey belched, still wrapped in nightmare thick as Shelob's web. With death only seconds away, he thrashed from side to side, desperately pleading, "No! No! Noo! Nooo! NOOOOOOO!" And with that, he was released, unbound, plopping back into the present with a *"Thup!"* as if he himself were a small, white ball arriving via pneumatic tube. In the process, his eyes, naught more than two small circles of fear, popped open and bounced frantically about until it finally started to sink in: *Wha... I, I, I was dreaming? That, that was a dream?*

Amid the rasp of his labored breathing, other questions rushed forward as well, and after a blurry glance around, came the answers:

Oh... the airport, right, right... which was followed by a wince and, *I was yelling, wasn't I? Like yelling out loud...*

Geoffrey Zukor had aced it on both accounts; he was at the airport, the Albuquerque Sunport to be exact, and yes, he had yelled *NOOOOOOO!* so loud a whole crowd of people were now staring at him. When he opened his eyes, a man standing several rows away even offered up a congratulatory cheer, followed by a few others seated off to the left.

"Great. Just great..." he grumbled under his breath.

Geoffrey straightened in his plastic seat and cracked an embarrassed smile to all. But then, in a panic, his eyes shot downward. *My—*

Oh, thank God...

Yes, his computer satchel was still tethered to his black *Tumi* roller bag, both resting undisturbed at his feet. Relieved, he exhaled into his seatback with an audible sigh. And there he sat.

It wasn't long before he started to drift off again, such was the weight of his weariness. His eyes slowly closed as his head rolled forward, extruding the ample fat of his under-chin like a thick smear of cream cheese out the backside of a bagel. He caught himself with a jerk.

Coffee... I really need some coffee...

Another squinty look around the gate area...

What? Why is everyone is still staring at me?

Again, he straightened up and for good measure brushed some imaginary dust off his two sizes too small and two years too old, size 42, dark green, single-breasted sports coat. Then he nodded toward the crowd as if to say, *Well, there it is then, people. I am now fully awake — Eyes wide open, see? — so please, just go on about your business. Show's over. I won't be embarrassing myself any further today... let's hope.*

But even without his glasses, Geoffrey Zukor could see his audience was not dispersing.

What is going on? Haven't they seen a guy doze off at an airport before? And then he wondered, *Maybe they're like a band of gypsies or something, just waiting for a chance to steal my luggage?* Geoffrey scooted his bag closer to his leg.

For most, all this unwanted attention would prove unnerving, but such was not the case with our man; no, never for the unflappable Mr. Z.

Well, that might be overstating things — *a bit.* For in truth, Geoffrey was rattled by the crowd of people eyeballing him, deeply rattled in fact, just as he had been his entire life whenever he felt put on the spot or was confronted with an awkward social situation. But at least this fact wasn't lost on him as it might have been on a lesser man. No, even early on, Geoffrey Zukor recognized his spinelessness as a liability and had decided to do something about it.

This realization first struck him after giving an oral report one afternoon in the third grade. His speech was the stuff legends were made of — no, not for its topic nor the depth of his research — but rather for his delivery. You see, just the thought of having to get up and speak in front of the class terrified Geoffrey, feelings that only grew while sitting there, waiting and waiting and waiting to be called upon. (When your name is Zukor, going last is not exactly a rare occurrence.) Finally, it was his turn. With all eyes upon him, he awkwardly made his way up to the blackboard, turned, cleared his throat, and then threw up all over some unsuspecting know-it-all who always wanted to sit in the front.

Those familiar with the latest findings in Quantum Physics can confirm the viability of the Law of Attraction, which simply stated means "like attracts like." While the credit for that discovery was bestowed on physicist John Lekner, Geoffrey deserves at least a nod, for one thing was indisputably clear: "Like attracts like" sure works with vomit! Several kids in the class (the one with Geoffrey's regurgitated cafeteria spaghetti all over her plus two other highly empathetic, grossed-out children sitting nearby) all screamed, screamed again, and then started gagging themselves, vomit not far behind. This, in most retellings, is considered the second round of hurling. I will spare you the details of what followed, but suffice it to say, with the sight, sound, and especially the smell of a Bulimics for Buttigieg fundraiser wafting through the classroom, said second round of hurling was followed by a third, a fourth, and even a fifth. In the end, spaghetti was everywhere (except in the children's stomachs, of course), dotted with the occasional bit of sack-lunch peanut butter and jelly, leaving such a lasting impression on the children that even a year later several mothers reported their kids barfing whenever they drove passed a Chef Boyardee billboard.

Geoffrey, whose report was on volcanoes, tried to explain away the mishap: "It was a special effect. I was erupting, get it?" But none of the kids bought it. Humiliated, "Zukor the Puker" (which was precisely what every kid on the planet called him from that day forward) vowed to never let anything like that happen again. And so, starting right then and there, whenever an uncomfortable social situation arose, he willed himself to stand his ground, paste an unbothered smile on his face, and above all else, try not to barf on anyone. In other words, he would pretend to be something he clearly was not— the sort of fellow who remains steadfastly confident and composed under pressure. And a brave stance it was too, especially since it was obvious to even a dead-drunk dodo bird that the truth was irrefutably to the contrary. This calls into question whether there was any benefit to his pretense at all, except perhaps to allow at least some small part of himself to hope against hope that maybe, just maybe, there might be someone out there who couldn't see through his all-too-transparent portrayal of a man who wasn't nearly as easily intimidated as he so painfully knew himself to be. Sadly, he has yet to encounter such an individual and each year received a world-class collection of Christmas cards from door-to-door salesmen to prove it.

And so, due to his lifelong insecurity surrounding his obvious tilt toward timidity, Geoffrey was determined to prove his manliness and show this crowd of airport onlookers that he was not about to be untied by their stares. Therefore, rather than simply up and flee like a urinary incontinent after three cups of coffee, he decided he would stay right where he was and ignore them, simply ignore them, or at least so he would pretend.

So go ahead, folks. You want to stand around staring at me, no problem. It doesn't bother me a bit! Not a bit!

To show just how unbothered and relaxed he was, he released a fake yawn into the air, always a good start in situations like these. Considering how tired he felt, it was surprising the yawn wasn't more of an award winner, but even lackluster as it was, the yawn remained a solid choice and he was off to a fine, fine start.

Mr. Cool, Calm, & Collected then leisurely leaned back and raised his right knee, his right foot lifting a few inches off the floor. With all the *Umpf!* his non-existent abdominal muscles could muster, he pitched his upper body forward as his hands strained to reach over his medicine ball of a stomach, which in profile appeared to be even larger than he was. With fingers quivering, he was just able to grab hold of his right shin, and then, as if reeling in a giant tuna, eventually managed to hoist his right foot onto the top of his left knee. *Et voila!* His legs were crossed! How relaxed can one guy be!

From this stunning display of agility, it probably comes as no surprise to learn that our man Zukor did not follow his doctor's advice and rattle off twenty toe-touches every morn. But then, how could he? The poor guy couldn't even reach the change in his pocket without a fair-sized grunt or two; how was he ever going to touch his toes? Now, upper thigh touches? Okay, he could probably swing that, but toe touches were going to have to wait for a foot to sprout from his belly button.

Sitting there, ever so *faux*-laxed, Geoffrey snuck a sideways glance back out toward the crowd.

Oh my God, they're all still staring at me! Every one of them! Well, fine. Fine, fine, fine!

But as he sat there feeling anything but fine, he felt his right foot starting to inch away from him and it wasn't long before it sat dangerously close to the edge of his knee. So as not to appear a fat guy who couldn't even cross his legs, he corralled the front side of his ankle with both of his hands, this to counteract the tension between his fat calf, his fat thigh, and his especially fat stomach, all trying to share the same small space with his apparently highly claustrophobic foot. As the pressure from these competing forces mounted, and mount rapidly they did, he was forced to repeatedly re-tighten his grasp and do what he could to wrangle his ankle back in. This man/leg tug-a-war went on for some time, although smart money was clearly on the leg. And right the smart money was, too. Much to Geoffrey's dismay, his leg's ever-increasing pull eventually wrenched his shoulder blades up around his ears and drew his upper body so far forward that his back collapsed into a large hump. *Yikes!* Now Showing: Geoffrey Zukor in *Invasion of the Overweight Turtle People from Planet X!*

As he sat there contorting into a tortoise, Geoffrey wondered, *What's happened to me? When did just crossing my legs start to feel like being a last-minute stand-in for Wetzel, The Human Pretzel?*

And yet he would not give up—Oh no, not he!—well, at least not until a blistering bolt of pain flashed wickedly along the inside of his right knee, causing him to wince so severely one would have thought he was trying to pop a pimple on the tip of his nose using only his cheek muscles.

Ooohhh! Okay! All right! Maybe the leg-crossing thing wasn't such a good idea after all...

As nonchalantly as possible, which you can imagine to be not nonchalantly at all, he released his white-knuckle grasp on his leg and — *Vroom!* — off it went, his foot launching straight into the air where it hung for a moment, wobbling as if he had suddenly sprouted the world's biggest *stiffy* and it was taking a moment to wave hello to the crowd. Then it flopped to the floor with a pronounced thud.

Ooooh! Ooh... I am ignoring the whole crowd of people watching me just as I am ignoring the friggin' cramp in my right leg... Ooooh!

People who I am ignoring, may I have your attention please? There is no excruciating pain in my right leg—none at all!—and the excruciating pain that is in my right leg does not bother me one teensy-weensy, excruciating bit. Got it? I am as loose and limber as a contortionist hooker after a Vegas weekend with Shaquille O'Neal. Now for God's sake, LEAVE ME ALONE!!

But disperse, they did not...

THE ART OF COINCIDENCE

Well, that was it! Now he was angry. *Really* angry. Geoffrey didn't know what they were up to, but whatever it was, he had had all he was going to take of it. It was time to bring out the big guns and do what every guy does when he's all-alone, not in pain, and no one is watching him. (No, not that! The man's in the middle of an airport, for Christ's sake!) No, Mr. Z was going to whistle. That's what men do to fill the idle moments of their day. They sit around and whistle! And what could be more appropriate. The whistling man, an icon of nonchalance.

And so, he began, his eyebrows rising toward his disappearing hairline, buoyed by a rush of incoming air ballooning his chest. Then he pushed his lips forward into an exaggerated pucker. To the casual passerby, it may have appeared that Geoffrey was doing a cheap Ed Sullivan impersonation, but no; the man was whistling!

He started off rather meekly, ever so softly whistling one of the little ditties he always whistles whenever he's alone, not in pain, and no one is watching him. In other words, he had no idea what he was whistling; he was making the damn thing up as he went along. The result was a tune so improbable it sounded like a cross between *The Andy Griffith Show* theme and *In-A-Gadda-Da-Vida*. But the funny thing was, once he got into it some, it started to sound pretty good, at least to Geoffrey anyway, which I guess is not all that surprising considering his musical tastes ran to the Perry Como side of The Captain and Tennille. And so, on he whistled, and as he did, he found himself starting to enjoy his newly discovered whistling talents, even throwing in slight head bobs here and there for good measure. And as his little tune progressed, so did his emotional involvement with the material, the swell of the music eventually transforming him into a full-blown, whistling Satchmo. *Go, Louie, go!*

His hooting continued, forging new sonic ground with a wholly unique blend of *fortissimo, tremolo,* and *squeaky screen door-o.* After a minute or two, he managed to squeeze out another glance around the room.

What? That's impossible! They're all still staring at me! What is going on? This can't be happening! It just can't!

He yanked his glasses out of his shirt pocket, slipped them on, and then blinked back at the crowd.

But they are! They're all still staring at me! Every single one of them! And look at their faces. Oh my God! They're so angry! What did I ever do to them? They look like they want to rip my head off! I mean, these folks aren't just angry, they're like zombie-angry... Maybe that's it! Maybe it's Zombie Thanksgiving and I'm gonna be the turkey!

A Rockwell-esque image floated through Geoffrey's mind of an idyllic, small town, all-American zombie family, lingering around the after-Thanksgiving table, each in repose with bloated stomachs and satiated smiles on their zombie faces. At the head of the table, sat ol' Grandpa zombie enjoying his corncob pipe while graciously declining another serving of leg from a platter held by Grandma zombie, the leg in this case still wearing one of Geoffrey's brown shoes.

Ohhhh! Geoffrey shuttered, trying to shake the image. *Okay, calm down, just calm down. Don't get all carried away. You don't want to start barfing on people now, do you? Deep breaths, deep breaths…*

Geoffrey felt faint, his whistling more squeaky screen door-o than ever. He wiped his brow, finding it cold and clammy. He was either going to puke or pass out. Or both. *Oh God…*

THE ART OF COINCIDENCE

Calm down. Just calm down!

Everything's going to be fine. Just breathe. Breathe. Long slow breaths... Long slow breaths? How am I supposed to take long slow breaths while I'm doing all this cockamamie whistling? Okay, maybe I should just get the hell out of here before they beat the crap out of me. But how? No one stops whistling right in the middle of a song. That would be like admitting I was just making it all up. I can't do that... I've got it! Maybe I should try being friendly and show them what a nice guy I am. That couldn't hurt, right?

He scanned the room, taking the time to make eye contact with most every onlooker and giving each a broad, overly happy, aren't-we-all-having-the-greatest-time-ever smile before moving on the next. What Geoffrey failed to appreciate, however, was just how strange someone looks when they're smiling at you and whistling at the same time. You might as well be wearing a big sign that says, *I am undoubtedly the weirdest person alive! Want to have a whistle party with me?* Go on. Try it in front of a mirror and you'll see what I mean.

See? Looking all caps STRANGE, aren't you?

And so, by the time the Pied Piper of Peculiarville had finished his round of whistling smiles, he was more worried than ever.

What's with these people? Look at them. They hate me. I haven't seen this many angry faces since I went to my in-laws for Passover... He winced at the thought, the memory still tender. *How was I supposed to know I hid the matzo in a drawer where my brother-in-law's keeps his adult videos?*

His mind drifted...

"I found it! I found it! I found the matzo!" exclaimed an excited little Ezra from his uncle's study. The other children were too busy to care.

"Yeah, well, look what I found, *Big, Black, and Booty-licious!*" exclaimed an even more excited little Benjamin.

Several boys huddled around him, mesmerized by the photo of the girls on the DVD case. "Whoa," one of them murmured. "Do you think they're Jewish?"

"They must be. Uncle Eitan keeps kosher!" one of the other boys answered.

"Hey, look what I found," exclaimed an utterly amazed little Moshe. "*Mondo Mammaries!*"

"Yeah, well, I'll have you know they're not really *mondo*," smirked Miriam, Moshe's little sister, "because *mondo* isn't even a real word! So there!" Miriam never missed an opportunity to rain on her brother's parade.

"I guess you're right," Moshe conceded. "These whoppers are more like mega-*mondo!*"

"Look at this! I've got *Chesty Cheerleaders!*" chirped a positively cheery little Charlie.

His cousin, Sammy, an aspiring Spielberg, murmured, "Now there's a camera angle you don't often see used to film someone doing the splits!"

Whether it was the custom of drinking four cups of wine during the Passover meal, their downing enough *charoset* to rebuild the ancient pyramids of Giza, or just the familial kibitzing that always accompanies holidays like this, their parents took little notice of the children's ramblings in the other room. All that changed, however, when a disappointed little Paulie approached the Seder table and said, "I found *Super-Stacked She-Male Tranny Whackers!* but I put it back. It was gross! I mean, mommies aren't supposed to have big hairy penises, are they?"

Silence. The parents just sat there, dumbstruck, staring at the little boy as if he were speaking a foreign language. The gulf between Passover, penises, and little Paulie's pouting was so great, it seemed like it took forever for it all to register. But when it did— *Holy Gefilte Fish!*— their parental shrieks were so loud and shrill several of the children suffered high frequency hearing loss.

The parents vaulted down the hall and discovering their worst suspicions true, ripped the adult videos from their children's hands. And all their parental *schrei-ing* didn't stop there. Oh, no, it did not! Once they got a good look at the DVD covers, they were so *fardeiget,* one would have thought they were watching a granny porno starring their own grandmothers.

Rapid fire, white-hot queries into how this could have happened followed.

"Don't look at me!" squawked Eitan. "I don't keep this stuff lying around. It was all locked away in a drawer. Geoffrey must have opened it. He's the one that hid the matzo, not me! It was Geoffrey!"

Two-dozen accusatory eyes turned to fix on Geoffrey with all the intensity of those freaky blonde kids in the final reel of *Village of the Damned*. "Uh, well, it, it mi, might have been locked," he mumbled. "But the key, the key was lying right there. I mean I didn't know what was inside — exactly. I was in a hurry. You can't be dawdling around when you're in charge of hiding the matzo! No, you gotta be fast! Fast! It's like I always say, *You can't be a slow man when you're hiding the Aficomen!*"

And that might have been the end of it had he the good sense to stop right there. Unfortunately for all involved, Geoffrey then turned to Eitan, who he never liked much anyway, and added, "When I was slipping it in there though, I did happen to see a bit of the cover of that she-males thing and I gotta agree with little Paulie here. It's creepy! I mean *Super-Stacked She-Male Tranny Whackers???* Trust me, Eit, you oughta have your head examined! And maybe even some electro-shock while they're at it!"

Well, that was it. Eitan lunged at him and just like that, it was the '71 Ali/Frazier fight at The Garden all over again, assuming, that is, that Ali and Frazier were two pudgy 5-year-old girls and the garden in question was in their mother's backyard. Interestingly though, despite the fact that neither man had an ounce of athletic ability (or muscle mass, for that matter), it actually turned out to be a pretty good bout. Right from the outset, the room exploded with terror-filled screams and weeping. And that was just from Geoffrey. Those looking on were pretty upset, too.

Amidst the chaos, Hannah Nettlebaum, perhaps the most religiously inclined of the children, looked around and said, "Boy, this night really *is* different from all other nights!"

It was then that a hyperventilating little Hiam said with DVD in hand, "Wow! *Big Boob Bangeroo! Volume 2, Collector's Edition!!* And look! Look! It's the Director's Cut! Man, this sure beats finding some stinky old matzo!"

Geoffrey blinked, *thupping* back to the present. The glares from the crowd showed no signs of letting up.

So, what should I do? From the look of things, I'd say I've got two minutes max before they come over here and beat the crap out of me! I could try scowling right back at them, maybe stick out my tongue or something? That might work... Or maybe I should just go sit someplace else and hope they don't follow. All this friggin' whistling is probably giving me a tumor anyway. Okay, I'll wrap it up with a big finish and then try and sneak off somewhere. All right... Almost done... Almost—

But just then, Geoffrey's rousing finale was interrupted by a booming male voice. "HEY! Would you knock it off ! We're trying to watch the game here, ya fuckin' fruitcake!"

???????????

The game...? What game?

Geoffrey Zukor froze. His eyes swept the scene in front of him and then continued cautiously to the right. As his pivot passed 90 degrees, he was caught off-guard by his first glimpse of green, the green of a baseball field displayed on a large, muted flat-screen T.V. hanging on the wall behind him just under a large Southwest Airlines graphic. *A baseball game? They're watching a... Oh God...*

He turned back to the crowd. Oh, they were all staring at him now all right, every single one of them, staring at him like the weird, annoying, bizarre creature he most certainly must be.

Geoffrey slouched, his head nearly disappearing between his shoulders. Then he turned, and with a pained grin on his face, he silently slid offstage.

THE ART OF COINCIDENCE

I have no money, no resources, no hopes.
I am the happiest man alive.

-Henry Miller

Great… Now I've got something to shoot for.

-Geoffrey Zukor

Dejected and demoralized, Geoffrey Zukor sat slumped in a seat at the far corner of Gate 9. Add to that, with his 5-foot 10-inch frame weighing in at a wobbling 255 pounds and what you're got was not exactly a picture of graceful aging. Sure, there remained something upscale, even oafishly charming about him, but it seemed his best days had undoubtedly come and gone. Little did he know how wrong he was.

To forestall the inevitable, he had religiously used both *Rogaine* and *Propecia,* which worked surprisingly well — he now had the hairiest back this side of Yellowstone. Unfortunately, only Geoffrey could see any benefit to his hairline, which remained shaped more like Bluff Cove than the pompadourian Rock of Gibraltar he had worked so hard to achieve.

He shook his head and sighed. *All this traveling, it's really getting to me.*

Actually, *everything* was getting to Geoffrey Zukor. Even the simplest tasks far too often erupted into mountains of stress-laden complexity, and whatever he did to try and put things right, only complicated them all the more. It was as if by some divine degree, the harder he worked at something, the more unworkable it would become. And the fault was clearly his. He was always *yinging* when he should be *yanging* or ebbing when he should be flowing, and it didn't look like things would be improving anytime soon.

Seems like I've been gone forever. Are the weeks getting longer or am I just getting shorter?

Although his trip had only been three days and two nights, it felt like a week alright — oh, it most certainly did — a long, dreadfully dry week. Looking back, these hours marked the early dawn of a startling new day for Geoffrey Zukor, but from his current vantage point, the familiar musty curtain of his blurred and parched existence numbed any inkling he may have had of the life-changing events that lay silently in wait. To him, this was just another long, wearing trip piled on top of what felt like a lifetime of long, wearing trips.

Geoffrey had spent the last three days stuck to a red vinyl seat in an insufficiently air-conditioned rental car, zigzagging his way across New Mexico, inspecting his string of retail stores there. It was a pilgrimage he made at least twice a year for the last twenty or so and stood as a testament to his hands-on management style. But on this trip, more than ever before, he had found his travels nearly unbearable, marked by days so bright and hot he began to understand why NASA had selected the state as the site for its new astronaut training center in support of their upcoming manned mission to the Sun. *Where else could they go to test Bain de Soleil with SPF 9,780,936,278?*

He squirmed, finding it impossible to get comfortable in his seat.

All this touring around... I used to enjoy it. I really did. But now, I don't know, it's gotten so old, so exhausting...

Poor Mr. Z had it backwards; it was *he* who was getting old. Not aging really as much as simply drying up — dry skin, dry hair, a dry soul now living a dry life. His once buoyantly affable personality had lost most of its youthful verve and pluck and even his robust wit had been replaced more often than not with the desiccated snicker of common sarcasm.

And so there he sat, drying up in the dreadfully dry air of the Albuquerque Sunport, gateway to the Land of Enchantment.

The Land of Enchantment? Now there's a cruel joke to play on tourists. I guess "Land of the Mile-High Melanoma" was already taken. Too bad! Well, I sure hope all the folks vacationing here get an opportunity to experience the "enchanted" intersection of Lead Rd & Coal Avenue or imbibe in the intoxicating effervescence of Smelt Street between Bleek and Bleeker, or any of the other half-dozen places I've visited over the last couple of days. The Land of Enchantment? Of course, it is! And when I'm traveling, my wife does nothing but sit home by the fire and sing along with Barbra Streisand...

Oh my man, I love him so,
He'll never know all my life is just despair, but I don't care,
When he takes me in his arms the world is bright all right...

His lips pulled thin. *Marriage… You start out with a plum and end up with a prune.*

Alas, there he was being all negative again, dry and negative. Thankfully though, his workweek would soon be over—just a one-hour forty-minute flight to L.A., a short walk to Parking Zone One, and then a twenty-five-minute drive to Brentwood. Okay, it was a twenty-five-minute drive that with traffic would probably take him an hour and a half, fine, but at least he'd be home and if he was lucky there might even be some fog rolling in — a thick, gloriously moist, blanket of coastal fog, covering everything and everyone. That was just what he needed. He closed his eyes.

Oh, let there be some fog, some cool, soothing fog…

With images of a lacy, white mist billowing over him, he felt himself starting to nod off again, which he surely would have had it not been for the sudden crackling of overhead speakers:

"Attention Southwest Airline passengers of Flight 2020. May I have your attention, please? Weather in Los Angeles this evening is a cool 60 degrees with patches of fog— Hold please." This was followed by an abrupt click.

Geoffrey immediately perked up. "Did she just say there's fog in L.A.?" he asked no one in particular.

"That what she said all right," answered a man seated a few chairs away.

"Great!" Geoffrey replied. "Wow, I can't believe it! I was just sitting here hoping there might be some fog. Isn't that great?" He was downright giddy over the news. Could it be that things were finally going his way?

The overhead speakers crackled again but this time the gate agent's voice was muffled, her words barely discernable. "I don't care. Tell that luggage luggin' ass I'm not here. Tell him I called in sick—of him!" Then, in a full, clear voice, she continued.

"Attention passengers of Flight 2020. As I was saying, we have just received word of fog in Los Angeles—"

"Yes!" trumpeted Geoffrey, his clenched fist rising above his head as if he were a member of the White & Blubbery Chapter of the Black Panthers.

"—limiting visibility at LAX. Therefore Flight 2020 has been delayed until 7:55 p.m. We're sorry for any inconvenience this may cause but the delay was mandated by Air Traffic Control. Please report back to the gate no later than 7:20 for boarding. And do not travel far, for if weather conditions change, we may need to adjust our schedule accordingly."

With the announcement, chaos descended upon the crowd, scattering aggravated passengers in all directions. The man seated a few chairs away, leaned toward Geoffrey. "Congratulations. Happy now?" he sneered.

Other passengers shuffled by, shooting him resentful looks as well, as if this was somehow all his fault. But then a sweet, old lady approached, her clear, blue eyes full of comfort and understanding. "You were hoping for some fog, weren't you?" she asked. But then her face skewed dark and cold. "Why? So you could bother some more people while they're trying to watch TV? You know, I've waited my entire life for the Soxs to sweep the Yanks — my entire life! — and now that's all I can remember about the game is you going like this—" She smiled as broadly as she possibly could and then started whistling, her eyebrows flapping up and down like the front bumper of a souped up '63 Impala. "Ya nut job!" she snapped, and off she went.

His Royal Dryness didn't know what to say to her or any of them. He just stood there, a nucleus orbited by a thousand angry electrons. "There's fog in LA..." he whispered wistfully. He could see the fog, feel the fog. He closed his eyes and he was there, *in* the

fog — the cool, moist, lovely fog… Well, he was in the fog until —
Ouch! — some guy banged into him with an enormous roller bag,
nearly knocking him over as he bustled passed to see what accom-
modations could be made on a more *adventurous* airline.

Oh, it's fine, fine… thought Geoffrey with a grunt while he
bent to rub the side of his knee. *No reason to stop and say you're
sorry, Mister. Really! I'll be fine. It's nothing a little minor surgery
won't take care of. I guess I should just thank my lucky coconuts you
weren't behind the wheel of an SUV. Well, goodbye, friend. It was
nice getting run over by you…*

And thus, there stood Geoffrey Zukor, plumb out of gas at the
intersection of Parched Place and Stuck Street.

He glanced glumly toward the check-in counter, behind
which a large plate-glass window revealed his waiting plane. A
glint of late afternoon sun reflected off its tail section right above
its call sign, L594. Something about the light held his attention.
The plane looked so shiny and new. It was like there was something special about that plane. *Five nine four… Five nine four…* He
mulled it over for a second before checking his watch.

It was now 5:25 p.m. He had almost three hours to kill. He
found himself moving through the airport like a rock-beaten
salmon, fighting an uphill battle against all the bitterly annoying,
petty inconveniences life could throw at him. His destination,
known only to his feet, lay at the mouth of the terminal.

After passing a gate or two, Geoffrey stopped and frisked himself for his cell phone. He knew he better call home. No, not
because his wife would worry — she probably wouldn't even get
the message until after he arrived — but he knew if he didn't call,
she would have yet another reason to be angry with him—and she
never missed an opportunity to be angry with him. It was as if Victoria Zukor was born with an innate, supersonically sensitized,

stereoscopic sonar system, honed to acquire just such opportunities floating through her universe, no matter how faint or obscure they may be. She had, through diligence and sheer determination, singled-handedly unearthed a host of new reasons for women to be angry at their husbands, reasons never conceived of by any woman before, making her no less than the Galileo of newly discovered woman's degradations. Then, as was her custom, she would take her latest find, be it malicious insult, callous slight, or snide, cutting remark—aka "Good morning, Dear"—and share it with her few close friends who would so dotingly sympathize with the righteous, operatic tragedy of her plight. Men, after all, are such stupid, insensitive bastards! This truth was a call-to-arms for women everywhere, inspiring them to demand "More Prince, Less Frog!" of their mates without ever once stopping to consider that the problem may be with their own kissing skills.

As expected, Victoria didn't answer her cell, forcing Geoffrey to leave a message. "Honey, my flight is delayed because of the fog in L.A. I can't believe it. Anyway, I should be home by eleven. Love you. Call me if you need anything. Can hardly wait to see you. Miss you. Love you. See you soon, you…" Not quite sure why he added that last "you", he stopped and then tried to gloss over it by adding another, "Love you." Just to make sure that was enough, he tossed in a rather anemic, "Miss you," which he immediately feared his wife would call him on, so he added an energetic, "I do. I do. I weelly, weelly do!" Why he was suddenly talking like Tweedy Bird, he had no idea. He heard his wife say, "Can't you just be normal for once in your life?" and so he blurted out a more awkward than ever, Hail Mary, "I love you!" and then forced himself to hang up before he opened his mouth again and made the situation even worse.

Geoffrey stood there for a moment in the wake of another self-inflicted loss, a worried look on his face. Then he turned, put his head down, and like an old mule pulled his roller bag passed another five gates before making a right onto the main concourse where he was promptly met by a newly installed moving sidewalk. Yes, a moving sidewalk! Just what an obese America needs. But even in his weakened state, Geoffrey chose to step around it and walk. This was exercise after all, and a little flame of pride was ignited within for making the right choice. Sadly, it was snuffed out only moments later when an overly competitive senior citizen, easily a hundred if he was a day and dragging a bum leg to boot, let loose a wicked little laugh as he and his walker shuffled passed Geoffrey with ease. Geoffrey looked at him incredulously and shook his head. Then he swallowed hard, put his head back down, and plowed onward.

At long last, he reached the end of the concourse where he was eyed as he inched his way passed Security before exiting through a pair of sliding glass doors that separated the secured gate area from the airport's main retail plaza. Immediately, he was hit with the smell of America's four basic food groups, those being the pepperoni pizza group, the hot dog on a stick group, the French fry/potato chip group, and lastly, the all-important Cinnabons/donuts group. His destination was now only steps away.

The fork in the road, cloaked in insignificance and wholly unrecognized, was at hand. What happens here, in these next few minutes, could change Geoffrey's life in ways he could never imagine.

THE ART OF COINCIDENCE

The notion of Free Will is flimsy at best.
It was probably first raised by God's legal department
as a prima facie defense against product liability claims
for the glaring mistakes He made in the creation of Man.

Although Geoffrey's destination was directly in front of him, once he was through the security doors, he found his path blocked by an old man standing like a rock in the sand, splitting the current of exiting travelers in two.

At first glance, he appeared average enough, though a bit frail with his gold rim spectacles and thinning skin. Yet beyond the mark of years, there remained an unmistakable otherworldliness about him. And indeed, there was. For here stood The Giver, no longer in his usual attire of black pants, pleated cummerbund, and ruffled lavender shirt cut with a black garter across his right bicep, but now reborn into another role altogether, the role of his youth, of his glory days and champagne nights. Yes, out from behind his retirement desk job, The Giver had returned for one final mission, draped in a long, billowing robe and holding out a brass cup of some weight and size.

The old man had gone great lengths to be there, first petitioning and then receiving special dispensation from none other than The Governors to make the trip. Then there was his costuming, the making of travel arrangements — never easy on such short notice — and lastly, finding someone to fill in for him without screwing things up too badly while he was away. But all the effort was worth it, there was no doubt about that, for this was his calling, the one thing he was born to do, the singular activity that made him feel truly alive and engaged. Here was an opportunity to be an operative again on assignment "in country." Oh, the thrill of it! This was involving work of the highest order, requiring a cunning and agile mind, a penchant for subtly and nuance, and even a certain savoir-faire. Most importantly though, his job required discipline, for he was there to plant a seed, an inkling, to conjure the pre-image of a déjà vu and nothing more; to simply do what his machine on-high had started but in the end, failed to adequately complete. He wasn't there as a guardian angel to offer celestial enlightenment or Jiminy Cricket advice. Nor was he there as a Jacob Marley wannabe, an apparition bent on using spectral persuasion to scare someone into submission. No, antics like those went out over a century ago with the advent and popularization of the camera, for evidence of his handiwork was the last thing The Governors wanted. It was one thing for an earthling to say, "I was dreaming and all of a sudden was awoken by clanking chains and this ghastly, ghoulish ghost!" It was something else entirely for them to add, "And look! I even have Polaroids!"

No, The Giver's job was to plant the seed of an idea and nothing more. Sometimes that seed took root and provided enough of a subliminal nudge to sway the outcome of events, later explained away as, "I don't know why I picked those lotto numbers," or "took the bus that day instead of a cab," or any of a zillion other small things that in and of themselves seemed so inconsequential. Yet, as a result of more than a googolplex of calculations by The Cube, once that "hunch" was acted on, that was it. Their path was set, their modified destiny ready to propel them onto a new and exciting trajectory, a new chapter, a new life even, perhaps one wholly unimagined before the intervention took place.

But whether "The Giving" took root or not was none of The Giver's concern. His one and only job was to plant the seed. No further meddling was allowed. *Ever.* Those in the know believed the highly curtailed nature of the guidance, subliminal as it was, was to ensure plausible deniability and insulation from recrimination, not to mention treble damages, should things end up going awry, something that's bound to happen from time to time when even the wisest of life's paths was chosen. And so, The Governors of The Given allowed only so much tampering in the lives of humans and not a bit more.

But since the old man's retirement, things rarely went as planned. The Governors had auditioned thousands of applicants to replace him but nary a one could get an earthling to follow their directive with any regularity. This was a particularly hard pill for The Governors to swallow for the man they were replacing had not only made it look easy but also had accomplished the extraordinary — a perfect track record — the baseball equivalent of hitting a home run at each and every at bat — while blindfolded. Yes, all those files over all those years and the old man had never suffered a single failure. Not one. Of course, that was before he came up against the likes of Geoffrey Zukor.

THE ART of COINCIDENCE

The Giver decided to bronze his face and use an Indian accent for the assignment, or at least as close to an Indian accent as he could muster. The goal was to make the encounter memorable, thereby making his message memorable as well. That, he believed more than anything, was the reason for his unprecedented string of successes and was the mantra he repeated over and over again in his lectures to each year's crop of new trainees. "What do you need in a situation like this? You need *m-e-m-o-r-a-b-l-e*."

As Geoffrey walked through the security doors, the old man's brows lifted in warm welcome. With just steps between them, the elder began reading from a small card he held in his left hand, his right still holding the brass cup. The Giver cleared his throat and then spoke in tones suggesting a tolling bell. "Five—Nine—Four."

The old man's get up and demeanor were spot on — ethereal, prophetic, and most importantly, succeeded in creating an image that would not soon be forgot. His Indian accent, on the other hand, pretty much sucked. He sounded like Yoda, assuming Yoda was played by Santa Claus on a three-week schnapps bender. The old man was obviously a bit rusty in the elocution department.

Geoffrey had no idea what The Giver was saying and frankly, didn't care. He just thrust his hand into his pocket, and after two fair-sized grunts, dropped a few coins into the old man's cup and kept right on walking. As he passed, he expected some sort of acknowledgement, a smile perhaps, a nod, maybe even a slight bow. Something. What he got was — "*Aaaawwwkkk!*" — a shriek so unexpected and shrill, it stopped Geoffrey in his tracks. Any kindness in the old man's face was suddenly replaced with that all-too-familiar *What-planet-are-you-from?* expression that seemed to follow our hero wherever he went.

Geoffrey winced. *What? I didn't give him enough??*

But before he could placate the guy with a few more coins, the old man sputtered, "Why'd you do that?!?"

Confused, Geoffrey followed the old man's stare down to his cup. It was filled with coffee.

Oh, no!

Oh, yes! Geoffrey Zukor had done it again. Another heave when he should have been busy ho-ing.

"What kind of weirdo runs around tossing money into people's coffee?" the old man bellowed. "Shouldn't you at least ask before doing something like that? Like, 'Would you care for cream? Sugar? INDIAN HEAD NICKELS?!?' Do you have any idea how long it's been since I've had a good cup of coffee? Where I'm from that's all we have is Starbucks and it always tastes like burnt rocks. *Uggggh!*" The old man shivered and then looked forlornly into his cup, adding, "And I had it just right, too."

"Oh God, I'm so sorry. I, I, I thought you were a beggar—" Geoffrey stopped. It dawned on him the fellow might not exactly take that as a compliment. He tried to backpedal. "Not that you—I mean, I didn't mean I thought you were one of those, you know, stinky ol' beggar people," he said, shaking his head. "No, I mean, look at you. You're like, like the opposite. You're like, uh…" Geoffrey scrambled to come up with the opposite of a stinky beggar. "You're like a… a sweet smelling… beggar?"

The old man looked at him incredulously. "You think I'm a sweet-smelling beggar?"

"Uh, sure," Geoffrey replied, nodding unconvincingly. He took a deep breath and forced an awkward smile. "Nothing makes you want to throw some change in someone's coffee like a sweet-smelling beggar — that's what I always say…" His voice trailed off. He knew it was definitely time to be moving on. He searched his pockets for his wallet. "Here. Sorry. Really, I am. Buy yourself another cup of coffee, all right? I'd go with you, but I've got to run go get my head examined." He held out a five-dollar bill, but the old man made no move to take it. He just stood there, motionless, staring into his coffee, a scowl affixed to his face.

Geoffrey moved the bill tentatively toward the old man's cup and asked, "You want me to put it in here?"

"NO!"

"I didn't think so. But then I thought, well, since my other money is in there, maybe you'd want to keep it all together?"

The Giver answered with a look and then checked his watch. Time was growing short, *very* short. He took a quick breath and tried to calm himself. "Five, nine, four," he intoned declaratively, careful to avoid any hint or gesture.

Geoffrey's head cocked to one side. "Excuse me?"

"Five, nine, four." The old man spoke louder this time, but his lousy Indian accent wasn't helping. Then, Geoffrey's face lit up. "Oh! Twenty? Twenty?"

Now it was the old man's turn to squint in confusion.

"Five times four is twenty. You want me to give you a twenty? For a cup of coffee?"

"No! Five, *nine,* four!" The Giver replied. He once again checked his watch and with the few seconds he had left, nearly shouted. "Five, *nine,* four! Five, *nine,* four!!"

"Oh," said Geoffrey, finally understanding. "Sorry, your accent is throwing me off a bit. Where are you from, Mexico?"

The old man looked offended by the question but before he could say anything, Geoffrey continued, "Flight nine-four, I got you now, but I don't know when that's landing. Go check — see the big sign over there, the one with all the lights? — that will have your flight information on it. See? It's the big one right there."

"No! No!" the old man yelled.

"Yes, it will. It's got everyone's. It's just right over there — the big black board with all the lights. Tu savay, lights? I wish I spoke Eskimo. You're an Eskimo, right?"

"I'm a what??" The Giver's watch started to emit a high pitch tone. Panicked, he yelled even more frantically, "NO! FIVE—"

Just then, a large group of people exited the concourse. Some scurried by on their right, others on their left, and still others angled between them. Seconds later, when the crowd subsided, The Giver was gone. Geoffrey looked every which way, but the old man was nowhere to be found. He had disappeared into thin air! Geoffrey did find something though; the change he put in the old man's cup was piled on the floor in the exact spot the old man once stood.

He grabbed the handle of his roller bag to steady himself and bent over to pick it up. *Weird… the coins… they aren't even wet.* And there was something else, too; there were so many of them. He didn't realize he had put so much money in the old man's cup. *I couldn't have, could I?*

After picking up the change, he took a minute to count it all. "Five ninety-one, ninety-two, ninety-three, ninety-four... Five dollars and ninety-four cents..."

Geoffrey stood there, rattling the coins around in his hand. *Five ninety-four... Five ninety-four...*

Then Geoffrey heard him, the old man's voice, clear yet strange in its sudden distance. It sounded almost as if it was coming through the vents in the ceiling. But how could that be? The only thing he knew for sure was that it was the old man. And he was laughing. It was the jolliest laugh he had ever heard.

He looked around. He had finally reached his destination, standing before the huge open mouth of a restaurant.

THE ART OF COINCIDENCE

In a town like Albuquerque, where "dilapidated" has been the reigning architectural style since folks first settled there, local restaurant designer's sole focus has been on trying to "out-dilapidate" each other. And they've gotten pretty good at it, too. So good, in fact, no matter what part of town you're driving through, it's often difficult to differentiate one of their newly constructed, dilapidated-looking restaurants from the truly dilapidated restaurant next door. This was undoubtedly the motivation behind *Fiesta!*, a stunning example of American one-upmanship. *Fiesta!* — a fabulously happy name for a restaurant designed to look like it has been serving up its delectable Ham and Cheese Tacos and kiddy-favorite fried Peanut Butter and Jelly Burritos for hundreds of years and was now falling apart under the sheer weight of all that undeniably authentic Southwest cuisine.

To make matters worse, the architect specified building materials for the construction of the establishment that were even less authentic than its food, with wall after wall covered in plastic sheets of fake looking plaster and used brick. Ironically, the polypropylene wall-veneers that were supposed to read "falling apart," will, in reality, never fall apart. Lucky us! Better buy stock in the local refuse company; they're going to be stuffed to the gills with the corniest, non-deteriorating crap to ever fill a landfill should this baby go under.

Geoffrey Zukor stood as if invisible before the *Fiesta!* reception podium while a heavily costumed hostess gazed intently downward, tapping her grease pencil on a plastic-covered seating chart. *Tap, tap, tap, tap, tap…*

Moments became minutes of nothing but more than greeting-less pencil tapping. There was no welcoming smile. No *"Buenos divas"* or other such greeting one might expect from an establishment of this authenticity. There wasn't even an *"Uno momentum."* In fact, there was no acknowledgment that he was standing there at all. More time passed, returning the exact same result. Geoffrey looked around, wondering what to do. He bent slightly to get an angle on the hostess' face.

She has to know I'm waiting; I'm standing right in front of her. Maybe she knows but maybe, maybe she's a paralyzed mute and she's trying to communicate with me via Morse code! That could be it! Hmmm… I wonder how many pencil taps it is to say non-smoking? The thought brought a smile. Although faint, it was his first smile in days.

Without the benefit of his own grease pencil and seating chart, Geoffrey, on a whim, began testing his theory by ever-so-subtlety clicking his front teeth together, loud enough so she might hear but not so obvious as to give passersby the impression he was trying to take a bite out of the young girl.

Click-click, click-click-click, click, click-click, click, click-click-click, click-click — but then he stopped, suddenly worried that for all he knew he could be tapping out anything. *With my luck, I'm telling her I'm wearing a pink thong. Or I have a dog biscuit stuck up my butt. Or— Oh, forget it...*

And so, he abandoned his little experiment and one by one began trying all the customary attention-getters. He cleared his throat. He checked his watch while tapping his foot. He even tried squirming restlessly from side to side as if to indicate he was about to urinate all over her podium—but alas, nothing worked. She simply refused to acknowledge him.

I know. Maybe I should start whistling! It sure got the attention of all those folks back there trying to watch TV! And there it was, a true Geoffrey Zukor strength: He could always laugh at himself.

Out of sheer desperation, he, the man who throughout his life had spent so much time beating around the bush that many believed he was the main cause of global deforestation, was forced into doing that which he dreaded most — use the direct approach. (Well, as much of the direct approach as he could muster, anyway.) And so, he inhaled, and then squinting as if he were peering at her through a very small hole, squeaked out a minuscule "Uh, excuse me?"

Without taking her eyes off the seating chart, the hostess replied with a flat, "Yes?"

Not exactly, *Welcome to the Magic Kingdom!* but hey, this was Albuquerque.

"Yeah, uh, hi. Could, uh, could I get a booth by a power outlet, please?" he asked the hair on the top of the head of the heavily costumed hostess as she continued to look down, tapping her grease pencil on her plastic-covered seating chart.

"You want dinner?"

"No, I'm standing here waiting for the bus," he mumbled.

"Excuse me?" Her tone indicated she'd like nothing better than to give a sharp yank to his pink thong if he bothered her a single second longer.

"Dinner. Yes, dinner. Dinner would be great. Thanks."

"So why do you need a power outlet?" she asked, rather suspiciously.

"Because I have an electric hibachi here in my bag. I thought maybe I'd roast some s'mores later. You wouldn't happen to have a spare tree branch around anywhere, would you?"

Well, at least that's what he felt like saying, or tried to say, or maybe just wished he was man enough to have said. But what he actually said, and said rather meekly at that, was, "So I can, you know, plug in my laptop. Just for a little while, if, if that's okay?"

The hostess stopped tapping her grease pencil long enough to turn her back to him to grab a menu.

"Smoking or non-smoking?" she droned, all the while continuing to comply with her personal radar that sensed he wasn't much to look at by never once bothering to look at him.

"No…" replied Geoffrey with a shake of his head. He reached down for his cell phone again, wondering if it was too late L.A. time to still catch anyone in the office.

"Excuse me?" she snorted, more than a smidge peeved by what she considered to be his unresponsive answer. "Was that *no* to smoking or *no* to non-smoking?"

"What?" Geoffrey replied, in the midst of dialing now and not quite following.

"Was that *no* to smoking or *no* to non-smoking?" spat la mucho annoyo'd, costumo'd senorita who had taken just about all she was going take from el Bozo standing before her.

Her being *mucho annoyo'd* was not lost on el Bozo; in fact, it was coming through the aridity loud and clear.

"What do you think I meant?" he asked in return. Had this been another time, he probably would have mustered a smile but unfortunately today it was nowhere to be found. Maybe it too was delayed due to fog at LAX.

"I don't know what you meant. I'm not a mind reader," she replied sourly. Her smile must have been delayed due to fog at LAX also.

"Well, you don't have to be a mind reader to know what no means, do you? Come on, you really don't know what people mean when they answer 'no' to 'smoking or non-smoking?' Really? Well, go on, take a guess. What does no mean?"

"You want me to guess?"

"Yeah, take a guess."

"Okay. I guess… I guess I'll have to go get my manager! How's that for a guess?" This she punctuated with a snotty little smirk, obviously pleased with herself that she was able to come up with what she considered to be such a quick-witted response. And with that, she curtly turned and wiggled away.

"Do you think he's in smoking or non-smoking?" Geoffrey asked her backside. Granted, the comment was unnecessary — unfunny and unnecessary — and he knew it, but, well, he just couldn't help himself.

THE ART OF COINCIDENCE

Herman Torres approached the reservation podium with the pomp, if not the circumstance, of a matador entering the arena. He was dressed in an all-white gaucho outfit that was cut with a large, red sash around his waist. Although his nametag read, "El Managero," everything else about his appearance said Grand Pooh-Bah of high school pot smokers. The largest sombrero Geoffrey Zukor had ever seen dangled off the back of the kid's shoulders, suspended by a small-caliber red rope that burrowed across the front of his neck. Perhaps the stupid look on his face was caused by the rope cutting off vitally needed supplies of oxygen to his brain.

Geoffrey stood transfixed. *Does he always lug that hat around or did he put it on for just this occasion?* he wondered.

Señor Torres, before saying anything to Geoffrey, gave a self-assured nod to his newly hired and definitely *spankable* little hostess, recognizing her for exactly what she was — a hot body living in a cheap world. Then he turned, and with far more seriousness than the task required, issued forth a condescending "Yes?" while doing his best to modulate his natural schoolboy tenor into a rich, hopefully babe-attracting, baritone. There was no polite smile, no "How can I help you?" or even a "What seems to be the problem?"— just a sour face and a stern, bicep-flexing "Yes?" Obviously, the apple doesn't fall far from the sombrero.

"Oh, it, it's nothing really," Geoffrey replied apologetically. "She just asked me if I wanted smoking or non-smoking and I said no. It's really no big deal." Then, with a darting little point into the restaurant, he added, "If I could please just get a—"

"Well, was that *no* to smoking or *no* to non-smoking?" asked la muy seriouso manlyo managero, as if he were speaking to a really stupido, annoyingo childo. The hostess, delighted, bounced in full support.

Geoffrey was stunned. Of all the things he thought the manager might say, he figured "Was that *no* to smoking or *no* to non-smoking?" was about as likely as being asked, "Hey, aren't you that chick on the cover of the *Sports Illustrated Swimsuit Issue?*" Yet asked he was, and to stress the point, both manager and hostess stood stone-faced before him, their stern, lowered brows demanding an answer. He couldn't believe it. He couldn't. He just stood there, shaking his head. Then a vision came to him. He saw the front page of today's New York Post spinning into view as if from an old movie. At long last, it all started to make sense...

It was official; the whole fucking world was against him.

Geoffrey figured the planning had probably started at the very top, perhaps with a secret meeting of world leaders, leaders who then passed directives through all levels of their respective bureaucracies. The airlines were obviously involved in the plot as were, most likely, other transportation sectors as well.

"Fellow Citizens of Earth, heed my call: Don't ever give that bastard a break! Ever! Run him over with your roller bag if you have to, but stop him, people, stop him! If we all pull together, stand steadfast and strong, we will wear him down, down, whittle him down into the broken stump of a man he most surely deserves to be!"

"Fight on, people. Fight on!!"

Geoffrey stood there, dazed, reeling. The phrase, *Was that no to smoking or no to non-smoking?* echoed through his brain as if repeated by a thousand demented souls. There was no escape, nowhere to run.

"And that's not all," the hostess howled, her nipples hard in anticipation of the kill. She pointed a long, accusatory finger at him, and then screeched in a voice so loud and shrill it reverberated through the entire food court causing everyone to turn in their direction. "This guy has a stuck a dog biscuit up his butt! That's what he told me! He stood right there and told me he's got a dog biscuit stuck up his butt!"

Geoffrey gasped. "What are you– You mean when I was clicking my–? Oh my God! I was afraid I said that!" He slapped a hand over his mouth. His eyes ricocheted around the room and seeing that he was once again the center of attention, added, "I mean, I *was* afraid I said that but then I realized, I didn't have to be afraid because I didn't say it. So there! Hurray for me! I absolutely never said that… did I? Did I really say I've got a dog biscuit stuck up my butt? Really?"

"You most certainly did, you Purina Chow pervert!" Then she stuck out her jaw and started clicking her teeth together. *Click-click, click-click-click, click, click-click, click, click-click-click, click-click.* "See! You're messing with the wrong chick, Sicko! I'll have you know my father is a paralyzed mute. He's been clicking code at me since I was two years old. You're not going to pull one over on me! I'm going to have you arrested, you weirdo!"

Geoffrey mumbled something or another, but no one was sure exactly what. He was so horrified his mouth was unable to form consonants. What came out was just a long vowel-y dribble. *"Iiiaah heeeuuuu eeaaa oohh uuieeee oooiiaaa…"*

Geoffrey was sinking fast but the hostess showed him no mercy. "And that's not all," she shouted to everyone around her. "Mr. Milk Bone Butt here told me he's wearing a pink thong! Can you believe it? Mr. Fat Ass is wearing a pink thong!!"

"AAhhhhh!" Geoffrey screamed. "I didn't say that! I didn't! At least I don't think I did, did I? Did I really say…? No, I couldn't have! And if I did, well, it was an accident! I didn't mean to say it! It just came out… by accident! You gotta believe me! And I'm not anyway. Here, look! Look!!" Geoffrey hands moved to his waist.

"HE'S FLASHING ME!" the hostess hollered. "This thong-wearing sicko with a dog biscuit up his butt is a flasher, too! Security! Security! The perv is flashing me! He's flashing me!!"

"NO, I'M NOT!" Geoffrey screamed back. Then to the crowd he shouted, "I WAS JUST GOING TO SHOW HER MY UNDERWEAR—" Geoffrey thought about that for a moment. "OH MY GOD! NO! NO, I DIDN'T MEAN I WAS GOING TO SHOW HER MY— I, I NEVER SAID, I NEVER SAID I, I, I—"

Spinning. His world was spinning, whirling like a Sandy Koufax curveball. A white ring of flesh wrapped his cinched, colorless lips. He couldn't breathe. He was going into shock.

And then…

THE ART OF COINCIDENCE

And then... Nothing.

That's right. Absolutely nothing!

His stress coupled with the dehydration of his soul caused his entire apparatus to lock-up tight. And there he stood, frozen in place — a Zukorsicle! His blood pressure and body temperature were skyrocketing but he couldn't move a muscle. If something didn't happen — and happen quickly — Geoffrey Zukor would be the first documented case of spontaneous combustion in Albuquerque!

As for Herman Torres, well, he wasn't faring much better. His face was now a blood-starved Barney purple — no, not out of anger — but from the prolonged pull of his super-sized sombrero across his neck. He was just able to choke out a "Buzz off, Perv, or

I'm calling the cops!" before growing so lightheaded he fell backwards with more plop than a shill at a Pentecostal revival.

Although the Grand Pooh-Bah was merely dazed, the hostess rushed to his side and engaged in enough mouth-to-mouth resuscitation to inflate the Snoopy balloon in Macy's Thanksgiving Day Parade. Then she helped him back to his office, where she continued to aid in his recovery until they both got the raise they were after. Geoffrey, barely able to stand, was left all alone, staring like an abandoned lover into the establishment he was forbidden to enter. He was Charles Foster Kane on his deathbed, except instead of "Rosebud…," he was mumbling, "Non-Smoking… Non-Smoking… Non-Smoking…"

THE ART OF COINCIDENCE

It was a palsied Geoffrey Zukor that made the long trek back, through security, towards his gate. The living dead had claimed another victim: Zombie, now be he.

After the incident at *Fiesta!,* he stood there for a moment, staring blankly across the food court at *Mama George's Italian All-You-Can-Eat Buffet.*

Mama George's? Really? Mama George's? Did a gay couple adopt and then go into the restaurant business? And what's with "Italian All-You-Can-Eat Buffet?" Shouldn't that be "All-You-Can-Eat Italian Buffet?" he wondered, numbly. *If someone was so bent on screwing things up, why didn't they just name the place, "Italian George's You-Can-All-Eat Mama Buffet?" That's got a nice ring to it...*

But alas, Geoffrey was so shell-shocked by the day's events, the only conclusion he could muster regarding whether to venture over there was, *Sure, why not?* A few more days like today and he'd be living on the streets, eating cat food, and wearing nothing but a pink thong. Whistling Barry Manilow medleys and clacking Morse code hellos to passers-by wouldn't be out of the question either. Geoffrey took a few steps toward *Mama George's* but then stopped, his fingers fiddling with all the change in his pocket. *Five ninety-four...*

He took another step or two toward *Mama George's* only to stop again. *I couldn't have put five dollars and ninety-four cents in his coffee. I think there was only a couple of quarters and a dime on the hotel dresser this morning. Did I buy something and get some change? I don't think so...* He frowned, the mystery of it weighing on him, pinning him there. He thought about the brute yelling at him to stop whistling, the old lady calling him a nut job, the old man with the funny accent (*Maybe he was French?*), the fiasco with the hostess, and finally back to the coins in his pocket. *Five ninety-four... Five ninety-four... Five ninety-four... There's something about those numbers...* he could feel himself being pulled back to the gate. And to the silent sound of rousing cheers worlds away, that was exactly where he went.

The Art of Coincidence

Ah, what a feeling! There was nothing like it!

Charts, gauges, three-dimensional planar scope readings, multi-expressive probability graphs, and raw data streams pulsed with mathematical precision across the wall of glass before him. The Giver stood there, letting it all sink in. And he wasn't the only one. Interest in what was likely The Giver's last mission had been high, and as a result, Geoffrey's feed had been broadcast throughout the entire complex. He'd even heard rumor that if things went as everyone now expected, a great banquet would soon be held in his honor. As if to confirm the matter, the vintage black phone sitting atop a Corinthian pedestal next to him rang. The old man picked it up without a word of greeting.

"He's heading back toward the gate."

"Yes, sir. It appears so, sir," The Giver replied.

"That was quite a show you put on down there. You're either the best there ever was or the luckiest," The Governor chided.

"I'm sure it's the later, sir."

"I'll bet you are. Anyway, I called to congratulate you. We've never shared this with you before, but that was an ultra-band operation, our broadest yet. The repercussions of the Zukor intervention will ripple through generations and its implications will be fascinating to watch. You very well may have ushered in a new era for us. Job well done."

"Thank you, sir."

"You know, in light of this accomplishment, of few of The Governors and I have been wondering…" His voice trailed off.

"Yes, sir?"

"Best to speak of this in person. We'll meet soon." There was a click on the line and The Governor was gone.

The Giver couldn't help but smile as he returned the phone to its cradle, his curiosity piqued. The Zukor case was closed. The Giver wondered if perhaps his mandatory retirement might not be so mandatory after all.

The Cube perked up, sniffing the air around him. *Hmmm… Is that a sequel I smell? Maybe I could even get my own spin-off…* The thought kept The Cube scheming for months.

THE ART OF COINCIDENCE

Things were decidedly less upbeat at the Albuquerque Sun-port where a glum Geoffrey Zukor had finally dragged himself back to where his long and restaurant-less trek had begun. As he approached his gate, he was greeted with disapproving stares from several of the waiting and obviously grumpy fellow passengers. Geoffrey, still numb from his encounter with the hostess, paid them no mind. He was heading back to his former seat when he saw the fellow that had sneered at him earlier still sitting right where he had been but was now joined by the elderly female Boston Red Sox fan that called him a "nut job!"

When they saw him, the old woman disparagingly flicked her finger in his direction and began recounting what had happened to her earlier when she was trying the watch the game. Numb or no, Geoffrey knew that's what they were talking about because suddenly the old woman puckered her lips and started whistling like a cat whose tail was caught in a garbage disposal. Geoffrey fought off the impulse to go over and offer her whistling lessons. Instead, he did an abrupt about face and walked toward a row of empty seats near the check-in counter. It was then that a single red flash from a light atop his waiting plane's tail section caught his attention. And there it was again, the plane's call sign: L594. *Five nine four...* His fingers fiddled with the change in his pocket. *Five nine four...* And then it hit him. *The change is the same number that's on the plane! That's why it sounded so familiar! I knew it was something! Five dollars and ninety-four cents!* Geoffrey smiled, glad he was able to finally solve the mystery. And the more he thought about it, the more he felt reassured by the strange coincidence, like it was some kind of sign, an affirmation that he was indeed right where he should be. If he only knew... He looked back at the plane's tail section and gave the coins in his pocket a good shake. *Five ninety-four. Five ninety—*

"Attention Southwest Airlines passengers of Flight 2020 to Los Angeles, may I have your attention, please?" blared the overhead speaker. "Well, good news, folks. We have been notified by your captain that your flight has been green lit for immediate departure and air traffic control has given us an expedited takeoff slot so will all ticketed passengers of Flight 2020, regardless of whether you're in Group A, B, or C, please approach Gate 9 for boarding. I repeat: All ticketed passengers of Flight 2020 to Los Angeles please approach Gate 9 for immediate boarding. This will be your final boarding call."

Geoffrey turned. *What?*

Surprised passengers looked around to confirm the news.

Really? Wow, I can't believe it... We're boarding now? Right now? And then it all became clear. *What if I would have gone over to Mama George's? I would have missed the flight for sure! And this is the last one back to L.A. tonight. I can't believe it!* His fingers fluttered through the coins in his pocket and in their jingling, he could have sworn he heard a faint echo of the old man's laugh. He nodded and smiled. *Well, I'll be... I'm going home! I'm going home on ol' five ninety-four!*

A strong, revitalizing wave of optimism swelled within, propelling him in an altogether new and unimaginable direction. Fasten your seatbelt, Mr. Zukor. It's gonna be a bumpy ride.

THE ART OF COINCIDENCE

We got trouble, right here in River City!
With a capital 'T' that rhymes with 'P'
and stands for pool.
We've surely got trouble, right here in River City!
Gotta figger out a way
to keep the young ones moral after school!
    -Meredith Willson's *The Music Man*

Although few understood its importance, its location was no secret, continually occupying the same plot of land for almost three-quarters of a century, eighteen miles north of the Albuquerque Sunport, near the southern rim of the Manhattoan Indian Reservation. And for all that time, this sleepy part of town remained quiet, as if immune to the viral onslaught of new development that had contaminated so much of America with a mind-dulling sameness. All that changed, however, with the recently completed, $261 million-dollar Manhattoan Casino. It was

Vegas with a side of green chile, its muted Southwestern architecture in direct contrast to the cacophony of *Ka-ching!* from its legions of tricked-out slot machines.

The Manhattoan Casino—where every day the tribe got the opportunity to repay hundreds of years of good ol' fashioned American hospitality with a thank you gift of a ceremonial necklace presented to each and every gambler upon exiting. Evidently, they figured it was paleface's turn to leave Manhattoan with nothing more to show for it than a handful of worthless glass beads.

Three short blocks away, on an unassuming two-lane road sat the Western States Regional Headquarters of the U.S. Air Traffic Control System. Behind its humble and unprotected facade, lay the hub of the world's most technologically advanced radar network. Here, in this single facility, the flight plan of every plane that either originates or concludes at a controlled airport in California, Oregon, Washington, Utah, Arizona, Nevada, New Mexico, or Colorado was coordinated.

Amidst the glare of four hi-def, thirty-six inch, finely calibrated video monitors, John Markum allowed a peek into the future of human evolution; here was the consummate multitasker, a juggler extraordinaire. With over five thousand lives in his hands each and every minute he sat behind those screens, he calmly barked Byzantine instructions almost simultaneously at no less than three dozen aircraft as they made their way across the western skies. Coffee? *Uh, yeah.*

Just barely discernable above the rumble of the twenty-seven other air traffic controllers in ATC Pod B, John felt a vibration from his cell phone. He made a sly but thorough glance over his left shoulder before reaching into his shirt pocket. No, chatting on cell phones while ordering planes about was not permitted at the ATC.

John Markum spoke quickly. "Yeah?"

"John, It's Bill. Ill Bill Berry."

"Hey man, got my hands full. I'll call you on break, alright?"

"Just a quick sec. I need some help. I'm stalled on SWA 2020 inbound for LAX at ABQ."

"Hold." John looked over his left shoulder again, issued two quick mods to planes on approach, then another quick glance over his left before saying into the phone, "Yeah?"

"Hey, get me out of here a-sap, would ya? I'm supposed to meet Dodge tonight. He's got this thing lined up and I don't want to miss it. I don't think you want me to miss it either."

"Hold." Again, a glance. "Hey Chuck, give me SWA 2020 stat, for the duration."

"I'll give you all you want, Cowboy."

And with that, SWA Flight 2020 popped onto John Markum's Screen C. He studied the patterns for a moment although he already knew what he'd find. "Bill, fog's got L.A. backed up to state line. Don't have any shorts available at all. I've got a long haul maybe I could squeeze you into but, man, it's gonna be tight, maybe too tight. You'd have to be tits up by 18:44. That's only fourteen minutes from now with a touchdown at 20:07. I don't see how you could— Fuck!"

Markum dropped the phone into his lap as he pumped an urgent stream of orders through his chrome-tipped, neoprene tube headset, then silently watched Screen B for a moment before he was able to exhale. He followed this with a round of D/C's, ATC-speak for duty-checks, after which noting the precise time on his shift log. It wasn't until after a thorough look left that he picked back up his cell.

"Fucking foreigners, man; I swear half of them have never been to flight school. Anyway, re 2020, that's all there is. And with the headwinds tonight, I don't see how you can get it done."

"Piece of cake, we're already loaded," he lied.

"ABQ's Tower is gonna have to cooperate. And even then, I don't see—"

"Don't worry about it. I've got a friend in the tower."

"Yeah, I'll bet you do. Well, all right, you got it, Illy, but it's gonna be real tight. And if you don't make it, you understand they're gonna make me send you to Burbank, right? And then you're gonna have a shitload of explaining to do. Sure it's worth it?"

"Dodge says she's 13, stacked like a motherfucker, and dumb as dirt. Says she'll do anything. *Anything.*"

"Shit. Get me the vid tonight if you can, Illy."

"You know I will. It's gonna be a scorcher. Girl's got no idea what she's walking into."

John Markum went immediately back to work, but somehow everything was different now. He was finding it hard to concentrate.

THE ART OF COINCIDENCE

The passengers aboard Flight 2020 ascended through 12,000 feet jangling like the clackity band of train-traveling salesman in Act 1, Scene 1 of *The Music Man.* No matter how often Geoffrey flew, he was never able to make peace with turbulence. He knew in his heart he was just one big bump away from falling right out the sky. He tried to look down through the small, scratched airplane window, wondering what kind of terrain they would soon be crashing into, but he couldn't make out a thing. Beneath them lay only a blanket of doom.

That's comforting...

He glanced around the cabin to see if anyone else shared his sense of impending disaster only to spot a suited businessman across the aisle and one row forward with his left index finger stuck two knuckles deep into his ear.

Whoa! That's either a world record or that guy was last in his class at Yakuza Prep School.

Geoffrey cracked a worried smile, took a deep breath, and tried to calm himself.

Two minutes later...

"Ladies and Gentlemen, this is Captain William Berry. From all of us on the flight deck, welcome aboard. My apologies for the turbulence we're encountering. We are currently on our way to 36,000 feet and are doing absolutely everything we can to make up for the delay leaving Albuquerque." Ill Bill had not spoken truer words in years.

Ten minutes later...

"Lima-5-Niner-4, this is ABQ ATC. Come in. Markum was all business, fully aware his every word while "on-com" was being recorded.

"Lima-5-Niner-4, over."

"Lima-5-Niner-4, you are late leaving ABQ airspace. May have no choice but to divert to Burbank."

"Negative, ATC. We are full throttle and will meet landing schedule. Request 47,000 feet."

"Green on 4-7-k but headwinds look to make on time landing impossible. I repeat, may have no choice but to divert."

"Don't sweat it; we're as good as there. Lima-5-Niner-4 out."

With each hand clinging dearly to an armrest, Geoffrey sat staring at the seatback in front of him. He was debating whether he should take out his laptop and go through some email. His answer came in the form of a large atmospheric pothole.

OOOoooooooooohhhhh! Ooohh! Ooh! I swear to God, I'm driving from now on...

He looked around. Even The Human Brain Tickler had removed his finger from his ear and was looking out the window.

"Ladies and Gentlemen, this is your captain again. The turbulence does not seem to be letting up. We're ascending to 47,000 feet to try and get on top of it. Please remain in your seats with your seatbelts tightly fastened."

Fifteen minutes later...

Mike Costello, SWA Flight 2020's co-pilot and thanks to Bill's indoctrination and sponsorship also a member of "*Dazz*", squawked to the captain, "Bill, we're still eighteen minutes long. We're not going to make it."

"Shit."

"Should I radio ATC?"

"No," Bill replied with a shake of the head. And then into his headpiece, he squawked, "ATC, this is Lima-5-Niner-4."

"Lima-5-Niner-4, ATC over," said Markum.

"Lima-5-Niner-4 requests 56,000 feet."

"5-6-k? Where you going, Tokyo?"

"No. Manhattan Beach, remember?" Ill Bill replied, pointedly.

"Okay to 5-6-k."

"Lima-5-Niner-4 out."

Captain Bill Berry was gunning for a new record. The extra fuel expense would cost Southwest Airlines a bundle, which would mean questions. But then there was a lot of turbulence, right?

THE ART OF COINCIDENCE

Geoffrey Zukor hated sitting at the rear of the plane; it was so noisy and certainly that night's flight was no exception. The aircraft engines' hard, strident whine rattled the luggage bins above him. After several failed attempts, he was finally able to draw down the gummy, beige plastic shade on the window to his left. Then, with the tips of two fingers, he picked up a small rectangular airline pillow from the seat next to him, a pillow he just knew was teeming with not only every germ known to Man but countless others still awaiting discovery. He covered it with his sport coat, which was made from of one of those new "no-iron miracle fabrics." When Geoffrey purchased it, he assumed that the jacket would remain relatively wrinkle-free no matter how it was treated, but after only a single wear, he realized what they meant was that this no-iron miracle fabric wrinkles so deeply, "no iron" could possibly get it out. He figured the "miracle" must have been they were able to sell any of the crap in the first place. *"We sold some! Thank you, Jesus, it's a miracle!"*

Geoffrey closed his eyes and nuzzled the side of his head into his makeshift pillow. He tried to get comfortable, which was difficult because one of his sport coat buttons kept getting lodged in his ear. But then Geoffrey always found sleep difficult. It seemed no matter how tired he was beforehand, there was something about the act of getting into bed that turned sleep into an impossibility. He would lay there for hours, the aftershocks of his tossing and turning reverberating through the mattress and sending his wife bouncing up and down like she was on the receiving end of a late-night booty-call from Wilt Chamberlain. He tried everything, even counting sheep, yet there too he failed miserably. You see, Geoffrey's sheep were always milling about, a behavior he found particularly bothersome because it made it impossible to tell whether he was counting some of the same sheep twice. *I mean, what's the point of spending all that time counting if you're not sure you've ended up with the right number?*

And then there was the night he discovered that his flock had almost doubled in size. Sheep were everywhere, stacked two and three high in some places. At first, he welcomed this turn of events, but his glee was short-lived, overtaken by a terrible feeling the whole thing was a setup and that he was being fingered as the fall guy. He just knew that at any moment there would be a crashing knock at the door, and he would be arrested for sheep-nabbing. If things went as he suspected, by morning every kid in America would hate him.

Little Bo Peep didn't lose her sheep.
It was big, fat Geoffrey Zukor who stole them!
Then he knocked her down,
And broke her crown,
And probably stole that too, the fat bastard!

And so, he decided to give up on the whole sheep counting business before things got out of hand. Or he was hit with a restraining order, case in point being the feelings he had developed for this sassy little Blackbelly from Barbados. Geoffrey, naive to the ways of the world, failed to pick up on the fact she was actually a lesbian and therefore completely misunderstood when she told him, "I'm into ewe. I'm into ewe!"

Hearing that, Geoffrey went all Barry White on her and replied, "Well, then, little lady, why don't you come over here and show me just how baaaaaa-dly you want me."

"I'm into ewe! I'm into ewe!!" the Blackbelly screamed in reply.

Regrettably, details of what of followed are sealed by court order.

And so instead of counting sheep, Geoffrey closed his eyes and tried to relax. His inner view turned cerulean as he watched an Olympic-trained version of himself dive ever so gracefully from a springboard on high, his perfect form piercing a sparkling, sun-starred sea. His momentum carried him downward, swimming deeper and deeper into the darkening, bottomless blue. Further down and ever deeper, he swam, he swam, into the waiting shadowy arms of the unknown.

THE ART OF COINCIDENCE

Don't worry. Be happy.
                              - Meir Baba

I am not a violent man, but does anyone have a gun?
                              - Geoffrey Zukor

SWA Flight 2020 made up considerable time over the next 45 minutes. Captain Berry's goal was now in sight but still out of reach; a tease — a tauntingly ripe, baited hook for the incessantly starving, slowly reeling him in, reeling him in. He kept thinking about the girl. *She's got no idea what she's walking into...*

On a typical approach, a commercial pilot begins to reduce speed and engage an orderly descent at the 180 miles mark east of LAX. Instead, SWA Flight 2020 remained static at 56,000 feet for another 40 miles.

"Lima-5-Niner-4, this is Albuquerque ATC, unless you are planning on vacationing in Hawaii, immediately reduce elevation to 18,000 feet and await further instruction."

"Roger, ATC. Good for 1-8-k. Lima-5-Niner-4 out."

Markum at ATC had seen that Lima-5-Niner-4 was flying high but hadn't focused on the fact they were also flying fast. Too fast. As a flight attendant made her standard cabin announcements, they began their descent. Their elevation and proximity to the airport meant having to push the aircraft into a steeper than customary glideslope, which translated into even greater airspeed, automatically tripping the cockpit's Aircraft Warning System.

"Reduce glideslope," blasted a robotic voice from the instrument panel. A flick of a chrome toggle next to a red flashing light on the console returned silence to the cockpit.

Two minutes later…

"Lima-5-Niner-4, this is Albuquerque ATC, altitude outside FAA Guidelines for landing. We will not be able to accommodate you on this approach. Turn 1-2-6 for an immediate redirect."

"Negative Albuquerque ATC, we will make our cue. Lima-5-Niner-4 out," replied the captain. He hit the com switch before Marcum could respond and pushed the plane's nose downward, resulting in a momentary sensation of quasi-weightlessness for all those aboard and a corresponding bit of nausea for those so inclined.

"Shit," John Markum said, off mic.

Captain Bill Berry was swinging for the fences, motivated by images of a waiting and willing thirteen-year-old girl. He had seen a polaroid of her with her top down. *She was perfect, so fucking perfect…* He had watched Dodge fuck a couple of girls and he was hungry to get some for himself. *Tonight… Tonight… Tonight…*

"Captain, we're too fast," Costello warned.

"15 percent flaps," Berry answered. "Just a bit more…" He continued to increase the rate of descent, but the flaps held the craft to 490 knots. This certainly *will* be a record.

One minute later…

"20 percent flaps and gear."

"We're way over spec. That's a negative, sir," countermanded Costello.

"Now!" ordered the captain.

Captain Berry was right, in one respect anyway; at the risk of possible damage to the landing gear or worse, blowing out the aircraft's hydraulic system, the added drag would certainly help to slow the plane as it descended. As Lima-5-Niner-4's landing gear lowered, the cabin vibrated with more rumble and wind noise than any of the passengers had ever experienced before.

"Albuquerque ATC, this is Lima-5-Niner-4, request to land 0-6-5." The fact that this was L.A.'s longest runway was lost on no one.

"You are still high Lima-5-Niner-4. Maintain elevation and turn 1-2-6 stat for an immediate redirect."

"Gear down, craft in full landing configuration, and rate of descent acceptable. Landing 0-6-5."

"Come on, you'll never make that," balked Markum.

"That's what they said to Earhart."

Costello eyes darted to the captain. He wondered if he meant to say Lindberg but didn't ask. This was no time for conversation.

"John, I've got this. It's *not* a problem. Lima-5-Niner-4 gear down, landing 0-6-5."

He knew he shouldn't, he knew he shouldn't, he knew he shouldn't... but John Markum felt powerless to stop him.

"Okay, 0-6-5," he squawked. He stared at his screen. All he could see was Lima-5-Niner-4. And what he saw, gave him a real bad feeling. "Shit. SHIT!"

THE ART OF COINCIDENCE

Four minutes later...

It was unbelievable! Truly unbelievable! SWA Flight 2020 was wheels down on Runway 0-6-5 exactly on cue: 20:07! Yes, 20:07! It was a new ABQ/LAX commercial carrier speed record and by all accounts, a real accomplishment — unless, that is, you consider a landing that's 115 yards long and 72 knots fast a bit of an overriding flaw. Most would.

"Reverse thrust full. Full flaps," barked Captain Berry. He stomped on the hydraulic wheel brakes as if a child were on the runway; soon enough, there would be.

The captain looked right, across an adjacent taxiway into a thick windbreak of mature eucalyptus trees. The speed of their passing confirmed the reversed thrusters were having little effect. His eyes shot forward. And then it hit him; he had walked this way before.

This was like his dream, his reoccurring dream. In it, a plane was speeding, always speeding toward disaster. But he was cool, always cool, confident in his natural, God-given abilities. He remained aloof, unworried, ever the star of his own feature film. The moment to save the day was at hand and so was the only man with skill enough to do it. It was perfect.

He would take charge with a blaze of activity, hurriedly barking orders, flipping switches, pulling levers; there was no time to lose. Against this dire backdrop, he cut a handsome silhouette, every bit the hero. Intelligence, grit, and raw, brazen talent— he wielded them all in glamour shot after glamour shot. And how he loved it. This is right where he belonged. And it is precisely then that Captain Berry's dreams always took the same nightmarish turn. His craft rocked violently from side to side; the beast had not been tamed. He continued to work frantically but soon came to realize that every move he made, every switch he flipped, every peddle he pushed, was to no effect, no effect at all. Faster and faster, he worked to save himself, save his aircraft, save his crew, but one failed effort after another was his only reward. And time was running out. And then it dawned on him; the instruments, the controls, they, they… they weren't real. Somehow everything in the cockpit was fake, there simply for show; all of it flaccid, unattached, meaningless. *Without meaning…* The bottom fell from ill Bill's stomach as he realized that those were not just dreams; they were both admonition and premonition. How he lived his life was exactly how he would die: *Without meaning.*

The inevitable could no longer be denied; Lima-5-Niner-4 was going long. The captain, against all hope, continued to pound the wheel brakes into the floor. The tires stuttered violently but the aircraft would not comply with his command, and no one could do a damned thing about it. Disaster was at hand.

THE ART OF COINCIDENCE

Merrily we roll along, roll along, roll along.
Merrily we roll along, t'ward the deep blue sea.
-Old English sea chantey

"FUCK! WE'RE GOING LONG, WE'RE GOING LONG!!" the captain blared into his radio, out of breath, panicked.

Seconds later, Lima-5-Niner-4 plowed through the thrust-guard at the end of the paved and grooved section of Runway 0-6-5, fracturing the right main landing struts, leaving it weakened, unable to support the immense weight of the Boeing 737. The plane listed hard right as steel support shafts plunged deep into the fuselage. Bent and bloodied but no less determined, the aircraft barreled across the airport's gravel over-run.

Yes, he had walked this way before but nothing in Captain William Berry's life prepared him for the view now present from his cockpit window: his imminent head-on collision with a thirty-foot, rebar and girder reinforced concrete street barricade.

Mid-scream, Ill Bill's 312,000-pound aircraft rammed the massive wall. The impact created an immense jolt, completely re-arranging the passenger cabin. Bodies slammed into seatbacks, cushioned only by the occasional dangling yellow plastic air-cup that had inadvertently gotten in the way. Carry-on luggage orbited madly about. The street barricade reluctantly gave way but did manage to strip the plane of its landing gear and most of its cargo hold. Screams of ripping steel trumped all others.

After clearing the block wall, what was left of Lima-5-Niner-4 pitched downward and slammed into the center median of West Airport Drive, reverberating in a spectacular multicolored explosion of sparks, so thunderous the impact it severed the nose assembly from the plane's main fuselage. A motorcyclist, speeding southbound on West Airport banked hard right to avoid the plane but his wheels lost traction and he ended up on the asphalt, sliding without his leathers. His Harley's last official act was a full triple-axel, spinning like Ronnie Robertson towards Yates' Airport Tex-aco, where it was joined by the decapitated flight-deck. No one could say which caught fire first but soon flames engulfed every-thing. Three minutes later, the subterranean tanks of the Texaco blew, its concussive force shattering windows blocks away. A huge fireball rose into the night sky, a fireball that could be seen all the way to a certain house in Manhattan Beach.

THE ART OF COINCIDENCE

Think what you will about the gay lifestyle, but every once in a while, all that working out comes in real handy. Donn Olson threw open the main cabin's rear emergency exit like Steve Reeves leaving the Temple of Narcissi. Performing exactly as designed, a bright yellow slide shot from the ravaged fuselage onto the street below, fully inflating in seconds. From inside the cabin, only flames flickering through thick smoke could be seen looking forward; no one was getting out that way. This slide was their only chance of escape. And Donn knew all too well they had but a few precious minutes to get what use out of it they could. After that, FAA studies showed the chances of surviving a crash dropped precipitously.

"THIS WAY! THIS WAY! THIS WAY! GO! GO! GO! WHEN YOU'RE DOWN, MOVE AWAY FROM THE PLANE! GO! GO! GO!" he yelled, almost throwing a string of dazed passengers through the emergency exit. "GO! GO! GO!"

Again and again, Donn looked forward toward the cockpit but the smoke, dense, black, and impenetrable, billowing aft, completely obscured his view.

"TIM! TIM! THIS WAY! THIS WAY!! EVERYONE, THIS WAY!!" he yelled as he continued to move passengers in rapid succession off the plane. "GO! GO! GO!"

When the main aisle was clear, he continued to yell forward. "TIM! TIM!"

Do they have the front hatch open?

"TIM! TIM!" Still no answer. "TIM!!!"

Donn could barely see ten feet in front of him. He stuck his head out the rear exit, tried to rub the sting from his eyes, took a deep breath, then ducked back inside. He kept his head low and began fighting his way forward. He didn't get far. It was then that the main tanks at the Texaco blew. A huge wave of ignited gas slapped the right side of the plane nearly rolling it, and in the process, tossed Donn into the seats on his left. And that was how Donn Olson came to find Geoffrey Zukor, who lay clumped on the floor, unconscious from his unrestrained bout with the seatback tray table; it was a draw, both now inoperable.

"HEY! HEY!! CAN YOU HEAR ME? CAN YOU HEAR ME?

Donn couldn't revive him and only with the help of angels was he able to drag Geoffrey out into the main aisle and then finally aft, to the rear door. He stood there for a moment, gasping for a breath of uncontaminated air as he wiped his tearing eyes. A final attempt looking back into the cabin revealed nothing. As flames and heavy black smoke surrounded him, he scooped Geoffrey into his arms and tumbled down the escape slide onto the street below.

Donn Olson was the first to board Five-Niner-Four that day, and now he was the last to leave.

THE ART OF COINCIDENCE

Cedars-Sinai Medical Center held a soup rich with human emotion. A hospital, like no other place on Earth, infuses a broth of both hope and loss, exhilaration and despair, where routinely those blighted by death share an elevator with the recipients of a newborn. It is here that the spared meet the forsaken, the diseased meet the pure, and the forgotten meet the expectant.

The cavernous hospital lobby, lined in large slabs of black marble, stood like the west coast reflection of Grand Central Station. Each of the hospital's three multi-level parking structures were connected via elevator to the large atrium, as were all of the elevator banks for the hospital's North, South, and East towers. The west wall of the lobby was constructed entirely of glass, soaring some sixty feet upward, and revealed a lush and varied park, filled with mature oak and cottonwood trees, perfectly placed to read as though parks naturally spring up on every large concrete slab in the country.

was the trademarked phrase italicized across the top of Braun Dinkerhoff's business card, the park's renowned landscape architect.

Braun Dinkerhoff—the genius designer whose latest work included the dense, musty, and omnipresent jungle at Las Vegas' newest, no-expense-spared, mega-resort *Lost!* themed after the hit TV show. And what a stunning achievement it was too. Dinkerhoff's jungle was so authentic that at the property's lavish grand opening most of its patrons, once off the strip and through the hotel's main entrance, were unable find their way through the overgrown maze of tangled greenery to locate the Faraday Front Desk, Locke's Lagoon swimming pool, Ben's All-You-Can-Eat Buffet, and most devastating of all, Kate's Casino, leaving a dazzling assortment of slots and gaming tables almost entirely empty, accompanied only by gum-chewing cocktail waitresses outfitted like Kate herself, assuming, that is, there's an episode where Kate goes to a costume party dressed as Lizzo after she squeezed into one of Ariana Grande's skimpiest bikinis.

"What size are you, honey?"

"I'm an eight."

"Okay, here you go."

"But sir, this is a size 2."

"Sweetie, you may be a size 8 on the reservation, but in Vegas, you wear a 2, capisce? If our customers wanted to see fabric, they'd stay home and stare at their couch."

Unfortunately for its owner/developer, the flamboyant Mr. Wynn, whose ferociously unrestrained bad taste was finally explained in a *60 Minutes* puff-piece when it was revealed that he is actually blind, *Lost!* was eventually lost, bankrupt, buried under an avalanche of its own debt. The resort's foreclosure dealt a devastating blow to those who financed it, a syndicate of small Midwestern banks, the loss so substantial as to move several to the brink of bankruptcy themselves. The hotel's construction loan and permanent financing had been arranged by none other than the financial services giant Citigroup, fresh off their stunning Enron, WorldCom, and Parmalat trifecta. Even still, their credibility was a notch above most other New York firms.

Lost! was sold at auction for just half of its original cost, shuttered for six months, and then re-opened, jungle intact, as:

TARZAN!

The Swingingest Hotel in Vegas!

Sadly, it wasn't long before the re-born star of the Vegas Strip found itself in its own tsunami of trouble, despite the obvious allure of Tarzan, Jane, and their lovable chimp, Chaiyo, all performing aerial feats of wonder in a jungle-themed trapeze act directly over the heads of the gambling public on the main casino floor—sans underwear.

"Dwayne, we better not do the triple-toe side-split flip-flap with Chaiyo tonight. He doesn't look well. I don't think he's up to it."

"Vasche, we must! The producers from *Boylesque!* are here to see me perform. They're casting the biggest show to ever hit the strip. It's an all-male, all-nude, all-black revival of *Fiddler on the Roof!* This could be my big break! We must do the triple-toe side-split flip-flap, Vasche, we must! Now hurry! It's showtime!"

Three minutes later, Chaiyo the Chimp was the first primate in history to *crap-out* in a Las Vegas casino. No one was sure if it was a rotten banana or his recently acquired appetency for Mexican food, but whatever the reason was, Chiayo really let it fly-o. From this vine to that, from one end of the casino to another, swinging back and forth, here and there, he zoomed overhead like a biplane crop-duster, or, perhaps more accurately, a biplane *crap*-duster, leaving his indelible watery-brown mark all over the casino and most of its patrons. *Ah, the smell of the jungle…*

Unfortunately, the hotel was never able to recover from the fiasco and thus it was that TARZAN! — *The Swingingest Hotel in Vegas!* quite literally swung itself right out of business, eventually selling in bankruptcy for about 40% of the cost of its acquisition and renovation. *Ouch!* Another huge loss for the consortium of fee-paying, Citigroup-lead, "partner" banks. Boy, it sure is nice having partners.

The purchaser this third go-round was a group of Hollywood types who blew into town with a savvy marketing plan and enough *chutzpah* to finally transform the twice failed property into a success. Once again, the resort was closed for a complete make-over, finally re-opening, yes, thank God, with jungle intact, as:

The
Flintstones
Go to Vegas!
The Hotel

which boldly advertised the world's largest massage parlor—

The Rub-ba Dub-ba Do!

where guests of the casino, for an extra twenty bucks, could get some very good Fred. Problem solved.

THE ART OF COINCIDENCE

It was almost seventy-two hours before Geoffrey regained some level of consciousness and opened his eyes — or eye, to be exact. His right cornea was badly mangled by a blunt force blow to the side of his head and his lid was now bandaged shut. No one could say for sure to what extent he would regain his vision.

Sweet sleep and advanced pharmacology had spared Geoffrey immeasurable pain over the last three days but like a dutiful dog it eagerly awaited his return to consciousness. He tried to turn his head; everything hurt.

"Dad! Dad, can you hear me?"

In a room so blindingly white as to be mistaken for Heaven itself, there she was, a blur yet unmistakably his daughter Charlotte. He could feel himself shaking, his head, his hands. He struggled to focus.

"Char…"

"Dad!"

"That's too loud, Charlotte!" ordered Victoria Zukor. She moved closer to him. Even in his semi-conscious state, Geoffrey could see his wife was angry. It came as no surprise.

"Look at you, look at you…" she said, slowly shaking her head. In her words lay the undeniable inferences of blame, sweet blame, her constant companion. Her voice though was softened with the tears of pity that ran past her elegantly pronounced cheekbones. Never mind that Geoffrey looked like a well-used practice cadaver at a medical school for the blind, this tragedy was all hers.

But that was a Victoria few ever saw. The outer, public Victoria was cool, aloof, mysterious even in her stylish, unapproachable elegance. She was a recherché breed, the modern-day Marlena Dietrich, whose soul's pronouncement was broadcast with her every move: *I don't want you and I certainly do not need you.* She was an object of desire yet was incapable of returning the love; that would be simply beneath her.

Today, Victoria Zukor stood posture perfect, wearing an impeccably tailored, obsidian blue Channel suit with its trademark piping, this time in black with matching black oyster buttons. A triple strand of black pearls lay across the ageless, even tone of her chest. Her hair, a lovely chestnut brown with multiple shades of golden highlights, was swept up into a perfectly coiffed French bun. This was what all the well-dressed mourners were wearing this season — it was Jackie at Onassis' deathbed — and while many were attempting it, few looked better doing so than Victoria Zukor.

Geoffrey tried to speak, perhaps even to apologize, but as his mouth groped for words gone missing, he slipped back into unconsciousness.

THE ART OF COINCIDENCE

Dr. Eric Alacombre, Director of Cedars-Sinai Level 1 Trauma Center, had come to the hospital with only the experience of a young Marine triage medic, schooled in bandaging the brutality of war. In his first decade at Cedars, Dr. Alacombre became widely recognized as a genius in his field, developing over a dozen surgical techniques adopted by doctors around the world. His work brought Cedars' trauma center to national prominence, earning the hospital its Level 1 accreditation, and establishing it as a marvel of cutting-edge science. And it wasn't only Dr. Alacombre that set it apart. The breadth of experience of the team he assembled was unrivaled, owing largely to the number of applicants who wanted to work beside him. Being a member of Dr. Alacombre's staff virtually guaranteed an individual their choice of jobs nearly anywhere in the world, should they be so inclined, although few rarely were. They also had the finest, most up-to-date equipment at their disposal, much of it donated by manufacturers well before it was released to hospitals at large. Experience had taught the device manufacturers that being able to say, "Alacombre at Cedars has 3 of them" was a powerful sales tool.

The trauma center at Cedars-Sinai had seen only one passenger from Flight 2020. Other hospitals were closer and despite the severity of the crash, miraculously not many were critically injured. This excluded the four pronounced dead at the scene of course. Geoffrey Zukor was originally transported via Medivac to County General, but against doctor's orders was transferred almost immediately to Cedars-Sinai.

Victoria Zukor's husband would have only the finest care and that was Cedars-Sinai. The fact that they had valet parking and opulent suites on the ninth floor did not factor into her decision at all. Nor did the chic cappuccino bar, *21 West*, in the atrium, nor *Restaurant Alain Ducasse Cedars-Sinai* located on the mezzanine overlooking the main lobby; and neither did the *Gucci, Prada, Hermes,* and *Louis Vuitton* gift boutiques on the Plaza Level, nor the finest collection of artwork in any hospital in the world; and certainly, Cedars unrivaled clientele had nothing whatsoever to do with Geoffrey's relocation. Cedars-Sinai offered the best care and for that reason and that reason alone, he was moved in such a precarious state. Really, that was the only reason. The singular, sole reason. That was it. Il Reasonotto Uno. The best care for her husband — *that* was all that concerned her…

Okay, you're right, Victoria Zukor couldn't give a cannoli about the care her husband would receive at Cedars-Sinai. She was not going to be seen roaming the halls in a blue-collar joint like County General and that was all there was to it. Period. End of story.

When Victoria had her thyroid surgery, (it was *not* a breast lift, it was thyroid surgery. Many people experience extra perky boobs following their thyroid surgery. Tons of people. Happens all the time.) anyway, she insisted her procedure be done at Cedars, even though the surgery cost twice as much as it would have had it been done in Dr. Douglas 'Dougie' Williams in-office surgi-center in Beverly Hills. You see, in Los Angeles people brag about going to Cedars. They say it with the same clenched-jaw inflection one might say, "We're going to Gstaad for Christmas, darling." And for Los Angelenos, Cedars-Sinai in the summer is nothing less than the West Coast's answer to the Hamptons. "Joan, I'd love to make your dinner party for the Bidens, but we already have plans to go to Cedars for the weekend. So sorry, dear."

THE ART OF COINCIDENCE

While Geoffrey was still in transit, Dr. Alacombre quickly read though his assessment from County, and as soon as he arrived was sent directly to Imaging for another set of scans, including films from Cedars' new MRSI unit, the world's most advanced, non-intrusive 3-D imaging system. Within fifteen minutes the doctor was reviewing a full complement of data with a diverse team of clinical technicians.

"We better go in, stat. Full torso prep in OR2. Get me a fresh second, an assist, and a full com of support. And call over to Jules Stein and see if they could send someone to work on his right eye. See if you can get Horowitz or the heavyset fella, I forget his name. If not, get me Bartini from upstairs or his best man, nothing less. And you better call over to Plastics and see if they can have someone on standby, available in say, four, maybe five hours for some prelim facial work."

Geoffrey Zukor was then whisked into surgery at near Flight 2020 touchdown speed.

Seven and a half hours later, Geoffrey Zukor was wheeled into post-op, minus his spleen and six units of blood. For seven and a half hours, Dr. Alacombre and team talked vacations, kids, *Curb Your Enthusiasm*, the sale at the new Bergdorf Goodman across the street, husbands, wives, kids, colleges, movies, restaurants, diets, and of course, the latest celebrity gossip — and all with the unsettling casualness of a Sunday brunch gabfest at Leisure World. Discussing politics, however, had been strictly off-limits since Trump took office. Peppered into the mix of topics were comments like "Losing O2 sat, central venous pressure near fail, anaplastic hemorrhage non-aspirating, warm ischemic perfusion to the spleen," and the always popular, "gastric perforation causing acute cardio-respiratory decompensation—clamp and cauterize stat."

The nurses all dotingly asked Dr. Alacombre questions about his golf game, questions they would never think to ask their husbands, and they listened to his answers like Dr. Alacombre's wife never had time to. They laughed at his jokes and often took turns asking him for advice on this subject or that. Their admiration for the man was palpable; here was the closest thing to a harem this side of rural Utah. It didn't hurt that Dr. Alacombre was soap opera doctor handsome, albeit in a more casual, unaffected, middle-aged Harrison Ford kind of way. Even from behind his surgical mask, his rich, warm eyebrows and vivid blue eyes brought many a dreamy smile from the O.R. nursing staff, even during the most stressful of surgeries.

Yes, doctor…

THE ART OF COINCIDENCE

Cedars' impeccably credentialed staff, its restaurants and pricey boutiques, its art collection and fabulously famous clientele were not the only things that differentiated it from other hospitals. Cedars-Sinai was the only medical center in the world to have a fully equipped Press Center, stocked with a complete array of klieg lights, low-impedance microphones, satellite transponders, radio antennae, and fax, data, and email terminals, all of which connected by hundreds of thousands of feet of subterranean A/V cabling, and all at the disposal of the media. Mobile television units needed only to pull into a specially designated section of the hospital's parking structure and run a short cable from a recorder in their truck to the appropriately labeled jack on a nearby wall, where they could select from either a live feed from the hospital's Sony HDC-2000 multiformat camera system or from their own equipment hauled up to the Press Center. Another wall-jack was available to take the A/V feed from their truck and route the signal to an array of satellite transponders on the roof, where it could be beamed back to their television network or radio station for broadcast. The Cedars-Sinai Press Center was undoubtedly the most convenient hospital remote on the planet, and, due to the nature of its clientele, the busiest—granted, not the most truthful—but certainly the busiest.

QUOTES
FROM THE 3 MOST ATTENDED
CEDARS-SINAI PRESS CONFERENCES OF THE YEAR

1. Cliff Maxford, P/M/K: "Our client, Ms. Lisa Rinna, known to her fans as, *You look familiar. Do you work at the dry cleaners on San Vicente?* is in stable condition here at Cedars-Sinai recovering from the first known attack of Africanize Honeybees in Southern California. Contrary to what has been reported in irresponsible fringe media outlets like *The New Republic* and *The Washington Post*, Ms. Rinna's lips did not explode from an over-fill of injectable collagen but rather were ruptured in a brutal assault by Africanized Honeybees. The Africanized Honeybees were obviously very hungry after their long flight in from Africa and probably just mistook her lips for the fruit of the Tzi-Tzi Tree. Ms. Rinna would also like it known that she is an animal lover and a proud supporter of PETA and that no bees were harmed in her attack."

2. Uber-publicist Pressley Groane-Melnick: "While I cannot confirm that my client is being treated here at Cedars-Sinai, I can unequivocally state that if she

were here, it would not, I repeat, it would *not* be for treatment of an eating disorder. Her weight is absolutely within normal parameters for a girl of her height and age. At this time, I would also like to dispel the false and vicious rumor floating around the Internet's cancel culture that she is here because when she sneezed yesterday, she went flying around the room like an untied balloon and ended up landing on her head. That is absolutely, one-hundred-percent false. I was with her all day yesterday and can personally assure you she landed quite squarely on her feet and was completely fine afterward. A little dizzy perhaps, but fine. And anyone that prints anything to the contrary will be sued."

"The truth of the matter is simply that she was so frustrated trying to get into shape for a demanding new project she starts in the fall, that after 24 hours of continuous exercise, stopping only long enough to eat, purge, and then down some laxatives, well, she was so frustrated because after doing all that, the poor girl didn't lose any weight at all, not a single pound, well, she was so desperate to at least lose *something* that she accidentally, purely accidentally, punctured both of her breast implants with a fork. It was nothing more serious than that. And that's the only reason she's here, if she's here at all, which she isn't."

3. Nevi Wyland, spokesperson for Ms. Courtney Love: "At 2:57 a.m. this morning, an unconscious Courtney Love voluntarily checked herself into the lockdown wing of the Tom Sizemore Psychiatric Unit at Cedars-Sinai Medical Center. Ms. Love's

recent episodes of what some have reported to be alarmingly erratic behavior were not, I repeat, *not* a result of illicit drug use but rather a chemical imbalance that Ms. Love's private team of physicians believe was most likely caused by an accidental overuse of peroxide in her hair dye. There is strong evidence to suggest that the peroxide seeped through her scalp and created a disturbance of neurotransmitter connectivity within and between the hippocampus, the prefrontal cortex, and the dorsal thalamus, resulting in severe over-activity in their glutamatergic and dopaminergic functions, known precursors of behavioral abnormalities. Due to the serious nature of her illness, we ask members of the press to be especially respectful and sensitive during this most difficult time."

"It is also worth clarifying that Courtney did not arrive at Cedars in handcuffs as some mean-spirited reporters have suggested. I am sorry to deprive you of a juicy story, but the truth is Ms. Love's bracelets just got tangled together and she wasn't able to separate them without the help of a highly-trained jewelry professional. And that's all there is to it."

"Oh, and contrary to various utterly false media reports that began surfacing this morning, the uniformed men that were kind enough to accompany her here and assist her with her *voluntary* admittance, were not "arresting" officers but rather special agents from the elite Beverly Hills Beauty Shop Police, Peroxide Division — men specially trained to handle delicate situations such as this.

And so, let's recap, shall we?

Tangled bracelets — YES.

Handcuffs — NO.

Accompanied to hospital by Beverly Hills Beauty Shop Police — YES.

Arrested for offering to blow an undercover cop for two tabs of "Hillbilly Heroin" and a cigarette — NO.

Bizarre behavior due to chemical imbalance caused by peroxide overuse — YES.

Bizarre behavior due to taking massive amounts of any drug she could get her hands on — NO.

Any questions?

THE ART OF COINCIDENCE

No matter how many times he did it, Dr. Alacombre never enjoyed it nor believed it contributed in any meaningful way to the benefit of the hospital. Considering all the important things that were left undone at the end of each week, that his participation at a press conference was a required part of his job seemed flat-out stupid.

"Why am I here?" he often asked. "Are we trying to assure people that there really are doctors at Cedars-Sinai by showing one on TV?"

Yet despite his grumbling, his presence was never excused, and on this day Dr. Alacombre stood uneasily several feet behind and to the left of a honey stained, bird's eye maple podium bearing a large, embossed emblem of the hospital. On top of the podium, sat no less than two-dozen microphones, perched like a close-knit family of finch. Dr. Alacombre glanced again at his watch while a striking, mid-to-late thirty-something woman approached the lectern with confidence and ease.

"Ladies and Gentlemen, my name is Laura Latman, Director of Media and Public Relation here at Cedars-Sinai Medical Center. At your request, Cedars-Sinai is making Dr. Eric Alacombre, Head of the Cedars-Sinai's Level One Trauma Center, available today to give you a briefing on the condition of Mr. Geoffrey Zacky, a passenger aboard Thursday's fatal crash of Southwest Airline's Flight 2020."

"Dr. Eric Alacombre has been a lead physician here at Cedars-Sinai for twenty-eight years. He received his training at Harvard Medical School and is a recipient of the United States Marines Corp's Silver Scepter for valor by a medic on the field of battle. Dr. Alacombre has also received the American Medical Association's Medal of Hope, their highest honor awarded to our nation's trauma center doctors for his career-long commitment and dedication to setting new standards of excellence. Ladies and gentlemen of the press, Dr. Eric Alacombre."

There was not a single reporter present that had not heard Dr. Alacombre's bio at least two-dozen times but then, given the opportunity, Laura Latman would put maple syrup on a hot fudge sundae.

"Thank you *soooo* much for the *opportunity* to be here, Ms. Latman," he said, turning toward her and away from the video feed and microphones to conceal his obvious sarcasm. He then faced front and began to read from the double-spaced text she had prepared for him. Laura wondered if his consistently awkward delivery was his way of telling her, *"You can make me do it, but you can't make me do it well."*

"Ladies and Gentleman of the press, yesterday, Thursday, May 9, at approximately 11:47 p.m., we received Mr. Geoffrey Zacky into our Cedars-Sinai's Level One Trauma Center, after sustaining multiple Class V injuries in the crash of Southwest Airlines Flight 2020. Mr. Zacky was immediately treated in a demanding and multifaceted eight-hour operation involving some of the most technologically advanced medical equipment available at any hospital in the world today. Mr. Zacky has yet to regain consciousness and remains in our ICU." Standard press *bla-bla-bla*, whose real message was more about the wonderful treatment patients receive at Cedars-Sinai than it was on the condition of the patient themselves. Laura Latman was no dummy.

"Sheila Stieger, KNBC Channel Four. What is Mr. Zacky's current condition?"

Laura knew to always leave plenty of meat on the bone for reporters to pick through. She considered this tactic one of the mainstays of her success. "You see," she would explain to anyone she was trying to impress, which oftentimes seemed like just about everyone, "leaving out key information from our prepared statements gives those covering the story an opportunity to display their 'finely-honed reporting skills.' This makes the reporters feel important, invests them in the story, and most importantly, gives them a bit of screen time. The result? Consistently more coverage for the hospital and our clients."

Laura Latman glided back to the podium. "Mr. Zacky remains in critical condition, but we have every reason to believe he will be upgraded to—" Here she waved her hand about in ambiguous circular motions as if to indicate those in attendance would, of course, know what one gets upgraded to after being in critical condition. "—you know, not-quite-so-critical condition in the very near future."

Okay, so she still wasn't very good with medical jargon, a fact that neither she nor the press corps ever seemed to notice. On the other hand, every time Dr. Alacombre heard Laura say something like "not-quite-so-critical condition," he would wince like someone just run a nail through his foot.

Fifteen minutes later, Dr. Alacombre and Ms. Latman left the briefing, one cool and confident, the other a bit confused.

"I thought his name was Zukor," the doctor said.

"Really?" replied Laura, entirely unconcerned and in a hurry to return to her office to finish up a few loose ends before dashing out to attend a planning meeting for this year's gala fundraiser at The Four Seasons, just a few blocks away.

THE ART OF COINCIDENCE

As Laura was pulling out of the hospital's parking structure, her cell phone rang. She saw that it was from the executive offices.

"Laura Latman," she announced to the caller in her best, "The white zone is for loading and unloading of passengers only" voice.

Laura's Effie-tweezed eyebrows lowered as gloom shadowed her face. She pulled to the curb. "Why? ...What? ...Really? ...Oh, come on. ...I couldn't possibly. I'm driving to the Four Seasons for my meeting with— ...But we're in the middle of the planning the Chinese Auction, sir. It's only three months— ...Yes. ...Yes. ...I understand. ...Yes, sir. Immediately, sir."

She called and left a message for the chairwoman of the event. It was fine; none of the ladies really cared about her missing the meeting. She was second wife material and always kept at a distance. *Always.*

THE ART OF COINCIDENCE

It's a little like wrestling a gorilla. You don't quit when you're tired; you quit when the gorilla's tired.

- Robert Strauss

Laura fumed. *How could he order me back to the hospital like that? 'I'm not asking you, I'm telling you!' That's how he speaks to me after everything I've done for this hospital? He should have retired a long time ago...*

She was referring to Dr. Sidney Sheinman, the father of Cedars-Sinai Medical Center, who in 1953 founded the beginnings of what would become the first Jewish hospital on the West Coast. In concept, one would think the task, although complex, was achievable; after all, there was plenty of Jewish money in Los Angeles and certainly a need within L.A.'s growing Jewish population. But if life teaches us anything, it's that things are rarely as simple as they first present themselves to be, and so it was with the founding of Cedars-Sinai.

While it's true, there was plenty of Jewish money in Los Angeles in the 30's and 40's, the problem, it turned out, was that most of it was held by individuals who were not particularly interested in being primarily identified as Jews. Nor, for that matter, did they feel bound to propagate an insular Jewish existence that was common in most cities were Jews lived at the time. No, this was California, the Promised Land, where Jews, for the first time in their long history, where not ghettoed by society or the orthodoxy of their religious beliefs. Here, Jews experienced an unprecedented level of anonymity and freedom. They were, to a far greater extent than ever before, just like those around them; after all, everyone in California was from somewhere else. Sure, there were country clubs, beach clubs, and men's clubs in Los Angeles whose admission policies were as clear as the invisible "No Jews Allowed" signs on their front doors, but that rancid bit of upper-crust L.A. society, try as they might, did not ruin the taste of the pie. For there was a feeling, a vibration, as the Beach Boys would extol some thirty years later about this place and right the Beach Boys were, the vibrations were good. The freshness of California, this new Jerusalem, practiced what America had only promised; here, a man could truly be known for what he did and not what he was. And opportunity was everywhere.

In California, Jews were free, free to do whatever they like—eat shellfish, date gorgeous gentiles, and hell, even have Christmas parties! *Christmas parties?!? This is the life!*

For the Jews who lived the Hollywood dream like Jack and Harry Warner, Louis B. Meyer, Harry Cohn, Groucho Marx, Samuel Goldwyn, and the like, this was Oz—who needed gefilte fish?

Here was a place largely devoid of ethnicity, a characteristic that remains both Los Angeles' greatest strength and greatest weakness. L.A. has no Greektown or Little Italy, no Polish Hill or

Spanish Harlem. Here, the Shultzes lived next to the McSweeneys who lived next to the De Lucas who lived next to the Liebermans who lived next to the Zielinskis who lived next to the Smiths who lived next to the Chens — and no one thought twice about it. And the few ethnic landmarks that Los Angeles had, namely Olvera Street and Chinatown, were far more commercial "tourist traps" than they were neighborhoods of teeming transplanted immigrants.

California: This was a new land and it called for new thinking. As such, it became the birthplace of Reform Judaism. Although most cultural historians will tell you that the origins of Reform Judaism date back to 19th century Germany, it wasn't until it was remixed with Californian sensibilities that it really got its groove on. Infused with the funky and fresh, laid-back rhythms of the golden state, Reform Judaism became the only religion in the world that you didn't have to "practice" in order to practice. In fact, the less observant Jew you are, the better Reformed Jew you're considered to be. Example: You don't go to synagogue on Shabbat? No problem, you're Reformed. You don't even observe the High Holidays? It's fine, you're Reformed. You marry a *shiksa* and have your son baptized at Saint Peters? Congratulations, you're Reformed! Keep this up and they'll make you a rabbi.

In any event, those pioneers, Mayer, Marx, Goldwyn, and the lot, believed Los Angeles needed a Jewish hospital about as much as they needed to be re-circumcised. The exception, to his great honor, was Eddie Cantor, Sidney Sheinman's first, and for many years, only significant contributor. It was not until the atrocities of WWII came to light, that the others came around.

Since then, Dr. Sidney Sheinman has worked day in and out to grow his one story, 12 bed, 6,000 square foot facility, into one of the finest healing centers in the world. And perhaps it's no coincidence that Dr. Sheinman, a man who had spent his entire life so that others should be healed, has himself never suffered a serious illness or injury. But most of this was lost on Laura Latman, who remained too wrapped up in her own small world to fully appreciate the great soul she had the privilege to work beside.

THE ART OF COINCIDENCE

It was a dark and aggravated Laura that swept like storm clouds into the Chairman's office. Normally, there would be a cute little tap at the door or one of her trademark moon-eyed inquiring looks seeking permission to enter, but there were no such niceties late this Friday afternoon.

"Thank you for coming, Ms. Latman. We have a problem here I think you are uniquely qualified to resolve."

She was *soooo* not interested; she should be at The Four Seasons and unapologetically wore her dark mood for all to see. A woman unknown to her stood beside Dr. Sheinman, arms tightly crossed.

"Laura, this is Mrs. Victoria Zukor. Her husband was the subject of the press briefing you gave this afternoon, the gentleman who was critically injured in the Southwest Airlines crash. I have been listening to Mrs. Zukor for well over an hour now describe how concerned she is by the manner in which you reported on his condition earlier today."

Victoria could remain silent no longer; after all, it had been almost 30 seconds. "*Concerned?* I think you know, sir, I am far more than just *concerned*. I am extremely hurt, and disappointed, and upset, and angered, and insulted, and deeply humiliated by the lack of professionalism displayed here at your hospital, for which I understand you, young lady, are to entirely blame."

"Excuse me?" said Laura, taken aback.

Dr. Sheinman put his right hand over his brows, shielding his eyes. He had listened to Mrs. Zukor long enough to have a pretty good idea where all this was heading and couldn't bear to watch.

"Do you have any idea what it's like to be in the middle of a Swusi manicure and all of a sudden receive word that your husband's plane has just fallen right out of the sky? I was sitting there with only one hand done! What was I supposed to do, just leave and wait another three weeks for an appointment? And then I hear they are taking him to County General! Without even asking me! How does someone handle something like that?"

"But what kind of support do I get around here?" Victoria continued. "You call me Zacky! Me, a Zacky? My husband lies near death and in front of the whole world, you have the nerve to call me Zacky! Do I look like a Zacky to you? Do I, missy?"

Laura Latman, never shy, swallowed hard and tried as diplomatically as possible to come to her own defense. "Excuse me, ma'am, will you please calm down? There is no need to speak to me like that. In rushing to meet a deadline, perhaps the press received certain inaccuracies I never intended."

Victoria turned sharply to Dr. Sheinman. "Ha! A dangling participle! Did you hear that? A dangling participle! Well, isn't that just perfect! Tell me, sir, what kind of imbeciles do you hire around here?"

Dr. Sheinman started to reply but then stopped; it was a hard question to answer, especially when worded like that. His proposed response — "*I assure you, ma'am, we hire the very best imbeciles we can find*" — didn't have a particularly reassuring ring to it.

Then Victoria inquired of Laura, "Is English your second language, moron?"

Dr. Sheinman jumped in. "Mrs. Zukor, I think what Ms. Latman is trying to say is that—"

"Well, she isn't saying it very well, now is she? What'll she do next, end a sentence with a preposition? I can hardly wait!"

"Ma'am," said Laura, "you are making it very difficult for me to—"

"Silence! How dare you interrupt me? I am not done with you, Ms. Latman, not by a long shot. Let me explain it in a way even a pea brain like you can understand. You have insulted a man lying in critical condition in this hospital and his grieving, heartbroken wife. You see, I may be many things, Missy, but I am NOT Zacky!"

"Well, I don't think I—"

"I've got an idea!" Victoria offered. "Let's have a press conference and I'll introduce everyone to Ms. *Slutman* here. How would that be, Ms. *Slutman?*"

"Slutman? Well, I've never!"

"You've never? Ha! Don't make me laugh! You've been pumped by more guys than unleaded gasoline!"

"How dare you! You, you… Zacky!"

"She did it again!!" yelled Victoria, appealing to Dr. Sheinman. "She called me a Zacky!!"

"Well, she called me a Slutman!"

"Buck tooth!"

"Grey hair!"

"Droopy lids!"

"Crow's feet!"

"Hunchback!"

"Boob job!"

Well, that was the last straw. Mrs. Victoria Zukor did *not* have a boob job. "It was a thyroid procedure!!!" she screamed, lunging for Laura's neck.

Grab the Crackerjacks, Ladies and Gentlemen, Los Angeles hasn't seen a wrestling card like this since Bobo Brazil faced "Classy" Freddie Blassie at the Olympic in '61. High heels flew as pearls dotted the carpet. Slutman grabbed Zacky's hair and took her hard to the mat. But wait— Zacky escapes! They were hair extensions!

Zacky slips left, does a 360-degree reach-around lassoing Slutman by the waist, spins her for another 360 and another and — *Ooohh!* — hurls her right over Sheinman's desk, popping several of her blouse buttons in the process. Better duck, Doc, you've got incoming! And then — *Ooouuu!* — Slutman hits the deck hard. She's down, folks. She's down!

Zacky, clearly with the early advantage, runs in the opposite direction, ricochets off the far side mahogany-paneled wall, and then leaps into the air. She springs off a red tufted leather ottoman, soars over Sheinman's desk with an aerial front flip and — *Oh, nooo!* — has Slutman directly in her sights! Pouncing petunias, Patsy, someone's gonna get pulverized! But no! No! Slutman survived! She survived! At the last possible second, Slutman regained enough strength to roll right, dodging Zacky's deathblow. Unbelievable! Now it's Zacky turn to take a tumble on the tarmac. *Whoa, Nellie!* Zacky hits hard, folks, slitting her skirt so high up her thigh you can see where Armstrong landed.

With Zacky down and badly shaken, Slutman searches the room for a weapon. Finding none, she grabs Dr. Sheinman! She's whipping him around like a whirling dervish and — *Howling Hurricane!* — slings him toward the rising Zacky! But wait— Zacky dives and — *Ooohhh!* — Sheinman smacks right into the wall. Get out the Epson Salts, Emma, that twister was a mister, Sister!

Slutman now climbs atop a burgundy leather occasional chair, launches into the air and — *Watch it! Watch it!* — she's going to pile drive her knee right into Zacky's back. But wait! Wait! It was a trap!! Zacky lunges left, away from the descending Slutman and — *Oooouch!* — Slutman's knee smashes right into the parquet floor! *Oh-me-oh-my-oh!* Her knee's as Republican Red as Ohio! Now Zacky grabs a serving tray from one of Sheinman's end tables, and — *Slap!* — she whacks Slutman across the heinie so hard Slutman sails across the hardwood floor face first! Holy Dermabrasion, Batman! Everywhere you look the girl's got a red cheek!

But Zacky's not done. She leaps at Slutman from across the room, pouncing on her back and whipping Slutman's right arm into a vicious half-nelson. Oh, Slutman's in pain! She's pounding the floor for mercy, but Zacky won't stop! Better call the power company, Edison, much more of this and Slutman's gonna blackout! But wait, Zacky stopped... she stopped—

"That's very pretty nail polish. What is it?" Victoria asked, bending Laura's arm in a direction arms most assuredly are not meant to be bent.

Laura squeezed out "Mac" through the pain.

"Mac? Don't give me that," Victoria shot back, with an even more persuasive twist of her wrist. "I've never seen this color before."

"It's ...an ...exclusive. They ...only ...sell ....it ....at ...one ....p-p-place."

"Where?"

"T-Truce?"

"Where? Unless you like hearing the sound of breaking bones, sweetie, you better give it up."

"Truce or no deal."

Victoria thought for a second. Then, rubbing the small of her back with her right hand, she answered, "All right, truce."

"Crossies don't count," Laura warned.

Victoria glared at her. After thinking this over, she slowly removed the hand she had tucked behind her, exposing her crossed fingers. Ever so reluctantly she uncrossed them. "Oh, all right, crossies don't count."

"It's exclusive to Neiman's."

"Really? Well, no wonder. I hate buying make-up at Neiman's." Victoria scooted off her, trying to catch her breath.

"I know, me too. The lighting there is terrible. Everybody looks green," Laura agreed, sitting up. She was finding it difficult to straighten her arm.

"Exactly. And the counter girls—"

"I know, I know, the worst! They must have learned about make-up while working at the circus."

"Century City?" Victoria asked, standing up and straightening her outfit as best she could.

"Yes, but my favorite is the Neiman's at Fashion Island, you know, down in Newport Beach. They have everything there. It's like a completely different store."

"Oh, I love Fashion Island," said Victoria, helping Laura to her feet. "It's so fun."

"And I love your lift. I mean, your thyroid procedure."

"Really? Oh, aren't you sweet. What a cute thing to say."

Laura had a thought. "You know, I'm going down to Fashion Island on Monday. Why don't I stop by Neiman's and pick you up a bottle? My treat. Or, if you like, we could go together?"

"Really? I would love that! I end up getting lost every time I go down there. I don't know why they made Orange County so confusing."

"I know!" Laura agreed. "Everything is so screwed up down there. How do they figure when you are heading toward the ocean you're going south? I mean, I'm no Jacques Cousteau but don't they know they're on the West Coast, as in the coast is west?"

"I think maybe it has something to do with Neiman's originally coming from Texas. The ocean is south down there. Maybe they did it to keep everything consistent."

"Oh..." replied Laura. "I hadn't thought of that. Anyway, if you're up to going, we could drive down together and make a day of it—that is, if your husband's feeling better, of course."

"Oh, he'll be fine. He always makes such a big deal about everything. I'd love to go. Here's my number, call me Sunday. Oh, and what do you think we should do about Dr. Sheinman?"

"Oh, he'll be fine, too. The guy could use the rest. He's been in a foul mood lately."

"Men," said Victoria, shaking her head.

"Exactly," agreed Laura.

The two ladies walked toward the door.

"Mrs. Zukor—"

"Call me Victoria."

"Victoria, I do want to apologize about the name mix up. I really am sorry."

"Oh please, don't be silly. It was nothing. I barely noticed. But aren't you just a dear for saying so!"

THE ART OF COINCIDENCE

"Thank you all for coming on such short notice. It's late and I know many of you have tight deadlines, so we'll keep this as brief as possible."

Laura Latman was all business, standing at the podium in Cedars' Press Room in a new wool-tweed Chanel jacket and matching skirt purchased yesterday during a day long shopathon at Neiman's and every other designer boutique at Fashion Island. She had spent far too much trying to keep up with her new bestie, Victoria Zukor. Power-shopping is *the* female mating ritual among the Los Angeles elite. Both women knew the game well and were determined not to receive an underclass ranking. They spent with abandon, demonstrating their self-perceived royal status. Laura knew that all of it, save her new *Fendi* wallet, would have to go back, including the outfit she was wearing today. She wanted to return the wallet too but was certain Victoria would notice if she wasn't using it, and of course, she was absolutely right.

"My name is Laura Latman, Director of Media and Public Relation for the Cedars-Sinai Medical Center." Leaving out this vital piece of information, no matter how rushed, was simply out of the question.

"We are here today to update you on the condition of Mr. Geoffrey Theodore Zukor."

Again, she introduced Dr. Alacombre, who dutifully read from the prepared text Laura had given him that consistently referred to their patient as "Mr. Geoffrey Theodore Zukor, husband of Mrs. Victoria Helena Zukor." During his vague assessment of Geoffrey's condition, he twice mentioned Cedars' new hundred-million-dollar Spielberg Magnetic Ion Imaging Center, the first of its kind in the United States.

"Any questions?" Laura asked with a straight face. "Yes?" she said pointing to hunky Josh Haskell from KABC, Channel 7.

"What is Geoffrey Zukor current condition?"

"Mr. Geoffrey Theodore Zukor remains in critical condition, but we are hopeful he will improve and be moved into one of our luxury suites on the 9th Floor soon. Dr. Alacombre has already referred to it, but it certainly bears repeating that his recovery is being aided immensely by the constant reassuring presence of his wife, Mrs. Victoria Helena Zukor."

Victoria will be so pleased; the fact that it was completely untrue would never even cross her mind.

THE ART OF COINCIDENCE

LOS ANGELES
Where the girls all look like candy,
And the gay boys dress so dandy.

In 1984, West Hollywood gained national notoriety when it became America's first fully incorporated "gay" city. Its citizenry unapologetically elected a gay mayor and a gay city council, which together ran a full complement of city services like police, fire, and sanitation. Payday at City Hall is something to see, resembling an open casting call for *The Village People — Butching it Up on Broadway!*

House on fire? Don't fret. The West Hollywood Fire Department is trained to save lives and fine china. "Excuse me! Will you hurry it up with the bubble wrap, please? My nuts are getting toasty in here!"

Serious crimes by outsiders are almost non-existent in West Hollywood. Even criminals are smart enough to know the last place they'd want to spend the weekend is in the West Hollywood jail.

All and all, West Hollywood provides its residents a feeling of security, of belonging, of family and community; a place that allows them the freedom to truly be themselves, many for the first time in their lives.

The Rage is to West Hollywood what the Mormon Tabernacle is to Salt Lake City, albeit with a lot less wives in attendance. It sits on a double-wide lot fronting Santa Monica Boulevard with its façade of a dozen sliding French doors all gathered to the right except in the most inclement of weather, receiving all who pass this street of many colors. The Rage features a restaurant, a bar, and of course, a dance floor, which sees almost as much action as the men's restroom — what with boys being boys. A stage at the far end of the room completes the picture.

From the look of the crowd on this Friday night, one might have thought The Rage was hosting a convention of Chippendale dancers or an AA meeting for male models, but that was not the case. Here was the Mayor, all twelve of the City Council, the Chiefs of Police and Fire, the City Attorney, and various other local dignitaries. Hundreds of regulars and a number of celebrities were also on-hand, what with boys being boys. The party was hosted by West Hollywood's new weekly newspaper.

A PAGE FROM
LOS ANGELES NEWSPAPER HISTORY

Although few will admit it, Los Angeles has always been a lousy newspaper town, lousy because any writer in L.A. who could string two sentences together went to work in the movies. Those that could almost string two sentences together went to work in

TV. And writers that weren't quite sure what a sentence was, went to work for a Los Angeles newspaper.

In 1962, when the failing *Los Angeles Evening Herald* merged with the failing *Los Angeles Examiner*, L.A. was treated to a fresh, new, failing newspaper, *The Los Angeles Herald Examiner*. Their creditors quickly approved the merger, although their reason for doing so was baffling. Perhaps they were trying to disprove the mathematical theorem that states the sum of two negative numbers is always another negative number. After all, *always* is such a vague and ambiguous term, who knows, maybe they thought it was worth a shot.

During its first few years, *The Examiner* was wretched — pathetically, bottom-of-the-barrel, Ben Affleck Batman, wretched. And then its beginner's luck ran out and it got even worse. How bad was it? My mother's scrambled eggs come to mind:

"Where are you going? You haven't touched your eggs," said Ma.

"Yeah, right, well, uh, I'm late for school, Ma," said very skinny me.

"Son, do you know right this very minute there are children starving in Africa?"

"Really? You cook for them too, Ma?"

After the City of West Hollywood incorporated, *The Examiner*, once again facing bankruptcy, reorganized, and sensing an unmet need refocused exclusively on chronically gay life there. To complete its transformation, the paper needed a new public image, something more, well, *Gay!* and so it changed its name from *The Examiner* to *The Examinhim*.

The Examinhim quickly became one of the nation's leading gay newspapers, second only in gay readership to *The Daily Oklahoman*.

"Ladies and Gentlemen, may I have your *atten-see-own, pul-lease*? My name is Calvin Foxxe, and I welcome you on behalf of *The Examinhim*, where I proudly serve as Editor-in-Chief."

"We are gathered here tonight to pay tribute to an American hero, a gay man who has been a resident of our very own West Hollywood community for nearly four years, having grown up in Wichita, Kansas, a lot of fun that must have been."

"It was just three weeks ago that Southwest Airlines, long a true friend of *The Examinhim* and our gay community, suffered the downing of Flight 2020. In that devastating crash, four souls lost their lives and countless more would have surely perished on that dark, dark night had it not been for the courageously gay spirit of tonight's honoree: Mr. Donn Olson, stewardess extraordinaire!"

"On impact, Donn Olson suffered numerous serious injuries. His leg was badly mangled and fractured in three places. The airplane cabin was filled with flames and thick, black smoke. The aircraft's fuel tanks had ruptured, and it was only a matter of time before everything exploded. And yet, despite all of those obstacles, without concern for his own pain or personal safety, Donn Olson stayed at his post and single-handedly ushered out 67 passengers from the plane's burning fuselage. If it were me, I would have run out of there like I was chasing Antonio Banderas at a Sadie Hawkins Day Race, but no, not so for our Donn Olson. It is his astonishing act of bravery that we salute here tonight. And it is in his honor that we dedicate next week's issue of *The Examinhim*. Behold!"

With that, Calvin Foxxe flamboyantly (as if he were capable of doing it any other way) removed a large, pink satin sheet that was draped over a nearby easel, exposing a 4' X 8' blow-up of next week's front cover. There was a huge photo of Donn Olson, covered in sweat, standing in the opening of Lima-5-Niner-4's emergency hatch as flames devoured the aircraft all around him. In his arms he carried a passenger — a fat, balding, unconscious lump of humanity. The caption, floated over the bottom of the photo and set in bold, italic Adobe Garamond Pro typeface, read:

He's here… He's queer… He's…

DONN OLSON,
GAY SUPERMAN!

and was followed by the sub-head:

Rescuing Passenger Geoff Zuckler,
President of the Gay Men's Archeological Society
from the Arms of Certain Death!

"Ladies and Gentleman," Calvin Foxxe continued, emotion filling his every word, "Wichita's loss and forever our gain, West Hollywood's favorite gay son and the best thing to happen to this town since the invention of the male thong… He's here, he's queer, here's Mr. Donn Olson, Gay Superman!" And from behind a rising red velvet curtain, Donn hobbled out into the spotlight, hindered by a thigh-high pink cast on his left leg. He was wearing a tight black tee-shirt emblazoned with a large pink Superman emblem, the painted cast and tee-shirt both being Calvin's idea. The crowd loved it. The moment he appeared, everyone went wild. It was like the reaction to Kirk Gibson's dramatic pinch-hit home run in the bottom of the ninth in Game 1 of the 1988 World Series, only higher pitched. The ruckus continued for what seemed like forever and still they gave no sign of stopping the love. A subgroup off to the left began chanting, "Our Hero is Queer-o! Our Hero is Queer-o! Our Hero..."

The DJ was quick to pick up on it and chimed in with Mariah Carey's *Hero*. Soon everyone was singing along; they all knew every word.

> *There's a hero if you look inside your heart;*
> *You don't have to be afraid of what you are...*

Donn looked out over the swaying crowd to the restaurant, the bar, and then down at dance floor... He couldn't hold it back any longer. Tears filled his eyes. For it was on his second night in Los Angeles, there, right there on that very dance floor, that he first met Tim, his roommate, co-worker, and the love of his very young life. They had been inseparable ever since — inseparable until the night of the crash, the night of Tim's death. Donn had not returned to their apartment and knew no matter how much time passed, he would never be able to. Donn Olson was broken and lost.

THE ART OF COINCIDENCE

The Ballad of Rosie and Rae
A Love Story
Part 1

(310) 278-4329 to (310) 278-7822
Wednesday, 9:30 a.m.

"Hello?"

"Rose?"

"Good morning, Rachael."

"No time for pleasantries. Patsy just called, and you are not going to believe what she just told me."

"What is it?"

"This is the shocker to end all shockers."

"Really? Worse than the Moskowitz Bat Mitzvah when every boy their daughter invited was black? That raised a few eyebrows. *Oy* God, I'll never forget the way they were all dancing with her, one on one side, one on the other, right up close to her like that. Every time I looked at her, all I saw was one big Oreo cookie. If I were her mother, that would have been it. I would have died right there. Everyone would have gone right from the party directly over to the cemetery."

"God forbid, Rose."

"Maybe we could get a deal from the caterer. You know, 'I'll give you the Bat Mitzvah, but you gotta throw in the after-funeral nosh.'"

"What are you talking about? You don't remember? Really? Minnie told everyone those boys weren't invited. They came with the DJ. They were the dancers — you know, part of the entertainment."

"Fine. Believe what you will. But I'll tell you that was the first Bat Mitzvah I'd ever been to where the candle lighting ceremony was replaced with everyone joining hands and singing, *We Shall Overcome*. Trust me, the girl thinks she's a schwartza."

"Schwartza or no, the Moskowitz Bat Mitzvah was nothing compared to what I heard today."

"Really?"

"Naw-thing!"

"So, tell me already. What happened?"

"Are you sitting down?"

"No, I'm standing up *pishing!* Of course, I'm sitting down! Now tell me."

"He's a ho-mo-sexual. A ho-mo-sexual! Can you believe it? He's been keeping it secret for years!"

"Who?"

"Who? What do you mean who? Who do you think we've been talking about for last five minutes? You don't remember? You know, next time you're at the doctors, you might want to mention to him that you're having a little trouble following conversations. Have him check it out for you. Better safe than sorry. It's no big deal. They even have a pill for it now. Really. I even take it — not that I need to, mind you. Even my son said it was ridiculous that I should take such a thing. In fact, when I told him the doctor put me on the pill, he said that even if I were 50 years younger and the last woman on Earth, I still wouldn't need to take it, which made me feel a lot better because sometimes I worry — I do — I worry that I get so confused sometimes, people can't even follow what it is I'm saying. You know how I worry unnecessarily."

"Rae, you never told me who we're talking about. You said someone's a homosexual, but you never told me who it was."

"I didn't? I thought for sure I said… Maybe I should start doubling up on those pills. Where did I put them again? I haven't been able to find them for months."

"Who's a homosexual?"

"Victoria Zukor's husband, Geoffrey."

"What?"

"Yeah. Geoffrey Zukor."

"Geoffrey Zukor's a homosexual? Oh, please. Don't be ridiculous."

"It's true! And that's not all. She said he's been outed!"

"Outed? What's outed?"

"I don't know, but that's what Patsy said they did to him. I was eating a bagel at the time, and I didn't want too many details. You know how my stomach is. Maybe it's something he had done at the hospital, I don't know."

"They outed him? Hmmm... Maybe that's when they take an *inny* and they make it an *outy?*"

"I don't know. Could be. Who can keep up with all the plastic surgery *michegas* going on today? I didn't even recognize Myra at the beauty shop last week. The girl's been doing my hair for twenty years — twenty years — and I didn't know who she was. I thought maybe I had Alzheimer's for a minute. Really, I was scared to death, but no, thank God, it turns out that My just had a little "procedure." Wonderful idea. I don't know what they did to her, but her lips are so swollen, it looks like she's finally given up on finding a man and now trying to attract a large fish. So sure, for all I know, getting an *outy* is probably all the rage."

"But why would Geoffrey do such a thing? Like his waistline wasn't big enough already, he needed to out his bellybutton? Please, it doesn't make any sense."

"Who knows why anyone does anything today. None of it makes any sense. Half the women at our temple look like they bought their boobs from one of those guys that make balloon animals. I was just at the Epstein girl's Bat Mitzvah. I've never seen such large breasts before in my life. And such low-cut dresses! Oy, everywhere I looked there was a boob pointed right at me. You could lose an eye in a place like that. It was disgusting. Trust me; it wasn't a Bat Mitzvah party — it was a Bat *Tits*-vah party. So, who's to say why anyone does anything today."

"Maybe Geoffrey did it because he trying to be the J-Lo of bellybuttons."

"J-Lo... *Oy,* there's another one. What kind of a name is J-Lo? I saw her on television the other day. The way her *heinie* shakes, her name should be Jel-Lo."

"And even if he did get an *outy*, that automatically means he's a homosexual?"

"Patsy says he's been leading a secret double life for years. He's even been going by another name and everything."

"Oh, please. Does Geoffrey Zukor look gay to you? He doesn't even go to a gym. Now Patsy's son, Ronnie, he's always at the gym. Him, I worry about."

"Patsy swears Ronnie is not gay. She says he's just a late bloomer."

"Rae, the kid wears bloomers! Have you seen the knickers he's always running around in, with all the rhinestone flowers up and down the legs? Hello? You don't think he's trying to tell us something?"

"Patsy says they were a gift."

"A gift? A gift from who? Liberace?"

"How should I know? But with Geoffrey, she's got proof. Real live proof! Listen to this: Geoffrey Zukor is on the cover of a gay newspaper!"

"Oh, sure, of course he is. And what's the occasion, National Fat & Gay Month?"

"Poor Victoria is beside herself. She's in shock."

"I still don't believe it. It can't be true."

"Was I right about Francine Walsenburg leaving her husband for that Mexican guy?"

"She says he's Portuguese."

"He's her gardener! How many Portuguese gardeners do you know, Rose? And the bum doesn't lift a finger anymore. He just floats around her pool eating tacos. Oh sure, he's Portuguese all right!"

"Rae, don't be too hard on him. Remember what the rabbi said, 'We all have our own lessons to learn and crosses to bear.'"

"The rabbi was talking about crosses? You must be going to that new reform synagogue. You know, the one with black cantor who's always shaking his booty to *Ain Kelahanu*."

"My point is that none of us is without our problems."

"Yeah, well, that certainly holds true for Geoffrey Zukor. And if you had a subscription to the homosexual newspaper you could see for yourself just how true that statement happens to be."

"Oh, and you know this because you're a subscriber?"

"No, Patsy told me all about it. In fact, she read the entire article to me."

"And how did Patsy get a hold of a gay newspaper?"

"From Ronnie, her son."

"Ronnie? The same Ronnie that Patsy swears is not homosexual? Does that add up to you?"

"Give her a break. Patsy was never very good at math, now was she? And apparently neither was Victoria Zukor. She had no idea about her Geoffrey. And I hear she's livid. Livid!"

"Really? Are they separating?"

"Oh, she's separating all right. She's separating Geoffrey's head from Geoffrey's body. Good thing he's already in the hospital. He'll save himself a cab fare."

THE ART OF COINCIDENCE

The other day I ate at a real nice family restaurant.
You could tell it was a family restaurant
because there was an argument going on at every table.

- the late great George Carlin

The following is an excerpt from *The Examinhim's* lead story for the week of May 22:

Aboard Flight 2020 that evening were 17 members of the West Hollywood Archaeological Society, returning home from a weeklong dig in the painted deserts of New Mexico. The group had traveled to the Land of Enchantment hoping to locate the ancestral home of the Sortoches Indian Tribe, whom they believe were the first predominantly gay Indian tribe on North America soil. It should be noted, however, that most in the narrow-minded, "red-state" thinking, Archaeological Institute of America have given little credence to their theory.

Undeterred by the skepticism, the West Hollywood Archaeological Society has worked tirelessly over the past decade to substantiate their claim. Their persistence finally paid off late last year when one of its members stumbled upon an ancient cave painting (see insert below), which they tout as the greatest scientific discovery since the creation of K-Y Jelly. After extensive analysis of the mural, the West Hollywood Archaeological Society compiled their findings in a comprehensive research treatise and submitted it to several leading scientific journals for peer review. The treatise irrefutably substantiates the Archaeological Society's claim of the Sortoches' overt homosexuality, concluding, "The left half of the mural clearly depicts two Sortoches tribesmen dancing with one another while holding umbrellas in one hand and condoms in the other." (The photo below with superimposed descriptors was provided courtesy of the West Hollywood Archeological Society.)

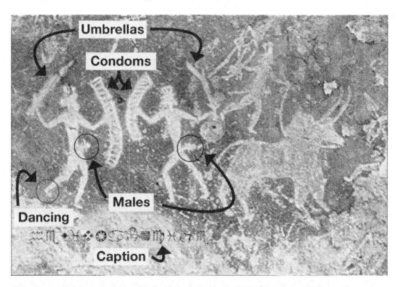

[Editor's Note: Our Science/Hair & Make-Up Editor here at *The Examinhim* wholeheartedly agrees with findings of the West Hollywood Archaeological Society. His exact words were, "Of course they're gay. When was the last time you saw a straight guy in L.A. carrying an umbrella? And get a load of the size of those condoms. Yikes! Makes you want to go out and cruise a reservation!"]

To further bolster their claim, the West Hollywood Archaeological Society has done extensive research decoding the Sortuches' native tongue and pictographs. This work allowed them to translate the caption under the two dancing young men, which they have determined reads, "I'll poka your hauntas, if you'll poka mine."

They believe they have discovered evidence that braves from nearby tribes visited the Sortuches' small but exquisitely appointed village and while being welcomed in a midnight ritual, all blindfolded and seated around a large bonfire, were often heard as saying, "Hey, what that you stick in my mouth? That no feel like peace pipe to me!"

As surprising as the discoveries they've made were, nothing could have prepared them for shock they received on their journey home, shortly after their plane touched down in Los Angeles.

Amid flames and explosions, all 17 members of the West Hollywood Archeological Society including their 5-term president, Mr. Jeff Zeekler, (see cover photo) were saved from certain death by flight attendant Donn Olson, a 9-year resident of West Hollywood. Mr. Zeekler, who was traveling with his lover, Paul 'The Doll' Vidal, owns and operates the 95¢ Stores, one of the nation's largest privately held discount sundry chains.

Neither Charlotte nor the three nurses stationed near ICU Bay 3 could remove Victoria from atop her husband as her violently shaking hands were pulling the ends of Geoffrey's I.V. tube in opposite directions, the center of which she had wrapped several times around his neck.

"How could you let them embarrass me like this? First, they call me a Zacky and now newspapers are saying I'm married to a gay man?" she screamed. He tried to reply but couldn't, his face a shade somewhere between Cobalt Blue and Paynes Purple. His eyes bulged forth like Elmo's. "Feeling gay now, are you?" ARE YOU?!?

Security arrived promptly in response to a "Code Yellow/ICB3" alert and after a full discharge of a stun gun into Victoria's thigh, she was flapping around on the bacteria resistant Hexyl-PVP polymer-coated linoleum floor like a giant Alaskan halibut on the deck of a trawler.

After a phone call from Dr. Sheinman, Victoria Zukor was released by Security and stormed out of the hospital, never to see her husband again.

Or did she? This, as it turns out, is a question not easily answered.

THE
ART
OF
COINCIDENCE

Genetics, you are the true Zeus, the Master Player,
the source of destiny for all mankind.
Around you, we turn.
Around you, we burn.

Although May became October, the passage of time was mocked by the unchanging weather pattern of Southern California. Since the crash and ensuing altercation between her parents, Charlotte had been a permanent fixture at her father's bedside. She was a fragile, slender girl with a full, round face, startled blue eyes, and a painfully shy heart the size of Texas. Like a dog rescued from an abusive owner, Charlotte's loyalty to her father was above all else. Throughout her childhood, he had been her savior, her protector, and her guardian angel in a world cruelly ruled by Queen Victoria. For try as she might, Charlotte was unable keep up with the appearance driven demands of her mother and was made to suffer countless indignities as a result.

Victoria, firmly rooted in the physical, shared nothing in common with her emotionally bent daughter. She would lower a branch with comments like, "Don't you think Cousin Amy is just stunning? That cute little figure of hers, that face, and oh, that beautiful hair. Doesn't she have the most beautiful hair you have ever seen?" But Charlotte could never find a way to climb aboard. Right or wrong, what she heard was her mother saying, *She's far prettier than you, Charlotte, far, far prettier.*

Other comments like, "That Bobbi is always wearing the cutest clothes, isn't she?" were understood as more criticism, as, *Why can't you dress like her, Charlotte? Why do you always look so disheveled and sloppy?*

"Oh, isn't that little Brianna something? Look at the way she carries herself. She's going to have all the boys looking!" was taken to be her mother's way of saying, *Oh, what I wouldn't give for a daughter like that. Instead, I'm stuck with you. Just look at you. How did I of all people ever end up with a daughter like you?*

And so, to the endless flood of remarks like these, little drowning Charlotte, always unsure of what to say in the best of circumstances, would say nothing at all.

Charlotte rarely received any encouragement or validation from her mother for simply being a wonderful little girl; in fact, she received few gestures of love from her at all. Victoria simply could not or would not communicate with her daughter on that level.

Naturally shy and timid, her relationship with her mother did nothing but feed her insecurities, leaving her terribly wounded and dependent as a child. The result was Charlotte's life-rafting onto her father, her fragility eventually reaching a point where she needed to know his whereabouts at all times. She would call his cell phone from a payphone at school during recess each day and at any other time the opportunity arose. In third grade, Geoffrey secretly, meaning without Queen Victoria's knowledge, bought Charlotte her own cell phone, in the hopes that knowing she could easily reach him whenever necessary, would somehow reassure her.

When Victoria found out about the phone, she was (*Surprise!*) angry, accusing Geoffrey of, once again, spoiling their daughter, coddling her, and purposely trying to keep her weak and dependent on him just to bolster his own lack of self-esteem.

How could she say such a thing?

That stunning accusation was a mystery, a mystery that stayed with Geoffrey for years. At first, he chalked it up to Victoria just being Victoria, a vicious comment spoken out of jealousy or feelings of rejection, being excluded from their little club. But the more he thought about it, the more he felt it was something else, something deeper, something about to the inner Victoria, the secret Victoria, and how she came to be like that. He realized that in some fundamental way, he really didn't know his wife at all. He didn't understand her, understand why she thought the things she thought. Why was she so tough on everyone? Where did her anger come from? And did she really think the tone she set with her daughter was in her daughter's best interest? Or perhaps she wasn't thinking at all, just being herself and letting the chips fall where they may? Was she even seeing the same wounded girl Geoffrey saw? Or was she seeing someone else, someone that actually had very little to do with their little girl?

Geoffrey knew little of Victoria's past and her life before him. When they met, he had been so captivated by her, so head-over-heals, crazy-crazy-crazy in love, that only the present seemed to matter. She rarely mentioned her childhood and to his knowledge she had just a single picture of her mother, a soft-toned studio portrait in a silver frame that had always reminded him of the young and beautiful Donna Reed, circa *It's A Wonderful Life*. It was a perfect photo, with an unmistakable dreaminess to it. In a country where beauty is more prized than brains, she could have had anything she wanted. And yet he doubted things worked out for her. There was something in her eyes, eyes that somehow signaled trouble ahead. They were the eyes of a victim.

As for Victoria's father, he was never discussed. In fact, his name was never even mentioned — not once, not ever. And she had no photo or remembrance of him either. It was as if he never existed.

Geoffrey wondered if the root of her anger lay somewhere within her threadbare back-story but doubted he would ever find out. He only knew that their home was filled with an undercurrent of tension and violence, an anger that could appear at any moment to wreak havoc; an anger, Geoffrey feared, that was drawing far too close to his beloved Charlotte.

Geoffrey Zukor took on the role the family mediator, or more accurately, its rodeo clown; he was not equipped to do battle with the bull, but he could at least provide some relief for others also trapped in the ring. Thankfully, he had the benefit of knowing something about the beast. Victoria's anger, he discovered, did have its limitations; the bull's horns, although devastating in their damage, could only be angled in one direction at a time. It was a weakness Geoffrey learned to exploit.

Whenever he felt Victoria was being too tough or harsh with their daughter, he'd go to the refrigerator, an act certainly in keeping with his character and doubly so in times of stress, grab whatever was handy, and "accidentally" drop it. If he were uncertain of it achieving its desired effect, he'd yell something like, "Oh, shoot! Sorry! Sorry! Don't worry; I'll clean it up. I can do it. Uh, where do you keep all those rags again?" That was all it took; the bull came running.

Another of his tricks was, "Oh, excuse me. Sorry to interrupt. I think maybe I got some peanut butter, just a little bit, not a lot, well, not really a lot, just kind of… Well, anyway, it's on the sofa. I tried to Clorox it off but…" And the bull came running.

And then there was the time Victoria was with Charlotte at the piano while she was practicing. It was late, too late for a girl her age to be pushed as hard as Victoria was pushing her, and it had been going on for far too long. Charlotte was crying, and Victoria was clearly angry about it. Geoffrey slipped into the kitchen and put a bag of popcorn in the microwave. He set it for twenty minutes, although it didn't take nearly that long. The resulting stink bomb was undoubtedly his best attention getter yet. Okay, it nearly burnt their house down, but still, what an attention getter!

From that night forward, Geoffrey was forbidden from doing any cooking in the house at all. Even the toaster was off limits, which was too bad, what with toasted bagels being the main component of his long-standing plan to pack on at least fifteen pounds per year. Toasted bagels… he just loved them. Bagels with cream cheese, bagels with butter, bagels with jelly, peanut butter, sliced bananas, or any combination thereof; any way you sliced it, there were few things he found more satisfyingly than bagels. They were right up there with his all-time number one favorite: Donuts. In fact, he loved bagels so much, shortly after his banishment from the kitchen, he became the only executive in Century City to have a toaster as a desk accessory.

And as for Charlotte, well, she knew the sacrifices her father had made for her and despite or perhaps because of all the family fire and chaos aimed in their direction, Geoffrey and Charlotte grew to share a bond few experience.

THE ART OF COINCIDENCE

The Ballad of Rosie and Rae
A Love Story
Part 2

(310) 278-4329 to (310) 278-7822
Thursday, 9:30 a.m.

"Hello?"

"Good morning, Rachael."

"Good morning, Rose. You know, sometimes I think you're the only reason I have a phone."

"What, you haven't heard from your kids?"

"Not a peep. Ever since I stopped giving them an allowance, it's been radio silence."

"Trust me, you don't know from *tsuris*. I just hung up with Patsy, and she told me that Alice Angel told her that when she was having lunch with Suzy Azar, Suzy said that when she was out with Bob and Beverly at some fundraising thing, she happened to overhear someone at the very next table say that Victoria was devastated, just devastated. In fact, she's so depressed by the whole newspaper ordeal, she's going shopping in Italy. Whatever works, I guess. For most people it's Prozac. In Beverly Hills, it's Prada."

"*Oy!* That girl goes to Rome like I go to the potty. Maybe this trip she'll finally get the recognition she deserves and the Pope will make her the patron saint of frequent flyer miles. Or maybe she'll run for President of Italy. Her slogan could be, Meaner than Mussolini!"

"Don't be so hard on her, Rae. This wasn't her fault."

"It's just like I told my son about this girl he used to go with. I forget her name, but—"

"You mean Sylvia, his wife for the past 18 years? You don't remember Sylvia's name?"

"She seems incapable of remembering my birthday, so I can't seem to remember her name. Fair is fair. It's like that expression — you know, what goes around, goes back around, and then goes around again, I guess, and before you know it, from all that going around and around, you're so dizzy you want to throw up. Because that's how I feel about her, I want to throw up. I can't stand her and that's all there is to it. She thinks she's such a *berryer*, meanwhile her house should be located on St. *Shmutzik* Square."

"Rae, Rae, Rae, what am I going to do with you? She called you on your birthday, you know that. You just wouldn't pick up the phone. You said you were screening your calls, remember?"

"Oh, and there's something wrong with that? I should speak with just anyone on my 76th birthday? She should have come by."

"They did come by, but you wouldn't answer the door."

"I couldn't. I was too busy eavesdropping on them through the intercom. You should have heard what they were saying about me. You wouldn't believe it. The girl David was with, uh, Miss Whatever-Her-Name-Is—"

"Sylvia."

"Sylvia, *Schmilvia*. Anyway, what's her name thought I should be down at Leisure World with her mother. Me! In Leisure World! What's next, the glue factory? I couldn't believe it. And then, like a shrew, she's yelling at my David for not having a key to the apartment."

"David doesn't have a key to your apartment?"

"Of course not. I don't want him barging in here whenever he feels like it. What if I'm entertaining a private visitor or something and he comes waltzing in?"

"Rae, the last private visitor you entertained was Mr. Kaminski back in 1987. And the only reason you had him over was so you could run into the other room and call his wife and ask her if she knew where her husband was."

"*Oy!* Don't get me started on that Gloria Kaminski. I couldn't stand that woman. She would vacuum her carpets for hours! Hours! They lived directly above me, and it was so noisy down here, it was like my head was stuck in the hair dryer at the beauty shop and I couldn't get it out. *Vvvrrrmm. Vvvrrrmmm*. Every single day that's all I heard. *Vvvrmmm. Vvrrmm. Vvrrmmm*. What was that woman doing up there, training for the Indianapolis 500 of vacuuming? But you should have seen her face when she came downstairs and found her husband in my apartment! Oh, that took the suck right out of her Hoover, all right. Oh yeah, she got the message loud and clear. Never heard a peep out of that vacuum again, thank you very much."

"Rae, you're terrible."

"You know, Mr. Kaminski still calls me every once in a while. He's got quite the phone voice, that one, and some very provocative ideas."

"Rae, Harold Kaminski passed. He died, what, six years ago?"

"He did? Are you sure? So, who's been calling me then?"

"Rachael, you're not seducing telemarketers again, are you?"

"Never! Those guys are such prudes. But there was this one fellow that wanted to put aluminum siding on my condominium... Now that man knew how to close a deal!"

THE ART OF COINCIDENCE

Sure enough, October found Victoria at the Spanish Steps, shopping in newly stocked boutiques with the assistance of courteous staff, freshly rested from August's vacations. Bella Roma — the center of the world for a thousand years and remains beloved today for its hospitality and good nature. A gentle smile from a stranger walking down the street is a commonplace act of grace in even Rome's poorest neighborhoods. And directions, although unintelligible and often wrong, are given by Italians as freely as the exchange of bodily fluids after an American high school prom. In contrast, ask a Parisian for assistance, in even the direst of circumstances, like say for directions to a hospital were your mother lays on her deathbed, and your request will go unanswered, mocked even, if it was not asked in their native tongue, which apparently is the only language Parisians understand.

Muggings are rare in Rome, but on this October evening, *La Polizia di Roma* found a man beaten just this side of consciousness, laying on a small side street off the Rio Appreacio.

"I don't a know what a happened," he muttered. "I saw this, this attractive a woman walking towards me. Not young, but attractive. I think I said a 'buona sera' or something, and, as she passed, I don't know, maybe I gave her a little squeeze of the cantaloupe. You know, it a was nothing really, just a nice, friendly, little squeeze hello. Well, she turned and glared at a me. Oh! I haven't seen such hatred in-a woman's face since I told a my wife I wanted to celebrate our twenty-fifth wedding anniversary by going on a nice long vacation — without her."

"Anyway — *Presto Change-o! Bing! Bang! Boom!* — this lovely woman becomes like a vicious ninja. True! A foot to the side a my head, a fist to my stomach, and then a she twisted my arm so hard, I go — *wuh-wuh-wuh* — flipping right a through the air and then — *Smack!* — I crash-a into that brick wall, right a there. And this you won't believe. I'm a standing there, woozy like my wife after I give her good slam with the ol' salami — *capice?* — and then this lady, she runs over and then runs right a up me, like I was a ladder or something — one afoot on my crouch, and then one on my chest, and another in my face — and then she does a back-a flip and lands a standing right in front me! Just like a movie show! Incredible! And then, before I knew it, I found-a myself raised above her head, spinning around like a pizza pie! Me! A pizza pie! Then — *Whammo!* She a dropped me to the street like a sack of pasta dough. I'm lying there so dazed I couldn't tell a difference between a fedelini and a fettuccini. So, what does she do? She picks up her purse, says 'Buena sera', and then gives me a pat on the bottom!

Yeah! And then strolls onto Rio Appreacio like a nothing happened at all! *Marone,* that is a woman!"

"You catch her, you tell a her that I don't want a press any charges. No! I want a marry her. You find her, you tell her, okay? If she says yes, I'll have her go tell it to my wife. That should be quite an afternoon. I could sell-a tickets."

THE ART OF COINCIDENCE

In a world where a hospital could cut off both of your legs in the morning and your friendly HMO mandate that you walk home that afternoon, Geoffrey Zukor was at Cedars-Sinai a total of 171 days. Four surgeries, a severe post-op infection, feeding tubes, catheters, I.V.'s, and enough monitoring equipment to put a man on the moon, filled his days and nights.

"How's my best customer?" Dr. Sheinman would ask during his twice-weekly rounds of the ninth floor.

"Doin' fine, Doc. Just fine."

"That's because you've got the best nurse in the business taking care of you," he said, smiling at Charlotte.

"And the best daughter, too."

"That is evident also. Charlotte, let's get him well and get him out of here. The man's got a life to live."

"Yes, sir. I'm trying."

During Charlotte's daily visits, between the tests, the shots, the x-rays and consultations, and a host of other medical procedures, she would read to her father, sometimes for hours, from her precious treasure trove of books. Books, books, books — these were her most prized possessions. At a very young age, Charlotte developed an uncanny connection to the written word. It was as if the girl was gifted with a sixth sense, able to form a visceral connection with text as real and direct as the thrill a rider receives from a rollercoaster. Growing up, books were always her favorite toys — the bookstore, her Disneyland. Her constant plea, "Could I buy this, Daddy?" was spoken with such intensity it was hard to believe she was talking about a paperback. For to Charlotte, a book was so much more than just a story; it was a portal into another world, a real world, a world far richer and more alive than the one she inhabited. Books were a place where plot twists would take her breath away, and where her relationships with characters would grow stronger and more intimate than with any members of her own family. Whereas Charlotte would never discuss any of Geoffrey's nurses, if she were reading a book about nurses, she could talk about them for hours, elaborately filling in details left untouched by the author and reveal their complex emotional states as if they were her closest friends.

Charlotte was always obsessed with books, reading fluently before entering kindergarten yet unable to legibly write her name until she was well into the third grade. In school, she was insecure, frightened, and out of sync with her peers. When confronted with an awkward situation that demanded a response, she found herself overcompensating, acting superior to others as if overtaken by some strange force. She hated the things she heard herself say, this unconvincing display of conceit, perhaps because she knew from where it came; she was acting like her mother.

Geoffrey remembered the days he would stop by her elementary school at lunchtime and watch her from afar as she sat in the cafeteria. She was alone, always alone, always with her head down, always reading. Detached from the hum of life, there she sat, unable to make a connection to the children around her. And she wasn't much better with adults. At her teacher's suggestion, they tried prohibiting her from taking books to lunch, hoping this might lead to greater socialization with her classmates. After a few lunch periods, she finally left her cafeteria seat and started exploring the perimeter of the playground, a promising sign. A few days after that, while Geoffrey noticed she appeared to be talking to herself. By the following week, there was no doubt; while on the playground she was either speaking to herself or to an imaginary friend, her gestures growing larger and more pronounced each day. He guessed she was telling herself stories but whatever she was doing he found the sight was so odd, so disconcerting, he brought the experiment to a quick and final close and gave the poor girl her books back. Since then, there she sat; head down, lost in inner space. And as he watched her, his heart would ache, the day in, day out ache only a parent of a child with special needs experiences. He would fight it though, fight it with the determination every such parent must have to survive; fight it, if not for themselves, then for their child, fight it so that he could sit with her for a minute at the end of her lunch period without her seeing the red eyes of his worry. And on most occasions, that's precisely what happened. But then there were days when it was all too much, when the tears would flow, and he was forced to leave without her ever knowing he was there.

THE ART OF COINCIDENCE

You only get something for nothing when the something you get
is worth less than the nothing you give.

Press interest in Geoffrey Zukor's recovery remained relatively high. Don't get me wrong, it was no unveiling of the latest
Pamela Anderson breast implants, her last set being so humongous
her doctors had to stitch ball-bearings into the folds of her buttocks just to keep her from toppling over; *that* was the all-time
attendance high watermark for the Cedars-Sinai Press Center. But
because the crash was such a big national story and the crash photos so captivating, local radio and 3 of the 5 local TV stations were,
when time allowed, broadcasting short weekly or biweekly updates

on Geoffrey's condition. It added considerably to the public's interest that his recovery was anything but smooth. It seemed at times he did nothing but bounce as if scripted from one medical crisis to another, making follow-ups a series of *"only time will tell"* cliffhangers. And, as a result, Geoffrey Zukor became something of a minor celebrity.

Throughout Geoffrey's recuperation, Laura Latman stayed updated on his progress and, at Dr. Sheinman's suggestion, began stopping by his room once or twice a week for short visits. She came to sense the very special bond between Geoffrey and his daughter, something that struck her as particularly endearing. With growing regularity, she found herself listening outside his room as Charlotte read to her father or as they discussed a book's latest twists and turns, visits that she always ended with a quick stop inside to say hello. It wasn't long before several nurses caught notice and wondered privately what was going on.

Late one afternoon in early October, Laura peeked into his room after receiving no response to her knock at the door. "Anyone home?"

"Oh, hi," answered Charlotte, barely audibly as she slowly broke from a deep stare out the window.

"Everything all right? Where's your father?"

"Down in x-ray. He's fine. He should be back soon..." Her voice trailed off as her head tilted downward, her gaze falling to the floor.

"So, what's wrong then?" Laura asked, venturing further into the room.

Charlotte looked at her but said nothing. Then her red-stained eyes pointed to a brown 9" by 14" envelope on her lap and tears began rolling down her cheeks as if racing.

"Darling, what is it?" she asked.

"I think it's from my mother."

Laura read the oversized white label with its stylish *Perpetua Titling MT* font:

BERÑA, LEICH, & WANETAAL, LLC
FAMILY LAW SPECIALISTS

"Oh," she sighed knowingly.

Charlotte's head sagged. Her cry was heart-wrenching.

"I'm sorry. I'm so sorry," Laura whispered. She moved to her and held her in her arms with the good sense to say nothing more. She just held her and held her as Charlotte cried and cried.

For a long while that was fine, but when Charlotte's crying grew even more intense with no let-up in sight, Laura tried to calm her by saying, "You know, Charlotte, sometimes, sometimes people start to separate and then end up getting back together. It happens all the time — it really does. No one knows what the future will bring. But one thing I do know is that you're a beautiful, young woman and a wonderful, loving daughter to your father. He's a very lucky man to have you taking care of him—maybe the luckiest of all the fathers I've seen at this hospital. You know that? It's true. And to see the way he looks at you, it's, it's very, very special. I can't imagine anything ever changing that." But her words were of little consolation. Charlotte was clearly distraught.

Laura looked at the envelope again. "You know what does worry me about all this though? Your father. I wish he were stronger. I'm just not sure he's in any condition to have to deal with all this right now, are you?"

Charlotte shook her head and said something that Laura couldn't quite make out.

"I've got an idea. Let's see. Why don't..." Laura looked around the room before fixing on the closet and walking over to it. "Why don't we take this and just put it up here for a while — we could put it right up here — just for a little while, just till he's a little bit stronger." She slid the envelope onto the top shelf and shut the door.

"But how, how could I keep it from him? I have to tell him, don't I?"

"Of course, you do. But do you have to tell him right this minute?"

"I don't know… How could I keep something like this from him?"

"Charlotte, did you ever smoke pot is high school?"

"Once."

"Did you tell your dad?"

"No."

"Well, it's kind of the same thing, right? And it's not like you're never going to tell him."

Charlotte looked at her.

"Let's give it a week or two. Just let him get a little bit stronger. And in the meantime, we'll try not to think about it. It's only a week. If you could do it, I think it'd be a lot better for your father. I really do."

Charlotte stared at Laura for moment then nodded and capped it off with a defeated shrug.

Laura wanted to tell her that everything was going to be all right, for her not to worry, but she knew better than to make promises she had no control over. So instead, she hugged her and said, "If you ever need anything, Charlotte, anything, I'm going to give you my number, and I want to you to promise you'll call me. It doesn't matter what time of the day or night it is. It doesn't matter if you need something big or small, or just want to talk. I want you to promise you'll call me. Do you promise?"

Charlotte nodded again but this time with the faintest glimmer of a smile.

"Great. Now, no more crying. We don't want to have to explain to your father why your beautiful eyes are all red and teary, do we?"

"No, I guess not."

"Now listen." Laura quickly checked her watch. "Unfortunately, I'm late for a meeting so I got to run but it won't take long. How about if I come back and check in on you in, say, thirty minutes, maybe even less, okay? Then if you want, we can go down to the cafeteria and have a cup of coffee together. How would that be?"

Laura bent over and dropped a kiss onto the top of Charlotte's head, who returned a grateful hug.

"And one more thing: I smoked pot a couple of times in high school too, so it looks like we have three things we're not going to tell your dad about, okay? Now let me see that beautiful smile."

Charlotte tried, although her heart clearly wasn't in it.

"Perfect. Just perfect."

THE ART OF COINCIDENCE

Want to feel like you've lived forever? It's simple — just spend five months in a hospital. The anemic second hands of hospital clocks move like they can barely muster the strength to make it from one tick to the next, the effort so monumental. It is as if they alone were faced with the task of pulling fearful patients into the future to meet their fate. Certainly, hospital time trumps all others as night after night once dependable internal clocks awaken sleepers expecting to face the light of day, only to be bitch-slapped by the cold, florescent quiet of 1:30 a.m. Even visitors are thrown by time's abrupt downshift here, their escape routes blocked by its slim passing. Yes, hospital time is hard time. It's like solitary confinement — with needles.

Even so, it was well over a month before Charlotte felt her father was strong enough to receive the large envelope Laura had stashed away in his hospital room closet. She sat beside his bed as

Geoffrey opened and quickly scanned its contents before sliding the documents back inside their manila home and then onto the over-crowded nightstand to the right of his bed. All the while, Charlotte's head remained bowed, her eyes fixed on the book in her lap she was pretending to read.

"It's alright, Charlotte. It's from a law firm representing your mother. She wants… She wants a divorce."

Charlotte knew this all too well, of course, but hearing her father say it, secrets never spoken and feelings never shared came at her anew, spewing her tears onto the pages below.

"It's okay, Charlotte. It's gonna be okay. Really. It's the right thing, the best thing for both of us, for all of us."

She was sure he was right, but that didn't make it any easier for her. There had been so much fighting in their house, she had often secretly hoped that her parents would divorce and that her father would run away with her somewhere, live by a beach maybe. She would daydream of sitting on the sand with him, then meandering south, together, along the shore. She, running slightly ahead, frolicking with the dog she never had, a golden retriever. Her father, relaxed and smiling, watching her, barefoot with his rolled-up pant legs, poking a driftwood walking stick into the soft, accepting sand. She ran and ran along the water's edge, laughing and running, running and laughing. The sun cast its amber net over them as breeze-swept waves danced in the distance. Their hearts, the sand, the breeze, the sound of the surf, the laughter, the love, all connected, all one. This was her favorite childhood memory, the memory that never was.

"Charlotte?"

She wouldn't look up.

"Charlotte? Charlotte, look at me please."

Her eyes glanced in his direction but missed their mark and then returned to the safe neat blocks of text below.

"Char, everything's okay. Are you listening?"

She nodded.

"Good, because I've got something to tell you that I have been thinking about for some time and I need you to really listen to me, okay? It's important."

"All right," she said softly, followed by a brief look up into his eyes.

"This doesn't come as a surprise, Charlotte, not to me and I'll bet not even to you. It's been hard living with your mother, hard for the both of us." And then softly, almost to himself, he added, "I can't even imagine how hard it's been for you..." His voice softened as he drifted off in thought.

Charlotte tensed, wondering what he was thinking. Suddenly scared, her eyes shifted to his. *He's not going to talk about...?* Instinctually, her left hand moved to the top of her head then down, her palm wide, pressing against her hair against her head with a downward stroke. She repeated the motion several times before catching herself and stopping.

"Boy, we fought a lot, didn't we? So many stupid, stupid, horrible fights. There were times when I, I didn't know how we were going to get through it." He shook his head and paused, searching for precisely what he wanted to say. "We've been given so much, haven't we, and have so much to be thankful for. And yet we were always fighting about all this stupid, minuscule little stuff..." Again, he drifted off, but caught himself, refocused, and continued, "But in spite of everything, no matter how bad things got, I could never leave your mother because that would have meant leaving you and I was never going to let that happen. I would have put up with anything, anything, because missing even one night of tucking you in, or seeing your funny, groggy little face in the morning, made it all worth it. And how could I ever leave my little girl, knowing a time might come when you'd need me and I wouldn't be there for you? I couldn't. I just couldn't. But Charlotte, those days are gone now. Look at you. You're all grown up and on your own, my beautiful little girl…"

Charlotte was looking away, toward the door, hoping, praying someone would interrupt them.

"Your mom's right. It's time to let go. As much as I love her, it's been impossible living with her, knowing that no matter what I did, no matter how hard I tried, I could never please her. Charlotte, it's time for me to let her go, let her find that someone or something that will finally make her happy."

Privately though, Geoffrey wondered if his wife would ever be happy. Certainly, given their life together, he doubted it. Yet he took no comfort in the fact for he knew her odds of finding happiness were nothing compared to the odds he faced of being able to let her go and find some kind of a life without her. But that he didn't dwell on, couldn't dwell on. Certainly not now.

The one thing that was abundantly clear was that whatever it was she was looking for, whatever it was she needed, it didn't include him, for it was as plain as the look on her face and the tone in her voice that Victoria couldn't stand her husband. She didn't like a single thing about him, not the way he breathed, or ate, or talked, or walked, or drove a car, and over the course of their life together, she made him excruciatingly well aware of it. No matter what he did, he could never please her, never make her happy. In fact, it seemed the harder he tried, the more aggravated she got with him. Once, he tidied up the kitchen after she went to bed, a good idea he thought, considering her constant complaints about his "*colossal*" messiness. The result? With anger and disgust, she regaled him for throwing out an empty cereal box that she wanted saved for Charlotte's box-top school drive. He tried to explain that he didn't know he was supposed to save it and was certainly sorry about it, but he was just trying to do something nice and shouldn't she be at least a little appreciative of his effort.

She shook her head. "You're always making excuses for yourself, aren't you?" A classic Victoria response.

Her dissatisfaction with everything Geoffrey Zukor was the only real constant in their marriage. Yet Geoffrey wasn't angry. He wasn't angry because he knew it wasn't really her fault. He knew the truth of it was that she just naturally, honestly, truly disliked every single thing about him. And how can you blame someone for the way they honestly feel?

THE ART OF COINCIDENCE

So why then didn't Victoria leave him sooner? Because of Charlotte, he supposed. Victoria knew Charlotte could never get by without Geoffrey, nor could she handle Charlotte without him. And she probably sensed that a divorce would mean, in all practicality, her losing her daughter as well, and that was a cost too high, a cost she couldn't reconcile. Perhaps she felt that no matter how distant and strained their relationship, there was a subliminal benefit for Charlotte to be in her presence, even if they rarely spoke. But whether that was true or not, mattered little. Victoria knew she could never give her up. And so, there she was, trapped. And for that, she resented Geoffrey and Charlotte all the more. And for that, they both paid dearly. Misery casts a wide net.

"A divorce is a good idea, Charlotte. It might seem a little weird at first maybe, but it's for the best. And I promise you — I promise you — it won't affect our relationship at all. In fact, I'll probably have even more time for you. It's the right thing and it's the right time. It really is."

Thoroughly defeated, Charlotte rocked forward, crying, her hands clasped together under her chin as if in prayer.

"Come on, don't cry. Please."

But there was no stopping her. "I'm sorry. I'm sorry. I'm sorry," she cried.

"You have nothing to be sorry about. You're not the reason we're getting divorced."

"Yeah, right," she mumbled between sobs.

"You're not. None of this is your fault. Charlotte, look at me. Come on, look at me. I know this is hard, but you've got to listen to me. Charlotte, if you don't look at me right now, I'm going to go home and get your high school yearbook — you know, the one with the picture of you with your eyes kind of going off in two different directions and your lips kind of scrunched up like you've just swallowed a frog — you know the picture, right? — well, I'm going to take that picture and show it to every doctor in this hospital. In fact, I may pass out flyers. Maybe even have a few posters made up. Across the top it's going to say, *Want a Date? Meet me in Room 908!*" You gotta admit, that's kind of catchy. So, either you stop crying and listen to me, or I'm hauling your senior yearbook down to Poster City right this very minute."

"Yeah, well, go ahead," she said. "But just so you know, I haven't a clue what picture you're talking about. I didn't even order my senior yearbook, you big dunce."

"You didn't? Hmm… Maybe I'm thinking of my high school yearbook."

"Yeah, maybe you are, Dad."

Geoffrey stared at her for a moment while she tried to compose herself. "You know, I love you."

Hearing that, she burst into tears again. "Oh, Daddy…"

"No, Charlotte, come on. We've got to talk about this. It's important. It really is."

Charlotte was trying but still her shoulders were shaking and tears continued to pool in her eyes.

"It was Grandma!" Geoffrey blurted out with a snap of his fingers.

Charlotte looked at him. "You're getting divorced because of Grandma?"

"No! The picture I was thinking of. It was of Grandma in the hospital when she had pneumonia. Remember, she was yelling at me to stop taking pictures of her because she looked so horrible."

"I remember. Not your finest moment, Dad. What woman wants to have pictures taken of her when she's sick in the hospital?

Geoffrey shrugged. "Yeah, I guess that wasn't one of my better days. I remember I just bought that camera. How can you buy a new camera and then not take any pictures? It's impossible. So I remember, I went home and started taking pictures of your mom while she was putting on her make-up. You can imagine how that went over. I had to go out and buy a new camera. Anyway, that picture of Grandma, that's what I'm gonna use on the flyer. I'll just tell all the doctors you're not very photogenic. Plus, you have that disease where you grow old really fast. So, if they're interested, they better get up here quick--before you lose the rest of your teeth! Who knows? You might meet someone really nice out of all this."

"Okay, okay, I've stopped," she said, wiping her eyes. "But I'll tell you something; you're the weirdest Dad in the whole world." Then she smiled at him. "The weirdest!"

Geoffrey smiled in return. "You know, the one thing we haven't talked about is your mom and how hard our marriage has been on her. The truth is, your mother loves you so much that she's spent her entire adult life with a man she doesn't love, in fact, can barely stand. And she did it so that you could have the best life she could give you. Can you imagine such a thing? For twenty-four years your mother has sacrificed her happiness for you. Sure, sometimes she's been resentful and angry but maybe she was entitled to be. She expected a lot from you because she's given a lot, maybe more than you appreciate. So, don't ever confuse her resentment and anger and high expectations with a lack of love for you."

"Okay, so she's not one of those touchy-feely moms that get down on their knees and hug their kids all the time and are always running around, taking care of them. But believe me, there aren't many moms out there that would do for their kids what your mother has done for you."

"What she did *for* me or what she did *to* me? Which is it, Dad?"

For the first time in her life, Charlotte had spoken the unspeakable.

THE ART OF COINCIDENCE

T' un-speak the spoken or un-say the said,
'bout as easily done as un-dyin' the dead.

Did I say that?

Charlotte flinched, her eyes panicked, darting around the room as if her words had unleashed something dangerous in their midst. She dared say nothing more as anxiety pushed its deep claws into her stomach.

"Charlotte, I—"

"I don't want to talk about it!" She was up now, gathering her things, making her escape. "I don't. I won't. I won't ever talk about it. And if you make me, I'll leave. I'll leave and I'll *never* come back!" She nervously ran her palm down the side of her head, flattening her hair.

"Okay, okay, just calm down. We don't have to talk about it now if you don't want to—"

"NOT NOW, NOT EVER! I WILL NEVER TALK ABOUT IT! DO YOU HEAR ME? NEVER!! NEVER!!!"

Geoffrey was shocked. He had never seen his daughter this angry before. In fact, he couldn't remember her ever yelling at all. Her distance from her feelings, from life, had always been one of his great worries. And so, despite the topic of her rage, he couldn't help but smile.

"You think this is funny?"

"Funny? No, I—"

"I DON'T WANT TO TALK ABOUT IT!"

"I was only smiling because my little girl is growing up."

"Yeah, well, if this is growing up, I don't like it very much."

"You don't?"

"No, I don't. I don't like it at all. Any of it!"

"Really?"

She looked at him sharply but said nothing.

"I don't know, seems like you do to me. You should, anyway. It's nice to be able to express yourself, not keep everything so bottled up inside. Feels good to let loose a little, doesn't it?"

Charlotte ignored him as she rummaged through her purse.

"Doesn't it?" he prodded. He thought he saw the slightest wisp of a smile creep across her lips. "And one thing's for sure: You are beautiful when you're angry. Wow. You're just like your mother, a real goddess of fire."

Charlotte shot him a black look, clearly resentful of the comparison. Then her eyes moved to his tray-table searching for what Geoffrey guessed were her keys.

"What I meant was, you must get that from your mom's side of the family. When my side of the family gets mad, we never yell.

We chew. We eat everything in sight." He nodded, adding, "And it's an angry chew too. It's like we're one of those zombies from *Night of the Living Dead. Grrr, Grr, Grrr...* We take all of our anger out on the food we're eating. *Grrr, Grr, Grrr...* And we'll eat anything. Oh, yeah. When a Zukor gets angry, nothing in the fridge is safe. Or the panty. And we don't wait to warm stuff up or cook it either. No way. We're too angry for that. We shove it in our mouth just the way it is. I was so angry at your mom once, I ate a whole box of apple turnovers — still frozen! I chipped 3 teeth! Now that's angry."

Charlotte turned her back to him. He wondered if she was smiling.

"You ever eat a frozen apple turnover? Trust me; it's not so good. My side of the family also over-eats if we're feeling anxious about something. Or when we're depressed. Or even really scared..." Geoffrey thought for a moment, then added, "Or bored. Or frustrated. Or, uh, you know, forlorned... Boy, can we pack it away when we're forlorned. Once during Passover, I was so forlorned I ate a whole box of matzo. Those things are so dry, I completely dehydrated myself. Couldn't pee for three weeks!"

"Nice, Dad. Thanks for sharing." Charlotte said sarcastically.

"Or when no one laughs at our jokes and we're feeling unap-preciated, you know, unloved, or just plain ol' lugubrious—"

"Lugubrious?"

"Oh sure, lugubriousness runs in the family. We also overeat when we're feeling, uh, you know, forlorned."

"You mentioned that already."

"Or nitpicked, or criticized, belittled— You know, once I was feeling so belittled ate spaghetti once right out of the box, no boil-ing or anything. I told myself they were breadsticks but trust me, they don't taste like breadsticks! Then there's—"

"Obnoxious?" suggested Charlotte.

"Disparaged," continued Geoffrey.

"*Very* obnoxious?" countered Charlotte.

"*Very* disparaged," Geoffrey shot back. "Then, of course, there's bleak. You know, when I'm feeling bleak, nothing tastes better than *31 Flavors*. Yep, all 31 of them. One right after another. Not a loser in the bunch. Even that bright blue one, completely delicious. I also overeat when I'm feeling—"

"Extremely, incredibly obnoxious?" Charlotte shrieked.

"Forlorned—"

"That's your third time with forlorned, Dad. Now stop it!"

"Then there's hungry—"

"Dad!!"

"What? I couldn't leave out hungry. Speaking of hungry, do you want to run out and get me a donut?"

"Are you joking? A donut? Is that really a healthy choice?"

"I also overeat when I'm deprived, depressed—"

"Diabetic?" Charlotte quipped. "Weren't both Grandma and Grandpa diabetic? And you want to start eating donuts again?"

"And also, when I'm demoralized, distraught, divorced..." Geoffrey thought about that for a moment.

"Divorced..." he muttered. "You better make it a dozen."

"Dad!!!"

"I'm joking. I wouldn't dream of having a donut. *Sheesh!* Do I look like the kind of guy that eats a lot of donuts?"

Charlotte looked at him. "Well, I was the only girl in my class to have a guy that owns a donut shop light a candle at her Bat Mitzvah!"

"That was Uncle Larry. What was wrong with that?"

"What was wrong with that? Oh, nothing, except you'd say, 'Let's go by and see Uncle Larry' so often, I grew up thinking he was really my uncle. It's a little weird, Dad, to be seventeen and find out that *Uncle Larry* isn't really your uncle at all. He's just some dude that sells my dad donuts."

"That's his name, the name of his shop, Uncle Larry's Corner Donut Shoppe. All his regulars call him Uncle Larry. You eat pancakes, right? Did you grow up thinking Aunt Jemima was really your aunt?"

"If you took me to see Aunt Jemima every single day after school, yeah, I'm sure I would have thought she was my aunt."

"We didn't go for donuts every day."

"Well, I'm guessin' you've got to be going there pretty regular for Uncle Larry to name a donut after you, *Zook.*"

"Oh, you had to mention it, didn't you? *The Zook.* Uummmm…. You know what happens when you die? You walk through those pearly gates and the first thing they do is hand you a warm *Zook.* Man, I'm really hungry now."

"Dad, please don't start up with the donuts again. You're doing so good. You don't want to wreck it, do you? The doctor said you've lost thirty-two pounds."

"I have," Geoffrey agreed, nodding. "But thirty-one of them was my spleen. Biggest spleen they'd ever they ever seen around here. I wouldn't be surprised if one of the surgeons had it stuffed and mounted in his den like a moose head or something. Who knows, if I end up losing a kidney, maybe I'll finally get below 400."

A disapproving look swept across Charlotte's face, softened by the smile she tried but couldn't keep from her lips.

"How much do you think tonsils weigh?" Geoffrey wondered. "Or an appendix? That's got be worth a good ten pounds right there."

"Don't even joke about stuff like that."

"Or what are you going to do, yell at me again?" he asked, smiling himself now.

"I'm sorry. I didn't mean to—"

"Don't you be sorry, Charlotte. If you feel like yelling, I want you to yell. And if you feel like screaming, I want you to scream. And if you feel like jumping for joy, Charlotte, you jump for joy. It's so great to see you expressing yourself. If you feel it, I want you to show it. The louder the better." And then Geoffrey began singing, *"I am woman, hear me roar. I am too big to explore. La, la, la, la, and I've fallen on the floor."*

Charlotte tilted her head. "Dad, maybe you should lighten up on the Vicodin."

"It's an old song. You've never heard it?" He continued on. *"I am strong. I am invincible. I am woman!* They used to play it on the radio all the time. Before you were born."

"Like no offense, Dad, but like your music was really corny."

"Just you wait. Your kids will say the same thing to you someday, God willing."

Charlotte grew quiet. "I'm not going to have any kids."

"You're what?"

"I'm not going to have kids. I don't want to be a mom."

"Oh, really," Geoffrey said skeptically.

"Yeah, really."

"And when did you decide that?"

"A long time ago."

"And you don't think you'll ever change your mind?"

"No."

"Not even when you're all grown up and settled down?"

"You said I was grown up, remember?"

"Well, you are. But who knows, maybe one day you'll feel differently. It could happen. You know, *after* you're married and settled." Geoffrey felt compelled to make sure that last bit was clearly on the record.

"You think you know everything, don't you?"

"Your mother used to say that to me all the time. All the time…"

A moment passed before Charlotte said, "I'm sorry I made your life so hard."

"What are you talking about?" Geoffrey asked, incredulously.

She looked at him as if she was being asked to state the obvious. "What were ninety-nine-point nine percent of your fights about?"

She didn't wait for an answer. "Me. And you know that's the truth. You were always arguing because of me. I made your lives miserable. And now she's gonna leave you and it's all because of me. I'm sorry, Dad. I'm so sorry."

"Really? It's all because of you? Well, if that's true, I want you to look at me right now and tell me that your mother loves me— really, truly loves me—adores me, admires me, feels that the best day of her life was the day we got married because that meant that she could spend her whole life beside her true love, her one and only dream-come-true husband. Me! Mr. Perfect!"

"Well, I, I…"

"What? That's the truth, right? The only reason your mother and I ever fought was because of you. She never had a single complaint about me, did she? Not one, right? If it hadn't been for you, your mom would never want a divorce because I'm so perfect for her and she's so crazy in love with me. Cause she is, right? You know, I don't know if she told you but not too long ago, she had my face tattooed on her stomach. Yeah. My whole face, life-size. I had to pose for it and everything. Took forever. But she really wanted to do it because that's just how much your mother loves me."

Charlotte couldn't help but smile visualizing Queen Victoria with a huge tattoo of her father's goofy grin across her stomach.

"What's so funny? I have that effect on a lot of women, and your mom knows it, too. She made the tattoo guy promise he wouldn't put my face on any other women's stomachs. Made him swear and everything. And then she broke his arm just to make sure he got the message. Poor guy will probably never tattoo again. But that's love for you. It makes you do all kinds of crazy things. But then you saw the way your mother was with me. She couldn't keep her hands off of me, right? She was always hanging on me, giving me hugs and kisses, rubbing up against me all the time. You know, the minute you went off to school, she'd always be dragging me upstairs, ripping off my clothes, then ripping off her clothes, and then she'd start to do this—"

"Dad, stop! That's so gross!"

"It wasn't her fault. The girl was just so darn in love with me, she couldn't help herself. I drove her wild! You know, sometimes she'd want me to cozy up behind her and—"

Charlotte covered her ears. "Dad! Stop! I'm not listening! I'm not hearing a word you're saying!"

"Why not? I'm agreeing with you. You and you alone are the only reason we're getting divorced. It's got nothing to do with how she feels about me. No, sir. You know, sometimes she would do this stripper thing for me. She would put on this music and do this wiggle dance while she took off her—"

"DAD, STOP! STOP!!" she yelled, laughing now, unable to shake the image of Victoria doing a "wiggle dance" with a huge tattoo of her father's face undulating across her stomach. "Okay, I get what you are trying to say. I understand!"

"You do? Really?"

"I do, Dad."

"Then you understand that our divorce has nothing to do with you, Charlotte, nothing at all. Your mother has been miserable with me for as long as I can remember. She found fault with every single thing I did. In fact, I probably hold the world record for most consecutive things done wrong by a husband. There's probably a plaque somewhere with my picture on it in the Clueless Husband Hall of Fame."

Geoffrey shook his head and continued. "You're too smart to think you're the cause of this or that this is somehow all your fault. In fact, if you think about it, *really* think about it, it's actually just the opposite. Your mom isn't leaving me because of you — she *stayed* with me because of you. Because of you, she stayed with a man she never really got along with. But she stayed with me for all those years, because of you, because of her love for you."

Charlotte looked away. *Could that possibly be true?*

Charlotte never felt her mother loved her — not for a day, not for an hour, at least not any that she could remember. And she certainly knew her mother never *liked* her. They were so different. They were like awkward strangers pretending to be mother and daughter, the feeling of detachment so strong she wondered whether Victoria was really her mother at all. She used to think maybe her dad was married before and her real mother died or was a drug addict or something; that would explain so many things. But now, after listening to her father, she wondered if maybe, just maybe, she had been wrong about her. *She stayed because of me?*

Geoffrey was satisfied. From the look on Charlotte's face, it appeared his words had somehow penetrated, opening a place in her heart that had been closed for a very long time. With his words, with that opening, Charlotte took the first small step toward feeling better about her mother than she had her entire life. And maybe, maybe, about herself as well. But just then, Charlotte's thoughts were interrupted by a soft tap at the door.

A bouquet of white tea roses appeared followed by the handsome, perfectly groomed face of a stranger.

"Mr. Zukor?" Dressed in pressed white jeans and a white tee shirt and walking with a grace so natural as to not even make a sound, the beautiful stranger continued, "I am sure you don't remember me..."

THE ART OF COINCIDENCE

Charlotte was shocked, eyes bigger than bicycle tires. Suddenly, she wanted to leave, *had* to leave, but then again, she dared not move a muscle.

"Hi. I hope I'm not interrupting. I'm Donn Olson. I was a flight attendant on your plane when it crashed. I heard you were still in the hospital, and I thought I'd come by and-"

"You're the one that saved my dad," said Charlotte's inner voice, which, to her surprise, was connected to her outer voice as well. Embarrassed, she quickly returned to her reading. Unfortunately, it was several minutes before she realized she was no longer holding a book. She slid hers off a nearby table hoping no one noticed.

"I just helped him out of the plane."

"That was you?" asked Geoffrey, straightening up in his bed. "I can't believe it. I've been meaning to look you up. I just haven't quite found the strength yet."

"Oh, I—"

"That was you, wasn't it?" Geoffrey said, now firmly making the connection. "I saw the footage. That plane was on fire and you went back inside to get me. I must have seen it a dozen times on the news."

"Well, no, that wasn't exactly... I mean I did go— but I, I..." Finally, he just gave up with, "Anyway, here, these for you."

"They're beautiful, son, thank you. Please come in. Charlotte, ask the nurse if there's a vase around somewhere, would you?"

Charlotte couldn't move.

"Charlotte?"

Again, nothing. Charlotte sat frozen, reading her book without ever turning a page, an extremely difficult feat usually only practiced by highly experienced literary critics.

"I'll go ask," offered Donn.

"No," Geoffrey replied. And then in a tone Charlotte knew she could not ignore, he added, "Charlotte, get me a vase from the nurse now please." On her way out, she brushed by Donn, at the last second looking up to find his stare. Their eyes met and then she was gone.

"Your daughter?"

"Yes."

"She's so beautiful. Really beautiful. You don't see girls like her anymore. It's like she's from another time."

"That's funny. I thought I was the only one that ever thought that. You'll have to excuse her shyness. It's been a terrible problem for her all of her life."

"No one was shyer than I was growing up. I would keep my head so tucked away from everyone, they used to call me Donn the Swan."

"Well, Donn the Swan, you saved my life, son. You went back into that burning wreck and you carried me out."

"It wasn't like that, sir, really. It was a fluke that I found you. You must have collapsed onto the floor in front of your seat. It was so dark and smoky; I didn't even know you were there. I was trying to get forward to see if, well… And I don't know, and then there was this explosion. The whole plane rocked, and I was thrown in your direction. I think I almost landed on top you. Like I said, it was a fluke. But I just wanted to stop by and tell you I hope you get better real soon."

"Say what you will, you saved my life, son. You picked me up and carried me out of that plane. You gave me a chance to see my daughter again. I owe you everything, young man."

Charlotte returned, vase in hand. She filled it with water and placed it on a nearby service tray. "They're so beautiful," she said, arranging the flowers in the vase.

"They sure are. That was very, very thoughtful of you. You are quite the hero. How can I thank you for all that you've done for me?"

"Please, sir, it's, it's…" Donn said, shaking his head. "Listen, do we have to keep talking about this? I just wanted to—"

"My father's right. We owe you everything," Charlotte said with surprising ease.

"And speaking of my everything, Donn, this is my daughter, Charlotte. And I am Geoffrey Zukor." He swung his legs off the side of the bed.

"No, don't get up—"

"Oh, it's okay," said Geoffrey with an obvious strain in his voice. "They want me out of bed as much as possible, which, unfortunately, hasn't been all that possible. But for you, I will stand if it's the last… thing… I… do." With help from both Charlotte and Donn, he was up.

"Not so bad, right?" Geoffrey said, apparently unaware he was listing badly to the left.

"You're doing great, Dad. Just great."

"He is?" Donn whispered to Charlotte, struggling to keep Geoffrey upright. His face was part alarm, part smile.

Charlotte smiled back, charmed by both his candor and his boyishness.

Geoffrey extended his hand, which was promptly met by Donn's.

"Thank you, son—for more than you will ever, ever know. Hey, they're threatening to kick me out of here in a few days. How about we have a dinner party in your honor, say a week from Saturday? Will you come? I'm not going to take no for an answer."

Will you please? asked Charlotte's eyes before she lowered them to the floor.

"You're not going to turn her down, are you?"

Donn found himself unable to say no.

"I'd love to, but on one condition."

"Anything. You name it."

"We don't talk about the night of the crash again. Ever again. Okay?"

THE ART of COINCIDENCE

From just past the door frame, two inquisitive eyes peeked in, immediately catching Geoffrey's attention. "Laura?" Geoffrey waved her in.

"So?" she asked, glancing around the room to make sure they were alone. "How'd it go?"

"She just left. I think it went great, I really do," he replied with a smile.

"Oh, I'm so glad. I was so worried about her. Did you tell her I told you about the papers?"

"No. She has no idea."

"Well, I probably shouldn't have butted in like that. I hope I didn't make things more difficult for you. The poor girl was just so miserable—"

"Are you kidding? The way you handled everything was perfect. I can't thank you enough."

"Really? You're not just saying that?"

"Without your help, our talk would have been a complete disaster. You gave me a chance to think about what I wanted to say to her. And it gave Charlotte some time get used to the whole idea. I don't know what would have happened without you. You made a huge difference. How'd you get to be so smart?"

"Yeah, right."

"I mean it. You've been so wonderful. Thanks so much for everything you've done for us. The way you've befriended Charlotte and helped her through all this. For, for everything. You've been incredible. I know she's really going to miss you. And I know I will, too."

Laura leaned over the side rail of his bed, very close to his ear, and whispered, "Well, maybe you don't have to." Then she shot him a mischievous little smile and left.

THE ART OF COINCIDENCE

"You wanted to see me, sir?" Laura asked, still smiling as she walked into Dr. Sheinman's office.

Over the past few months, something had begun stirring in Laura, a small thing really, as big things usually are. It was as if she had grown more gracious, more mature, more naturally feminine in manner, something even Dr. Sheinman had privately noted. It did not appear to him as so much of an act but a real transformation, a small cellular awakening, a bloom he had never seen in her before. It was as if she were coming into her spring.

"Yes, come in. Tell me, what are you planning for the Zukor discharge on Friday?"

"There will be a press conference at 10:30 a.m. in the Press Center. Mr. Zukor will be there, Dr. Alacombre, and maybe you'd like to join us as well?"

"No thanks, but perhaps you could also have his daughter there, standing beside him?"

"That's a great idea, sir."

"Fine then. Thank you," Dr. Sheinman said, discharging her. But as she started toward the door, he added, "You know, you two are not the only ones around here that smoked pot in high school."

"What?"

"And you're not the only one with a young friend on the ninth floor."

"I guess not, sir."

"You've been a big help to her, Laura, a very big help. And don't think it's gone unnoticed or unappreciated. You've done a fine job, young lady, a fine, fine job."

"Well, thank you, sir."

"Thank you, Laura."

In all of her days at Cedars-Sinai, she had never felt better than she did just then; it was as if she had finally figured out what it meant to work in a hospital.

THE ART OF COINCIDENCE

Days later, the following AP news item appeared in the *Los Angeles Times*:

Mysterious Person Halts Attack

By Frieda Volapanucci, Associated Press

(ROME, Italy) Domestic violence was no stranger to the home of Dugo and Francesca Torino, 48 Via Lanza, near S. Maria Maggiore. On countless occasions over the last decade, the Rome Police had been summoned by neighbors to the Torino residence in response to the emotional cries of physical battery. In four of the five incidents this year alone, Mr. Torino was removed from his home for aggravated drunkenness and although Mrs. Torino displayed clear signs of spousal abuse, charges were never brought against her husband. Following each occurrence, Mr. Torino spent but a single night in jail.

At approximately 11:45 p.m. on November 14, a heavily intoxicated Mr. Torino came home to find the meatballs his wife had prepared for him not to his liking.

"These no meatballs, these baseballs," Mr. Torino jeered, and following a lengthy tirade, he came to the fine idea of hurling them at her. With each hit, Mr. Torino yelled, *"STRIKE!"*

After exhausting his supply of *meat-ammo,* Mr. Torino began beating her with the 22" iron skillet she used to prepare the dish. With each smack, he roared triumphantly, *"HOME RUN!",* shouts that could be heard almost a block away amid his wife screams.

In a sworn affidavit filed with Rome police, Mrs. Torino said that it was then that a mysterious stranger burst through their second story living room window, ripped the pan from Mr. Torino's hands, spun around, and then struck him with it on the buttocks so hard as to bend its handle.

Exploding forward from the force of the blow, Mr. Torino's head rammed a nearby plaster wall, leaving a 3-inch-deep crater. With a single hit, Mr. Torino was incapacitated.

"GRAND SLAM!" the intruder yelled and then withdrew to the kitchen, returning a moment later with a large pot of Mrs. Torino's marinara. As if he weighed nothing at all, the mysterious stranger flipped the 265-pound man onto his back and then proceeded to douse him with sauce. As the wet splat covered his face, he returned to at least some level of consciousness.

"How do you like playing hardball now, slugger? It's not quite as much fun when you're the one taking the beating, is it? And I've got something you're going to like even less—a whole lot less. If you ever lay so much as a finger on your wife again, I will boil the sauce before I cover you with it. Do you understand me?"

When Mr. Torino failed to reply, the intruder pressed one of her high heeled pumps into his groin and said, "Oh, two tiny baseballs. Maybe I hit another grand slam with these, huh? Huh?" Then she straightened her leg, pressing her point all the more.

"No! No! Ohhh—" yelled Mr. Torino.

"Then are you ever going to lay a hand on your wife again?"

"No! No, I never!"

"Promise?"

"Si. Yes-ah, I promise! I promise!"

"Pinky promise?" Again, she dug her heel deep into his groin.

"Yes, okay, okay, pinky promise! Pinky promise!"

"Good. I'm glad we understand each other. See what a good boy you can be when you try? Don't make me comeback here again. You won't' like what happens."

The mysterious stranger moved to the living room window from which she entered. At her back she heard, "Help me up, Woman!"

There was something in his tone she didn't like, something familiar, something unchanged. On a small wooden end table, an uncapped bottleneck protruding from a rumpled paper bag caught her eye. She stopped and turned back around to find Mrs. Torino still sobbing.

"Oh, so you're a drinker, aren't you, slugger? You know, my father used to drink. And when he drank, he was *especially* mean, to both my mother and to me. But then one night, just like you, he promised me he would stop. And just like you, he even pinky promised. But you know one of the many, many things I learned from my father was? When people drink, sometimes they forget their promises. Isn't that sad? I was just thinking that for your sake maybe I should leave you with a little something just so that no matter how drunk you get, you will always remember the importance of keeping your word." Then she leaned over him and whispered, "Because, trust me, you don't want to end up like my father."

In a blur, she grabbed his right hand and brought it up, close to his ear. Then she latched onto the top half of his little finger and said, "So listen and never forget the sound of a broken pinky promise..." And with that, she snapped it back upon itself, shattering the bone.

Neighbors had endured years of yelling at 48 Via Lanza, but they had never heard a scream like that.

"A broken bat single! I better run!"

At the living room window, she stopped to tell the woman of the house not to fear. "Although I may be gone, I will never be far," she assured her. And then the mysterious intruder disappeared into the night.

Minutes later, Mrs. Torino told the Rome police, "It was a woman, but strong. So strong. She was wearing a Prada jumpsuit. I know it was Prada because I do sewing for them on Via Condotti. Pink with orange silk trim and belt. Matching shoes, pink with an orange bow. And she was wearing a mask—again pink with orange trim. Everything fit her so beautifully. She was stunning, really. She saved my life, that woman. That woman, she saved my life."

THE ART OF COINCIDENCE

It was 10:38 a.m., the waning moments of Laura's customary ten-minute grace period before beginning any press conference. The Press Center was unusually full for what looked to be the culmination of the SWA Flight 2020 crash/Geoffrey Zukor recovery story, and several reporters were still partaking of the varied pastries and coffee she had, as always, laid out for them, another smart Laura Latman *exclusive* in this very news-competitive city. It was not lost on her that there were more press conferences held in media-rich Los Angeles than in New York, London, and Paris combined. Today, all of the locals were present and even cable outlets like *MSNBC*, *CNN*, and *Fox* had sent over crews. The papers were represented by *UPI*, *AP*, *Reuters*, *The Los Angeles Times*, and *USA Today*. It didn't hurt attendance that word had somehow leaked that even *Time* magazine was sending a reporter as part of a cover story they had in the works. The source of the leak wasn't much of a mystery (Laura) but what wasn't revealed was that the magazine's coverage was a result of one of her emails to their Health & Science Editor, pitching him an idea for an article along the lines of, *The Resurrection, the Miracle of Modern Medicine*. Sub-

Head: *How could this man survive this crash after sustaining multiple fatal injuries? And what does this mean for your chances to live to be 100? 125? or even...?*

Whether it was the day's first slap of sugar and caffeine or the feel-good nature of this particular press conference, was unclear, but for whatever the reason, the upbeat mood in the Press Center was unmistakable. This was one media event that even Dr. Alacombre was happy to attend. As notebooks flipped open, pencils dislodged from behind ears, and small, red LEDs ignited atop expensive, new, wide format 8k video gear, Dr. Alacombre took his place between Laura and Geoffrey, who was seated in a wheelchair, bordered on the opposite side by his daughter.

With a nod from Laura, two large banks of recessed floods came to life drawing everyone's attention forward to the stage-less stage area, intentionally kept at a more flattering, lower line of sight than the row of cameras standing on an elevated platform at the rear of room. There was no worse fate one could suffer in image conscious Los Angeles than being shot by a camera angled up into your nostrils. It was for that very reason that the Screen Actors Guild had sponsored recent legislation prohibiting dwarfs from working as handheld video-cam operators within the state.

Although the main room of the Press Center remained lit, the view of the reporter pool from stage was now obscured behind a luminescent curtain of white haze. Laura, Dr. Alacombre, Geoffrey, and Charlotte were suddenly fish in a fishbowl, each of their faces reacting differently to all of the attention directed their way. As a group, their facial expressions read like the varied pictographs on an anxiety disorder clinic's wall chart:

HOW DO YOU FEEL TODAY?

Please point to the picture/caption below that best describes
your current anxiety level.

I feel good. Everything is fine. I am CALM & RELAXED.

I feel okay, kind of, but have this lingering feeling that
maybe something isn't quite right. I'm a bit tense and on-guard. I
am able to get by but still, I am SLIGHTLY STRESSED.

I'm a mess, a complete mess. Things are lousy and I can't
see them getting better anytime soon. I can't remember the last
time I had a good night's sleep. Trust me, I have a whole bunch of
reasons to be VERY NERVOUS AND IRRITABLE.

How am I feeling? What kind of question is that, numb-nuts? You think I just popped in here to sell you some Girl Scout cookies? I'm a wreck, asshole, and can you blame me? How would you feel if you were waiting in line, minding your own business, and standing right next to you is this fidgety, dark-haired guy, wearing a big, bulky vest? It's probably nothing, right? But then you over-hear him ask in this thick accent of his, "Do you think there will be signs directing us where to go to pick up all of our virgins?" How would that make you feel, huh? That's got to raise the old blood pressure a few points, don't you think? And that's not the half of it.

Then this other dark-haired guy who's standing on the other side of me and is also wearing a big, bulky vest, answers, "Oh, yes, Sahib, I have heard there will be many signs directing us where to go. Locating our virgins should not be a problem. But I was wondering, do you think they give us our virgins all at once, or do they dole them out a few at a time?"

So then this guy right behind me, who's obviously also hit the sale at *Big & Bulky Vests R Us*, answers, "I was told they offer sev-eral different plans from which to choose. They range from the top of the line, *Grab-All-Your-Virgins-At-Once Plan,* to the very popular, *Get-One-New-Virgin-Delivered-Right-to-Your-Door-Each-Year-for-72-Years Plan.* Personally, I'm going for the *Get-One-New-Virgin-Delivered-Right-to-Your-Door-Each-Year Plan* because I worry if I receive them all at once, by the time I get around to the last one, she might not be a virgin anymore."

So then a guy right in front of me, whose vest was even big-ger and bulkier than the rest, turned to the others and said, "I hear you, my Brother, but personally I think I'm going for the *Grab-All-Your-Virgins-At-Once Plan* because what happens if you take the *Get-One-New-Virgin-Delivered-Right-to-Your-Door-Each-Year-for-*

72-Years Plan and then they go out of business or something before you get all your virgins. What are you going to do then, huh? On the other hand, the *Get-One-New-Virgin-Delivered-Right-to-Your-Door-Each-Year-for-72-Years Plan* does give you a little something to look forward to every year, so I don't know. I keep going back and forth. I guess I'll decide when I get there. I'm sure they'll have a 4-color brochure or a PowerPoint presentation that will help us decide."

Vest-in-Front looked at his watch and ominously raised one finger. The three other vests nodded solemnly. Then Vest-in-Front added, "You know, the only thing that bothers me about all this is that my Imam must have told me a million times that sex outside of marriage is strictly forbidden, but now, all of a sudden, they're throwing virgins at me like I'm an all-state quarterback at a C.U. recruiting party. I mean, why is it okay to have sex with some virgin after you've been blown into itty-bitty pieces but not okay with one of your cousins down by the creek—you know, while you still have your head attached to your body?"

"And your arms attached to your body," sighed Vested-Man-to-my-Right.

"And your legs attached to your body," sighed Vested-Man-to-my-Left.

"And your body attached to your body," sighed Vested-Man-to-the-Rear.

"Oh well," sighed Vested-Man-in-Front-of-Me. "On the count of three. One. Two. Thr—"

"STOP!" I said, wondering if I as a mere bystander might also be eligible to participate in *The Great Virgin Giveaway of the New Millennium,* which was undoubtedly the largest and most generous offering of its kind since the Nevada Gaming Commission first began tracking virgin giveaways back in 1952.

Personally, I'm a bit skeptical. I mean they're giving away virgins by the boatload, right? Well, you gotta ask yourself, where are they getting all these virgins from anyway? Virgins don't grow on trees, you know. Heck, ever since my wife discovered the joys of over-fertilizing, not even leaves grow on our trees anymore. And

I wouldn't be surprised to learn that someone was over-fertilizing down at the *Vern's Virgin Making Factory* as well because just one quick look around L.A. will tell you that they ain't cranking out nearly as many virgins as they used to.

And what happens if they run out? Talk about a lousy job, how'd you like to work at the Virgin Dispensary Facility in Heaven and have to tell all the guys slithering in piece by piece that their gonna have to take a rain check on the virgin part of the deal? (And here I thought taking AT&T complaint calls about their nearly non-existent cell phone coverage would be a tough gig!) Still, as curious as I am about the legitimacy of *The Great Virgin Giveaway,* make no mistake, I'm in no big hurry to take the trip to check out what's really going on.

And so I said, "Sorry to interrupt you gentlemen but I couldn't help overhearing some of your discussion and as a Certi-fied Public Accountant and someone who deals with the intricacies of numbers all day long, I feel compelled to tell you that the *Get-One-New-Virgin-Delivered-Right-to-Your-Door-Each-Year-for-72-Years Plan* you were just discussing is actually quite deceiving. You see, because you are getting your virgins spread over an extended pe-riod of time, *without* the benefit of interest I might add, the net present value of your virgins is actually far less than 72."

"Net present value? What do you mean?" asked Vested-Man-in-Front-of-Me skeptically but interested, nonetheless.

"It's quite simple. Let me give you an example. Say some-one owes you one hundred dollars but rather than repay you all at once, they give you one dollar a year for one hundred years. Now because of inflation and the lost opportunity cost associated with not being able to put your money to work elsewhere, the real value of receiving one dollar a year for one hundred years is much, much less than receiving one hundred dollars today, right? Well, same thing is true with virgins. Even considering today's lousy interest rate environment, if you selected the *Get-One-New-Virgin-Deliv-ered-Right-to-Your-Door-Each-Year-for-72-Years Plan,* it's like you're actually only getting 33 or 34 virgins, tops."

"We're only getting virgin tops?" asked Vested-Man-to-my-Right, suddenly quite concerned. "Nobody ever said anything to me about only getting virgin tops."

"Nor I," exclaimed Vested-Man-to-my-Left. "I think they are trying to change the deal on us!"

"Well, are they really big tops?" wondered Vested-Man-Behind-Me. "I mean, if they're really jumbos…?"

"How can you tell if a girl's top is really virgin? Do they look different?" asked Vested-Man-to-my-Right.

"They're probably not all sticky," answered Vested-Man-Behind-Me. "If they're all sticky, that's probably a sign they're not so virgin-y."

That seemed to make sense to Vested-Man-to-my-Right and Vested-Man-to-my-Left who both nodded and said, "Right."

"What are you talking about? Don't be ridiculous," admonished Vested-Man-in-Front-of-Me. "That is not what this gentleman is saying. You're not going to be getting just the top half of virgins. I assure you, you will be getting your virgins whole."

"Just the hole??" asked Vest-to-my-Right, Vest-to-my-Left, and Vest-to-my-Behind, in unison, suddenly more concerned than ever.

"That's kind of weird, don't you think?" added Vest-to-my-Behind, not at all sure he wouldn't prefer just virgin tops if, in fact, they really were jumbos.

"Very weird," agreed Vest-to-my-Left. "Don't get me wrong, portability is a nice feature, but how would you carry the virgin hole around? I wouldn't want to keep getting pocket lint on it all the time."

"You could wrap it in tin foil," suggested Vest-to-my-Right. "Kind of like baked potato."

"Or maybe put it on a chain around your neck?" suggested Vest-to-my-Behind. "That might be nice. And an interesting conversation starter, too!"

"I don't know," said Vest–to-my-Left, unconvinced.

"Well, if they did give you just the hole, there would be a lot less complaining," offered Vest-to-my-Right.

"And a lot less pointing and snickering, too," said Vest-to-my-Behind.

"Come to think of it, just the hole sounds pretty darn good to me," said Vest-to-my-Left. Right-Vest and Rear-Vest nodded in agreement.

"You pork-brains! That is not what this gentleman is trying to explain to you either! What he is saying, and please, sir, correct me if I am wrong, is that the *Grab-All-Your-Virgins-At-Once Plan* is a wiser choice. It's like I read in *Rich Sheik, Poor Sheik.* I think it was Chapter 27: *You Can Work For Your Money Or Let Your Money Work For You.* Well, it's the same thing with our virgins."

"We should put our virgins to work for us?" asked Rear-Vest.

"I think that is what my uncle does," offered Left-Vest, "and he makes lots of money at it too. Lots of money. And trust me, his girls aren't virgins. In fact, his girls don't look like they were even born virgins."

Right-Vest considered this for a moment. "I guess putting them to work is okay with me, as long as they all remain pure and chaste."

"Well, maybe the good-looking ones will be chased," replied Left-Vest, "but from what I've seen, it's mostly the girls that do the chasing. They're always running up and down the street, wobbling around in their high heels, hollering stuff like, 'Hey sweetie, come on back here. I'm havin' a pre-Ramadan special!'"

"Guys, as you can see there's a lot to consider," I interjected, "and I don't think your decision is something you should rush into blindly. Here's my card. Why don't you come by my office in the morning and we'll make sure you don't end up making a choice you might seriously regret later."

"Look! It says here his name is Hiram Goldfarb!" said Right-Vest to Left-Vest and Rear-Vest. "Goldfarb! This man is a—!" Both Left-Vest and Rear-Vest recoiled in horror.

"So?" said Front-Vest. "Your father never taught you the first rule of business? Get yourself a Jewish accountant."

"Well, maybe my father did mention that a couple of times," mumbled Left-Vest begrudgingly.

"Mine too. A bunch of times," agreed Rear-Vest.

"Yes, mine too," nodded Right-Vest. "Even the Mosque uses the accounting firm of Israel, Levy, Cohen, & Abdul."

"Israel, Levy, Cohen, & Abdul?" said Left-Vest. "Really? Abdul?"

"That's right," I confirmed. "The firm's name is actually Israel, Levy, Cohen, & Abdul. I've got a few friends over there and from what I heard, Abdul was added at the Mosque's request—you know, just in case word should get out. In any event, it's the first time in accounting history that a janitor has ever made name partner."

Front-Vest checked his watch. "Guys, we're way off schedule. What shall it be then? Do you want to put this thing off until tomorrow afternoon so we can go see Goldfarb in the morning or should we get on with it now and just wing it when we get there, with whatever wings we have left, that is?"

As the four men debated their futureless future, I am EXTREMELY, and I mean *EXTREMELY FUCKING ANXIOUS.*

THE ART OF COINCIDENCE

Laura gave Geoffrey and Charlotte a reassuring little nod and then approached the Cedars-Sinai Press Center podium.

"Shall we get started?" she asked no one in particular.

"Ladies and Gentlemen, my name is Laura Latman. For the past eight years, I have had the great pleasure to serve as Director of Media and Public Relation for the Cedars-Sinai Medical Center. In all that time, I have never as pleased as I am today in announcing the successful discharge of Mr. Geoffrey Theodore Zukor." And with that she turned and flashed a sincere smile, first to Charlotte and then to her father.

"As you know, Mr. Zukor was the most severely injured among the survivors of the crash of Southwest Airlines Flight 2020, and as such, has been a patient here at Cedars-Sinai for the last 179 days. Over half of that time was spent in our Trauma Center and Critical

Care Unit under the direct supervision of Dr. Eric Alacombre. Cedars-Sinai is making Dr. Alacombre available here today to give you a full briefing on the recovery and discharge of Mr. Zukor."

"Dr. Alacombre has been a lead physician at Cedars-Sinai for over twenty years and during his tenure was the youngest recipient of the American Medical Association's Medal of Hope, the highest honor given to our nation's trauma center doctors. Before coming to Cedars, Dr. Alacombre served three combat tours as a forward triage medic and was commended for his heroic service to others on the battlefield. On a personal note, Dr. Alacombre is a first generation American, a Sephardic Jew, whose parents immigrated to this county from the island of Rhodes virtually penniless and with little knowledge of English. As a result of their daily sweat and toil, spending little to nothing on themselves, they afforded their son an opportunity to go to one of this nation's finest medical schools at Harvard University, where he graduated at the very top of his class. Ladies and Gentlemen of the press, the finest man I have ever had the pleasure of beating at checkers, Dr. Eric Alacombre."

Alacombre laughed and shook his head, revealing just how much she had caught him off-guard. That was the first time Laura had ever acknowledged the kindness he showed her on her first day at Cedars all those years ago. Although her previous experience in public relations had been limited and without much in the way of authority, she was hired on to be the first full-time PR Director that Cedars had ever had, which, taken together, basically meant she didn't know what she was doing and had no footsteps to follow for a clue. Certainly, there had to have been a dozen more qualified applicants than Laura Latman and why Dr. Sheinman chose to hire her, she never understood. After a morning of calling people by the wrong names, repeatedly misspelling Cedars-Sinai in press releases (she spelled it as most people say it, Cedar-Sinai), and then trying to exit her office by walking into her closet, an act unfortunately witnessed by Dr. Sheinman's secretary, Laura Latman sat in a corner of the hospital cafeteria staring blankly into her cup of coffee, into which she had forgotten to add cream, sugar, or even coffee.

It was Dr. Eric Alacombre who walked up, introduced himself, and then explained to Laura that it was mandated by Dr. Sheinman that all new hires must play at least one game of checkers with the reigning Cedars-Sinai Checkers Champion, "…and that be me." On a board he plopped down on her table, Dr. Alacombre began casually making every unobvious wrong move he could think of, all the while retelling the latest round of jokes that had been circulating the Trauma Center that week. Soon Laura Latman found herself smiling, laughing even, and, to her surprise, winning. He peppered their conversation with comments like, "You're not one of those professional checker players that go around to all the parks to swindle old men out of their pocket change, are you?" and "Do you really work here or did Sheinman just hire you to come down here and embarrass me like this?" His joking and bumbled moves culminated with, "I can't believe it! You're the first person to beat me at checkers since I started here seventeen years ago! If your PR skills are half as savvy as your checkers game, you're going to be running this place in no time. Are you sure you've never played professional checkers? Really, you can tell me. You have, haven't you? I know you have. You have, right?" Laura left the cafeteria that day not quite sure what just happened, but certainly feeling a lot better than she had when she walked in.

It was almost a year later before Laura caught Dr. Alacombre in the cafeteria cozied up to some other new hire who looked like she too were having a rough first day of it, using the same losing strategies and the same well-rehearsed lines, all of which ending with the same relieved smile on the face of a new friend who was starting to believe her new job might just turn out to be okay.

"I see a checkers rematch in your future, Ms. Latman," Dr. Alacombre said with a wry smile. He resisted the temptation to improvise further and instead faithfully recapped for the press the highs and lows of Mr. Zukor's hospitalization, outlining his emergency splenectomy and the three surgeries that followed, totaling over thirty-seven hours in the O.R.; his sixty-four days in the Intensive Care Unit, thirty-seven of which he was listed in critical condition; the various angiogenic gene-based therapies used to help facilitate his recovery from what not too long ago would have been considered incurable injuries; and two robotically-assisted combination neuro-retinal and corneal transplants, the second operation required due to tissue rejection following the first.

"Many of the technologies used to save Mr. Zukor's life were unavailable to us as little as three years ago. And had this accident happen in 1995, Mr. Zukor's recovery could have easily involved twice as many hospital days and still face a great likelihood of ending up with a far more catastrophic result."

At this point, Dr. Alacombre stopped while his eyes quickly scanned the paragraphs of prepared text that followed. It didn't take long; he was well aware of what it said, having spoken a variation of these words perhaps a hundred times before. Without a second thought or even a glance back to Laura, he folded his speech and instead said, "But, to be frank, the real miracle here was the not the technology we used to keep Mr. Zukor alive but Mr. Zukor himself. Throughout all of the operations, the painful procedures, the needles and around-the-clock prodding, the day in-and-out ache of recovering from near fatal injuries, and the prolonged uncertainty of his chances for a full recovery of both his sight in his right eye and his ability to walk without assistance;

during all of that, Mr. Geoffrey Zukor has shown more heart and grace than this doctor has seen from a patient in a long, long time. To my standard opening line, 'How are we doing today?' Mr. Zukor always answered, 'Perfect, Doc. Just perfect.' In a dire predicament like the one Mr. Zukor has faced, I have often witnessed patients ask some version of, 'Why did this have to happen to me?' And yet, despite the horrific plane crash and all that he has subsequently endured, I have never heard Mr. Zukor say anything other than, 'I am the luckiest guy in the whole world.' No, the miracle here is not technology; the miracle here is the man."

"Mr. Zukor, on behalf of all of the doctors, nurses, and our support teams here at Cedars-Sinai, we are so pleased to see you going home. It has been an honor for us to be of service to you, sir, and we wish you Godspeed on your continuing recovery."

With that, Dr. Alacombre turned to find Geoffrey Zukor standing and extending his arms in gratitude and friendship. As the two men embraced, more than a few reporters noticed a circle of light radiating around them, an event even watchful eyes see only on the rarest of occasions. In that moment, these two became the hypnotic focus of all in attendance, yet exactly what was transpiring was both impossible to explain and impossible to ignore. The radiating aura and corresponding feeling that permeated the gathering was so rare a thing, so distinctly special, that although it would never be discussed or publicly acknowledged, in that moment, the room was somehow brighter and the world somehow younger, as witnessing hearts were touched with a light that somehow made them all the purer. It was as if through these two, Heaven itself opened to show a glimpse of its glory.

"Yes?" said Laura, acknowledging the raised pencil in the second row.

"Mark Scene, CNN. Question for Mr. Zukor, please. Mr. Zukor, would you share with us a few of things you will always remember about your stay here at Cedars-Sinai and perhaps a few you'd like to forget?"

One didn't need a master's degree in non-verbal communication to decipher the "Who me?" expression on Geoffrey's face. His eyebrows rose nearly to the top of his head and his lips pursed together so tightly as to completely obliterate any sign of a mouth. Geoffrey's eyes darted to Laura, who returned a smile and an encouraging nod. Geoffrey looked at the reporter and began to mumble something or another; no one was sure exactly what.

"Geoffrey?" Laura said, interrupting him. Then she motioned for him to join her at the podium, adding off-mic, "From here, you silly."

Laura thought he might be asked a question or two but didn't say anything to Geoffrey. She didn't want to rattle him unnecessarily and thought he might come off better, more natural, if he spoke extemporaneously. Yep, she was wrong.

Geoffrey slapped a stiff smile on his face. "What should I say?" he asked her, trying to conceal his question from the audience by not moving his lips.

"Anything you want."

"Well, like what?" Geoffrey urged nervously.

Laura leaned very close to him and whispered, "You could tell them that a certain Director of Public Relations who works at a certain hospital has been flirting with you. But I'm just not sure if you're going to tell them that was one of the things you'll always remember or one you'd like to forget. I wonder which it is?" Then to the reporter she asked, "Mark, would you please repeat the question?" Before leaving Geoffrey's side, she added, "Just answer their questions. You'll be great, I promise." Without thinking, she kissed him on the cheek and walked away.

Mark Scene, a 35-year veteran of L.A.'s press corps said, "Well, if that's how all plane crash victims get treated around here, I'm going to start flying a lot more and hope I get lucky."

An hour later, Geoffrey Theodore Zukor left the hospital.

THE ART OF COINCIDENCE

The Ballad of Rosie and Rae
A Love Story
Part 3

(310) 278-4329 to (310) 278-7822

"Hello?"

"Rae, did you see it? Geoffrey Zukor is being released from the hospital today. It was just on TV and everything."

"No, I haven't turned on the television all morning. I've been too busy staring at the phone, waiting for my children not to call."

"They had his doctor on again. Oy, what a handsome man! Him, I could watch for hours."

"You know, David was going to be a doctor."

"Your son? He was?"

"Sure. But then he changed his mind and decided to be an imbecile instead."

"Rae, you should count your blessings. At least your kids are married. It kills me that my Sophie is alone and has no one to share her life with."

"I don't want to talk about it. Last time you and I discussed Sophie, you got so mad, you wouldn't talk to me for a month."

"Five weeks."

"Exactly."

"So why? Why can't she find a man? You really think it's the weight?"

Rae thought for a moment. "It's either her weight or her mustache."

"There you go again with the mustache comments! My daughter does not have a mustache!"

"No? So, what's stretched across her upper lip? Her pet caterpillar?"

"Rae, you're so cruel."

"What are you talking about? No one loves Sophie more than I do—no one! So let me help her. I saw this ad on TV for this wax that removes unwanted hair. It was so simple. They showed it working fabulously. I'll buy some for her."

"You think we haven't tried that nonsense already? She made the mixture. She put it on. She let it dry. And then I yanked it off. We nearly had to have her lip surgically reattached."

"Was that why her upper lip was dangling down below her chin for a while?"

"Exactly. Sophie was so embarrassed, the poor dear, she didn't want me to tell you, but yeah, that was the reason."

"That was not a good look for her."

"Well, thank you for that, Mr. Blackwell. We had no idea."

"You don't have to be so sarcastic. I'm just trying to help. And if it were me, I wouldn't be sobbing that she hasn't found anyone yet. Better no spouse than the one my son married. Out of all the nice girls he dated, the *schmendrik* chooses her?"

"What nice girls? She was the only date you son ever had."

"Sure, because she scared all the nice girls away. You think I'm not on to all of her little tricks?"

"My Sophie should have married your David. I've said that since they were kids."

"They can't marry. They're second cousins."

"Please, don't be so naïve. Sophie's father and I were second cousins. No one checks. It's fine."

"Oh sure, it's just fine — 'til one day your daughter starts growing a mustache!"

"There you go again with the mustache comments! My Sophie does not have a mustache!"

"Rosey, wake up. The girl's a dead ringer for Groucho Marx!"

"I'm warning you. Say it again and it will be eight weeks this time. Eight weeks!"

"Okay, fine. Your daughter doesn't have a mustache. And I suppose she doesn't weight 280 pounds either."

"She doesn't. She's been on this new diet for the last couple of weeks. She only weights 279½ now."

"Swell. If she lives to be 700, she'll be a regular Twiggy."

"Well, she may be a little overweight, I'll give you that. But I think she carries it very nicely."

"Oh, sure. For someone 4-feet, 10-inches tall, she carries 279½ pounds just fantastic. Hardly notice the extra weight at all."

"You're so cruel."

"No, I'm not. I just find it helpful to be realistic when it comes to our children, for their sake as much as ours. Believe me, Rose, it's not helping Sophie any when you tell her that the new black blouse she bought is slimming. The only way that blouse could be slimming is if she wore it in a closet with all the lights turned off. Then maybe you've got slimming."

"Rose," Rae continued, "we've got to face facts. Our true children were stolen from us at birth and replaced with babies from a circus sideshow performer. Sophie and David are not our real kids. They're not, Rose. Your true daughter is out there somewhere, probably one of those pretty girls on a soap opera or maybe even in the movies. You know, a girl who's always had a bad relationship with the woman that she *thinks* is her real mother but isn't – a woman who doesn't look like her or act like her and who lives in a rundown trailer park somewhere and even sells her daughter's nude baby pictures and crappy report cards to *The Enquirer*. That poor girl... She is your true daughter, Rose. And my son... my real son is a doctor somewhere, a surgeon, a tall, handsome surgeon, who has always been baffled by his so-called father; a man so dumb he would starve before he could figure out how to open a can of beans. Those, those are our real kids, Rose. They're out there somewhere, their hearts calling to us. We must never forget them, Rose. Never forget them!"

THE ART OF COINCIDENCE

Wilshire Boulevard: The quintessence of Los Angeles.

Wilshire Boulevard: Six lanes of very important cars being driven by very important people wearing very important clothes as they hastily motor their way to their very important destinations, all the while remaining steadfastly focused on their life's core mission, which apparently is to never let anyone forget just how very important they undoubtedly are.

This is Wilshire Boulevard and the location of The Remington, which, in accordance with the terms of a lease signed just days ago, will be Geoffrey Zukor's new home.

The Remington was a newly constructed high rise near the center of the L.A.'s Diamond Necklace, a phrase coined by a local realtor to describe the string of prestige residential towers along Wilshire as it links Brentwood and Holmby Hills to Rodeo Drive and everything Beverly. Residences in even the worst buildings along this stretch of the boulevard can easily fetch five-million dollars with some selling for as much as five times that, or more.

The Remington stood twenty-seven stories and featured a total of ninety-six luxuriously appointed *penthouse* suites. Never mind that the term *penthouse* means, *"...a premium residence on the upper most floor."* Here, by divine degree of the developer's advertising agency, always the best arbiter of good taste and judgment in these matters, every condo was deemed a *penthouse*, even the ones on the second floor just above the noisy and exhaust-ridden driveway.

The tires of the black Lincoln Towncar were the first to herald Geoffrey Zukor's arrival as they warbled over the entrance's palette of slate gray, beige, and rust cobblestones. The car circled a scaled down replica of the main fountain at the Piazza Navona. Unfortunately, the Remington version seemed to share the same ring of authenticity as say, Sara Lee bagels. Moments later, they arrived under an Art Nouveau flavored porte-cochere.

"Welcome to The Remington," chirped the doorman while promptly opening the rear passenger-side door. Charlotte took his gloved hand and exited, keeping her head down as if trying to disappear into this new landscape via the biomorphic power of bad posture.

"Thank you," answered Geoffrey. "I think I'm going to need a bit of help also, if you'd be so kind."

The driver had already hopped from the car and both men now extended their arms deep into the back seat.

"Ooohh, oh! No, no, I don't think that's going to work. Would you mind coming around the other side?" Geoffrey suggested, hoping to save himself some painful shimmying. Exiting the car turned out to be far more difficult than falling into it had been.

"Visiting someone today, sir?" asked the doorman, not quite sure he should completely let go of the man's arm for fear of him toppling over.

"Nope. I'm coming home today. I'm moving here."

"Well, that's fine, sir. Welcome home." The doorman's smile was warm and generous.

Geoffrey reached for his wallet but was met with, "No, but thank you, sir, all the same. We can only accept gratuities from residents at Christmas, should you be so inclined. Can I help you up with anything, sir?"

"No, I just have this," gesturing to the satchel in the driver's hand. "Everything else should be here already. At least that was the plan."

"Fine, sir. Well, my name is Asa Washington. Please let me know if there is anything at all I can do for you."

The rear wall of the pickled-oak elevator cab was fitted with a large, beveled mirror above the wainscot and grab bar. Mirrors, always a safe bet in *"It's All About Me"* Los Angeles. Veins of black lightning ran across the antique marble squares that patterned the floor as polished brass doors closed with modern precision.

In the whoosh of the elevator's ascension, Glinda the Good Witch announced from nowhere, "Eighteenth Floor" to the surprise of all.

The lift opened onto a small but similarly paneled elevator lobby to the sounds of two men speaking excited Chinese, as if the customary sequence of talking and then listening had been replaced with talking and then talking even louder, streamlining the whole conversational process by removing the apparently unnecessary listening portion altogether. A few steps away, a third

Chinese man spoke in broken English to a scruffy, blurry-eyed and pale Caucasian, wearing jeans and a weathered red t-shirt fronted with the faded words, TV SUCKS. (I know the Chinese man was speaking broken English, because broken English was my language elective in high school, wherein I consistently received B's and C's with only a moderate amount of studying, my teacher referring to me as "naturally gifted in the tongue." Sadly, despite numerous energetic efforts in the years that followed, that was the only context in which I ever heard the phrase "gifted in the tongue" uttered. In hindsight, perhaps my efforts were a bit *too* energetic, for one young lady did spout, "Geez, save some for the next guy!")

"Oooohhh, it very bad! Very bad! Problem is here. You see? You feel it?" explained the Chinese gentleman, pointing to the front door of Geoffrey's neighbor. "This door solid. It block chi. It trap dragon. No way out so dragon is angry. Very angry! So, of course, you lose money. Of course, you sick. Of course, you fearful. It is dragon. He is powerful, very powerful. We must free the dragon! Free him now!!"

"Really? That's it?" asked the blurry-eyed Caucasian.

"Yes, it is dragon. We must free him now! Then chi will flow and natural balance be restored."

"And everything will be fixed, like, like back to normal? Really? Everything? Just like before?"

"Better than before. The fix very simple. The problem is front door. We must replace old door with new glass door. Then chi with flow, dragon will fly, and natural balance be restored. I will explain all, but you must act quickly. Here, call this number. Tell them front door must be replaced with glass door. Tell them Geo-Ming said it must be done immediately. Go now. Call. And don't forget, tell them Geo-Ming sent you. I get small referral fee."

As the modern-day Maynard G. Krebs scurried back into *Penthouse* 1802, the Chinese man, noticing the hobbling Geoffrey, asked, "You live here too, right?"

"Yes."

"You have bad luck, right? Very bad luck. You fall down, right?"

"Well, no, I—"

"No? Hmm... worse luck...You in car crash, right?"

"No, I—"

"No?? Even worse luck? Hmm... Some big guys beat you up, right?"

"No. I was in a plane crash."

"Plane crash? Plane crash??"

Geoffrey nodded.

"*Ooohhh!!*" yelled the Chinese gentleman, his two eyes and mouth suddenly a triangle of small round holes, giving his head the distinct appearance of a bowling ball. He turned and said something in Cantonese to his two associates. It was either about Geoffrey's plane crash or it was a pre-automatic-ball-return spell because after an *Ooohhh!* from each of them, their heads were suddenly bowling balls, too.

All three Chinese men then broke for the opening of 1802, each chiming in with their own version of: "Quickly! Call quickly! You got one pissed-off dragon here, buddy! You call now! Call now!! Hurry! Hurry!! And don't forget, use my name. I get small referral fee!" Then one of them scurried back to Geoffrey with his card. "Here, we help you too, friend. Call me. I give free estimate." Then he stopped, his eyes narrowing and head tilting to the right. "You look familiar. Plane crash... Hey, you that fat guy on TV! That you, right?"

"I don't know. I—"

"Yes. You in hospital, right? You have problem, then you get better. But then you have even worse problem, but then you get better again. But then, you have extra, extra bad problem. No one knows if you get better. Everyone worried. But then you get better! That you, right?"

"I guess it—"

"Yes, that you! You very good show! My wife be very excited I meet you. Tell me, what you do next season? Maybe arm fall off? Maybe leg? No, no, I got it! Maybe you head shrivel up? That happen to my uncle, and he no get better! Maybe you try that. That be good one. Everyone watch! Anyway, you call me. I give free estimate. Plus, celebrity discount just for you!"

"Oh," said Geoffrey, not at all following and pretty sure he wanted to keep it that way.

"That's right, free estimate! But you better call quickly. You got big problem here, buddy. You want dragon crap all over you again?"

"Probably not."

The Chinese man thrust his nose toward Geoffrey's chest, his nostrils bobbing like a bunny's. "That's dragon crap all right. Phew!"

"You know, my wife never liked this cologne much either but even she never said I smelled like dragon crap. And she was a tough grader."

Charlotte tugged on her father's sleeve, whispering something. He nodded and turned back to the Chinese man. "Well, I guess there was this one time she *did* say I smelled like—"

"You call for appointment. Call quickly! I help you. Plus, I give free estimate!"

"Free estimate. Well, all right then, I'm going to give this some very serious—"

"And don't forget about head shrivel. Everyone love head shrivel! I guarantee it!" the man hollered one last time before disappearing into Penthouse 1802.

"Great," Geoffrey replied. He stood there for a moment, motionless, and then added faintly, "Great, great, great…" But it wasn't. Nothing about this was great. He looked around, his eyes eventually locating the door to 1804. Yet there he stood, unable to take another step. He shook his head. Something was wrong, very wrong. Everything felt so strange.

He had been feeling this way for the last couple of weeks, the last week especially, but kept shrugging it off, which became harder and harder to do as his discharge date neared. Only now was he beginning to understand why. It was Victoria. Without thinking, he looked around for her, knowing full well she wouldn't be there. He had a sick, hollow feeling in his stomach.

Victoria…

In the surreal, hectic world of Cedars, their separation had taken a back seat to more pressing issues—medical procedures, exams, lab tests, more procedures, more tests, more exams, etc.—and then, of course, there was Charlotte—but out here, out here in the real world, the full impact of his wife's absence was just now beginning to be felt. He was going home without her and no matter how many times he would walk through that front door, she would never be there. He was alone, all alone. He suddenly felt so lost without her… A tear dropped from his eye. Then another.

What's happening…? He took a deep breath and tried to steady himself, but it was no use; something was pressing in on him, something far bigger than he could cope with. Under its weight, the world dimmed and fell away, taking all light and sound with it. And just like that, Geoffrey was locked in the dark, singular silence of his own thoughts.

He blinked at the darkness around him, trying to get his bearings. He needed to understand, to figure out how he ended up here. He needed to make some sense of it.

His mind flashed back to Albuquerque, to the airport. He saw himself whistling in front of the large crowd of onlookers, and then clicking his teeth to the hostess at the restaurant. He saw the old man with his stunned face looking down into his coffee cup. Then watched as he boarded the plane and that golden glint of late afternoon sun reflecting off its tail section right above its call sign — 5, 9, 4… 5, 9, 4… He remembered how happy, how truly happy he was. *"I'm going home. I'm going home…"* he heard himself say. And with that, he reached the only conclusion available. "And now here I am."

From his jacket pocket, he took out a brass key. It glistened in his hand, cold and heavy. Geoffrey slid it into the lock on the door to 1804 and turned. The tumblers reluctantly gave way. Shafts of white light streamed out into the lobby, welcoming him.

"I guess I'm home," he said. "I guess I'm home." Geoffrey smiled a certain smile; it was more sad than happy. And through the door to 1804, he walked.

Some seconds later, his front door swung open again and Geoffrey re-appeared. He peered out into the still dark and murky lobby. Undeterred, he reached out, groping left and right. Finally, he hit upon something and pulled. Out came his Charlotte, her eyes stunned by the light as if she had just awoken. He laughed and put his arm around her, and together they walked into 1804, the door closing behind them.

And thus it was how Geoffrey Zukor came to cross the threshold of a new life, a life he will soon find filled with surprise and sorrow, a life of…

THE END OF PART ONE

JUST
ONE
LIFE
PART TWO

SEASON
OF THE
WITCH

SEASON OF THE WITCH

The first day of a new life...

"Hello?"

"Geoffrey Zukor, how's my best customer?"

"Dr. Sheinman?"

"Yes, Geoffrey. I thought I'd give you a call, check in with you, see how you managed on your first night out of the hospital."

"Gee, Doc, that's, that's really nice of you."

Geoffrey was clearly surprised. He thought he might hear from Dr. Alacombre or maybe one of his nurses at Cedars over course of the next week or so, but he never expected a call from the hospital's chairman and chief of staff.

"Last night was, uh, yeah, it was all right. It... it was fine." He knew he sounded less than convincing but that was about was all the enthusiasm he could muster. He wondered if he could confide in him; tell him how damn strange it felt to be out of the hospital, to be out in the world, out on his own. Tell him how everything on the drive overlooked the same, the same streets and buildings, yet it all felt so different, so *unfamiliar*. It was so weird. But should he tell him that? Tell him that maybe, somehow, he'd gotten used to the hospital, used to having everyone around, the endless barrage of smiling, familiar faces; tell him how maybe he had even come to feel part of something, something larger than just his own recovery. But now, all that was gone. Everyone's gone. It's as if they've dropped him at the curb and the circus had moved on without him, like he was never really part of their world at all. He was just another patient, soon to be forgotten altogether. How could he tell him that he missed being in the hospital? Who says something like that? Everyone had worked so hard to get him well and *out* of the hospital… And then he wondered if that was even the truth of it; that maybe, maybe what he was really missing was his… his… He couldn't say it, not even to himself. It hurt too much, hurt in a way not all the bandages at Cedars could ever heal. So instead of saying anything, he just swallowed and tried to shake it off with, "But I'm, I'm fine. I'm feeling fine. Just great."

"Geoffrey, when someone's been with us for as long as you have, their adjustment to homecare is often difficult, both physically and psychologically—especially psychologically. I won't bore you with all the research, but basically the longer one remains in a hospital, the greater likelihood of their having to be readmitted for further treatment. This is especially true in facilities like ours, where doctors and nurses are encouraged to go beyond objective patient care and form personal bonds with those they're treating. Many in my line of work believe our approach is a mistake, that it's actually detrimental to our patient's ultimate recovery. They argue that anything that interferes with objectivity, interferes with our ability to provide sound medical judgment and treatment. And they might be right. But I'll tell you, if I were forced to practice their kind of medicine, I would have retired long ago. So, anyway, unless you have some objection, our protocol would be to send over one of our nurses, someone you've become familiar with here, to oversee your care for the next couple of weeks until you're better acclimated to your new surroundings. I'm sure Southwest's insurance will cover the cost, no problem. It's a lot cheaper for them to send out a nurse than having you end up back here for a spell."

"Oh, I don't know if that's necessary, Doc. Maybe it's better if you don't. Not having someone around forces me to get out of bed more often."

"I am not going to take no for an answer. I'll have a nurse there tomorrow. Maybe Mena, she's a hoot and one of our very best." Mena Benico was one of Geoffrey's favorites, a large block of a woman, standing six foot three, and weighting in at two-hundred-eighty-pound. She was a Filipina with the ability to know just what to say to put a smile on Geoffrey's face. Prior to her career in nursing, Mena was the captain of the Philippines' Women's Greco-Roman Wrestling squad. As such, she was the recipient of her country's only Olympic medal in the event, an accomplishment later called into question amid a controversy over her birth sex.

Dr. Sheinman continued. "If you'd like, we could start with just afternoons for the next few days. And if you need her more, you'll tell her. Let's make sure your transition home is as smooth and successful as possible. And don't worry; I'll make sure she gets you out of bed and on some long walks around the neighborhood."

"I thought there was a law against walking in Los Angeles."

"There is, unless you're in a hospital gown and your tush is sticking out. Then it's fine."

"That'll certainly shake things up along Wilshire Blvd. I won't be responsible for any accidents I cause."

"I'm sure you'll catch the eye of every UCLA coed within a five-mile radius. They'll probably be circling around the block just to get another look."

"Yeah, I'm sure that'll happen."

"I don't know, you do pretty good with the ladies from what I've seen. I know our Laura has mentioned your name more than a few times."

That picked up his spirits. "Really? Well, like I told you, she's been very kind to Charlotte. Those two have struck up quite a friendship."

"Maybe that's it, maybe it's not. Who among us knows the heart of a woman?"

Their call didn't conclude so much as drift off. With the mention of Laura, some of the gloom he felt since leaving the hospital seemed to lift.

SEASON OF THE WITCH

A few hours later, Geoffrey gathered the gumption to embark on his first solo-walking excursion since arriving at The Remington. Once in the elevator, the voice of Glinda the Good Witch announced Geoffrey's arrival at "Lobby Level" to an audience of one. As the tower's front doors opened onto the porte-cochere, he was met with a crush of traffic noise, completely masking the sound of water tinkling from the driveway's circular fountain, which was supposed to provide exactly the opposite effect. To accomplish that, however, the developer would have needed a water feature along the lines of, say, Niagara Falls; what be bought was a statue of some naked kid peeing on his toes.

"Good morning, Mr. Zukor. Nice to see you out and about, sir," the doorman said with a tip of his hat.

"Well, thank you. It's Asa, right?"

"That's right. Very good, sir," he answered, a bit surprised. And then he added, "I've got residents been coming and going for years now, and they still can't remember my name. I get Astro, Peso, whatever comes to mind, they just say it. One nice ol' lady on the 16th floor, Mrs. Greenblatt, she calls me Assho. Her daughter nearly dies every time it happens. I just smile and say, 'It's Asa, ma'am' but she never gets it right. I used to think it was just because she's getting up in years, but then she started wearing one of those MAGA hats, so now I not so sure."

Geoffrey smiled. "It's quite a world we live in, isn't it?"

"It sure is, sir. Down that way to your left is a little less steep, if you're thinkin' of venturing further."

"Well, I thought I might but, I don't know. Maybe I'll just grab a bit of fresh air and then head back upstairs."

"Don't know how fresh the air is around here, sir, but you're welcome to have your fill."

"Oh, the hospital called. Said they're gonna be sending over a nurse. Her name is Mena. Not sure if it will be today or tomorrow."

"No problem, sir, I'll be sure to send her right up. 1804."

"That's right. I see I'm not the only one with a good memory round here."

"Thank you, sir. I work at it."

228

Geoffrey settled into bed early that night, exhausted, the strangeness of his new life pressing in hard on him. Lying there, he wondered if he were really up to all this, if he truly had the strength to begin again…

With questions unanswered tumbling around him like so many blank dice, he found an uneasy sleep, a sleep with no rest. Turning the midnight pages, he scoured the world but found no homecoming. It was all too foreign, too cold; impenetrable, there was no place for him. And then he felt himself slipping, slipping, beginning to fall…

No…, no…, no…

He was slipping, falling away, away from Earth, from life, from everything he had ever known. He tried to stop it, to wake, but couldn't. It was all slipping away. He tried harder still, his arms flailing, his body twisting, turning, but it was no use. He struggled in vain until he was finally devoured by the void.

It was there that the terror, the panic, the mad groping, all subsided. There, at last, he was delivered into the arms of peace, and in that sweet embrace he finally found the rest he so desperately needed. There he stayed as time perambulated through the stars.

And it was there that he saw something, there in the distance, radiating out into the thick charcoal of soul space, a beacon burning bright, dissolving the dark and calling him from his rest onto a plaza, a plaza at the fall of many steps. There, alone, he waited...

In the gray and groggy morning, suddenly there she was, her edges feathered to the mist. It was Victoria, standing ever so straight, wearing on her face that contradiction of push and pull he could never decipher. A dress of pale chiffon flowed across her body that had not a gained a single pound since the day they met. Her hair looser now, poured over her shoulders. She seemed younger, stronger, somehow more natural here.

He wanted—needed—to hold her, to press himself against her stiff, unloving body; to climb inside, and maybe, just maybe, after a lifetime of searching, finally find a place beyond the reach of her rejection. How he missed her, her every rigid, unyielding impulse, even her cold and constant dismissal of him. With a single look from her, his tears covering the cobblestones like so much rain.

"Forgive me. Please forgive me," he said, trained by the years to bend and bow, as he buried his head deep into her. In his arms he held his first and only love.

"Geoffrey," she said, pulling back slightly to look into his eyes. "I am the one that needs to be forgiven, forgiven for the unforgivable. Look at what I've done to you, Geoffrey, my Geoffrey. Look at what I've done to everyone I loved. I'm so sorry — about everything. I never should have married you."

Geoffrey balked. "You know that isn't true."

Despite her flaws and his private complaints, he was always mindful that Victoria had given him both life's most precious gift, his daughter Charlotte, and the drive to succeed, to make something of himself beyond his own ambition and natural abilities. She was his missing piece, the catalyst for his metamorphosis, his reason to be, to achieve. And like a vulnerable king, he laid his golden tribute at her feet, which she never once acknowledged, always just assuming it would be there.

"But it is true, Geoffrey. Forgive me. I have been so stupid, so stupid and cruel…" And she started to cry, holding on to him with a fullness, a humanity, she had never expressed before. Her cry so deep, they touched; for the first time, they touched.

"I love you."

She nodded softly. "I know. I've known that since the first day we met. I remember that day, the day I first saw my sweet, young, shiny Geoffrey… But you must hear me now. Time is growing short." She wiped the tears from her eyes and then looked directly into his. "Yes, you've always had this love for me, but I've never let you love me. Never. You mustn't settle for that, Geoffrey; that's not living. Life is not about love, it's about loving."

"No," he said, shaking his head. "Don't do this. Please. We can start again. I know we can. Please. Please."

"Listen to me, my dearest boy. Something very special is waiting for you out there. A life of loving. You've got to find that life, Geoffrey, find that someone to love, and not just someone to be in love with. Without loving, there can be no happiness." She held him and whispered, "Be happy, my Geoffrey. Be happy my little boy, my husband, my love…"

Those words, unspoken, were the last he would ever hear his wife say.

SEASON OF THE WITCH

He was, without a doubt, the most beautiful man she had ever seen. Beautiful as if a breed apart from mere work-a-day mortals, perhaps even a descendant of another race altogether, the elves of lands so long ago their entire existence has been reduced to fable. And as such, those of this rare pedigree and purity of soul, walk this earth but remain apart, subconsciously searching for a place, a land far different than the one they see around them — a land that is kinder, gentler, and far more saturated with the wonders of true enchantment. Seeking that which they cannot find, they spend their days following rainbows and majestic sunsets leading nowhere, their breadcrumbs home now scattered to oblivion. So here they linger, stranded, aliens all, amidst a sun too bright, a wind too harsh, and a rain too cold. And all too soon they perish, like so many once perfect blooms; alas, this world, this life, was not for them.

"Hi."

Charlotte smiled but said nothing in return as she opened the door wider, finding herself a hiding place behind it in the process.

"I brought these for you."

Two eyes peeked back out at him. "For me?" she said, surprised. "Thank you. They're, they're beautiful."

Donn wanted to say something in return, something about her, something like beautiful flowers for a beautiful girl, but the words somehow got stuck, leaving him only with, "Your home is lovely."

Charlotte glanced around the room before looking back at him and shrugging indifferently. He thought he saw a slight smile cross her lips.

"How's your father?"

She nodded 'fine,' and then added, "He'll be out." This time it was Donn's turn to smile, a smile so dear, so tender, Charlotte blushed as if she had just been kissed. Her eyes raced back to her flowers. "I, I better put these in some kitchen — I mean some water…" She grimaced and then off she ran.

A few seconds later, a mad crash of pots and pans rumbled out of the kitchen. Donn turned. He listened for a clue as to what to do but was met with only silence. Complete silence. Then sweet Charlotte yelled, "I'm okay!"

Donn had to smile. "Are you sure?" he yelled back.

"Oh yeah. Yeah, it's nothing. But don't come in. I'll be out in a second. I just have to find some glue… And maybe a welding torch."

He smiled again, laughed even. "Ok, well, I'm here if you need me." He moved to the large wall of glass framing a glistening panoramic view of Los Angeles. Saturday night, just after 8 p.m. Streams of headlights and taillights packed the streets below as cars struggled to make their way through the residential canyons of the *haves.* Random lit squares marked trailing towers and downtown Los Angeles gleamed in the distance as if it really were something to see. On the left, the hills of Bel Air descended into the foreground, its green camouflage cleverly hiding the rich, and to the right, planes cued over distant Inglewood, patiently waiting their turn at the tarmac parade. From here, it all seemed right, a rhapsody of intricate movements churning days into lives and lives into something of meaning.

"Donn, I'm so glad you came," interrupted Geoffrey. Donn wasn't sure how long he had been lost in his motionless gaze but came to life with a startled twist.

"Oh, well, thank you for the invitation. Sorry, I was just admiring your view. It's very special, isn't it?"

"It sure is. I think I stood right where you're standing for an hour today. I wasn't sure if it was the view or the Vicodin."

Geoffrey joined Donn at the window. "It looks so complicated, doesn't it? So many things going on, all at same time. And then when you realize that this is but a speck, a tiny corner of the world, that this is happening right now, everywhere, in Moscow, in Paris, Beijing and Mexico City, São Paulo, Mumbai… so many things happening, all at this very moment… in an alley in New York, on a cobblestone street in London… So many people, going so many places, doing so many things, all at this very moment… I don't know, it's kind of unsettling. I keep thinking about it, but I haven't been able to make peace with it yet."

And then, the doorbell rang.

There she stood, softly backlit and perfectly framed in the doorway, all eyes upon her, locked in the transcendence of the moment.

"Who is it?" asked Charlotte, leaving the kitchen. "Laura? Laura?" She gasped, both stunned and thrilled.

"I wanted to surprise you," said her father.

"Oh, it's a wonderful surprise. I'm so glad you're here," she said, running to deliver a hug to her newfound safe harbor.

"We're all glad," Geoffrey said warmly.

Laura, Geoffrey, Charlotte, and Donn, together at last. This gathering had been foretold in fragments of dreams these four had shared but could never individually decipher. They knew this was right, they could feel it, but were unable to explain the source of their knowing. This meeting, a checkpoint in their communal destinies, created by events that could never have been imagined, revealed at last. Four old friends finally came together for the very first time.

Laura's eyes touched Geoffrey's, the connection tangible, a ticklish vibration delighting both. He walked to her better than he had in years, straighter, taller, lighter, lifted by her presence.

"Hello," he whispered, kissing her cheek close to her ear. "I'm so glad you came."

"Hi," she replied with a schoolgirl's smiling eyes.

That there was something going on between these two was not lost on either Charlotte or Donn. Charlotte was aware of their attraction at the hospital but was unsure much would come of it once they left, despite vague comments to the contrary. But now she was more excited than ever by the possibilities.

"You're so beautiful," Geoffrey said, his voice a soft breeze.

Again, Laura's endearing smile ignited his. Her eyes quickly swept the room and then fell to the floor.

This was the first time Laura and Geoffrey had seen each other since he had left the hospital a few weeks earlier, although they had spoken on the phone several times. Most of the women in Geoffrey's past — okay, *all* of the women in Geoffrey's past — never considered him particularly skilled when it came to the rituals of dating, unless, that is, one prefers their dates stiff, tense, and painfully awkward, a fact that was not lost on Geoffrey. And he had no reason to think that twenty-something years of dating inactivity had done much to hone his meager skill set. His first call to her was met with voicemail. With the pressure of the upcoming beep mounting rapidly, he wasn't sure what to do.

Should I hang up and call back later? I should, right? Then again, maybe I shouldn't. What if she sees that I called but didn't have the guts to leave a message? But then what if I do leave a message and it turns out really lousy? She could play it over and over again and maybe decide she'd be better off just ducking my calls all together. So, what should I do? What should I do?

In the end, to his credit, he leapt, leaving a charming, albeit slightly bumbling, message and was rewarded with a prompt reply and the sweet, sweet words, "I was hoping you'd call."

"Laura, this is Donn, Donn Olson. He's the young man that rescued me and all the others from the plane."

"How do you do?" said Donn, with perfect Cotillion etiquette.

"Oh my gosh, it's you!" she replied, extending her hand. "I saw you on the news, saving everyone. It was such a wonderful thing you did. You were so brave."

"The mayor even gave him the key to the city," chimed Charlotte, unexpectedly.

"The Mayor of West Hollywood. It was a joke as much as anything. They gave me a key to the—" He shook his head. "The whole thing was stupid, really. And Mr. Zukor, I thought we agreed we weren't going to talk about it."

"And we're not going to talk about it. A deal's a deal, my boy. But we *are* going to drink about it." Geoffrey continued as he poured champagne. "To heroes, new friends, and a new life — a life that you made possible." And drink, they did.

Geoffrey noticed Laura glancing around the room rather nervously he thought. When she saw him looking at her, she returned a smile, a worried smile, fooling no one.

Laura moved towards Geoffrey but was stopped by the sound of the doorbell.

Charlotte looked to her dad, who shrugged in return.

"Yes?" Geoffrey said to the tall, tan, hip and handsome stranger standing at his door.

But the stranger paid him no mind, none at all, just walked right in as if he owned the place. "Sorry I'm late, everybody, but do they really expect me to let ol' Amos down there park my Lamborghini? I don't think so! I had to go five blocks to find a decent spot. Took forever. I wouldn't have been so particular if I brought the Ferrari but the Lambo, she's my little baby. Only twenty-six of them made last year. Twenty-six! And guess how many are in Los Angeles? Anybody? Anybody? Three! Three! It's sick, man! That's like one for every chick in L.A. with real tits! Am I right or am I right?" And then to Charlotte, he added, "Oh, you must still be getting your coins together, right honey? Great idea. You'll be smokin'. Call me when you're ready. I know all the best doctors."

Charlotte didn't know what to say. None of them did. They all just stood there, wondering who in the world was this strange creature that just blew through the front door.

"Hey, I'm Perry but my homies all call me P-Dawg." He shook Geoffrey's hand. "It's a pleasure meeting me."

Geoffrey replied with a half-hearted chuckle.

Then P-Dawg approached Laura and seeing the strained look on her face said, "It's all right. Daddy's back." And with that he planted a wet one on her, complete with tongue and a small but noticeable thrust of his pelvis. He had the good taste to finish off his public show of affection with a sharp little slap to her backside. "Baby's got it goin' on, doesn't she?" he said with a knowing nod to

Geoffrey and Donn. Then, as if his crowd of onlookers weren't already stupefied beyond legal limits, he threw his hands into the air, yelped like a flamingo dancer, and gyrated around in a circle. "Let's party! Party! Let's Party! Party! Uh huh! Let's party! Party…"

Geoffrey, Charlotte, and Donn's dropped jaw silence lasted longer than an all-pantomime version of *The Iceman Cometh* and was finally broken by Laura, who blurted out as if she was going to explode if she kept it in a single second longer, "I invited someone. You don't mind, do you?"

SEASON OF THE WITCH

In life, we are sometimes asked questions to which there is only one true answer — the obviously untruthful one.

With the sound of "I invited someone. You don't mind, do you?" still ringing in their ears, Geoffrey, Charlotte, and Donn, the three founding members of the pop group, *The Nervous Overcompensators,* answered as if there were eighteen distinctly different characters in the room, with overlapping choruses of, "No, of course not." "Are you kidding? The more the merrier!" "Oh no, it's fine, fine." "Not a problem at all." "Terrific!" "Mind? Good gracious no. I doubt anyone will even notice!" And finally, "Don't be silly! What's a party without uninvited guests?" A liar's fugue, if you will.

And once the ball got rolling, it was hard to stop.

Charlotte got a little carried away when she added a completely insincere, "We were all hoping you'd bring someone."

"We sure were," declared Donn, in full support. "Charlotte was just saying that very thing right before you arrived. But then I guess she must have forgotten that you were coming which explains why she was so surprised when you walked in. Right?"

Second verse, same as the first: "Right!" "How true, how true!" "Hooray!" "You know, a lot of people we don't like are going to be here. What's one more?" "What a grand idea!" "Well, aren't we the lucky ones!" "Any friend of yours…" And so on, and so on.

The piece finally ended with "STOP!" as yelled by Geoffrey, trying to reign in the *jam infinitum*. "Stop even thinking like that, Laura. No, of course we don't mind. In fact, it was a grand idea!" Then he turned and added, "Charlotte, tell Charles there will be one more for dinner."

"Charles?" she asked.

"Charles, the chef. He's in the kitchen."

"Oh, that was Charles? I, uh, kind of bumped into him earlier. I don't think he's in the kitchen right now. He needed to run out and pick up something real quick."

"He did? Like what?" ask Geoffrey.

"Like dinner. Long story." Charlotte replied with a grimace.

"Maybe he's back. I'll go check," offered Donn, eager for any excuse to leave the room.

"Good idea. I'll go help you check," said Charlotte as she followed Donn out of the room. "Just so you know, he might not be in the best mood. And careful, there might still be some roast beef on the floor… And maybe a matzo ball or two…"

"How do you do? I'm Geoffrey Zukor. Welcome. So, we should call you P-Dawg?"

"Beats what most people call me."

Geoffrey replied with another half-hearted chuckle. "Right. Well, would you care for some champagne?"

"Oh, no, no, not for me. I better not. I'm trying to cut back. There are those that think I get a little obnoxious when I drink. Can you believe that? Beware the comments of jealous little minds. But still, I better pass. We're gonna be heading back to my place in a little while and I've got a reputation to live up to." Then, on the not-so-sly, he added, "And so does she! *Ouch!* Oh yeah, that reminds me..."

Mr. Dawg patted the front of his pants but finally found what he was looking for in his shirt pocket. "Vitamin V, the little blue thrill! Rock hard, baby. Rock hard."

Once again, he threw his hands into the air, this time adding finger snaps while his hips circled so widely both Geoffrey and Laura had to step back, out of the way. "Go baby. Go baby. Go baby. Go baby. Go baby..." he chanted. "Who knows? Tonight, could be a tripleheader, sugar. Huh? Huh?" he said, nodding and pointing at Laura. "Oh, is that *Vive Clique*? Nice. Maybe I will have just a taste to wash this down. After all, it is a party!"

"And they say you're only obnoxious when you drink?" asked Geoffrey, having a hard time finding a congenial smile as he filled a flute about half full.

"Hey, old timer, let's not be stingy now. You shouldn't bring out the good stuff if you're too cheap to pour it. Come on, sock it to me, gramps. There you go. That's a little better."

With one tip of his glass, both the pill and his flute full of champagne were gone. Then he whispered to Laura in a voice so loud he could be heard by Geoffrey's neighbor next door, "A real sport, you got there, isn't he?"

Laura didn't respond. She was in shock, and it wasn't the good kind of shock, either. You know, the Steve Harvey/Publisher's Clearing House kind of shock. No, this was the bad kind of shock, the "Oh my God, a baby alien has just burst through my chest and is now shrieking down the hallway" kind of shock, leaving her standing there, wondering, *Is it possible to hold your breath until you die of suffocation?*

"Here, you look tired, old boy. Why don't you let me hold on to that for you?" P-Dawg said as he grabbed the bottle from Geoffrey and refilled his glass. Then to Laura he added, "Sweet cheeks, would you run see if there's any more of this anywhere?" He nudged her off in the direction of the kitchen.

"Hey, don't take this wrong, but when she asked me to come to this clambake, I wasn't exactly thrilled. I mean, I was thinking I'd just take the chick back to my place and play some tonsil pool, if you read me there, Grandpa. Eight ball, corner pocket!" Then he broke into dance again, chanting, "Uh, huh. Uh huh, Uh, huh. Oh, yeah!"

"Truth is, when girls take one look at my house, they're down for anything! *Anything!* It's sick, right? Am I right or am I right?"

"P-Dawg, would you excuse me for a moment, please. I think I better run check on my internal hemorrhaging."

Almost twenty minutes passed. No one wanted to return to the living room. Geoffrey was holed up in the bedroom while Charlotte and Donn were trying to get Laura to stop crying in the kitchen.

"Yoo-hoo? What happened? Everybody go to sleep. Come on, it's boogie time! Where you at, old buddy? Come on out and turn on some music, will ya, man? You gotta have some Lawrence Welk records around here someplace." P-Dawg, with a near empty Champagne bottle in hand, then rolled into a Sly Stone impersonation, adding an air of authenticity to it with his growing lack of sobriety. "Ba-da da, ba-da da, ba-da da, Hey! Hey! Hey! Everybody polka!"

"Oh, you're still here," said Geoffrey, as he re-entered the living room.

"Dinner is ready. If you'll all please have a seat," announced Charles, entering the room followed by Donn, Charlotte, and a red-eyed Laura.

"Thank you, Charles," said Geoffrey, more than a little grateful that either Charlotte or Donn had decided it was best to serve dinner earlier than originally planned.

"Whoa there, Mr. Boy-ar-dee," protested the Dawg. "What's the rush? We're just getting warmed around up here. Why don't you put the peanut butter sandwiches back in the fridge and I'll call you when we're ready, all right? Oh, and here, take this empty too. I grabbed another bottle from the mini-bar but there's only a couple left so dig up what you can in of the kitchen and bring it all on out, would ya, buddy?"

Charles looked to Geoffrey who nodded and discretely held up his hand, mouthing the words, "Five minutes."

"You know, I used to have a dog named Buddy, a big ol' dog. You should have seen him, man. Ol' Buddy gave it to every bitch in the neighborhood — every single one. I wonder who he learned that from, right? Am I right or am I right? And my neighbor used to have these two little poodles. And they were always getting out and guess where they'd end up? Huh? Anybody? That's right.

244

Scratching at my front door." P-Dawg then to turned to Charlotte and asked lasciviously, "All you girls like a big dog, don't you, Sugar? Huh? Am I right or am I right?"

"P-Dawg, this is my daughter, Charlotte, and I would appreciate it if you'd tone—"

"Whoa! Don't be such an old fuddy-duddy. This is nature, man. I'm talking fucking Discovery Channel here, so relax, will ya? And anyway, you think I'm telling her something she don't already know? Why don't you tell him, sweetie? I bet you got yourself some good ol' stories, don't you? Yeah, you do. I know you do." P-Dawg leered at her, the wag of his finger slightly out of sync with the rhythm of his speech. Then he turned back to Geoffrey. "You see, gramps, it ain't like it was when you were coming up. Back then, if some chick let you feel her chi-chi's, you'd go home with a big ol' stain on your pants and enough memories to last you a senior year full of showers, right? Am I right or am I right? Let's all drink to the olden days, shall we?" which, of course, no one did but him.

"So, what kind of work do you do, sir?" Donn asked Geoffrey, in an attempt to change both the subject and the speaker. But before he could respond, P-Dawg answered, "D.M. — Direct Marketing. In fact, I've got the largest D.M. firm in the county. That's right. Numbero uno."

"Really?" replied Donn. "And what do you do, Mr. Zukor?"

"Yep, that's right. You're looking at the big dog right here, kid. And I've got the big doghouse to prove it. Don't I, baby?" But Laura didn't hear him. She was too busy concentrating on holding her breath.

"Really?" asked Donn skeptically, having grown more than a little tired of his new friend. "Your company is larger than the Home Shopping Network?"

"Well, no, but they're not strictly D.M. like we are." P-Dawg drained another flute nearly as quickly as he filled it.

"I see. And what about QVC? Your firm is larger than QVC?"

"Well, no, we're not as big as QVC but you just don't get it, do you? They're not strictly D.M. either. They think they are, but they're not. Anyway, they're a bunch of assholes. Who gives a shit about them?" he asked with a snarl.

"What about—"

"Hey, what is this, kid, a deposition? Knock it off or I'll have to tell your Mama I caught you blowing your PE teacher under the bleachers. Are you reading me there, buddy?"

The Dawg continued, turning to the others. "Anyway, D.M. is all we do. And we're number one, baby. The Trip Light? You've all heard of the Trip Light, right? The round, little plastic light, runs on batteries with adhesive on the back so you can stick it anywhere? That's mine. Sold 1.2 gazillion of 'em. Made a fucking fortune with that one, a fucking fortune. And ya' know why I named it the Trip Lite? Anybody? Anybody? You're gonna love this. I named it the Trip Lite because, yeah, their bright as fuck, they really are, but the bulbs burn out so fast, if you put them on steps, like in my commercials, it's *Trip City, baby.* Maybe I should have named it the Sprain-Your-Fucking-Ankle Light! Or the Fall-On-Your-Fucking-Face Light!" His laughter only stopped long enough for him to take another drink.

"Oh, and you gotta hear this: My big one running now is The Amazing Inflate-O-Matic Mattress. You've all seen that on TV, right? Am I right? Well, I call it the Amazing in-*flat*-o-mattress be-cause the fuckers always leak! And they're still just flying out the door. I can't ship 'em fast enough. It's sick! Those dumb *snuckers* will buy anything, and I mean *anything*, just so long as you use the magic word."

P-Dawg looked around the room but there weren't any takers. "Come on, I know you're dying to know what my magic word is. Raise your hand if you want to know. Come on, raise your hand." Still, no takers. And then to Donn he said, "Hey, you want to know, don't you, kid? So, raise your hand or I'm going to have to tell your daddy I saw you walking Santa Monica Boulevard wearing hot pants and a tube top."

"Excuse me," Geoffrey said, "but that is completely—"

"It's okay. I've got this, Mr. Zukor," Donn said with a reassuring nod.

"You want to hear about it, don't you, little boy pink?" P-Dawg sneered.

Donn turned and stared at him, conceding not so much as a blink of an eye.

And then in a clearly threatening tone, P-Dawg asked, "Yes or no?"

"No."

"No? That's funny. You're funny, kid. What's your name?"

"Donn."

"Donn? How do you spell that, D-A-W-N?" P-Dawg laughed through a vicious grin. His eyes were starting to glaze, and his face was fully flushed in *I'm-Gonna-Bust-You-Up Red*. He slowly wiped his sweaty palms across his shirt front. Then he brought a fist within inches of Donn's face and shouted, "NOW RAISE YOUR HAND, YOU FUCKING—"

"I would love to know the magic word," interrupted Geoffrey.

"Me, too," chirped Charlotte, nodding like a bobble-head doll.

"Me three. Please tell us!" agreed a lavender Laura, who immediately went back to holding her breath and waiting for the Grim Reaper to arrive.

"Well, since you all asked so nicely… You see, I've discovered that you can sell the shit out of anything *if* you use my magic word — a word that I, and I alone, just me, made famous. And the word is? Anybody? Anybody? Come on, anybody think they know what it is? Huh? I can wait if you need more time…"

"Sale?" guessed Geoffrey, praying he was right so he could put an end to all this.

"No."

Geoffrey tried again. "Uh, limited time offer?"

"Limited time offer? Ha! Not even close."

"Call now?" Again, Geoffrey.

"Way off — but no worries. Take your time. We can play this little game all night long if you want. Hey, anybody else need a refill?"

Geoffrey, Donn, Charlotte and Laura all looked at each other, each mouthing the words, *"All night long???"* The pressure was on.

"Magic word… Uh… Buy now?" suggested Geoffrey.

"Good answer," cheered Charlotte.

"Wrong answer," replied P-Dawg. Then he turned to Donn.

"3 easy payments?" guessed Donn.

"Good answer," cheered both Charlotte and Geoffrey.

"Lousy answer," replied P-Dawg. Then he turned to Charlotte.

"Fantastic?" offered Charlotte.

"Good answer, good answer," cheered Geoffrey and Donn.

"El stinko answer," replied P-Dawg. He then turned to Laura, who was definitely near faint from self-inflicted suffocation.

"You can do it, Laura. I know you can," said Charlotte.

"Yeah," agreed both Geoffrey and Donn.

Laura nodded and then yelled out, "Circumcision!"

The room grew suddenly quiet. Geoffrey, Charlotte, and Donn exchanged worried looks before turning to Laura with forced smiles. "Good answer," they all said, although their hearts clearly weren't in it. Charlotte helped Laura over to a nearby chair.

"Circumcision!?! That's it!" yelled P-Dawg.

"It is?" asked Geoffrey, Charlotte, and Donn in unison.

"Gotcha!" replied P-Dawg with a sloppy grin. Then, to everyone's disappointment, he added, "Anybody? Anybody?"

Laura shot up immediately. "I've got it! Uh… Circumcision?"

"Magic word… Magic word…" Geoffrey said, trying to think. "I've got it. Alakasam!"

"Shazam!" suggested Charlotte.

"Presto Change-o?" suggested Donn.

P-Dawg shook his head. "You're ice cold, all of you. If you get any colder, you'll bring an end to global warming. Anybody? Anybody?"

With a hopeless shrug, Charlotte suggested, "Circumcision?"

"Good answer," said Laura enthusiastically.

Geoffrey snapped his fingers. "I've got it. Please."

"Or thank you," someone else offered.

"You're welcome?"

"Nice to see you."

Someone even suggested, "Gesundheit!"

"Maybe our dinner's ready?" suggested Geoffrey, hopefully loud enough for Charles to hear in the kitchen.

"No, no, no, no, and no!" said P-Dawg. "You guys are way off. The magic word is you! You! And the more you use it, the more shit you sell. It's that simple! Like, '*You* can dice. *You* can slice. *You* can use it to grind up mice! *You* do some of this, *you* do some of that, buy one today, and you'll lose all that fat. *You* put it on here, *you* put it on there, all of a sudden, you've got tons of hair.' See? It's not about the product. No one gives a shit about the product. It's about *you* and all the great things *you'll* be able to do once you buy it! Before I burst onto the scene, no one was using the word and now it's all you hear. I've even contacted a lawyer to see if I could sue those bastards for using my magic word. And he thinks I've got a very good case. I know I do! My case could be worth millions, baby! Millions! I'll drink to that!"

"But it don't matter," P-Dawg continued, wiping his mouth with his sleeve. "I'm making so much fucking money, I'm going to have to buy a Hummer just to carry around my wallet. It's sick, man, it's sick!"

"Oh, and listen to this. I'm working on a new product now, and it's gonna be my biggest one yet. You're gonna love it! But it's top secret, so you have to promise you won't tell anyone, okay? So, if you promise, raise your hand, and I'll tell you all about it, all right? Come on, who promises?"

Hands were not exactly flying into the air. Charlotte looked to her father, who was looking toward the kitchen. P-Dawg was focused on Donn. "Hey, Barbie Boy, you're not raising your hand. You wouldn't try and steal my idea, would you? Oh, I bet you would, you little cocksucker."

Geoffrey could tolerate no more. "All right, that's enough! Enough!"

But P-Dawg didn't stop. "Oh, you'd just love to run and tell all your *faggity* little friends, wouldn't you? Am I right or am I right? So, listen, dick-breath, you raise your hand right now or I am going rip you a new asshole."

"Stop it!" yelled Geoffrey.

"Oh, but you'd like that, wouldn't you? You show me a gay with two assholes, and I will show you one happy little homo. Am I right, or am I right?"

"Stop it," Geoffrey said sternly. "I'm going to have to ask you-"

"I think we've all heard more than we can stand," Donn said, staring defiantly at P-Dawg.

"I'M COUNTING TO THREE," screamed P-Dawg. "IF YOUR HAND ISN'T UP BY THE TIME I GET THERE, YOU'LL BE SPITTING OUT TEETH FOR A WEEK!"

"STOP IT! STOP IT RIGHT NOW!" yelled Geoffrey.

"ONE!"

"STOP IT! I'LL CALL THE POLICE. NOW STOP IT!"

"TWO!!"

"GOD DAMN IT! I AM ORDERING YOU TO—"

"TTTHHHRR—"

SEASON OF THE WITCH

The sound of 232 blood-filled beats per minute pulsed through P-Dawg's ears, leaving room for little else. The background dimmed and his view constricted, leaving Donn's head the sole focus of his attention. Time slowed to a trickle as thick, oily beads of sweat ran down along his sideburns, past his puffed, tension-filled cheeks and onto his shirt. Instinctively, his weight shifted forward to the balls of his feet, and he began weaving ever so slightly from left to right. P-Dawg was clearly in the zone; here, anything seemed possible—except a change of course.

Still, Donn gave him nothing as they stood nose to nose, not but inches between them. He braced himself.

"TTTTHHHHHRRRR—"

But a millisecond after he started to release his saliva punctuated *THREE*, P-Dawg's pant pocket began emitting a piercing high-pitched sound, cutting through the fog of war and catching his attention before he could finish the word. Anger immediately shifted to panic. With far more effort than the task required, he managed to remove his key chain from his tight, black leather pants, exposing a bright-red flashing light.

"Fuck! Fuck!! Someone's stealing my car! FUCK! They're stealing my car! Call the police! Call the police!! Call— No, no don't. I'll get 'em. I'll get those fucking bastards. You guys don't mind if I skip out for a minute, do you? Huh? Don't worry; I'll be right back. Keep the party going. This ain't gonna take long." With that he grabbed a half empty champagne bottle and left as abruptly as he had arrived.

With P-Dawg's slam of the front door, Laura disintegrated into tears again.

Geoffrey was immediately at her side, comforting her. "Hey, don't cry. Come on, everything's okay. Please. Please don't cry." To Charlotte and Donn, he added, "It must be very hard for her to be separated from him for even a minute. But Laura, you don't have to worry. He'll be back before you know it."

Laura looked up at him, so surprised by what he just said she stopped crying entirely. And there she stood, teetering between laughter and tears. But when she looked over and saw Charlotte's face, it was all too much; the weight of her humiliation dragged her down into a sea of even louder sobs.

"Dad!" admonished Charlotte, taking his place beside Laura. "It's okay... It's okay... Men are just jerks. I met a guy once, a Brit with an accent so thick I couldn't understand a word he said. Then I came to find out he wasn't from England at all. No, he was just some stupid kid from the Valley. The closest he ever got to London was east Tarzana. And I still went out with him four times."

"You did?" asked Geoffrey incredulously.

"Dad!" replied Charlotte, waving him off. "Laura, I've got an idea. Let's all pretend that none of this ever happened, like it was just a bad dream or something."

"Sure, that's a great idea," agreed Donn. "It was all just a bad dream."

"Yeah, a bad dream that never really happened," said Charlotte.

"That's right," said Donn. "It never happened. What a relief!"

"You can say that again," chimed in Geoffrey. "Thank goodness it was only a dream." He looked around. "So, it's unanimous then, right? If you think it was just a dream, raise your fucking hand. Go on. I can wait all night—"

"Dad!" said Charlotte.

"What? He said we should keep the party going while he's gone."

"You're terrible," said Laura, finding her first smile in an hour.

"That's better. That's the face I've been waiting to see," Geoffrey said, with a tender brush of her cheek. "I hope I never see anything on that face but that beautiful smile right there. Can I get you some water or something? Or are you hungry? Is anybody hungry? If you're hungry, raise your fuc—"

"Dad!"

"Okay, all right, I'll stop. Instead, anybody want to hear about my big ol' dog Buddy? Anybody? Anybody?"

SEASON OF THE WITCH

It's amazing really, how many different ways someone can find to apologize in a mere ten minutes. And in so many different languages, too. When Laura finished with the Eastern European tongues and began begging forgiveness in Mandinka, Charlotte turned to Donn and her father and whispered, "You know, it's been a while since he's been gone. What if he got beat up or something?"

Donn agreed. "Yeah. Or even worse, what if he didn't get beat up and he's on his way back?"

Geoffrey picked up the phone and dialed. "Asa, it's Geoffrey Zukor in 1804. I don't know if you saw him, but a fellow left here a while back to check on his car and—"

"Yes, sir. He ran by here real wobbly-like a few minutes ago and spoke none too kindly to me as he did."

"Oh, Asa, I'm so sorry. I feel terrible. What an— Well, he's certainly not a friend of mine, that's for sure. I guess he's a distant acquaintance of—"

"Oh, no apology necessary, sir. I could tell the pretty lady he dropped off here couldn't stand him anymore than I could. I watched him try and give her a little kiss, and she knocked him upside-the-head just 'bout put him down. That girl's feisty-like, she is. Kind of reminds me of my wife. Last time I said anything to her other than 'Yes, dear', my head hurt for a month. Still kind of sore in the back."

"I understand, Asa. Believe me, I understand. Anyway, I don't know why I care but do you think he's okay? Should we call the police or—?"

"No need, sir. They're already here. Looks to me like your friend's distant acquaintance just had his car repossessed. When he ran by me all panicky-like, I followed just close enough to make sure he wasn't about to get himself into any major squabbles, which, sure 'enough, he was. When he saw what was happening to his car, he took a swing at the tow truck operator with a big ol' bottle he was holding. Don't know what that boy was thinkin'. That driver was about as big this building. Then he took a swipe at the police officer who was trying to calm him down. That be about when the tow truck driver reciprocated with the ol' right, left, right. Say goodnight, Jasper! The boy doesn't know it yet, but his ornery self be in handcuffs on his way to spend the night with some of L.A.'s finest."

"Oh, no."

"Oh, yeah. Hope he calms down before he meets the boys in lock up. They about as understanding as my Mammy was when

Daddy came home smellin' of the widow Ferguson. Say goodnight, Jasper."

"Goodnight, Jasper."

"Goodnight, Mr. Zukor."

Before Charles corralled the four to the dinner table, the girls found time for a moment of private conversation.

"You must think I'm horrible. I'm really so sorry about tonight, Charlotte. I've ruined everything."

"Are you joking? That was the most brilliant thing I've ever seen a woman do! It was incredible. Showing my Dad you've got all these handsome guys chasing after you? It was, it was legendary! Laura, promise you'll teach me how you handle men? Do you promise?"

Laura couldn't believe her ears. She had been vacillating between whether she should see a psychiatrist or just check herself directly into an insane asylum. *Brilliant? Legendary?*

"Dinner is served," Charles announced. "And I don't want to hear a word from any of you about not being hungry. As my Yiddisher momma used to say, 'So what does hunger have to do with eating?'"

A brief but wonderful meal was peppered with conversation like:

"Don't get me wrong, Mr. Zukor, Geoffrey's nice, but have you ever considered G-Dawg? Come on, it's sick! Sick!"

"You're sick! Sick!" Charlotte said, laughing and feeling relaxed enough to throw her napkin at him for good measure.

"Dessert was delicious, wasn't it? I finished it in three bites. That's like one bite for every chick in L.A. with real—"

"Stop it! Screamed Charlotte. "You're both disgusting!"

"Don't worry about it, G-Dawg," said Donn. "Some people just aren't interested in statistics."

SEASON OF THE WITCH

At D-Dawg's suggestion, Donn's newly adopted name, he and Charlotte went for a walk through the neighborhood after dinner, leaving Geoffrey and Laura on the balcony, contemplating more than the view.

"I really do feel terrible about tonight."

"Oh, I'll bet you do."

"You know I do! I didn't know it was going to be just the four of us. I was expecting like a welcome home party kind of a thing," she said, looking but not looking at the street below.

"It's okay. I should have been more clear. So how long have you known P-Dawg?"

"Not long."

"He made it seem like you two were pretty close."

"Oh, that was just stupid guy-talk. You know, trying to mark his territory."

"Yeah, well, he did everything but pee on your leg."

"Maybe he was saving that for after dinner."

"Well now you have something to look forward to next time you see him."

"Thanks."

"What? It's obvious that you're quite attracted to him. And for good reason, I'm sure. The joy of driving around in his soon to be repossessed Lamborghini, his cute little slaps to your… you know, *slappable* area, the feel of his tongue sliding down your throat—"

"Geoffrey Zukor, you are disgusting! If you haven't figured it out already, that was the first time he ever kissed me. The *very* first time. And he only reason he got away with it was because he caught me off guard. After he walked in, I was so embarrassed about inviting him, I was trying to figure out what to do and before I knew it his lips were all over me. I almost barfed in his mouth, not that that's any business of yours."

"And the only reason I went out with him in the first place was because he kept pestering me, calling me all the time, sending all kinds of gifts to my office, and I just happened to be reading this article about dating and it said you've got to make a conscious effort to go out with people you might not think are your type because, first of all, someone might not appear to be your type but actually they really are; or, secondarily, you might find out that the type you had been looking for is not nearly as perfect for you as the type of guy you didn't think was your type. And then it went on to say that the only way you can figure out if either of those two things is true is to go out and be open to someone who you might not think is your type in the first place. That makes sense, right?"

"You know, you have the most beautiful lips I've ever seen."

"Are you listening to me?"

"Sure, of course I am. It's just that your lips are so—"

"Geoffrey! It's important to me that you understand. Please don't make this harder than it already is," she said with a mixture of mock anger and delight.

Or was that real anger and mock delight? wondered Geoffrey. *With women you can never tell. And even if you could, even if you got it right, they'd probably switch it on you at the last minute just so they could give you that You-Must-Be-The-Most-Clueless-Man-Alive look, which is probably the truth anyway.* And so, Geoffrey just plowed ahead because plowing ahead is what us clueless guys do best.

"Maybe it would help if you cover your mouth when you talk." He thought about that for a moment. "Hmmm, I don't know. I think then I would just end up being distracted by your eyes, and that would probably be even worse." Geoffrey raised his hand to cover Laura's lips. "Oh sure, see, that's definitely worse. Look at your eyes. They're so incredible. The color... it's so— What color do they call that?"

"Brown," she replied flatly.

"Brown? Well, technically they may—"

"Could I borrow two-hundred dollars? I'd like to go bail P-Dawg out of jail. At least he doesn't pretend to be a gentleman just to get some girl to take an interest in him."

"Hey, of course I'm listening. I've heard every word you've said. In my day, girls referred to that as kissing a frog — you know, to see if they'd turn into their prince."

"Well, I've gone out with so many frogs, I speak *Ribbit.* Fluently."

"Say what you will, it didn't seem like you were having all that bad of a time with P-Dawg tonight. Asa told me you two were smooching downstairs."

"What?"

"He said you couldn't keep your hands off each other."

"What are you talking about? Before he left to park his car, he *tried* to kiss me and I elbowed him so hard, he almost landed in the fountain. Did he really say that to you?"

"No," Geoffrey said with a smile.

"You are disgusting. You know, I wish I did kiss him downstairs. It would have served you right. I don't know what it was I ever saw in you anyway."

"You saw something in me?"

"Yes, I did. And it goes to show you how wrong a girl can be. Did it ever dawn on you that maybe I just brought him to make you jealous? And it would serve you right if I did! You know, a lot of girls think he's a real catch."

"And so is a cold. Personally, I rather have the cold."

"Well, I have plenty of other guys calling me too, just so you know."

"Of course, you do. And one of them is selling Trip Lites to his mates in Cell Block 14 right now."

"Are you ever going to be nice about this?"

"Are you ever going to stop talking… and kiss me? I feel like I've been waiting my whole life for you to kiss me." This was definitely a new Geoffrey Zukor.

Their eyes met, the attraction between them so strong they fell into each other's arms. A kiss, a perfect kiss—long and perfect, her body radiating with a warmth, a sweetness, way beyond Geoffrey's expectations. He had long wondered if such a kiss genuinely existed outside of the movies; at last, he finally knew the answer.

"You're not going to elbow me now, are you? It's a long way down to the fountain."

"I might — if you keep talking."

And they kissed again. And again. And perhaps Geoffrey *was* elbowed because he definitely felt himself falling, and falling, and falling…

The Ballad of Rosie and Rae
A Love Story
Part Four ◈ Seven Weeks Later

(310) 278-4329 to (310) 278-7822

"Hello?"

"Rae? Rae, is that you?"

"Of course, it's me. After all these years you don't know the sound of my voice?"

"I thought maybe it was that voicemail of yours. Today, everyone's got voicemail. What ever happened to, 'She didn't answer. I guess I'll call her back later.' What was so wrong with that? Now everyone leaves these messages and you have to listen to them rattle on and on about nothing, like I've got nothing better to do? Please. What a waste of time. So, I've figured out how to get even. I'm going to record a greeting that says, 'Hi, it's Rose. If this is Tuesday, I'm probably at the beauty parlor getting my hair done by Myra. She's been doing my hair for 18 years now. Lovely gal. Doesn't cut hair so good since she got the cataracts but hey, what does it matter? I'm not such a looker anymore anyway. If it's Thursday, I'm probably at market or the kosher butcher to buy chicken so I'll have it all ready for when my children don't show up for Shabbat. If it's Friday, well, it's Shabbat so I'm probably either cleaning the house, or cooking the chicken, broiling it maybe or maybe making matzo ball soup with celery. I like plenty of celery. Etcetera, etcetera, etcetera. When I'm done, the greeting is going to be an hour and half, minimum. Then we'll see how many messages I get! I tried to do it yesterday. I tried for like an hour and I still couldn't figure out how to turn my phone on. Would it kill them to put a button on the phone that says, 'On?" Is that too much to ask?"

"I know," replied Rae. "I can't figure out how to work half the things in my house. Thank God for David. At least he can tell me what to do. He knows all about these stupid contraptions. In fact, my son's an expert on anything that no one will pay you to know anything about. It's true. If it's impossible to make a living knowing about something, then my son will know everything there is to know about it. In fact, he may be the foremost authority on the subject."

"Rae, *luzzem di kinder*. You're lucky to have such a smart boy."

"Oh, sure. He's a genius, an encyclopedia of worthless information. Like last week, I go by my son. All of a sudden, his TV changes the station. It's flipping around here and there and then somehow it starts recording and everything's happening like magic. The kid is like the David Copperfield of television watching. And then, suddenly there's this big picture right in front of you, huge, and some guy is talking and talking, and his head is so big, God forbid he should sneeze, he'd blow you right into the powder bath. And then, before you know it, my son is watching something else, another movie or something beaming in from a satellite somewhere into the corner of the screen inside of the big picture. There's like two pictures going on, all at the same time! It's enough to make you seasick."

Rae continued. "So, Rose, you don't have to remind me how smart David is. The boy's a genius, I know this. The only thing he cannot figure out how to do, the only thing that has him completely *fartshadikt*, is how to pick up the phone and call his mother. That, for some reason, is totally beyond him."

"Rae, he's a fine boy."

"What? Who's *k'vetching*? Of course, he's a fine boy. I'll be dead a month before he notices, but he's a fine boy."

"*Oy!* God forbid."

"So, anyways, I says to him, 'Boychick, why don't you take all those TV watching skills you're so proud of and get yourself a decent job, a job you can be proud of. I got an idea for you. You should go to work for that kid from Mayberry. You know, the one who's dad was the policeman.'"

"Mayberry? You mean the old TV show with the cockamamie whistling?"

"Yeah, that's the one. You remember the little boy, right? His name was like Sloppy or Slopey, something like that, right? Anyways, I turned on TV the other day, and who do I see? Little Sloppy. He's all grown up now, but he looks just the same. I recognized him immediately. He still has that funny hair and the freckles. And guess what he does? He runs this big company, huge, that makes all of the windows for the computers today, which I guess is a very big business, although why a computer should need a window is beyond me. Like there's not already enough things to clean? I figure he must be in cahoots with those Windex people, right? Anyways, it turns out that Slopey is selling so many windows, he's now like the richest man in the world. He has *gelt* like I have gas. And he seems like a nice man, too. And so smart, you wouldn't believe. My son should go to work for him."

"Let me ask you, this Sloppy-Slopey character, do you think he's Jewish? You know, he might be perfect for my Sophie."

"Rose, let me ask you, do you remember a synagogue in Mayberry? Did you ever see any *peyes* at Floyd's barbershop? And the sheriff's girlfriend, you know, the *shayna*, where do you think she worked, the Mt. Pilot Judaica Shop? I don't think so."

"Well, maybe he could convert?"

"*Oy*, don't get me started on that converting business, please. What a waste of time. My neighbor Phyllis's son married a Catholic girl who converted. Now at Christmas, she runs around the house singing, *Deck the halls with balls of matzah, tra-la-la-la-la-la.* Poor Phyllis almost had a coronary. It's like I always said, converting to Judaism is a bit like converting to Negro; you can do it, but it loses a little something in the translation."

"Well, at least our son is married. He's got a lovely family and a good job—"

"A good job? Who are you kidding, Rose? You think I'm blind to what has been going on? I can't even go to the Temple Sisterhood meetings anymore because of my son the big-shot stockbroker. Oh sure, he's a great broker all right. He broke her, he broke her, he broke her. Everywhere I look, he broke somebody! What do people expect when they give their money to someone called a broker? It's like going to the track and betting on a horse called Limpy."

"Rae, David didn't know—"

"Even little old Mim Revo walked up to me last week and said, 'Rae, Rae, G.E.'s up a point today. One hundred and thirty-nine more and I'm even. Maybe then I can buy the medicine that I need.'"

"Rae, it's not your son's fault. He didn't know all those stocks were going to go down and ruin everyone in our Temple."

"Even that *schlub* Marty Bienner called me and was so upset with his portfolio he wanted the Bar Mitzvah gift back he gave my son twenty-seven years ago. So I sent him an eight-track tape of Barbara Streisand."

"Rae, don't let it bother you. Jews *k'vetch*. That's what we do. It's like our national pastime. Jews *k'vetching* is as natural as gentiles painting themselves funny colors when they go to football games. It's like the same thing."

"Children, *feh!* If I knew then what I know now, I would have spread my wings and not my legs."

Rose was stunned by her lifelong friend's statement. "You spread your legs? You mean when you were having— *Oy* God! Where did you grow up, in a brothel?"

Rose continued. "Really? You spread your legs, like, like wide open? *Oy*, I can't imagine! And you weren't afraid of catching a draft or something? Now I know why you were so popular in high school."

"Rose, tell me honestly, what am I left with? A son who has forgotten he has a mother, a daughter-in-law *sie haut gevain a courva in de momma's bouch,* and grandkids that don't even say hello when I walk through the door. From them, I'm more likely to get streptococcus than *naches*. These are my fruits? *A klog iz mir!*"

"*Bubee*, I hear my father, *mich tatenui*—may he rest in peace— I hear him in heaven right now speaking as clear as day. He's saying to me, 'Rose, tell Rae she has no business complaining. She doesn't know how good she's got it. It's much worse up here. The deli is from hunger. The pastrami has more fat on it than Maddie Goldfarb's thighs. And pickles? *Oy*, don't ask! Up here it's pearly gates everywhere you look, but pickles are nowhere to be found. Go figure!'"

"Very funny, Rose. You know, you're the only one that can bring a smile to this face of mine."

"Rae, my father always told me, 'Joy is not where you find it. It's where you make it.'"

"I remember. He was a good man, your father, a good man. I miss him."

"Me too, but let's not light the *Yortseit* today, all right? How about lunch? Patsy is coming over to pick me up at 11:30 and then we will come by you."

"Where are you going to eat?"

"Like it matters? One stale bagel is as good as the next. But wait till you hear what she has to say about Geoffrey Zukor. This, you won't believe."

"Again with the Geoffrey Zukor stories? He's turning out to be the Jewish Meghan Markle."

"He's dating. Geoffrey Zukor is dating!"

"*Azoy gich?* He's still married!"

"Patsy said he met someone when he was at Cedars, maybe a nurse or something."

"I can't believe it."

"And she's young, *very* young—half his age, if that. She walks around wearing skirts so short, you can see what she had for breakfast!"

"*Oy! A tsatskele!* Of course! That's all men want today are *tsats-keles!* You lose your taste for meat when that's all you eat is candy. That's what I always told my son, but did he listen?"

"Rae, where the penis points, the man follows. That's why it's kind shaped like an arrow."

"What's shaped like an arrow?"

"A penis! Oy, Gd, I'm not listening! I am not listening! Where did you learn to talk like this?"

"Fine, don't listen, but come to lunch. We're going to have a nice day. And get this; afterwards, Patsy wants to go by Cedars and see if we can sneak a peek of Geoffrey Zukor's hot little tomato."

"Rose, you're shameless. I could never!"

"What? It's Patsy's idea. We're just tagging along."

"How are you going to find her in a big hospital like that?"

"Patsy has all the information. Come on, it'll be fun."

"She knows this home-wrecker's name?"

"Yeah. Turns out Patsy has a friend who lives in Geoffrey's building and actually sees this girl coming and going like all the time. So, they got to talking and she got the girl's name and everything. So, join us. What else do you have to do, sit home and be thankful your kids aren't on *Jerry Springer?*"

SEASON OF THE WITCH

Nothing worries me more than when my wife

all of a sudden starts being nice to me.

That, I find very unsettling.

Geoffrey Zukor awoke and turned to find a note where a beautiful body had been.

Good morning, my darling. I can't think about last night without smiling. You are so funny! Thank you for another evening I will always remember.

Since I've met you, so much has changed.

The world is more magical and my thoughts ever clearer. I am the luckiest girl alive.

Hawaii sounds wonderful! I don't think I'll have a problem getting the time off. One thing I know for certain – as beautiful as travelers over the centuries have reported the islands to be, they were never as magnificent as they will be through the eyes of a girl in love.

I'll pick up your dry cleaning and await your call. Can I burn dinner for you again tonight?

Laura
(I'm still smiling)

The crisp white down pillow next to him still bore her imprint, and yes, her smell. That smell… Suddenly, he was taken to a place where the world was new, where the air was sweet and ripe with feeling, where everything was part of everything. Oh, this was a new world all right, his new world, their new world.

And then there was the sex… Laura had made it all so easy. He didn't even get a chance to agonize over when or where, or if he even wanted to, or if he even could. Somehow, they ended up in the bedroom. He thought they would kiss, just kiss for a while, talk, touch, hold, dream, wonder, share a breath, share a smile, an intimate, wordless smile. But beyond that was uncharted territory. He had no plans, no strategies for male conquest.

Before he knew it, he was in her hand. And hard. Thank God, he was hard. And then their clothes disappeared. And she was so beautiful — her face, her breasts, her stomach, her hand so warm. And then she was on top him, her breasts towards his face, his hands reaching beyond her hips then up. So smooth, the small of her back, so young, so beautiful. How could a back feel so perfect, so strong, so sexual? He watched her from every angle and from every angle she glowed. The bounce of her breasts, the rhythm of hers against his, the look in her eyes… Oh, there was a God all right, and a Garden of Eden, and a Heaven, and a Promised Land, and the portal to them all was Woman. And they found their rhythm. And her breathing grew louder and then louder still. And her legs quivered, and her back arched, and her chest lifted, lifted high. And in one magnificent motion her hips thrust back, down and back, and her body shuttered and rolled forward and then shuttered again, her breath now, this intimate staccato. And he held her, held her tight. And he came inside her, and she held him, and he held her, and she started to cry. And he told her that he loved her, and she cried louder still. And she held him. And she told him that she loved him. And he held her. And she cried. And he loved her.

SEASON OF THE WITCH

·12·

The seeds of that intimacy grew in perfect soil, and they spent each night thereafter together, so together. Right from the start, Laura was a delightful addition to the family. Charlotte accepted her without question. And just like that, without any effort or pretense, they were suddenly best friends, naturally best friends. To Geoffrey's amazement, Laura had a seemingly magical way of making Charlotte laugh. Yes, laugh! It astonished him. He had never seen Charlotte laugh much before, never thought of her as the kind of girl who's given to laughter, strange as that may seem. Yet there she was — laughing! More and more, laughing! Out loud! He wondered if he had ever really known his daughter at all. Could this really be his Charlotte, this giggling girl with Laura? Was this a new Charlotte he was seeing, or had she always been like this but was never given the opportunity to express herself before? Or was this somehow all Laura's doing? Had she brought this out in Charlotte? And what was it they were always talking about? Whatever it was, it was certainly in another language. Yet there they were, so content in a world all their own, discussing things no man could understand or appreciate. There was Geoffrey's lover, now Charlotte's older sister. It would have been so natural for him to say, *"Okay girls, off to bed…,"* but then Laura would look at him and it was clear; her place was in his arms. It was a new world, indeed.

As Geoffrey put on his robe, catching a glimpse of himself in the mirror. Looking in mirrors was something he found himself doing more and more of lately. He took notice of his newly refined shape. Over the last months, his physical therapy had grown steadily more rigorous, and he was enjoying it more than he ever thought possible. He not only felt fit, he felt strong. Maybe he would even join a gym. A gym?!? Could this possibly be the same man? Behold the motivational pull of newfound romance.

And his new black, tufted silk robe? What was he thinking when be bought that robe? It was so male, so virile. Was it ridiculous? Who did he think he was, Hugh Hefner? Where was his frayed, white, waist-always-too-tight, arms-always-too-short, old terrycloth robe with *G.Z.* scripted in burgundy on the left chest pocket? He had worn that tired robe for years and never once thought about replacing it. But where was it now? If he ever caught sight of that old robe again, it would be straight to the trash. Laura would never see that robe, or the man who wore it.

The double-wide, brushed-chrome elevator doors had barely parted when Patsy Grenawitz slipped through, pulling Rose and Rae in her wake. The force of Patsy's presence, her perfect posture and long sweeping strides, were enough to straighten the geometric Agam originals that lined Cedars' hallway. She was one of kind, Ms. Patsy was, a seventy-six-year-old *ballaboosta*, whose black bra was far too exposed through her sheer, leopard print blouse tucked into her black tights. No, no skirt for this three-time saddled but never broke mare, just an eight-inch, black, patent-leather belt, capped with an oversized, rhinestone-laden, bright gold, tangled snake belt buckle, complete with ruby red glass eyes. From a distance, her belt could easily have been confused with ones given to the victors at a WWE Smackdown Match. Stiletto heels in black patent leather topped with leopard skin uppers pitched Patsy dangerously forward but the obstacle proved no match for the elegant determination of this lady. Well, maybe elegant was going a bit far up the ladder. Classy— yeah, that's it, *classy*. Patsy Grenawitz had more class than Brooklyn Tech in late September.

Her rings were apparently the only size Patsy thought jewelry came in: Extra-Extra-Extra-Large. On her right hand, two halves of natural pearl, the size of quality macadamias, sat like islands in a pool of rippling yellow gold, perhaps depicting the interstellar landscape of the homesick alien who was now stranded on Earth and supporting himself by working as a discount jeweler. On her left hand sat another pearl, this one whole and floating loosely inside a cage of golden branches, rising a good two inches off the back of her hand. Her neck was adored with enough chains to make any one-hit rapper proud — Snoop Dog Patsy, *keepin' it gansta*. And then there was the anklet with the dangling rhinestone horseshoe charm, so large it could have come off real horse. *Go, Patsy Girl, Go!* Truth is, they don't make her model anymore and haven't for a long, long time; she was the last of a breed— a pink Cadillac with fins. *Yeah, baby. Fins.*

You don't look like Patsy Grenawitz and not love to dance or be without a string of willing dance partners. Monday nights at this social club, Tuesdays at that, and so it was for the rest of the week as well. For years, she danced, and danced, and danced. That was her Broadway and she put on a show like few others. She knew all eyes were glued to her the moment she hit the dance floor and accepted the attention as a matter of fact. It just couldn't be helped; that was the way of the world and her place in it — the way it always had been and always would be. Until, that is, over the course of a single year, her seventy-fourth, she lost all interest in dancing.

"Today, men only want one thing and frankly, I'm just not interested — not with those old guys, anyway. With them, it's like making love to a tom turkey after a starvation diet — all loose skin. It's enough to give you the heebie-jeebies. 'So take your little blue pill, Mister, poke a hole in your mattress, and have a nice day.' That's what I tell 'em." And that's exactly what she told them.

So more and more she filled her days with her new favorite pastime: gossip. Patsy Grenawitz could tell you anything about anyone. She was shameless, blunt, and very funny. She would get the general outline of a story and then fill in all the details herself; the skin maybe orange but the juice was all hers.

Want to know who has had what done, where, and how long ago? Patsy could tell you. How about which husband has been calling his best friend when he knows he's not home just so he can speak to his young new wife? Just ask Patsy. And why was it the Peruvian nanny is going to live with Frieda Klein, when Joe Klein is getting custody of the kids? Oh yeah, Patsy has all the details on that one, too.

Today's mission, which she undoubtedly was going to accept since it was all her idea in the first place, was to catch a peek of that cold-hearted tart that broke up Geoffrey and Victoria after twenty-three years of wedded bliss. The rumors of Geoffrey Zukor being gay were nonsense, Patsy argued emphatically.

"He adored his wife and she idolized him. They did everything together, everything—grocery shopping, errands, the works. They were inseparable. He would even drive her to the beauty parlor and wait for her in the car just so she wouldn't have to touch the steering wheel or the gas pedal with her wet nails! They were that close."

Patsy the Troublemaker knew that every woman she told that little piece of fiction to would be mad at their own good-for-nothing husbands for a month.

"The last time my husband and I spent an afternoon shopping together, we went to Woolworth's Five and Dime," grumbled one of Patsy's friends. "When was the last time you saw a Woolworth's Five and Dime?!?"

After hearing the same story, another replied, "Oh, that's so *beu-dee-ful*, it makes me want to cry. If I *ev-va* asked my husband to drive me for my nails, I'd end up in the Home Depot parking lot. The man is from another planet!"

Patsy looked back to find both Rose and Rae lagging sheepishly behind. With a stern look and a constrained hand gesture, she motioned them forward. "Okay, it's almost time. Get ready. Now, I'll do all the talking. That's all you have to do is smile and nod. Got it? Just smile and nod."

Rose and Rae, unable to hide the nervous tension in their eyes, both looking like deranged crazy people as they smiled and nodded.

"Isn't that a picture," Patsy said sarcastically. She put an arm around each of the ladies and nudged them along the corridor. She was nervous too, quite nervous actually, but other than her rambling, thousand-mile-a-minute, Ellen DeGeneres speech pattern, you never would have guessed.

"Excuse me? Excuse me? Hi! Excuse me? Hello?" Patsy blurted, before finally catching the attention of two nurses that were huddled together synchronizing dosing charts.

"Oh, hi. Hello. How do you do? Maybe one of you could help me? I'm looking for Mena. A friend asked me to bring her a card.

A thank you. She asked that I give it to her personally. I don't know, maybe there's money in it. Not that she doesn't trust any of you. I mean, of course she does. You're nurses, for God's sake! Nurses are like angels — with needles. Loooonnng needles."

"That's Mena there, standing in front of the nurse's station. "Mena, you have a visitor."

Mena turned and approached the three ladies.

"Hi, I'm Mena," said the deep voiced, muscular, six-foot three-inch, two-hundred-eighty-pound Filipina towering over them.

"No, no sorry. I think there's been a bit of miscommunication, Miss — " Patsy stopped and cocked her head to the side as she took a good hard look at the huge block of a nurse standing before her, and then tentatively added, "-ter?"

"Ter?" asked Mena, not following.

"Never mind. I'm looking for Mena. Meeeee-naaaaah."

"That's me. I'm Mena."

"Your name is Mena?"

"Yes."

"You're Mena?"

"Yes."

Patsy paused, looked around, and then broke out laughing. "Ok, where's the camera? You got me! You completely got me! Is Alan Funt back there somewhere? Alan, very funny!" She then turned to Rachel and Rose. "Were you girls in on it the whole time? Funny! Very funny! I mean, look at her. *Aaaaahhhhh!*" And then to Nurse Mena, "You were good. You were *very* good."

"Is there something I can do you, ma'am? If you're looking for Mena, you've found her."

"Really? This isn't a… And you're sure there's not another Mena around here somewhere? You know, maybe one that's a little more… Well, maybe not quite so…" And then, out of frustration, she blurted, "You, you, you don't know Geoffrey Zukor, do you?"

"Geoffrey Zukor? Of course, I do. I'm getting ready to head over to his place right now."

"*REALLY???* I mean, really! My, what a small world. You know Geoffrey Zukor. Really? You go over to his house a lot now do you?"

"Quite often, yes. Sometimes it feels like I live there."

"Right!" Patsy squeaked. "Sure. Of course. Okay then, well, guess we've got to be going. Oh, uh, I, I got something for you, but I just remembered I left the car in my card. Downstairs. So, I'll be right back. Very nice Mena you. I meana, very nice… Never mind.

She could feel it; change was in the air. A door was opening, a door to a place that had held her captive her entire life. Suddenly, she could breathe. She was feeling less stressed, less afraid, less anxious. That's what she noticed first; she was less anxious. Her behavior didn't change much, certainly not at first. She would catch herself acting as she always had, avoiding people whenever possible and certainly never making eye contact with anyone. But recently she began to wonder why. Why didn't she reply to Asa's warm welcome whenever she arrived at The Remington? There was no reason for her to shy away from him, and yet shy away from him she did. Without saying a word, she would run right past him and into the lobby as if she were trying to get out of the rain. Why? Certainly, he deserved a smile, didn't he? Or maybe even a kind word? He was so nice. In fact, although she had never spoken to him, he was one of her favorite people! And yet, upon arrival, she always did her best to avoid him. *Next time, I'm going to smile back,* she promised herself. But old habit always took over, leaving her with one failed attempt after another. No matter how hard she tried, she was incapable of changing, until one day she got so mad at herself, before getting in the elevator, she ran back outside and stood there staring at Asa until she exploded with the loudest, "HI!" he had ever heard. It scared the b'Jesus out of both of them! Then she shrugged her shoulders as if say, *I don't know what just happened,* which he answered with a shrug of his own. Then she smiled, he smiled, and then she turned around a ran like hell. Afterward, she was flying, she felt so good! Charlotte was changing.

Geoffrey noticed it, too. Last week, they ordered in Italian food, after privately plotting together for a one-night reprieve from Laura's cooking and her uncanny ability to burn dinner to a crisp while leaving portions of it gooey and almost raw. When Geoffrey walked into the kitchen and found their takeout sitting on the counter, he yelled, "Laura?"

"She's not here yet," Charlotte replied from another room. "She had a late meeting at the hospital."

Geoffrey stood, staring at the brown bag of takeout still in cartons. "So, how'd the food get in here?"

"I brought it in. And I gave the delivery guy a 20% gratuity. I put it all on your card."

Geoffrey was so shocked by her reply, he didn't question whether 20% was too much to give the driver. No, the big news here was that Charlotte had met the delivery guy at the door!?! And she even gave him a gratuity! Maybe she even spoke to him! Geoffrey was beyond shocked but dared not say a word for fear of making her feel self-conscious. In the past, whenever the doorbell rang, Charlotte not only wouldn't answer it, she would usually escape into another room and not come out until long after the stranger was gone. *But not tonight! Tonight, she answered the door! That's a first!* And Charlotte had done it without even realizing.

So what had brought about this transformation? And why now? Was it the astrological pull of unseen planets? Or was the change charted by numerological values coded into her name and birth date? Or simpler still, perhaps her newfound well-being was the result of prescribed magical dope, that oblong spec of sunshine that filled her head with notions of better days. Her daily dose and weekly appointments with Dr. Elder had remained her secret, known only to Laura and Dr. Sheinman, who had arranged her therapy with the esteemed psychiatrist. But even they were not privy to how he had worked his magic, or the secrets unlocked in his inner sanctum.

Yet despite her progress, questions remained. Serious questions, chief among them being was she free of her past? Free to start anew? Dr. Elder knew she was not. He knew more road lay ahead; a road far more dangerous than that which they've traveled thus far. And he knew there was nothing, absolutely nothing, he could do to protect her from it. He had lost patients on far firmer ground than she now stood, lost them to suicide, or freak accidents, or even cancer. Yet he believed their real cause of death was rooted in their inability to change, to make the transition from one life to the next, to let go of who they were and start to live their life as who they would become.

And so, question remained. Could Charlotte do it? She had spent her life sequestered but now was beginning to feel free, free to attempt the crossing, free to discover her future, and free to finally face her past. Now, she was free.

The air, the air, I feel the air...

SEASON OF THE WITCH

The wind ran its fingers through the golden highlights of Donn's brown hair as the mid-afternoon sun reflected off the corner of his aviator sunglasses in the unmistakable shape of a star, as if a subliminal confirmation of his standing as a perfect one.

Born on a different day, at a different time, he could have been, should have been, the *pop*-est of celebrities, the next in a long line of primarily American products, idolized wherever televisions and movie tickets were sold — the gay Brad Pitt, an image large enough to fill a small screen.

His white convertible mustang streamed north along Pacific Coast Highway, passed mile after mile of sparkling beauty and the unmistakable mystique of Malibu.

To the sad, unfortunate few, namely those crippled with a firm grip on reality and inoculated against the hypnotic power of myth that otherwise had so entranced the power-elite in Los Angeles for well over a half of century, here lies nothing more than the world's largest, freeway close, garage door showroom. Yes, here you'll find mile after mile after mile of mobile home inspired, cracker-box houses, many crammed onto lots no wider than thirty feet, whose entire facade consists of a twenty-five-foot garage door. And adding to the esthetic, they all sit without benefit of a front yard, right smack dab on the shoulder of the always hectic, six-lane Pacific Coast Highway, referred to by locals as simply PCH; PCH, whose 65 mile an hour speed limit signs were ignored almost as often as celebrity wedding vows.

If you park on the street, getting to your front door can feel like being trapped in a real-life version of *Frogger;* unfortunately, your frog has only one life and once you've been clipped by a speeding Humvee of Malibuians, well, that's game over. So, if you're walking in the area, you best watch your step because despite Malibu culture's well-publicized mantra — *Life is a Journey, not a Destination. Sit Back and Enjoy the Ride!* — these folks are sure in a big fat hurry to get somewhere.

True, the pay-off for the cramped quarters and the price tag only a soon-to-be poor man would consider, is your backyard — the glorious Pacific Ocean — there, right there, within arm's reach, presenting itself to you as if it were your very own. Of course, there would have to be a hurricane outside before you could hear it above the rumble of the non-stop traffic roaring by, but still, the Pacific, *your* Pacific, is right there.

Another benefit of Malibu homeownership is that during an *El Niño* winter, you can enjoy all the thrills of scuba diving without ever having to leave your home. It's great to be so close to all of that marine life, especially during the high tides of a winter's storm when it's all right there before you, swimming around your credenza.

It should be mentioned however, that if one does decide to spend what could be as much as a $135,000.00 a month on a Malibu Colony summer rental, before you take a dip in that sparkling sea just beyond your living room window, it's best to consider making like Jesus and walking on the water, not in it. That way you'll be able to ignore the posted signs advising beach visitors to — no joke — "avoid all contact with ocean water at this location."

What???

Yes, that right. There are signs posted alongside homes in the Malibu colony, homes that cost more than the average American makes in 800 years, that read, "Avoid All Contact With Ocean Water At This Location."

That's ridiculous! Just because the surf zone is teeming with enough bacteria to give someone the stomach flu, an ear or upper respiratory infection, or even a nasty rash after just a single dip, doesn't mean you gotta go post a sign, for Christ's sake! Haven't you ever heard of "sign pollution?" And what's the big deal anyway? If I'm going to spend the day swimming around in fecal matter, at least I know I'll be swimming around in celebrity fecal matter! I mean, that's got to be like the Beluga caviar of human excrement. It doesn't get any better than that!

SEASON OF THE WITCH

·16·

Donn drove Charlotte northbound for over an hour to where Pacific Coast Highway edged slightly to the east, finally creating some breathing room between it and the shore. He turned left onto a small, unmarked dirt road that quickly fell away from the highway and then disappeared under a long canopy of one-hundred-year-old oaks. Closer to the shore, the white mustang emerged only to meet the road's end, marked by a dilapidated steel barricade.

"Come on," he said, hopping out of the car. "You're going to love this."

Donn grabbed Charlotte's hand and pulled like a child on his first trip through Disneyland as they made their way up a small footpath. Before Charlotte knew it, they were perched atop a grass bluff overlooking the vast, blue Pacific.

"Oh…" she said, taken aback by the expansiveness of the view before her. "It's so beautiful…"

Although she had spent her whole life in California, Charlotte had never seen this side of the Pacific before. This was far from the customary view of a protected, sunny, Southern California *Baywatch* beach. Here was a glimpse into the true nature of the Pacific—dark, cold, wild, and unapologetically dangerous; a glorious ocean of cerulean majesty topped with an invasion of swells from the distant Far North. On-shore winds whipped the surface water forward into explosions of white curls, curls from the head of the Tethys herself. Beneath its vastness lay the lost secrets of the Ancients, for the ocean knows no time; it remains a windswept portal to all that ever was. The Pacific Coast: Who was to say this was not the rocky shore of Heaven?

"I can't believe it. Its, its…"

Donn turned to see Charlotte lost in her surrounds, the wind whipping her dress against her young body and sweeping her hair off her face as it danced in the aging sun. She fit in exactly as he thought she would. He was right to have brought her there.

"It's the most beautiful thing I've ever seen. Can we move here?"

"That's exactly what I said when I first saw it. Exactly."

"Is it always like this?"

"I don't know. I've only been here once before and that was a long time ago." Donn looked around, and then added as if he were talking to himself, "But it kind of feels like it was yesterday…" They exchanged smiles, solemn and soft. He said nothing for a moment, and then, "Come on. This way."

Donn led Charlotte onto a small, barely worn path that parted a billowing sea of young spring grass as it ran its way down to the cliff's edge and then north, parallel with the shore.

Somehow, they were holding hands, holding hands and walking as if it were as natural as sea before them. "Tim and I were invited to a party by a friend of his who owns this big record company or something and lives a couple of miles further up the highway. His house was incredible, the most spectacular house I'd ever seen. The party though, wasn't really our thing— well, it wasn't my thing, anyway. I'm not really much for parties, unless, of course, P-Dawg's there to liven thing s up a bit. But Tim, Tim was just the opposite. He loved them. Any party, every party, he couldn't get enough. Tim could go to the opening of a carwash in Barstow and have the greatest time ever. By the end of the night, he would have made so many friends, they'd probably name the carwash after him. But then that was Tim…"

"Anyway, after we gawked our way through every room of the mansion, I convinced him to just duck out quietly. But David, Tim's friend, saw us leaving and handed Tim a bottle of some outrageously expensive champagne that one of his guests had brought him, two Lalique champagne glasses, and scribbled a map showing us how to find this place. He loved Tim; he really did. But then everyone loved Tim. Everyone, well, except his parents."

Charlotte looked at him but said nothing. He had volunteered only bits and pieces of his past life before, and then only in conjunction with a problem he was having with Tim's estate. Sure, she knew Tim was very special to Donn, *very* special. She knew they were lovers and were living together at the time of the crash, at the time of Tim death. She wanted to know more but wasn't sure it was her place to ask. Or maybe she didn't ask because she was afraid of what she might hear.

"I just don't get it," Donn continued after a moment's pause. "Tim was an only child, the only kid they had, and growing up he was so close to his parents, especially his father. I mean I'm sure he loved his mom and all, but he idolized his dad. He used to talk about him all the time. His father was a doctor, a surgeon of some kind. And very religious. He was like a deacon or something, whatever that is. Over the summers, he would take Tim on trips all around the world — into poor villages in Mexico and South America. They even went to Africa a couple of times together. And wherever they went, Tim's dad would spend weeks providing free medical care to anyone who needed it. Tim said people looked up to his father like he was a god. Tim sure thought he was."

"Tim even went to medical school to please his dad. He didn't last a semester, but still he tried. I don't know what his father was thinking. I mean Tim couldn't make toast, how was he ever going to be a doctor? I'm not kidding. Once he put bread in the toaster while he was rattling on about something or another and twenty minutes must have gone by. I kept looking over at the toaster, but Tim just kept talking and talking."

"Finally, I had to say something, so I said, 'Tim, don't you think the toast should be ready by now?"

"Alarmed, Tim threw up his hands and let out a gay little scream. He was so funny that way. And then he popped the bread up and looked at it. It was completely un-toasted. Without giving it second thought, pushed the black plastic lever down again and went right back to whatever it was he was talking about."

Donn interrupted again.

"Uh, Tim? What's the story with the toast?"

"It wasn't quite ready. Maybe a few more minutes."

"Why? Why do you think it's not ready?"

"Because it's still white."

Donn smiled. It was hard to be irritated with someone who gives you answers like that.

"Yes, I know. I saw. And why do you think it's still white?"

Tim shrugged. "How should I know. Sometimes it just takes a little longer than others. Maybe today's a slow toast day. What's the big deal?"

"A slow toast day? Tim, do you know how long it's been sitting in there? You could have baked a turkey by now. Do you see the plug lying there on the counter, the one coming out from the back of the toaster? Don't you think plugging it in might help the toasting process along a bit?"

Then Tim said what Tim always says in situations like that. "Oh, why don't you just do it then. If I could figure out stuff like this, I would have been a surgeon and the hottest thing to hit the O.R. since Dr. Kildare."

"So, I guess just when Tim's father had finally accepted the fact his son wouldn't be following in his footsteps, he found out he was gay. You can imagine how that went over. I know nobody wants to hear that their son is gay, but in Tim's case, I can't believe the news came as much of a surprise. Seems to me it must have been obvious to everyone since Tim was seven years old, but his dad just couldn't handle it. In the last conversation they ever had, his father really laid into him. He told him how disgusted he was by his *immorality*. He said he couldn't even stand to look at him and told him to get out of his house and never come back. And he meant it, too."

"He wouldn't have anything to do with Tim after that. He cut him off completely. Wouldn't talk to him on the phone, nothing. Tim would write him all the time, but every single letter was returned, unopened. It devastated him. He missed his father so much, it almost killed him."

Donn took a moment and looked out at the last sun, the sky ablaze to mark its passing. "Of course, I never knew any of that.

Tim kept it all a secret, even from me. I never heard him say one bad thing about his father. Not one. From listening to Tim, you would have thought they had the world's closest relationship. He was always talking about the things he and his father had done together, or things his father used to say to him, or what other people had told him about his dad. Anyone who knew Tim knew how much he idolized his dad. He never told any of them that his father hadn't spoken to him for nearly a decade. I knew him almost two years before I found out, and then it was only by accident."

"Maybe that's why he liked parties so much," offered Charlotte.

Donn nodded softly. "Yeah. Maybe that's why he liked a lot of things so much…" Donn twisted his foot in the dirt as if extinguishing a cigarette. "I was so young and stupid. I knew Tim drank, of course, sometimes way too much, but I never knew about all the drugs he was taking. Isn't that amazing? How could I have missed that? I guess I just didn't want to know."

"He took a lot of drugs?"

"Enough to nearly kill him," Donn said with a nod. "I came home from an overnight and found him lying on the bathroom floor, barely breathing, a pile of returned letters from his father all around him. That was how I found out about the drugs. And that was how I found out about what really happened between him and his dad. Tim ended up spending a few of nights in the hospital and even went to a couple of AA meetings, but then he started right back up again. He either couldn't stop …or he wouldn't stop."

"That's so sad…"

"Yeah, the whole thing was really sad."

Donn stopped and turned toward Charlotte. "Anyway, I'm sorry. I don't know why I'm going on like this. I didn't come here to talk about Tim. This must be so uncomfortable for you."

"Are you always such a gentleman?"

Donn wasn't exactly sure what to make of her question. He looked into her eyes, beautiful and blue, the inner Pacific. They both smiled, then Charlotte looked away.

"Come on. Just a little bit further." Donn motioned toward a rocky bluff ahead.

But after a few steps, Charlotte stopped. "So he never reconciled with his father? Ever?"

Donn shook his head. "No, he never did — not in the way he should have anyway." He looked out and slowly drifted out, into the horizon…

Beneath his feet, he saw the familiar Canyon Blue carpet out-stretched before him. He remembered voting for Canyon Blue, not that he had a choice. He smiled, hearing Tim defiantly state that he would quit, right then and there, if Southwest Orange won.

"I am not going to spend my days flying around in a pumpkin!" Tim, always so dramatic.

Moving aft, Donn noticed a string of tube lights out: port, rows 6 through 8. A quick check confirmed that all overhead aisle lights were operational, as were the No Smoking icons and passenger reading lights. Good. He wouldn't have to call Spot Maintenance; the tube lights could go on the aircraft's *E.O.D.* report.

Donn continued to make his way toward the galley. Tim was making coffee, always an adventure. Unfortunately, Donn's progress was stalled again, this time by a large black man trying to squeeze his large black suitcase into the small, beige overhead bin. Experience had taught him it was better to let his passengers exhaust themselves a bit first before stepping in with the bad news. After a few more grunts and groans, he said, "I'm sorry, sir, but I think we're going to have to check your bag."

"Oh, no," protested Leonard "Leon" Lewis. "This bag fit into the box which means it's fine, just fine." The buxom Mrs. Lewis stepped in front of her husband as if to run interference and nodded in full support.

"Well, I'm not sure whose box that bag fit into," replied Donn, smiling politely at Mrs. Lewis, who smiled in return only to withdraw it as she began to wonder what exactly the young man was implying, "but it's not going fit into the overhead bin. Let me get it checked for you, sir." Without allowing time for further debate, Donn called forward, "Martin, we've got a Driz at 12E. Would you get the gentleman a claim check please? Thank you."

It wasn't easy but Donn managed to shimmy past large Leon, large Leon's large luggage, and large Leon's large-lunged lady, but before he could complete his getaway, he asked, "What's a Driz?"

"Oh, it's nothing," Donn replied, "just flight attendant lingo for a passenger who tries to stuff a big object into a small space. We call them a Driz, short for Drizella, you know, one of the stepsisters from *Cinderella*, the fairy tale where she tries to stick her big foot into a little glass slipper."

"Well, then he be a Drizella all right, and in a lot more ways than one," chimed in Mrs. Lewis. "You would not believe what that man tries to stuff into my itty-bitty glass slipper, if you catch my meaning. And it's a lot longer than a foot, son. The man's built more like Godzilla than any Drizella. I can assure you of that!"

"Oh, you poor dear. I know *just* how you feel!" said the approaching Martin. "The things we must endure to please our men." Martin was as gay as *Par-ee* and a master buttinski to boot, capable of ease dropping on a conversation twenty rows away. He fanned himself with a claim check before handing it to Mrs. Lewis. Then to Leon, who was still trying to cram his carry-on into the overhead, he said admonishingly, "You big brute!" Leon the Large looked down at Martin the Minuscule. It was unclear whether it was love at first sight or fear of bodily injury that brought about the abrupt change in Martin's demeanor. Suddenly, he was smiling coyly and unabashedly batting his eyelashes at the big man. Leon begrudgingly handed him his luggage, the weight of which was so surprisingly heavy, Martin went reeling backwards nearly all the way to the forward hatch. *"Aaaaahhhhhhhhh!"*

Donn smiled. "You're free to take any open seat. I'll be back after takeoff for your beverage order."

Once again, he was moving aft. Row 13, 14, 15, 16, 17... Donn remembered every step. And then he arrived at Row 18. Flight 1005, Row 18, Seat F. There, next to the window... All of a sudden, Donn couldn't breathe.

Is that...?

He turned away. Looking forward, he started counting heads on the port side of the plane, or at least pretend to. Rows 13, 14, 15, 16, 17, 18... Donn's brow fell as he counted the couple in 18E and F.

No, maybe it's not... I mean, it couldn't be...

He moved quickly to the galley where he found Tim completely beside himself, having spent the last 20 minutes trying to lower the black plastic safety latch over the stainless-steel coffee carafe. Tim looked up and was about to tell him that the damn thing was broken again, which everyone knew to be Tim-speak for, *Would you do this for me, please?* but seeing the look on Donn's face instead asked, "What's wrong?"

"18F. Well, E and F. I don't know. It's probably nothing. It was just so freaky."

"What?"

"It's… well, you go look — but be careful. Don't let them see you."

Tim made his way toward mid-plane, slowing at Row 22. Donn followed, lagging a safe distance behind. Tim stopped just beyond Row 21. He looked back, alarm on his face. Donn shrugged his shoulders. Tim turned and just stood there, staring for a moment. He was sure but then again, he wasn't.

He inched a few more steps forward, almost to Row 19, before stopping again. Now sheet white, he turned back to Donn, who wanted desperately to help but wasn't sure how. He watched as Tim turned and briskly walked forward — 18, 17, 16, 15, all the way to Row 5. Then he turned again and slowly, tentatively began creeping back toward Row 18, seats E and F, his view remaining partially obscured by the seatbacks between them. He paused near Row 14. It had been ten years, ten years, but he knew that hair, that forehead, those brows. There was no doubt about it. It wasn't until he got closer that the whole of the man's head in Seat F scrolled into view. Tim stopped, unable to continue. Donn wondered if he should go to him.

"Dad?" Tim's voice was a whisper, inaudible to all but himself.

Dr. Douglas Conklin, 18F, removed his lips from the chubby, thirty-something brunette in 18E, who looked as if this were the very first time on an airplane. Tim stared at her. Whoever she was, she was not Mrs. Douglas Conklin. He watched as she playfully slapped his father's chest while releasing a mock-embarrassed chortle.

The good doctor responded with an overly assured, devilish grin. *That was nice. She's going to be a fun little weekend.* He lazily rolled back into his seat, every bit the community theatre James Bond reaching for an after-sex cigarette. As he did, he thought he caught sight of someone staring at him. He didn't mind. To his way of thinking, he had just put on a pretty good show. *Let 'em stare.* A second glance from Dr. Conklin revealed it was a flight attendant.

A flight attendant. A flight attendant...

It seemed like it took forever to register, so removed from his consciousness was his son, but when it did, he gasped.

His hands moved to the armrests as if to steady himself from the jolt. He looked again. Yes, it really was his son. It really— and then he caught a peripheral glimpse of his travel mate and remembered who he was with and what he was doing and— *Oh God...*

"Tim? Tim, Son..."

"Dad?"

"What?" squeaked Conklin's companion in 18E.

The doctor ignored her as he awkwardly tried to stand, his stature diminished by the arched seatback in front of him and the low-flung overhead bins above. He tried to hide his panic behind a smooth, forced smile as he searched for the best way out of this.

"I, I didn't know you..." Douglas Conklin should have stopped right there, should have left it at that, but instead added, "...worked, uh ...as a..." His heart was pounding. *Would Tim call his mother? Yes, of course he would. He'd do anything to get back in her good graces — even if it meant burying me to do it.*

"Who's this?" squawked 18E. Her screeching was not out of any sense of alarm; apparently that was just the way she spoke.

Douglas Conklin watched Tim look down at 18E and politely half-smile. Dr. Conklin shot her a quick glance too, but this time saw her through Tim's eyes; it wasn't a pretty picture. He looked back at his son, who seemed to loom large over him; the Grim Reaper had finally come to collect his due. The pit in his stomach confirmed something vital was slipping away and he was helpless to stop it. James Bond, where art thou?

He extended his hand, the bend of his long, articulated fingers reaching toward his son. He opened his mouth hoping to find words capable of extricating himself, but none came. *Damn it!* None came.

Maybe I should just act like nothing had happened? But he saw us... Or I could laugh it off, like, like with an old frat buddy... But he knew that wouldn't work either. Tim was about the furthest thing possible from one of his frat buddies. *Fuck! Fuck!! Maybe I should just deck the little prick. He's always been such a fucking little—*

"This is your son?" shrieked 18E. "But I thought you said you didn't have any kids."

Dr. Douglas Conklin looked down at the stupid expression on hes face, and as he did, could feel the heat of his son's eyes upon him. That was it. Caught or not, he wouldn't allow himself to be played like this. Not him. Not Dr. Douglas Conklin. He threw down his hand in disgust and absent his usually grace, stumbled out into the aisle, in the process accidentally stomping on the foot of his travel mate in 18E. With the sound of her shrieks at his back, he stormed past his son and off the plane.

"*Oooowwww! Oooowwww!* Dougie! *Oooowwww!*" She stood and finding it impossible to put any weight on her throbbing big toe, hopped out into the aisle and then forward as fast as she could after him. "Dougie? Where you going? Dougie? Dr. Conklin? Stop! You said we could go on a trip…"

Just as 18E was about to *Boing!* herself right off the plane, Tim stopped her.

"Ma'am? Ma'am, you better take this," he said, handing her a red vinyl purse. "And do me a favor, will you? When you see my dad, tell him that I miss him… a lot. Like every day, I miss him. But most of all… tell him that I love him. Please don't forget, okay?"

She nodded. "Sure." And then she turned and resumed her stick-less pogo-a-thon off the plane. But before she hit the boarding ramp, Tim stopped her again.

"Oh, and ma'am, if you see my mom, be sure to tell her I miss her too, will you?" Tim smiled. A smile and a tear.

Donn and Charlotte stood beneath the shelter of a lone cypress tree near the tip of Old Algiers Point as he finished the story.

"That day changed everything for Tim. It was like he was a different person after that. I know he wrote his dad a couple of times afterwards and even though he still never wrote back, it was okay. It didn't hurt like before. Seeing his father like that, seemed to put everything in perspective somehow. It was like he was finally free. That meeting was a real gift. A gift before dying..."

For a long while Donn stood silent and for the first time since they met, Charlotte began to feel uncomfortable in his presence.

"So, the problem with you and his parents, is that okay now?"

"No. I don't see how that's ever going to be okay."

"Well, you still have your car."

"Only because I didn't turn it in like I said I was going to. I just couldn't. Tim loved that car so much. He wouldn't want me to give it up. We got it right after the incident with his dad on the plane. It was like his symbol of freedom. He even put a personalized plate on it, 18E+F, so he'd always remember that his father wasn't some larger-than-life moral authority. He was just a guy, flawed like everyone else."

"He was so funny about it, too. After that, whenever he'd see a chubby girl with brown hair wearing kind of dumb, hokey clothes, he would pretend to be that girl from 18E and start bouncing all around, yelling 'Dougie? Dougie? Dr. Conklin? Wait! Where are you going? You said if I gave you a blowjob we could go somewhere. You promised! Dougie, come back! Come back!' I'd be so embarrassed, but he didn't care who heard him. He'd go on and on, flitting around all over the place. He was so gay, and crazy, and funny. He could really make me laugh. He really could…"

In the age-old battle between the gods of comedy and tragedy, it was usually the relentless, ravaging ache of tragedy that prevails, and this evening would be no different. Donn could see Tim's face, his hair, that shimmering glint in his eye, every detail as real as if he were standing right there before him. And again, he felt the bottomless pit of his loss, that sickening emptiness that had eaten away at him for so long.

"I'm so sick of this! I don't want to cry anymore! I can't! I can't!" he yelled with a burst of pent-up frustration that startled Charlotte.

But in the end, it was no use, and he knew it. He looked at her and said, "I don't know what to do. I'm sorry. I'm so sorry…"

She rushed to him, and he fell into her arms with a cry as deep as the ocean they stood before. And she held him as she had never held another. This was her son, her brother, her shipwrecked lover. And it was there and then, as the five o'clock sky blazed across the horizon, that their tearful eyes met, and they cast their fate into the sea with a kiss. A long, glorious, desperate kiss.

"I'm not sorry," Donn whispered, as much to himself as to Charlotte.

Of all the things a girl might hope to hear after someone kisses her for the first time, "I'm not sorry" scores only slightly higher than, "Did I mention I get these sores on my lip?" Charlotte, perplexed by such a glowing affirmation of love, found herself asking, slightly incredulously, "You're not sorry?"

"No, don't take it wrong. What I meant was that, well, I, I wanted to kiss you. I meant to kiss you."

"You did? I'm so relieved. For a minute there I thought you just lost your footing and your lips smashed into mine. You know, by accident."

Donn let out an embarrassed little laugh. "Okay, fine, I'm a dork. I admit it. I say the world's stupidest things. You feel better now?"

She smiled at him. She was irresistibly beautiful when she smiled.

"What I was trying to say was, well, I…" He paused, tried to gather his thoughts, compose himself. "…well, that I've wanted to kiss you for longest time. I think since the very first time I saw you. But I wanted to make sure that I did. And that it was for the right reasons, you know, considering everything. You understand, right?" Without waiting for an answer, he added, "I mean, I didn't just kiss you."

"You didn't?" She was playing with him now, enjoying the emotional upper hand.

"Well, I did just kiss you, but it wasn't just a spur of the moment kind of kiss." He thought about that for a moment. "Well, maybe it was a spur of the moment kind of kiss. But that wasn't all it was. You understand?"

"Do you always make things so complicated?" Her eyes smiled into his but when she saw him still struggling, it faded.

Donn took a moment, a long moment, and then told her the truth. "Charlotte, I've never kissed a girl before."

His confession stood like a wall between them.

Charlotte, of course, had wondered about this, worried about this, and about so many other things in Donn's past. And she was not alone. She had fended off repeated rounds of questioning from her father, awkwardly inquiring about Donn and "the nature of your relationship." But it was far too unwieldy of a subject to discuss with him and in any event, she had no answers to his male-oriented, black or white questions. She knew where she wanted their relationship to go but wasn't at all sure it was heading in that direction. She thought it was, but then when nothing happened between them despite several opportunities, she began to think that perhaps she was wrong, although she knew in her heart that she wasn't. She had wanted to discuss it with Laura but wasn't sure how to bring it up. She didn't need to worry. As with so many potentially uncomfortable situations, Laura had a way of making things easy, and thus she did for Charlotte.

Laura was naturally in tune with the sometimes awkward but always beautiful young lady she had grown so fond of over the last many months, and she seemed to be able to anticipate many of Charlotte's concerns and questions without her asking, offering her sage advice and reassurance. Laura was, after all, no stranger to the world of male/female relationships, particularly less than ideal ones. The first time they discussed Donn at any length was while shopping one afternoon. That it came up then was ideal for Charlotte because it not only added an air of casualness to their discussion but the hunt for that perfect "little black dress" — perfect meaning both perfect and, of course, on sale — broke up their conversation into smaller, more digestible slices that allowed her time to think things through. Charlotte never knew shopping could be so much fun.

In the end, there was nothing that Laura said about Donn that Charlotte hadn't already figured out for herself, but hearing Laura say it boosted her confidence in her own judgment.

Together, they concluded three things: First, and perhaps most importantly, that Donn was a true gentleman. "Perhaps to a fault," Laura added with a sly smile. This meant he would be as much if not more concerned about Charlotte than he would be about himself. Therefore, things would probably progress slowly, perhaps painfully so, but that was as much for her good as for his, given his circumstance. She, in turn, would need to be patient and remember that "slow progress was not no progress." And lastly, if things did start to move in a romantic direction, Charlotte was not to advance beyond a certain point sexually, should she be so inclined (which she clearly was or at least thought she was anyway), without an honest and frank discussion about HIV. Laura felt almost certainly that Donn would bring it up, and would probably already have taken one if not more HIV tests prior to any romantic behavior but, in the strange event he did not, Laura made Charlotte swear on her father's life (the only thing Laura could think in the moment) that she would suggest (suggest in this case meaning, "insist, but with a smile") they take at least one HIV test together. Charlotte was surprised to hear that Laura had taken an HIV test with every man she had slept with in the last 15 years or so. Every single one. No exceptions. (In truth, there had been one exception — Laura's father — but thankfully that never came up.) Evidently the courtship rituals of decades past like the soda fountain date, getting "pinned," and the exchanging of class rings or St. Christopher medallions has been replaced with the infinitely more romantic visit to the clinic for joint AIDS testing.

Ah, Love is in the Air...
Can't you just smell the rubbing alcohol?

Charlotte looked down. From where she gathered the courage, she had no idea. She just opened her mouth and the words fell out. "So, was it... all right? I mean, did you like kissing a girl?"

Donn smiled. "You couldn't tell?"

She swallowed. "I don't know. It seemed like you liked it, but I think maybe I was so busy liking it myself, I couldn't be completely sure if you were liking it too?"

"I more than liked it, Charlotte. I loved it. I loved it as much as I love everything else about you."

And beneath the canopy of the lone cypress on Old Algiers Point, they kissed, and they kissed, and they kissed some more as high above the stars danced as they only do for lovers.

Charlotte sat with her back nestled deep into Donn's chest, the warmth of his arms enveloping her as they looked out upon a world revealed to but a precious few. This was one those moments, one of those rare, perfect moments she knew she would remember forever.

How long they stayed there like that, neither could say. But it was Donn who eventually broke the silence, the mood, with a whisper. "There's so much you don't know about me, Charlotte. Are you sure this... is a good idea?"

"Do you want to go?" she asked, rocking forward.

"No."

"Are you sure?"

He thought for a moment. "I don't know. I don't know what to do. Every time we've been together, I've wanted to kiss you and hold you like this. And I've been so mad at myself afterwards for not doing it. But now, I don't know. I mean, I think this is right, it feels right, but I don't know. There's so much I don't know." His voice trailed off to a whisper. "I just don't want to hurt you... I don't know. Am I just being crazy? Are you worried about any of this?"

"Worried?" she repeated. "I'll tell you a secret. I've been seeing this doctor lately, a psychiatrist. And we've been talking—well, *I've* been talking. He just sits there and asks these questions, these difficult, impossible-to-answer questions. And mostly what we've focused on is all of my worrying. I never really realized it before but almost every single one of my childhood memories are somehow tied to me worrying about something. It's like all of my memories are worries. Isn't that weird? I was such a strange kid. I mean, what does a kindergartener at a private school in Brentwood have to be worried about, for God's sake? Or a first grader, or a second grader, or a third grader? And yet that's just about all I did."

"I've always felt so… unsafe, so vulnerable, as if there was something lurking out there, just out of sight, just waiting to jump out and grab me. People always thought I was shy. I wasn't shy. I was hiding. I was terrified and I was hiding. I think that's why I read so much. I learned how to escape into books."

"But lately, lately everything's been changing. I've been challenging myself to accept that I'm better and I'm going to stay that way no matter what happens. I know that probably doesn't sound like much to you, but for me, well, I've never felt this way before — ever — in my whole life. For the first time I can remember, I don't have to worry about what's going to happen because no matter what happens, it'll be okay. I'll be okay. I don't have to worry that I'm not good enough, or smart enough, or maybe even pretty enough that someone might like me, maybe even love me. I feel like for the first time, I can relax a little. I can finally breathe. I look around now and, I don't know, maybe I'm just imagining things, but I see beauty, so much beauty. For the first time in my life, I see the beauty in your eyes, in the stars in the sky, the beauty all around us. There's so much beauty all around us, and I feel it. I do. And in the midst of all this beauty, I'm beginning to understand that there is nothing really to worry about at all, that life is beautiful, more beautiful than we can possibly imagine, and that it always has been, and that it always will be. And just to be here, surrounded by all of this, makes me the luckiest girl in the whole world."

"Wow," sighed Donn. "I should definitely go see your doctor. Whenever I start feeling good about things, I know something really bad is about to happen."

"You must be Jewish."

"Probably," he nodded. "I know I look Jewish. People are always pointing at me and saying, 'Hey, there goes that Jewish kid.'"

"Now that you mention it, you do kind of look like David Lieberman."

"David Lieberman?"

"The first boy I ever kissed."

"You kissed David Lieberman?"

"Three times."

"You know, if I ever see that guy, I'm going to punch him right in the nose."

"You are?"

"Definitely."

"Well, that shouldn't be too hard. He was pretty much all nose. He almost poked my eye out every time he kissed me. A couple more smooches and I'd probably be blind today."

"That's what you get for two-timing me!"

"I was in eighth grade. I didn't even know you then."

"And that's my fault? You could have moved to Kansas if you wanted to meet me sooner."

"I should have. Instead, I wasted four days of my life going steady with David Lieberman."

"So, you two aren't still smooching on the swings?"

"No, but I still don't think I've completely gotten over him. He told every kid in school the reason... he broke up with me was..." Charlotte's voice left her.

"Why? Because you wanted to go to second base with him and he wouldn't let you?"

"Very funny," she replied with a slight backward jab of her elbow.

"Wait a minute. You're saying he broke up with you? I don't believe it."

Charlotte nodded.

"Impossible. Not even an eighth grader could be that stupid."

"He did. And then he told everyone that I had…" Again, her voice trailed off.

"What?"

Charlotte said nothing.

"What? What did he say?"

"Oh, he said I had… It doesn't matter."

"Come on, tell me. What did he say?"

"He said I had… big ears," she answered uneasily.

"He did? Really? Boy, I'm really going to let him have it now. The *duffuss* was probably just trying to deflect attention away from his big nose. I mean your ears can't be that big, right?"

Charlotte barely heard him. She sat there, motionless, ashamed.

It struck Donn that he'd never actually seen Charlotte's ears. He started to comb his fingers through her hair along the left side of her head when suddenly Charlotte jerked forward. "No, don't. Don't—" She abruptly swatted his hand away and got to her feet. "Don't do that."

"Wow, I just got a peek of them and they are pretty large, aren't they?" Donn said, looking up at her. "You know on a windy day, you might try jumping off a box or something. I'll bet you could get some real lift out of those babies. Worked for Dumbo."

"Very funny but there's only one Dumbo around here — Donn the Dumbo!" There was genuine agitation in her voice.

Donn hopped up. "Hey, I was joking! They're the prettiest ears I've ever seen. I mean it. Here, let me have another look." He reached for her.

"Don't!" She swatted his hand away even more forcibly than before. "Don't you know what don't means?" Clearly upset, she moved away from him, stopping several paces beyond the shelter of the lone cypress and out into the moonless night.

"Charlotte, I'm sorry. I didn't know you were so sensitive about them. But you don't have to be. Look at you. You're so beautiful. You don't need to be self-conscious about your ears just because of what some stupid kid said in the eighth grade, right?"

Charlotte shook her head, looked at him. Her eyebrows inched upward as she leaned slightly forward, all in an effort to speak. She tried. She really tried. She knew what she wanted to say but couldn't find the courage to say it.

Donn gently approached her, leading with his most endearing smile. "Let me ask you something, all right?" He bent slightly to her level, looked directly into her eyes, and with all the charm he could muster said, "Do ears that big give you like supersonic hearing? I mean, let's face it — you're like a walking satellite dish. You could be Miss DirecTV!"

Still, he was unable to coax a smile out of her. He tried again. "Would you mind if I crawled up in there and maybe had a little look around?" The silly goof raised his right foot high off the ground as he grabbed the side of her head.

"DON'T! DON'T!!" she screamed at him, leaning back and angrily batting his arms away. "I have to go." She spun right past him and darted off to the left between two large shrubs, disappearing into the night.

"Char? CHAR!!" he shouted. "NOT THAT WAY!!! THE CLIFF!!! CHAR!!!!"

Charlotte's scream, shrill, pierced the sky. For one brief moment it seemed to fill the entire world…

and then it was gone.

❖   ❖   ❖

THE END OF PART TWO

JUST ONE LIFE
PART THREE

THE SILVER SHOES

THE SILVER SHOES

There are sounds once heard that can never be forgotten, sounds that propagate the terror from which they were born. Forever reminders, these, no matter the lengths one goes to hide from their echo, that chase subjugated souls through daily alcoholic stupors or into desperate narcotic sleeps, clawing at the few gutter scraps of humanity that remain. Screams that foretell of fates so horrible that their details lay beyond the realm of words are some such sounds. Charlotte's was one of these, a scream so filled with panic that no matter the outcome, she would be forever changed.

"NO! CHAR—THE CLIFF!! NO!!!" Donn yelled, already on his feet. Charlotte tried to stop but couldn't, the cliff's edge so suddenly upon her. She reared back but her momentum was too great. Her feet slipped out from under her as if the darkness below had her by the ankles and was dragging her down, thirsty for another bloody grave. Donn cleared the bushes in time to see Charlotte's upper body falling backwards, then twisting, as first her side and then her chest hit the ground. As she slid, her fingers clawed deep, desperate rows into the gravel, trying to stop her slide. But it was all happening too fast. She arched her back, screaming, searching. She saw him. Their eyes locked as her thighs slipped over the edge of the cliff.

Donn leapt for her, diving forward, his outstretched fingers just barely reaching her hand. He hit the ground with a hard, dusty thud.

Donn latched on, but still they skidded forward. Charlotte's waist disappeared over the ledge adding momentum to her slide. Donn thrust his left hand into the dirt for what support he could find. Finally, they stopped. Donn struggled to maintain their position. Only Charlotte's head, shoulders, and arms were visible; the rest dangled, taunting the Dark Angel below.

Donn secured his grip on her wrist and slowly inched his legs around, moving from prone to sitting position. He knew that if he lost traction now and was pulled forward again, he probably would not be able to stop their slide a second time. Charlotte pressed her elbows into the ground and as she did, her legs swung forward, her right shoe hit the side of cliff. Shifting her weight onto her left arm, she was able to raise her right leg a bit. Her foot searched for a toe hold to ease the pressure …

As it searched, the tip of her shoe caught the slightest of ledges. She dug her foot into the wall while stepping up on the ledge. She rose maybe an inch.

"I think–"

Then her toehold gave way. She screamed, slid back down onto the lengths of her arms. Donn reeled back with all his might.

"Don't move! Don't move!!" he yelled. "I've got you! I won't let you fall!"

Charlotte looked down and watched as a portion of the cliff under her rumbled onto the rocks below. She was just able to make out the faint, white foam outlines of waves crashing against the jagged jaw of the shoreline.

"Charlotte, don't. Don't look down." But she couldn't turn away, couldn't remove her stare. She saw herself down there, her desperate outstretched limbs, her angled broken body, her bloody dress draped across cold, wave-swept rocks. Then her world went dark and slack.

THE SILVER SHOES

Donn lay panting on the ground beside her, her body shaking. He had muscled Charlotte to safety, not stopping until she was well away from the cliff's edge. Long bloody scrapes ran along both of her arms and legs. "It's okay. You're okay. You're okay..." It was some time before he was able to get her to her feet and it was longer still before she was steady enough to move.

Even with her arm around Donn's neck and his right hand around her waist, navigating the uneven terrain on that shadowy night made for slow going as they started their trek back to the car. After 30 minutes and scant progress to show for it, Donn couldn't shake the feeling that the trail too was conspiring against them, having grown immeasurably longer and more difficult since they first traveled it on what seemed like an afternoon so long ago.

"Charlotte? Charlotte, let me help you, okay?" She looked at him, her face ghostly pale. She didn't answer. He didn't know if she could hear him or not. "Charlotte, I'm going to pick you up and carry you to the car. If you don't want me to, just tell me and I'll put you right down, okay? I'll count to three."

There was no response from Charlotte. He lifted her into his arms and made his way along the cliff's edge.

Asa Johnson opened the passenger side door, his smile quickly turned into concern. Donn was immediately at his side to help Charlotte out of the car. They were both rumbled and stained, but it was obvious that Charlotte had gotten the worst of it by far. He saw the nasty scrapes down her legs and another even worse on her forearm. Despite his alarm, he said nothing.

"Charlotte, I'm going to help you upstairs, all right?" Donn asked.

Charlotte looked away, whispered, "Asa. Asa…"

The two men looked at each other. "Mr. Olson, sir, why don't I help the young lady up? You look plenty beat yourself."

"Yeah, okay. If you can, make sure Laura or her father knows she's home, will you? And if they're not, call me and I'll come back and stay with her."

"Of course," Asa said with a nod.

A few minutes later, Donn's cell phone rang.

"Donn, it's Geoffrey Zukor. What happened?" His voice, cold.

Donn relayed the evening's events in some detail. When Geoffrey interrupted to ask about the scrapes along Charlotte's legs and arm, he told him about the fall. If he was less than forthcoming about anything, it was Charlotte's proximity to the edge of the cliff when he grabbed her. He couldn't imagine any father taking that very well, and certainly not Geoffrey Zukor.

"I feel so bad. I wanted to bring her upstairs myself, but she said 'Asa' like she wanted him to do it or I would have. Maybe I should have anyway, I don't know. I was going to call in a little while and make sure she was okay and see if there was anything I could do. Maybe I should run out and get some bandages and hydrogen peroxide or something? I'm so sorry about everything. It just happened so fast. At first, I thought she was just, I don't know, pretending or goofing around. I mean, she's so beautiful. But then she got so upset, like out of nowhere. I didn't know she was so sensitive about her ears. I had no—"

"Her ears?" interrupted Geoffrey.

"Yeah, that's what she said. I didn't know—

"I'll get back to you." With that, Geoffrey Zukor hung up the phone.

Sex Ring Exposed

933 Nabbed Across 7 Western States in Largest Pedophile Bust in U.S. History

Investigation Also Links 8 Foreign Countries to Massive On-Line Child Pornography Ring

By Sloane McManus, *Los Angeles Times* Staff Writer

LOS ANGELES, California — In a sweeping multi-state crackdown yesterday, coordinated between local law enforcement agencies and the Federal Bureau of Investigation,

933 men and women were arrested on suspicion of possession and trafficking in child pornography. The arrests were made in synchronized pre-dawn raids in California, Oregon, Washington, Nevada, Arizona, Utah, and New Mexico, and resulted in the confiscation of more than a 1,200 computers and peripherals that are believed to contain over 150,000 still images and computerized videos depicting children engaged in illicit sexual activity. It is estimated that the number of minors involved could easily be in the hundreds. The raids yielded the single largest seizure of illegal pornographic material in U.S. history.

Suspects taken into custody were allegedly all part of an international electronic child pornography ring known as the Dazzletown Club. The club was organized as a giant lending library of kiddy porn, allowing members to exchange indecent materials online. Membership in the club was by invitation only and all prospective applicants were subjected to a rigorous screening process prior to admittance. According to police, admission required each member to provide a minimum of 1,000 illicit images to share among other club members and the payment of a $499 membership fee. It is unclear at this time how long the club has been operating.

"The FBI is continuing to comb through the material confiscated in yesterday's raid, which is said to include stacks of club records, credit card receipts, and bank deposits. Leads garnered from this material could easily result in the arrests of hundreds more," said a source close to the investigation.

One officer involved in the case from the outset has confirmed that the probe began several months ago when a computer was donated to Good Will Services, allegedly from the estate of a deceased individual. No additional information was released regarding the donor pending further investigation. When the disturbing images were discovered by Good Will staffers, the computer was turned over to the Los Angeles Police Department Special Investigations Unit, the same crack outfit that after months of harrowing undercover work and nearly $400,000 in expenditures was responsible for the arrest of that notorious menace to society, Pee-Wee Herman, for the crime of masturbating in an out-of-the-way X-rated movie theater.

"Word on the street had been circulating for months that Pee Wee Herman was involved in masturbation. Thank God, he tried it once in an adult movie house and we were able to nab him. I think we all feel a lot safer now, knowing Mr. Herman has been publicly humiliated and is finally behind bars where he belongs," said Chief of Police Willie Wachs at the time.

Although names are being withheld pending arraignment, those arrested in the Dazzletown Club child pornography raid yesterday are said to come from all walks of life and include elementary and high school teachers, Boy Scout and Cub Scout pack leaders, a professor from Brown, pastors, priests, officials at the U.S. Justice Department, and even police officers. Workers tied to commercial aviation, namely employees of various airlines and related F.A.A. staff, are thought to represent the largest block of those arrested for their Dazzletown Club activities.

Twenty-seven individuals who work in the entertainment industry were also charged but have all vigorously denied any wrongdoing, each spinning their particular version of the old threadbare line, "I was just doing 'research' for an upcoming project."

An actor starring in one of those omnipresent crime scene investigation television series went so far as to say, "This is all a big misunderstanding. You see, I was undercover, gathering detailed forensic evidence to bring those to justice who are involved in this despicable behavior. I was just about to turn my findings over to my commander in Vice when I was mistakenly caught up in the dragnet. Therefore, I am asking you to please refrain from using my real name or using any photos of me as it will only make my future undercover work all the more difficult."

When the actor in question was confronted with the fact that he was not actually a cop but merely played one on TV, he began shaking like a recently "homosexuality-cured" evangelical preacher whenever he passed a young male hitchhiker. Then he grabbed his shoe and, a la Maxwell Smart, radioed for backup. He has since been placed under around-the-clock psychiatric observation.

"This kind of delusional behavior has plagued actors since the earliest days of television," said Vesdin Guerst, one of three dozen physiatrists the Screen Actors Guild keeps on staff to combat the identity disorder. "The issue first came to light when Steve "Superman" Reeves, late for a meeting, opted to jump out a four-story window and fly across town rather than take his car. Unfortunately, dealing with an actor's psychotic behavior is extremely difficult, as anyone who has even casually dated one can testify. This is because their delusions are often deeply embedded in their psyches. For example, after Mr. Reeves hit the ground, his last words were, "Fuck, I forgot to make the wind sound! Everyone knows I fly a lot better when I go, 'Shhweeesshhhuuussseeessshhh!'"

As a result of the probe, links to foreign individuals and websites suspected of trafficking in child pornography were also uncovered, involving at least eight other countries. Evidence turned over to foreign authorities has already resulted in arrests in Austria, Belgium, Finland, France, Germany, Hungary, and Russia.

Last week, the Iranian Government publicly castrated a man as a result of evidence garnered in part by the probe.

During his arrest, the Iranian police discovered he was in possession of a small cache of highly suggestive children-sized lingerie. And that was it. Next stop, a guest spot on the long running, *The Holy Fazolli Show starring Rasheed Fazolli*. (For those unaware of Mr. Fazolli, he began his career as a Tom Jones-esque singer, billing himself as *The Don Juan of Tehran*. A falafel fetish in his 30's led to severe weight gain which cost him his singing career and precipitated his move to television, where he starred in the wildly popular *The Rollie Pollie Fazolli Show*. Following Iran's Islamic Revolution in 1979, the show was deemed "unworthy" and "not in keeping with Islamic values" and was immediately cancelled. But Rasheed changed with the times and soon reappeared on Iranian TV in *The Holy Fazolli Show*. Because of his longevity in the entertainment industry, Rasheed Fazolli is often referred to as the Regis Philbin of Iranian television.) At the request of his government, Mr. Fazolli broadcast the castration live for all to see. And it wasn't even Sweeps Week.

Sadly, new evidence has subsequently come to light casting doubt on the eunuch's involvement with the Dazzletown Club. One would have thought the fact that the man lived in a rural village without electricity, telephone, or a single computer within at least a 100-mile radius would have been a bit of red flag to the arresting officers, but no. It turned out it was DNA evidence collected from the children's lingerie found in his hut that led to his conviction. But subsequent testing determined that the lingerie in question had been worn exclusively by Wanda, the man's pet goat.

Several high-ranking U.S. officials protested the apparent lack of due process afforded the accused and the barbarity of his public castration. In response, Raif Susani, the Harvard-educated Iranian Foreign Minister, replied that they had simply followed the lead set by the U.S.

Government, whom he charged has consistently shown little concern over the number of innocent American men imprisoned and, in some cases, executed for crimes they did not commit.

In what proved to be a stinging indictment of the American judicial system, he went on to say, "Far more often than not in the United States, blacks are born in the face of brutal adversity, spending their youth in blighted neighborhoods where unemployment rates are five to six times that of the national average, where the only thing more plentiful than powerful and cheap narcotics are guns of every shape and caliber, and where their only chance for social redemption is severely undercut by the most inadequate and undercapitalized schools in the country. So, does it come as any real surprise that when white America sends their boys off to college as a commonplace rite of passage, far too many sons of the black community end up being shackled off to cold and dark prisons? And befitting their stature in American society, these young black men consistently face the most serious of criminal trials without adequate legal representation and, as a result, are regularly given the harshest of sentences; whereas whites in America, even those who commit the most heinous atrocities against the most trusting and vulnerable imaginable, i.e. a mother who slaughters her very own children for reasons so frivolous as to make one question the true nature of Man, are given far more lenient and compassionate sentences."

"Of course, blacks cheer when O.J. Simpson is allowed to go free, to the shock and disbelief of a white and fearful America. And why shouldn't they? Finally, a black man is afforded a slice of good ol' fashioned white man's justice, the same justice that has shielded whites from prosecution for their crimes against blacks since they were first brought to America as slaves. Ask yourself, in America's 250-year history, how many whites have killed blacks and yet never spent a single night in jail for their crimes? How many? More than most Caucasians would ever dare ponder, no less admit. But when one black man kills a white and gets away with it, when just a single black male is finally afforded the same justice as countless whites have enjoyed over the centuries, black America naturally rejoiced, having gotten their first notch on the scoreboard of equality, while the whites of your nation seethe like petulant poor sports at the loss of their shut out, even though the score is tens of thousands to one," Raif Susani said.

"I should also like to inform those Americans who so enjoy criticizing us with that all too familiar stare of U.S. superiority that even though the public castration may have been unjust and difficult to watch, they were not nearly as painful to sit through as some Ben Affleck movies. *Daredevil,* please. It was so bad, I had to walk out. And I saw it on a plane! And *Gigli*? I'd rather be castrated myself then sit through that turkey again!"

THE SILVER SHOES

After the incident at Old Algiers Point, Donn tried and tried to reach Charlotte, but she never answered her phone nor return any of his text messages. His attempts to bring her flowers, always found her not at home, or at least so he was told by Asa Washington. During the first week, Donn stopped by at least once a day, and usually more. By the middle of the second week, when it started to look as if Charlotte might have cast him aside for good, a sadness took hold of him. This was confirmed a few days into the third week after their disastrous date when he parked across the street and sat there for two maybe three hours keeping an eye on the entrance of the Remington for any sight of her. Nothing. Nothing.

One last try, he said to himself, three or four days after that. It could have even been longer; he didn't know. Days were melting together. Giving up hope, he started to think about leaving Los Angeles, but for where? Where would he go? Back home, no. New York? He loved New York, especially at Christmas, but couldn't see himself moving there. Seattle maybe. He always felt a certain fondness for Seattle but even that held no spark.

Maybe after one last try. Maybe then I'll be able to figure it out. Maybe after one last try…

And so, Donn returned to The Remington only to find Charlotte, once again, away. He politely asked Asa if he could wait. Although he didn't mention it, he would wait all night if he had to before giving up for good.

"Well, sir, I'm not one to say no, at least not often, but as much as I'd like to, I don't have the authority to allow you inside."

"I see. Okay, well, thanks."

Asa watched as Donn began a slow walk back to his Mustang. "Now if you was inclined as to wait out here, say in your car maybe, that might be construed as some kind of gray area, what with this bein' a free county and all. That is, should you be so inclined."

"Sure, that's no problem. I just want to see her, make sure she's ok. I'll just pull over there, out of the way, and if you need me to move, just holler. I really appreciate it, Asa. I really do."

Asa nodded and watched as Donn started his walk back to his car. 'Women…,' he thought, shaking his head. *God's got himself a wicked sense of humor, that's all I can say.*

Donn stopped, turned. "Have you seen Charlotte around much lately? Is she okay? I've been trying to reach her but I guess she's been busy or something."

Asa walked Donn back to his car. "You know, son, on my wedding day I was scared something awful. But I remember my pap lookin' me right in eye and sayin', 'Nothing to be frightened about, boy. Come on in, the water's fine.' And then he looked at my momma and gave her a little squeeze and that big ol' toothy grin of his. But then he looked right back at me, leaned over, and whispered, 'Water's fine, all right, especially if you like swimming in water so cold your willie just about breaks right off. Way I figures it, God created women to keep us from gettin' too happy and doin' even stupider nonsense than we already does. I's seen it a lot in my day. When a man starts gettin' too happy, before you know it, he finds his'self gettin' involved in all kinds of shenanigans. It's like automatic. One minute he's as happy as can be and the next he's up to his eyeballs in mischief he would have never even thought about doin' if he was miserable. So God made woman's job to be like, like, like a happiness vacuum cleaner, like their whole reason for bein' is to suck the happiness right out of us, every bit they can find — for our own good, of course. And I's gotta tell ya, from my experience, the ladies, they take their job very seriously indeed. Frankly, we don't stand a chance.' So, you just hang in there, hero. Things have a way of working out."

Donn pulled his car around the silent fountain and parked along the curb to the right of the porte-cochere, down closer to the side street that flanked The Remington's east property line. And there he waited.

Three o'clock became five without a sign of Charlotte, Laura, or Geoffrey. Donn sat and watched as Asa greeted everyone who passed his way. No one left without a smile on their face, such was the grace of the man. Every half hour or so, Asa did just as he was doing now, namely picking up the house phone, dialing, and then looking in Donn's direction. This time though he spoke at some length, but even then, Donn couldn't tell if he was actually having a conversation with someone or just leaving a message. After Asa hung up, Donn hopped out of his car and asked, "Was that Charlotte? Will she see me?"

"Who?" Asa asked in reply, his response delivered so unconvincingly as to make one wonder if he hadn't studied lying by watching Donald Trump anytime he opens his mouth.

"Charlotte. Was that Charlotte you were speaking to?"

"Son, did I ever tell you about the time before I was married, I waited nearly ten hours in front of her parent's house? Ten hours. We had just started courtin', it was like our first or second date or something, and all of a sudden, she flies off the handle for some reason or another and then takes off with one of her girlfriends. I went back to her house, but she wouldn't answer the door, so I just waited in my car. Well, I must've fallen asleep 'cause the next mornin' the police came 'round, woke me up and nearly arrested me for vagrancy. Me! I explained to 'em why I was there but it turns out I was waitin' in front of the wrong house. She actually lived one block over."

"I never told my wife about that. I mean, she thinks I'm a jackass for the smart things I do. You can just imagine what she'd think if she knew about that! Oh, mercy me."

"Asa, why won't Charlotte see me? She won't return my calls or texts. Is she okay? She hasn't said anything to you, has she?"

"Son, from my experience, it's better you don't know because as crazy as it makes you not knowing what you did wrong, if you *did* know, it would drive you right to the bughouse trying to figure out how that itty-bitty, teensy-weensy, microscopic bit of nothingness could possibly make someone — someone who says they love you sooo much — want to give you such a world of grief just for doing it. It just won't make no sense, no sense at all. So, trust me, son. You're better off not knowin' what ya' did. A lot better."

Asa put his hand on Don's shoulder and continued. "Anyway, just be patient. Like I said, things have a way of working out."

With the time nearing 6:30, Donn's cell phone rang.

"Donn, it's Geoffrey Zukor. I'm calling about Charlotte…"

Donn got a sick, hallow feeling in stomach, his heart beating faster and faster.

"What?" He couldn't believe what he was hearing. He pressed the phone hard against his ear, his head lowered. The world fell away.

Really? From the fall? He wondered. *Oh, my God…*

Thirty seconds later, Donn tossed his cellphone onto the passenger seat and gunned his Mustang. He slammed it into gear, tires instantly screeching across the stamped concrete drive. Asa turned, instinctively stepping back. A puzzled look came over his face. In response, Donn yelled, "I've been waiting in front of the wrong house, too."

THE SILVER SHOES

Dr. Isaac Elder's office was exactly as one might expect. Warm, dark woods paneled the walls and shuttered the windows, shutters that probably hadn't been opened once in the last twenty years, except for the occasional cleaning. The wall opposite the entry door was lined with floor-to-ceiling bookcases. Between their fluted edges sat row after row of neat leather volumes, the chattel of his trade no doubt, all of which serving as a backdrop for the room's focal point, an exquisite Chippendale writing desk. The desktop was largely without accessory, save a cut crystal glass filled with a variety of vintage fountain pens bearing the markings of Michel Perchin, Pelikan, S.T. Dupont and the like, and a small, weathered brass plaque with the inscription:

TRUTH

Behind the desk, with a nod to comfort over aesthetics, sat a somber, high-backed leather chair, whereas in front and to the right sat the desk's complement, a Georgian, which served as the doctor's usual perch while *in session*. A large button-tufted leather sofa was centered on the wall to the left, over which hung a mahogany-framed original oil. It was a landscape of sorts, a depiction of a man in shadowed silhouette standing alone under the canopy of a billowing tree, looking out across a darkened body of water onto a distant but beckoning shore.

Taken altogether, this was a solemn and earnest setting; there was no room for the inconsequential here.

A single buzz broke the tension. Dr. Elder's long sculpted fingers reached for the phone.

"Thank you. Please show him in."

Not but seconds later, the door opened, and Donn bounded forth, winded from his hurrying. His heart thumped heavy in his chest. It didn't help that from the doctor's waiting room he thought he heard Geoffrey Zukor yelling.

As he entered, both Geoffrey and Laura turned to greet him. Donn grew more worried than even when he saw the strained look on Geoffrey's face. Laura's eyes were red.

"What is it? Where's Charlotte?"

"Donn, this is Dr. Isaac Elder. He's Charlotte's psychiatrist," said Laura.

"How do you do."

"It's very nice meeting you," Dr. Elder replied, his well-steeped British accent conveying both charm and authority. "Thank you for coming so quickly."

"Sure. Is Charlotte here?"

"She's in the hospital next door. She's been there for several days."

"Why? What happened? Is she all right?"

"She's fine now. I met with her earlier today. She wants to see you. All of you."

THE SILVER SHOES

The glistening Otis elevator cab delivered them to the ninth floor. At the end of the corridor, they exited the building, traveling a sky bridge that connected the offices of the Cedars-Sinai Medical Center to the main hospital tower. As they reached the other side, Dr. Elder removed his clip-on hospital identification card and slid it through an almost imperceptible card reader attached to the right side of the bridge's guardrail. A small green LED flashed three times confirming his status and triggered the glass door, which was absent of any entry hardware, to open.

As they entered the hospital corridor, Dr. Elder glanced back toward Laura's feet and then stopped.

"If you don't mind walking down one flight of stairs, we could save some time?"

Both Geoffrey and Donn started to turn toward Laura, but she beat them to it with, "I do it every day."

The seriousness of their steps reverberated against the steel treads of the service stair. No one spoke until Dr. Elder opened the metal fire door to the right of a sign which read, 5th Floor. "Sorry about the noise."

Geoffrey wondered how they ended up on the fifth floor after leaving the office tower on the ninth and then going down but a single level, but he didn't ask. He needed to see Charlotte and didn't want to interject anything that might lead to even a moment's delay.

Geoffrey had been the second to arrive at Dr. Elder's office and the doctor was no more forthcoming with him about Charlotte's condition than he had been with Laura. Donn arrived less than 20 minutes later, but even that wait had proved almost unbearable for Geoffrey. The idea of his Charlotte being in the hospital without him knowing why and that he was still being kept in the dark regarding her condition, was simply too much to ask of him. Shortly after he got there, he leaned over to Laura and whispered, "Maybe you could excuse yourself for a minute and then go see what you can find out. Maybe you could check the hospital's computer system or something."

Laura looked toward Dr. Elder, who was working at his desk. Geoffrey wanted to look also, but didn't, afraid it might alert the doctor of his plan.

Before Laura could reply, Dr. Elder looked up and said, "I know this must be very hard, but Charlotte specifically asked me to try and gather all three of you so let's give Mr. Olson a few more minutes, shall we?"

"Sure," said Geoffrey as if the thought of doing anything but had never crossed his mind. "We'll wait. It's fine. We'll just wait right here," which he followed with, "Wait. Wait. Wait." Laura shot him a look, a warning. She knew that tone and was afraid where it might lead.

"Waiting's no problem at all. I mean I just found out that my daughter, my one and only daughter, has been seeing a psychiatrist, which no one bothered to tell me about and now for some reason she's ended up in the hospital, where I guess she's been for a couple of days without me even knowing about it, but hey, what's the big deal, right? I mean that's no reason to be alarmed, is it? People get pedicures and end up having to spend a couple of weeks in the hospital, so I'm sure this couldn't be anything serious, right? So, we'll wait. Waiting's fine. Not a problem. We'll just wait, wait, wait. In fact, if anyone's hungry, I know this great little Italian joint on Pico. You'll love it, Doc. The food's not very good but it's expensive as hell which kind of makes up for it, don't you think? Anybody want to run over there? And maybe afterwards, we could all catch a show. We can always stop back by here later on just to make sure that good ol' what's-her-name is feeling all right. What do you think, Doc? Sounds good, right?"

When the doctor failed to reply, Geoffrey looked sharply into his eyes. He raised his index finger and through clenched teeth said, "I don't know what in the hell you think you're doing, but I am going to see my daughter now. DO YOU UNDERSTAND? RIGHT NOW!"

Laura's eyes grew tall, almost erasing her forehead. She looked down and away, raising her right hand to shield her view; this, she couldn't watch. What she knew of Dr. Elder did not bode well for

Geoffrey in the least. In all of her years at Cedars, she worked with him but once, a particularly unpleasant experience. He had returned a press release she wrote for him with a stinging handwritten note across the top saying,

-No thanks. Not in the market for girlish hyperbole at the moment, but I'll be sure to give you a ring when I am. I do have a question for you though: Do you come from a long line of used car salesmen? Perhaps you should consider returning to the family business.

-Isaac

It angered her for months. She repeatedly brought it up with Dr. Sheinman, on each occasion demanding an apology, which, despite her threats to quit if not promptly tendered, never arrived.

Dr. Elder slowly rose from his chair and inhaled deeply, a dragon warming his breath. His eyes flickered in the two dark caves beneath his craggy brows. As if in slow motion, his lips began to form the first syllable of his response. But then, a single buzz of his phone succeeded in doing what few in his lifetime had ever even attempted — namely, to keep him from speaking his mind. Donn had arrived.

THE SILVER SHOES

Dr. Elder stopped near a nurse's station and addressed those following. He spoke softly but with great command. "Okay, we are here. I must speak to Charlotte's nurse for a moment and then we'll go in—*if* she's not sleeping. If she *is* sleeping, we will fix a time and reconvene back here later tonight. Do you understand?"

Geoffrey nodded in mock agreement, knowing that if she was sleeping, she wouldn't be for long, unless she could sleep through his harangue at the side of her bed, demanding to know what in the hell was going on.

"Wait right here. It will literally be less than two minutes." Then, looking directly at Geoffrey, he asked, "Can you wait two minutes?"

"Of course," Geoffrey replied, with a nod.

But the instant Dr. Elder turned away, Geoffrey began scanning the corridor around him, trying to figure out which room his daughter was in. Laura stopped him.

"Geoffrey, listen to me. Do you know who that guy is?"

"Charlotte's physiatrist." Then he turned to Donn. "Laura knew Charlotte was seeing a physiatrist. Did you know Charlotte was seeing a physiatrist?"

"Yes."

"You both knew? Then why didn't I know she was seeing a physiatrist? Fine. I'll just start keeping secrets from the both of you. Let's see how you like it!" Granted, not the world's most mature response.

"Geoffrey, listen to me," Laura interrupted sternly. "He'll be back in a minute. Dr. Isaac Elder is not just Charlotte's physiatrist. He is perhaps the most highly-regarded physiatrist practicing today — in the world. He has been on the cover of both *Time* and *Newsweek* and has been credited with reinventing the art of psychotherapy and making it relevant for the 21st century. Many believe he will take a place beside Freud and Jung before his work is through. I could go on and on but there isn't time. The only reason he agreed to see Charlotte was because Dr. Sheinman asked him to as personal favor."

"Dr. Sheinman? Even Dr. Sheinman knows??" Geoffrey asked incredulously. "I can't believe it!!"

Laura threw up her hands. "You're impossible."

"I might agree with that," Dr. Elder chimed in, returning to the group.

None of this stopped Geoffrey from leaning toward Laura and whispering, "If I find out Asa knows, I'm gonna jump right off my balcony. I swear to God I will."

"All right, if she's not sleeping, we'll go in," Dr. Elder continued. "Here are the conditions. After the pleasantries, I will steer the conversation. This is *not* a social gathering. You are here to be listeners. Do you understand? Listeners. Many people find my approach to the work cold, harsh, and unsympathetic. They are right—it is. I have one goal and one goal only, to actively assist my patients to acknowledge, admit, avow, confess, or concede the essential truth of their lives. Truth is often like pus in a boil. It must be freed with a lance, not coddled. You might do well to remind yourselves not to interfere. This is not about you. Tonight, we are here for Charlotte. Agreed?"

His eyes swept from Donn to Laura and finally to Geoffrey, lingering on the latter as if to reinforce the importance of his compliance. With nods all around, he said, "Follow me."

As Dr. Elder began walking, Geoffrey whispered, "Truth is like pus? Pus?" Laura waved him off. Then she took his hand and followed the doctor to the far side of the nurse's station and then made a right at the next corridor to the second door on the left. The doctor made eye contact with each of them and then knocked lightly. Geoffrey raised his eyebrows as if to say, *What? You call that a knock?*

But before he could decide whether or not to say something or just push it open himself, someone inside said faintly, "Hello?"

Dr. Elder opened the door and stuck his head inside. "Charlotte? It's Dr. Elder. I have some people here to see you."

"Great," she said, but her tone said otherwise.

THE SILVER SHOES

TRUTH IS THE ARROW; COURAGE IS THE BOW.

"If you're not up for some company now, we could—" But before Dr. Elder could finish his sentence, Geoffrey sidestepped past him and was through the door. Once inside though, the sight of Charlotte stopped him cold. Suddenly, he found himself wanting, needing to step backwards.

"Oh my God, Charlotte…" He thought he might be sick. He had seen her like this before. The memories came so strong he felt as if he were in two places at once. "What, what happened?"

Dr. Elder cracked the door wider. Laura moved through, stopping at Geoffrey's side. Donn followed, hanging back several steps to their left. All were stunned into silence.

The room was dark, save the cold, blue blur of a fluorescent lamp above Charlotte's headboard, the fixture casting an eerie backlight on the beehive of bandages wrapping her head. The image was far more disturbing and strange than any of the three dared imagine.

Dr. Elder's voice split the gloom. "All right if I turn on a light?"

From what Geoffrey, Laura, and Donn could make out in the dark, they were not so sure.

"Please," replied Charlotte.

With the flick of a switch, the newly minted bride of Frankenstein before them vanished in thin air, and in her place sat sweet, wounded Charlotte, her eyes blinking to adjust.

Geoffrey moved to her. "Are you alright? What happened?"

Laura and Donn followed, their faces also full of concern.

"I'm fine, I'm… fine. You don't need to worry."

"I don't need to worry? I think I've heard that before," replied Geoffrey.

Laura stiffened; there was that tone again and this was certainly neither the time nor the place for another rant. And so as subtly as possible, she grabbed Geoffrey's right hand with her left and then pressed her thumbnail deep enough into his skin to make an impression. He got the message. Without turning away from Charlotte, he nodded his compliance. He took a deep breath and tried to smile. Laura withdrew her nail.

"First of all, I'm fine. Really, I am. A lot better than I look, I'm sure. And I'm sorry, really sorry I didn't tell any of you about this beforehand, especially you Dad. I'm sorry, but I couldn't. I wanted to. I've wanted to for so long, to talk about things, but I couldn't…" Charlotte looked away, her eye's filling with tears. Geoffrey could feel the stares from both Laura and Donn, but his focus remained on his daughter.

"Charlotte," her father said, "we don't have to talk about this now. Why don't we just focus on getting you better and then we can–"

"That's what I found out, Dad. I'll never be better till I talk about it. That's why I wanted everyone to come. Is that okay?"

"Of course. Of course, it is," he said softly.

"It's okay to talk about… mom? In front of everyone?"

Geoffrey didn't know what to say. He didn't *want* to talk about this, not any of it. And certainly, Victoria was the last thing he wanted to discuss, but how could he say no? He glanced over to Dr. Elder who was staring at him over the rim his glasses, clearly expecting him to do the right thing.

Geoffrey inhaled, trying to relieve the painful ball of tension in his stomach. "Charlotte, we can talk about anything you want. Anything… —if you really want to."

Charlotte looked over at Donn. "And you…, I'm so sorry." And she started to cry, a deep cry. She buried her face in her hands. "I wanted to call you. I tried and tried but I just couldn't. I didn't have the words." She moved her hand towards his. He took it immediately and their thoughts returned to the lone cypress on Old Algiers Point, holding each other, staring up at the stars.

Then Charlotte looked to Laura, who stood so lovingly next to her father, his perfect complement. "And you… I want to thank you for all the things you've done for me… and my dad. I never had anyone in my life like you before." And she started to cry again.

"Charlotte, don't be silly. I'm the one who should be saying thank you… to both of you." She moved to the other side of Geoffrey and put her hand over Charlotte's, just below the tape securing an I.V.

"He really loves you," Charlotte half-whispered.

"And I love really love him," Laura replied in kind.

"Charlotte," interrupted Dr. Elder flatly. "Everyone knows you're a sweet girl. Is that why you gathered us here, so you could tell everyone how much you love them and how much they should love you?"

Charlotte looked down. "No."

"So why *are* we here?"

Although her head remained bowed, her eyes moved up to meet his, uncertain she could really heed his call to arms.

"Charlotte, before we started our adventure together, I told you we would meet six times and six times only. This is the sixth. If you have something to say, and I think you do, then find the courage to say it. Either that, or we can have our final session privately in my office next week or the week following." He looked at his watch. "What would you like to do?"

Charlotte closed her eyes and took a deep breath. When they first met, Charlotte could not speak. Dr. Elder cut their initial session off after just ten minutes, handing her the card of another psychiatrist and shooing her out the door with, "Of my patients, I ask only one thing: Courage. You have disappointed me, but far, far worse, you have disappointed yourself. Goodbye."

Charlotte showed up for her second session anyway. He kept her waiting for an hour, finally walking into the waiting room and greeting her with, "What are you doing here?"

When she didn't answer, Dr. Elder barked to his secretary, "Grace, grab the Yellow Pages. Missy here is looking for a mind reader. Or perhaps you could find her someone that reads palms, or tealeaves. Or maybe an astrologist. The girl might like that, you know, the stars and all — so romantic. And the best part is, it doesn't take any courage at all. Perfect for a little coward like her. And if none of those suits her fancy, try and hook her up with a babysitter, will you?"

With that, he turned to Charlotte. His eyes burned beneath the sharp ledge of his brows as he peered out at her over the upper rim of his glasses, glasses that looked every bit as old as its wearer. "Missy, save yourself the bus fare and don't come back again, all right? Grace will take it from here. Oh, and please don't leave without dropping off a check. I was told last time you forgot as well. Funny, I wouldn't have taken you for a coward or a cheat, but I guess I was wrong on both fronts, now wasn't I? Well, thank you for coming. I hope one day you will be able to eke out at least some small morsel of enjoyment from that miserable little life of yours." Then, as he passed, he leaned toward her and whispered, "Though in the direction you're heading, I sincerely doubt that will be possible. And that is the truth. Good day, Missy." And with that he retired back into his office.

THE SILVER SHOES

Three minutes later, she stood before his desk. Dr. Elder did not acknowledge her presence.

"My name is Charlotte."

He looked up briefly. "Lucky you."

"I thought you helped people like me."

"Sorry. Can't be done."

"That's not true."

"Really? And what do you know of truth? Without courage, there can be no truth."

Charlotte considered this. "So," she shrugged, "maybe I do need a little more… courage sometimes. I know that. So how do I, you know… get some?"

"What kind of question is that? Who do you think I am, the Wizard of Oz?"

Charlotte wanted to respond but had no idea what to say. Dr. Elder let her stew, staring deep into her as if he were looking beyond her eyes to the spirit within. She found his study of her so painful, she suddenly wanted, *needed* to get out of there. She leaned away from him but was unable to break his stare. The door was calling her, but try as she might, she could not answer. She knew now that coming back into his office had been a mistake, a big mistake. The distant lights may be beckoning, but the water was far too deep and dangerous to cross.

When his stare did break, she was finally able to breathe again. She put her head down, and not daring to look back into his eyes, turned to leave, to run, to make her escape, her escape from a room she knew she would never return. As she reached the door, her hand found the brass doorknob surprisingly cold. From behind her, a voice said, "You already have the silver shoes, Dorothy."

She stopped.

Silver shoes? He knows they were silver shoes?

Charlotte turned, carried by her curiosity.

The doctor continued. "And a fine brain, and good heart, and all the courage you will ever need. You already have it all. This old wizard has nothing for you for you are perfect just the way you are. It's just as Glinda said, 'All you have to do is to knock the heels together three times and command the shoes to carry you wherever you wish to go.' And that's what makes it all so tragic. You have the potential for greatness, you've had it all along, but you refuse to use it. Here—"

Dr. Elder stood and moved to his right, sliding a bookcase ladder with him as he went. From a shelf near the top, he carefully removed a stout beige volume with large squares of green filling both its front and back covers. He stared at it admiringly.

"*The Wonderful Wizard of Oz.* First edition. Over one hundred years old now and still perhaps the most important children's book ever written. And although its story is woven deep into the fabric of Americana and is known to virtually everyone, the book goes largely unread, its revolutionary message completely overlooked, mistaken for the crudely sentimental, *There's no place like home.* Ah, Hollywood and the power of cliché." He shook his head in silence and then returned his attention to Charlotte. "You're an avid reader, probably always have been, right?"

"Yes, sir. How did you know?"

"Your obviously intelligent, yet you've mis-buttoned your blouse. The first time you were here, there was something askew with your belt, if I'm remembering right. All signs that you're more there than here. Those observations, coupled with my finely honed intuitive sense, was how I reached my conclusion," he said, nodding, every bit the professor. "Well, that and the fact you've had a book with you both times you've come to see me and, if memory serves, the first one was different from the one you're holding now. Perhaps that might have been a bit of a tip off as well," he said with a sly smile.

"Oh, right."

"I'm guessing you've already read this," he said, handing the book to Charlotte, "but if you'd like to have another go at it, just drop it by Grace when you're done."

She was stunned by his generosity and the trust he put in her. "Oh, I—"

"What is it you want from your life, Charlotte?"

Feeling suddenly on the spot, Charlotte didn't know what to say.

"I see. Well, like I said, just drop it by Grace when you're through. Have a good day." He returned his attention to the papers on his desk.

"Other people seem to be happy. Do you think they're really happy or just, you know, kind of pretending to happy?"

"Why would they pretend to be happy?"

"Well, because everyone pretends to be happy. They think everyone else is happy, so they pretend to be happy too, just so everyone around them won't see how unhappy they really are."

"A world in which no one is truly happy... That's not as original an idea as you might think. And not an accurate one either," Dr. Elder replied with a dismissive shake of his head. "Charlotte, I'm going to ask you one last time. Find the courage to do nothing but simply answer the question. What is it you want from your life?"

"Well, do you think that it, it might be possible for—"

He pushed a button on his phone. "Grace, come get the girl, darling. Straight off, please."

"I'd like to be happy—," and then she added "—er... A little."

"A little, I see. And is there something wrong with wanting to be a lot happier? Say gobs and gobs and gobs happier? Wanting not just a tiny taste of happiness but a huge quadruple scoop of happiness on a sugar cone? Is there something wrong with wanting that?"

Charlotte didn't know. How could she? She had never been "happy," at least not that she could ever remember. She'd even come to accept the fact that it wasn't part of her make up, it just wasn't who she was. Happiness was for others, fine. Let them enjoy the forced laughter, the imbecilic antics, and all the other screeching gaiety she witnessed walking the corridors of her high school. But that life was not for her. It just wasn't. She watched, always the silent spectator, the perennial outsider, as the happiness parade passed her by. So disconnected and detached from all the goings on around her, she might as well have been watching it on television. And so, she turned her back and walked away, shunning everyone happiness seemed to come so easily to. More and more, she found herself even looking down on "the happy," privately dismissing the whole lot of them as frivolous, fake, stupid; theirs was an idiotic pastime, a waste of a life even. The pursuit of happiness… Certainly that was not the road less traveled. Anyone could see that. Or at least so she told herself.

But was that really the truth? Was it? A part of her wondered if her feelings were just a wall she had carefully constructed, nothing more than an ever-continuing rejection of a lover who, in reality, had rejected her long before and moved on. Was it not important to her because it truly wasn't important, or had she shunned happiness because happiness had already shunned her? Whichever it was, the one thing she knew for certain was the most obvious truth of all: She wasn't happy and despite what she told herself, she knew she wasn't happy about it.

"I do want to be a lot happier — I do. I need to be — gobs and gobs happier. But I don't think I can be. I don't. I don't…" Her voice was soft and sad, her words an admission of how helpless and unhappy she truly was.

"I had a patient stand right where you are standing now and he told me he wanted to fly. Then he stretched out his arms kind of like Superman and started jumping up and down. He stood right there and jumped up and down for a good five minutes. When he stopped and told me he used to know how to fly but he forgot and he wanted me to help him remember. All of this true. You know what else is true? He was a lot closer to being able to fly than you are to being happy. At least he could tell me what he wanted. You know, the funny thing about him, funny to me at least, was that he was afraid of heights! Isn't that hysterical? Even he thought that was funny! We had quite a laugh about that, we did. He was truly a lovely chap."

"Think what you will about him, but he had courage. It takes courage for someone to change their circumstance, to take charge of their life. Do you have the courage it takes to knock your heels together and finally take command of your silver shoes?"

Charlotte thought for a moment. She wanted to get this right. "I guess I do. I mean you said—"

"There can be no guessing. There is only yes. Every other answer, at its heart, is a hedge. It lacks commitment. It's nothing more than a form of no dressed up to look like a yes. Do you understand?"

"Yes."

"Good. And so it comes down to this: Do you have the courage it takes to sit in this office? To speak the truth, no matter how ugly, or scary, or disgusting, or humiliating, or revealing it might be? No matter how bad it may make you look or feel? No matter whom it may hurt or incriminate? Do you have that much courage, Charlotte? Do you really?"

"Yes," she replied, but then added, "I th—"

Dr. Elder's brows lowered like storm clouds over the room. "You what? There is only yes. Anything else is a form of no. If you want to say no, that's fine. Go ahead and say it. Shout it out for all I care, but don't sugarcoat it. Don't lie to yourself or to me. The truth requires clarity. And so, I'll ask you again..." The doctor removed his glasses and clamped a hand over his eyes, as if divining from a source far beyond that room. Then he asked in all solemnity, "Do you have the courage it takes to sit in this office? The courage to speak the truth, no matter how ugly, or scary, or humiliating, or revealing it may be? Do you? Because there's no point in starting our grand adventure together if you don't; there's no point at all." And the doctor sat there, motionless, and said nothing more.

Finally, Charlotte spoke. "Yes, I... do."

He opened his eyes. "Yes, that's right, you do. You most certainly do," he said, smiling, his face suddenly alight. "Can you feel it, Charlotte, that small kindling of courage inside you? Can you feel its power, its conviction, its authority?"

Charlotte nodded. She could. She really could. Or at least she thought she could.

"It's a wonderful feeling, isn't it?"

"Yes, it is. It's a wonderful feeling." Charlotte was now smiling too.

The doctor nodded, shot up from his seat, and briskly walked right past her, out of the room. A moment later, he poked his head back in. "Why are you just standing there? Come on, follow me!"

With five long strides, he was back in the patient waiting area. Charlotte ran to keep up. "Grace, pop in next door and ask Lorraine and, oh, the terribly big girl, what was her name again?"

"Shaquana, sir. But I don't think—"

"Right, Shaquana. I don't know why I can't remember that. Shaquana." To himself, he muttered, "Shaquana. Shaq. Shaq, like that basketball fellow, Shaq. As big as Shaq. Right. Shaq. Shaquana. I think I've got it." Then he added, confidently, "Right! So, Gracie, do run next door and ask Lorraine and Shaquana to stop over directly, if they'd be so kind."

Grace sprang to her feet, despite being what appeared to be the doctor's senior by a decade. She did not start walking though, but rather, standing ever so erect, she removed her glasses and said, "Sir, about Shaquana. Last time she was here, she took it rather badly. I was told she was a wreck about things for a week. She's a federal employee, and as you know, even lodged a complaint against you with her guild. They've been calling and wanting to meet with you, sir, to discuss the matter."

"Her guild? Fat people have their own guild in the States? Well, that makes perfect sense, now doesn't it? Anyway, run fetch them, will you? Both of them. Tell them oh, whatever you need to. You could even tell them Snoop Dogg is here if you have to, but do have them pop over directly, if they'd be so kind."

"Sir, Shaquana was very angry—"

"Grace, I am not asking you," he barked with a dismissive wave. And with that, she was out the door.

"Charlotte, consider this your entrance exam to Happiness University. If you pass, I will take you on. If you fail, you will have to look elsewhere for guidance. I say this with all sincerity. It is not posturing or a bluff. Do you understand?"

"Yes."

"Good. My work is my life, Charlotte, and with the precious small morsel I have left, I have chosen to work only with the courageous, the truth tellers. If you are one of them, you will be welcomed here. If you are not, I cannot permit you to waste my time or yours. This will be your one and only opportunity to show me you are capable of speaking the truth, no matter how humiliating, or scary, or embarrassing it might be, without regard for whom it may hurt or incriminate. To pass this test, you only need one thing: Courage — courage enough to speak the truth."

Dr. Elder knew the enormity of the thing he asked. Most who had attempted it had failed. He had. For 27 years he lived the straight life of a married heterosexual man.

THE SILVER SHOES

Lorraine Diamante and Shaquana Saunders stood before them, a picture of opposites. Lorraine was blushing, clearly flattered to be invited back into the prestigious doctor's office again. Shaquana, on the other hand, glared at him as if he were her good-for-nothing husband who just returned from a two-week *humpathon* at the Mustang Ranch, where he managed to squander their entire life savings. Every cell in her clenched body oozed, *Just give me one good reason...*

"How nice of you to drop in, ladies. Charlotte, these are our friends from next door. This is the lovely Lorraine and her co-worker, uh, oh God, uh, Shaq... uille... oneila?" Dr. Elder would have been beaten to a pulp had Shaquana not been so preoccupied looking around the room.

"Where's Snoop? You said I could meet Snoop Dogg!" barked Lady Shaquana with all the gentility of a Marseille dockworker.

"Oh, right, right… Uh, he called a bit ago, Grace, while you were out, and said he was running a wee bit late but should be here anytime now. Well, actually it was one of his people that called for him. Did you know he has his own people? I thought that sort of thing was frowned on here in the states, but apparently not. Grace, when he does pop in, be sure to ask him how much his people were, will you? Perhaps he might know where to get some on the cheap? I mean, maybe we should pick up a few of our own. It seems like we're the only ones in this town that don't have our own people. It's rather embarrassing, really."

"Anyway ladies, while you're waiting for Snoop, maybe you could help Charlotte and I clear up a few things, if you'd be so kind. So, Charlotte, about your mother then, you say her breasts are large. Would you say they're as large and firm as Lorraine's here?"

"Dr. Elder!" exclaimed Lorraine, trying to hide her delight over her anatomy once again being the topic of conversation. "Why are you always talking about my breasts?!?"

"Because there's so much to talk about, now isn't there?" He then turned to Charlotte. "So are your mother's breasts as large as Lorraine's?"

Charlotte looked up at him, horrified to be asked such a thing, especially in the company of others. She lowered her head so much it seemed to disappear between her shoulders. Perhaps she was regressing into a past life where she worked as a guillotine tester.

Immediately, Dr. Elder stepped between Charlotte and his visitors, obscuring their view. With his right hand, he forcibly grabbed her jaw and raised her head with sufficient squeeze to transform her mouth into fish lips.

His harsh, fast whisper penetrated her fortress of solitude. "Look at me! That behavior will get you nothing except more stifled suffering, misery, and loneliness. Is that what you want for your life? Because if it is, I'll have no part of it. The decision is yours, Charlotte. I will ask you a half dozen questions, maybe less. Most will only require a simple yes or no answer. But you must be truthful and that will take courage. Courage! Let the chips fall where they may. Your only allegiance is to the truth. I will not coddle you. Repeat this over and over to yourself: *I speak the truth. I speak the truth. I speak the truth.* And then answer my questions loud enough for all to hear. If you do not, I will leave this room and not see you again. On that, I swear. Do you understand? Now speak the truth, damn it! Speak it!"

Dr. Elder turned back to his visitors with a polite smile. "So, your mother's breasts may be large, Charlotte, but are they as large and fantastically buoyant as Lorraine's here?"

Charlotte looked toward Lorraine, her eyelids a dam of tears. She was trembling. It took nearly all of her strength for her lips to mouth a silent, "No."

"What did you say, probably so?"

Charlotte could not answer.

"Charlotte?" She could say nothing more. Tears ran down her cheeks.

Dr. Elder turned to her and said softly, sadly, "Goodbye, my dear," and walked away.

THE SILVER SHOES

Down by two with less than a second left on the clock, Charlotte trembled from head to toe, bound in pent-up silence. Tear tracks lined her cheeks. Then, out of sheer desperation, she opened her mouth and hurled a full-court *Hail Mary,* bursting forth with, "THOSE ARE THE BIGGEST BOOBS I'VE EVER SEEN IN MY ENTIRE LIFE!"

Dr. Elder reappeared instantly. "Yes, they are! They most certainly are!" he said, overjoyed. To Grace, he added, "I think she's got it!"

"So Charlotte, you would agree with me then that Lorraine's breasts are rather large?"

"LARGE, NO! THEY'RE HUMUNGOUS!" Charlotte shouted even louder.

"Humongous?!? By Jove, she's got it!" exclaimed the good doctor once again. "I think she's got it!"

And with that, music blossomed from the My Fair Lady Orchestra as Dr. Elder's waiting room took center stage at Broadway's Mark Hellinger Theatre for a very special rendition of *The Rain in Spain.*

[VERSE]

DR. ELDER

And how is she built, our sweet Lorraine?

CHARLOTTE

Like a freight train! Like a freight train!

DR. ELDER

Oh, please won't you describe them once again.

CHARLOTTE

I won't refrain! They're big as Maine!

[CHORUS]

DR. ELDER

Lorraine, your frame is driving me insane!

CHARLOTTE

Their like two planes!

DR. ELDER

Lorraine, your frame could make this gay man wane!

LORRAINE

I'll bring champagne!

[VERSE]

GRACE

And who has far more breasts than brains?

CHARLOTTE

It's Loraine! It's Loraine!

GRACE

How can she lug them all around without back strain?

CHARLOTTE

She needs a crane! A crane!

[CHORUS]

DR. ELDER, CHARLOTTE, GRACE, & SHAQUANA

Lorraine, your frame is utterly insane!

[A spot hits PATSY as her head rises from the orchestra pit]

PATSY

So what's her name?

DR. ELDER, CHARLOTTE, GRACE, & SHAQUANA
Lorraine, your janes are larger than Ukraine!

[ASA WASHINTON appears Stage Left, handing
Loraine an umbrella whose canopy is shaped like
the top-down silhouette of a woman with two
large breasts]

ASA

In case it rains!

[VERSE]

PATSY

Won't someone please tell me her name?

CHARLOTTE & GRACE

It's Loraine! It's Loraine!

[RAE appears Stage Right as ROSIE appears
Stage Left, both talking on the phone]

RAE & ROSIE

A girl like that should be ashamed!

PATSY

She's Geoffrey's flame!

RAE & ROSIE

(Spoken) Oy vey!

His flame!

[CHORUS/FINALE]

(Dr. Elder takes one of Lorraine's hands and kneels as if proposing.)

DR. ELDER, CHARLOTTE, GRACE, SHAQUANA, ASA,
PATSY, RAE, AND ROSIE

Lorraine, your frame could make that gay man wane!

DR. ELDER

No question, she's got it!

DR. ELDER, CHARLOTTE, GRACE, SHAQUANA, ASA,
PATSY, RAE, AND ROSIE

Lorraine, your frame is utterly insane!

After the song reached its rousing conclusion, they were returned to Dr. Elder's office where he shouted, "Well done, Charlotte, well done! I knew you could do it! Bravo, my girl! But now, take heed, for your most difficult trial is at hand. The time has come for us to discuss… your mother's weight." And with that, Dr. Elder executed a long, slow head movement toward Shaquana.

"OOOoooohhh no you don't! I'm in no mood for any of your tomfoolery unless you're hankerin' to be carried out of here with a lump on your head bigger than both of Lorraine's *chimichangas* combined. And that be some major league bump, Doc! Do we understand each other?"

"Shaq uh… laka… laka? I would never do anything to insult you, dear. Is that why you think I invited you over? No, no, no, no, no. I am a doctor, a scientist of the mind. My interests are in healing souls, not belittling them. But I am certain you would not mind, understanding that it is purely in the interest of medicine, if I asked Charlotte here a few questions about her mother's weight, now would you? And just so that we have a common frame of reference, we might, from time to time, compare her mother's figure to yours. Just like we did with Loraine's. Nothing more than that. Now that's not a problem, is it?"

"Oh, I see. In the interest of science? Yeah, right. And is that why, Doc, last time you invited me over here you said something about me being bigger than the houseboat you rented on Lake Havasu? Hmmmm? Was that in the interest of science?" Shaquana's face compressed into the world's most sensitive insult detection system, with safety off and built-in "auto-retribution" feature fully engaged. "Bigger than a houseboat on Lake Havasu? Is that how you described my figure, Doctor? Hmmmm? I just want ta hear you say it one more time…"

"Me? Oh, uh, I don't think that I uh, well, you know, ever, probably, compared you to a houseboat on Lake Shaq-asu, I mean Havasu, I don't think, exactly. I mean, I guess some might say, perhaps, you might be, you know, considered, perhaps by some, a few I'm sure, a very, very few, in fact, to, well, in some very small way resemble, kind of, uh, but certainly, not all, I might add, certainly not all, but perhaps some might, you know, might, uh, well—"

Grace interrupted. "Charlotte, the doctor seems to have misplaced his courage. You don't see it lying about on the floor anywhere, do you dear?"

"No, no I don't," Charlotte replied. "And there aren't any chips down here either. There must be someone around here that's afraid to just, 'Let them fall where they may.' Any idea whom that might be, Grace?"

"Yes, come to think of it, perhaps I do," Grace replied. "Terribly sad, isn't it? I mean, you try and *suggest* that inviting a certain someone to our offices was perhaps ill advised, but what do you get for your efforts, for all of your concern? You get ordered about like a dog. That's what you get! Well, there she is, Doctor, and she's waiting. Why don't tell Shaquana what you really think of her figure?"

"Charlotte, do not fall under the influence of this woman here," Dr. Elder cautioned, flicking his right index finger toward Grace. "Seems lovely at first, doesn't she, lovely. But, in truth, she's a bad sort, this one is. Particularly wicked to those who have shown her every kindness over the years. By the way, if you ever need to reach Grace at home, just dial 1-800-I-TOLD-U-SO. International callers can reach her at: 1-800-AND-I-RUB-IT-IN-WITH-RELISH-AT-EVERY-OPPORTUNITY. Wicked sort, this one. Don't say I didn't warn you."

Grace, completely unbothered by his comments, countered with, "Doctor, if you won't be needing me for a moment, perhaps you wouldn't mind if I ran outside, lifted my leg, and had a tinkle on a nearby tree? The bladder on this old dog isn't what it used to be."

Dr. Elder ignored her and continued speaking to Charlotte. "And don't be taken in by all the cutesy little pictures of children on her desk. I don't have a clue who they are. I wouldn't be surprised to find out they're photos of people she's actually bumped off over the years. She can be vicious, this one can. Vicious. Keep your distance."

"Charlotte," Grace added, "you are witnessing the same charm that brought Dr. Elder the rare distinction of being the only person in history to be dismissed from both Oxford and Cambridge, as both a student and a professor. That's quite an accomplishment when you think about it. And as for these *cutesy little pictures,* they are of our grandchildren." Her voice softened when she spoke of them. "I can't say our marriage turned out as expected, but still, warts and all, the very best thing I did in my life was to marry this man."

Dr. Elder looked down at his wife of twenty-seven years and best friend for nearly fifty and shook his head. "Sorry I barked at you, love. I don't know where I'd be without you, I truly don't. Can you forgive this old fool?" Dr. Elder wrapped his long arms around her and then said to Charlotte, "She's the finest human being I've ever met, which, granted, isn't saying much since I've spent most of my life sitting in an office chatting it up with lunatics."

"Present company excluded, dear, of course," Grace added reassuringly.

"In all seriousness, Charlotte, I am not suggesting that you spend your days running around speaking truths that need not be spoken. But you cannot run nor hide from them either. Above all, you must not fear the truth, for if you do, it will destroy you. With courage, you can acknowledge the truth of your life, and when you do, you will find, beneath all of its horrors, there is liberation and energy. And more importantly still, you'll find a certain strength, a freedom, a beauty, a light that can be found nowhere else. Acknowledging truth is a life-changing event; it is the beginning and the end of many paths. Truth is essential to us all. Try as we might, we cannot live without it. It must be faced. It must be spoken. That is our journey. That is our quest."

With a lilting chime, the door to Dr. Elder's office opened and Calvin Broadus, a.k.a. Snoop Dogg, loped in, to the delighted screams of both Lorraine and Shaquana. He was followed by at least two-dozen hipply dressed characters. Some carried clip-boards, some pulled various sized roller-bags filled with God-knows-what, and some lugged boom boxes and headphones. One of the women, obviously the Grand Mistress of Shimmy, vibrated across his threshold, her belt lined from one end to the other with a rainbow of *iPods*.

Dr. Elder watched as his usually sedate waiting room filled to overcapacity. He looked down at Grace. "Are we having a sale?"

Grace Elder smiled as he kissed her softly on the cheek, a smile that stayed with her long after the good doctor disappeared back into his office.

THE SILVER SHOES

Charlotte was looking down, looking lost and far away. There was a bruise under her right eye that grew wider and more pronounced as it continued along the side of her head and then disappeared under her bandages.

With all eyes upon her, she tried to speak, needed to speak, but the weight of what she had to say and the stares of the people she needed to say it to blocked her path forward. She closed her eyes and then out of the darkness came Dr. Elder's voice, as if he were communicating with her from across the room.

Does this thing need saying? If you know the answer is yes, then say it. Say it any way you can. Blurt it out, if necessary, but say it, by

God, say it, and do it quickly. Just open your mouth and speak. Say anything, anything, it doesn't matter what, but don't stop talking until you've said that which must be said.

Charlotte knew this was going to be hard but now with the task as at hand, it felt more like impossible. She had never discussed this with anyone before — not Dr. Elder, not even her father, not anyone — but the events on Old Algiers Point had shaken her badly, providing her with undeniable proof that indeed it must be spoken, it must be faced. There was no hiding from the fact that the secrets of her past still lived and were fully capable of destroying her future if she stood by and let it. Those secrets, she discovered, had but one aim: to finish what was started. They would rise up and strike again and again at each and every opportunity and would not stop until they had finally destroyed her. She knew she could run no longer; the next time there might not be anyone around to save her from the jagged rocks below.

Yes, it needs saying… And so, she opened her mouth and spoke.

"I have something that has been weighing on me for a long time. Something I've been too scared to talk about." Charlotte's left hand squeezed her right. I don't know why I was like that, but I was so scared I couldn't talk about it and then did things that made me so ashamed of myself…" She was rambling, and she knew it, but she knew she had to keep going, even if none of it made sense. She had to say it.

"I, uh, I was good in school. Growing up, I, I was a good student— you know, straight A's and all that. I even had a perfect attendance record."

Geoffrey shifted his weight. Dr. Elder noted that in the process he turned ever so slightly away.

"I never missed a day of school from kindergarten up through nearly the end of the fifth grade. I almost made to the end, but…

but that didn't mean I never got sick. I can remember being sick plenty of times. But no matter how sick I was, my, my mother would send me off to school. Coughs, or colds, even fevers, it didn't matter. She would fill me full of medicine, God knows what it was, and she would take me to school. She told me to put a smile on my face and that I better not to take it off till I got home... So, I smiled..." With that she sat silent, walking the corridors of her past.

"You were sent to school sick and none of your teachers ever noticed?" Dr. Elder asked. He had stationed himself, with pen and pad in hand, furthest from the bed, in a chair near the corner of her room.

"No one noticed — not 'til the end of fifth grade. My mother told me if I ever complained to anyone, she would send me off to boarding school as fast as she could pack my bags and I wouldn't be able to come home for a year."

"Why? Why would she do that to you?"

"She said that I had to learn to be tough, to be strong. That I couldn't grow up to be weak... like..." The words wouldn't come.

"Say it," Dr. Elder said, barely audibly.

"She said that I couldn't grow up to be weak... like my father." She immediately looked over at him. "I'm sorry, Dad."

"Was your father weak?" Dr. Elder asked, redirecting her attention.

"My father...," She stopped. She had to think. "Uh, my father really, really loved my mother. I think he would have done anything for her, anything to make her happy. I think sometimes that can make someone look like they're weak."

Dr. Elder nodded slowly. On his pad, he scribbled:

Her father would do anything for his wife. Anything.

374

Geoffrey shifted, arching his back slightly, inadvertently moving another step away.

"So, you believe that's the reason she would send you to school sick, to toughen you up so you wouldn't be weak like your father?"

"That's what she told me, but I don't think that was really the reason. I think she did it because she was so unhappy, she wanted everyone else to be unhappy, too."

So no one's really happy... Idea from her mother...?

Dr. Elder nodded but wasn't entirely convinced.

"*Unhappy* covers a lot of emotional territory. What did she do that gave you the impression she was unhappy?"

"She was always angry, always…"

"Why? What made her angry?"

"Anything. Everything. Big things, little things. Anything could set her off. You never knew what it was going to be."

Dr. Elder nodded, wrote:

Cause of mother's anger???

"As a child, did you believe that your mother was unhappy and she wanted everyone else to be unhappy, too? Or was that something you came to understand as you grew older?"

"As a child… I thought my mother hated me." Tears and shame.

"Hate is a very strong word. Why would you think that?"

"Well, she was just so perfect and I, I, wasn't. I wasn't anything like her. I was just a big disappointment. I wasn't as pretty as she wanted me to be, or as stylish, or as social, or as popular. I wasn't anything like she wanted me to be. And eventually she was so disappointed with me, she ended up hating me."

She looked up and saw Dr. Elder staring at her, frowning. Their eyes locked. He was saying something to her, but she could see he wasn't speaking. His face, a blank stare and yet as clear as day she heard him ask, "What — did — she — do — to — you?" Then she watched as his gaze turned almost robotically toward her father and asked something that stopped her cold. "Or was it him?"

THE SILVER SHOES

Charlotte's eyes juddered left and right. She was disoriented, a little faint even. The back of her hand moved to her forehead with a long, slow wipe. Laura saw something was wrong and moved to her. "Are you alright?"

"She's fine," Dr. Elder replied flatly. "Charlotte, look at me please." She blinked in his direction, as if struggling for focus. To Donn, he said, "Get her some water," and nodded toward to a blue plastic pitcher on a nearby tray.

Then Geoffrey spoke up. "Doctor, I don't think she's up to—"

"She is stronger than you could possibly imagine. Do not undermine her efforts," the doctor snapped. His attention returned to Charlotte, watching her as she held a clear plastic cup with both hands and sipped. Then he said, "Charlotte, do not be distracted or lose focus as to why we are here, although God knows you'll be tempted. For speaking an unwelcome truth is always difficult. Perhaps one of the most difficult things you will ever do. You are like Frodo on the steps of Mount Doom. You must stay strong and no matter what, keep pushing, keep climbing that mountain — and do not stop until you have. So tell me, why are we here?"

Charlotte glanced not so much at her father but near him and then quickly away. "The reason I told you about my school attendance was because one morning when I was, I don't know, maybe I was ten—" She stopped and corrected herself, looking toward Dr. Elder as she did. "I *know* I was ten… Anyway, I woke up sick, really sick. I was shivering and my body ached. I must have had the flu. But I was sent to school and spent the day trying to make sure no one noticed. I was doing all right until I got to P.E. and our teacher made us run around the track. I ended up falling and I scraped my knee pretty badly. I still have a little scar. I tried, I tried to get up and finish, I really tried, but my leg hurt, and I was feeling so sick and I started to cry. Then our teacher came over. I kept telling her I was okay, but my leg was bleeding, so I was sent to the nurse's office. The nurse could see how sick I was, but I asked her not to call my mother. I remember pleading with her. I begged her and begged her. And finally, she said okay. She said she wouldn't call her. She looked right at me, and she promised. And then twenty minutes later my mother showed up to get me."

"In the car, I kept telling her how sorry I was, but she wouldn't say anything. I was so worried she was going to send me away to boarding school." Charlotte shook her head. Tears rolled down her cheeks. She felt sick but continued on.

"I kept apologizing and telling her it would never happen again and that we could just wait a little while and I could go right back to school. No one would know. But she kept telling me to sit there and be quiet. I told her we could tell the school that she'd just taken me to the doctor's and he said I was fine. I told her it'd be easy. But she wouldn't listen. She just kept telling me to be quiet. But I couldn't. I was so scared. I really needed to make sure she knew that it would never happen again and that I was okay to go right back to school. I just wanted to make sure she wasn't going to send me away from my dad because I always thought he was the only person that really loved me."

Her father loved her, but he would do anything for his wife...

"We were at a stoplight a few blocks from our house. And I didn't want her to even mention about boarding school because once she said something, I knew she'd never change her mind so I kept telling her that I was feeling so much better, that I could even walk back to school. She wouldn't even have to drive me. But she wouldn't say anything. She kept telling me to shut up. I remember pleading and pleading to just pull over. I could walk back to school and everything would be okay. They would never find out. And it would never happen ever again. I don't know, I must have really been bothering her and she just couldn't take anymore because she just exploded. She picked up her hairbrush and started hitting me with it and yelling, *Shut up! Shut up! Shut up! Shut up! Shut up!* And she was just hitting me and hitting me with her brush and really hurting me. I remember I was screaming and screaming but she just wouldn't stop. She wouldn't stop. She kept hitting me and hitting me. And I looked up and I saw the red traffic light, and I said, *It's green! It's green! Go!! Go!!* And we did. And I heard screeching, and a horn I think... and I don't know. I don't remember anything after that."

"When I woke up, I was in the hospital, this same hospital. My father was standing beside my bed. I could see how worried he was. I told him, 'I'm fine, really, I'm fine.' That was why when I told him a little while ago that I was fine, he said, 'I think I've heard that before.' Right?"

Her red eyes looked toward her father. He barely nodded.

"But after the accident, he knew I wasn't fine. The left side of my face and my arm were pretty beaten up. I had a chip, a bone-chip on my left shoulder and three of my fingers were broken. And the worst of it, at least for me was…" She stopped.

"The worst of it was what?"

Charlotte nodded. "The worst of it was a tear on my scalp that ended up getting infected. By the time it healed, I was left having to wear this," she said, reaching into the drawer of her nightstand and with both distain and reverence she slowly removed a swatch of fine netting, slightly smaller than the size of her hand. Wire hooks looped its circumference. On top of the netting appeared to be pink flesh but was actually a resin-based polymer through which flowed several feet of long blonde hair, an exact match of her own. The way she held it, there was something very unsettling about it.

"The doctors said once I was healed, I could have another surgery to remove the scar tissue and have the sides of my scalp sewn together so maybe I wouldn't need this at all or at least not one as large. But afterwards, whenever anyone brought it up, I, I, I wouldn't talk about it. I, I couldn't. I just wanted to push the whole thing away and forget it, pretend it never happened. I was just so… There aren't even words…"

Charlotte looked over to Donn and then back to the hairpiece in her hands. "This is the reason the kid in my class broke up with me. He surprised me and put his hand on the side of my head and felt something strange so I kind of vaguely told him what it was. I guess I didn't do a very good job, or he was too grossed out to listen or something because he told every kid in school, I had a big piece of my skull missing and had to wear a wig to cover it up. He told everyone he saw my brains. That's why I wanted to leave Brentwood Elementary," she said to her father without actually looking at him. "I told you it was too easy for me but…" She finished her sentence with a shake of her head, then she briefly looked at Donn. "And then when we started to talk about it, I thought it was going to be okay. For once in my life, I thought I could talk about it. But then when it came to it I just couldn't. It didn't have anything to do with my ears. It was so stupid. I was so ashamed that after all this time I still couldn't tell you the truth. And you were so sweet and kept calling me. I'm so sorry. That night, everything was so beautiful. It was so special. I just didn't want you to touch it because I was afraid it would wreck everything… and then I wrecked everything. I feel terrible about what happened. And you were so wonderful. I'll never forget that night and everything you did for me, the way you took care of me." She started to cry again.

"Charlotte, I'm so sorry," replied Donn. "I was being such a dope. I should have figured out it was more than you were saying."

"No. I should have told you the truth. Afterward, I was so ashamed I couldn't even speak to you. I didn't want to keep covering it up. So, I decided to do something about it. That's why I'm here. I've had it fixed, completely fixed. So now, I can finally put it all behind me, finally, finally be like it never happened. I know I should have told you, Dad, but I just couldn't. I…, I'm sorry."

Dr. Elder remained silent for a time, letting the others hover over the young girl, offering their sympathies before he interrupted. "Why have you been in the hospital so long? I wouldn't think that kind of repair would require such a long stay?"

"I guess I had a fracture that wasn't visible at the time of the accident but became more pronounced as I grew up, so they wanted to address it."

"Really?" asked Geoffrey.

"Yeah, but I am okay now. Better than before, they said. No restrictions."

"Are you sure—"

"Was your mother hurt in the accident?" interrupted Dr. Elder.

"My mother?" asked Charlotte, regaining her focus on the doctor. "No. No, she wasn't."

"Not at all?"

"Not that I know of, no."

"So your injuries then, they were strictly the result of the beating? Or were some also from the accident?"

"None of us were hurt in the accident. Including the people in the other car."

"None of us" were hurt. Not in other car either.

Dr. Elder nodded. "Did the hospital report your injuries to Children's Authority, or whatever you call it here in the states?"

"CPS. Child Protective Services," Laura replied.

Charlotte took a deep breath, exhaled slowly. "No. I think everyone just assumed I was hurt in the crash. Maybe that's one of the benefits of driving a Jaguar."

"Did your mother ever acknowledge what she did to you?"

"No."

"She never apologized or tried to justify her actions?"

"No."

"Did she even try and bring it up, try to discuss it with you."

"No, not that I recall."

"And you've never discussed this with anyone else before? Not even your father?"

Charlotte eyes shifted downward. Her hands were stroking the strands of blonde hair flowing across her lap. "No, we've never talked about it either. I think Dad tried to bring it up a few times, but I couldn't, I wouldn't talk about it."

"Dad tried to bring it up..." Dad? Not Mom?

"And why is that? A terrible wrong had been done to you and the person responsible was never even questioned about it, just allowed to go about her life as if nothing ever happened. Why didn't you say something to someone, speak to your father about it? Were you angry?"

"I was devastated."

"I'm sure you were. And yet you never mentioned it to anyone, never even told your father what really happened, what could very well happen again."

"Well, that's what I'm doing now. I'm facing it. I've fixed it. Now I can finally let it go. I've lived with it for so long."

"You've fixed the physical manifestation of your beating, not the emotional ones." The doctor paused, thinking, then added, "not the betrayal."

Charlotte twitched. She shook her head. "My father loved my mother. He really loved her. And they already got along so terribly. I didn't want to make things worse."

"That's the reason?" Dr. Elder, skeptically. "In a book perhaps, but not in real life. Fear makes liars of us all. You can't resolve something that you're afraid to face. Humans aren't built that way. Why didn't you tell your father? Because your mother trained you to tough it out?"

Charlotte's voice grew quiet. "I... I don't know."

"If you want to skate through on vague half-truths that is your decision, but I hoped by now that you would understand the importance of demanding more of yourself. I tell you, young lady, this would be a terribly bad note on which to end our relationship. Let's not do that, shall we? Let's show the world how courageous you can be."

Charlotte looked at him, her face slightly cross. Her head was beginning to ache.

"Come on, you can do better than that. What aren't you telling me?"

She glared back at him, this dark sorcerer before her.

"Charlotte, does it need saying?"

"I don't want to keep talking about it. I don't. I don't. We've gone over it. I've faced it. I've fixed it. It's finally behind me know. That's all that matters." She closed her eyes and with the palm of her hand applied pressure to the side of her head. *It hurts...*

"The choice is yours, but I tell you this: No matter how hard it is to speak the truth, it is always easier than it is to live with lies."

"It's not important. It just doesn't matter." She wondered if she could call the nurse to get something for the pain. She looked for the buzzer, the buzzer to call the nurse. *Call the nurse...*

"It doesn't matter? It matters so much you can't even talk about it."

"Doc," Geoffrey interjected, "I think maybe she's getting—"

But the doctor ignored him, continuing, "What are you afraid of, Charlotte? Tell me. Tell me why you're so very afraid?"

"I'm not! I just don't want to talk about it anymore! I just didn't tell anyone. I'm so tired. Can't you get that?" Her incision burned, her head ached. *Where's the buzzer for the nurse?*

"You're not afraid? You're terrified, more terrified than I have ever seen you. Why? Why??" Dr. Elder said, raising his voice.

Charlotte's head sank lower. She winced with pain.

"I know you can do this. I wouldn't have taken you on if I didn't. Now tell me, Charlotte, tell me," he demanded.

Geoffrey interrupted again, this time more forcibly. "Doc, she's-"

"Speak it!" His voice nearly a yell now.

Charlotte eyes shut tight; her head rattled from side to side. The pain, that's all she could think about was the pain…

"Speak it!"

Her lips parted slightly—they did—but nothing came out. Nothing.

"NOW!" the doctor roared.

"Leave her alone!" Geoffrey ordered.

"NOW!"

Charlotte rocked forward, moaned.

"Stop it!" yelled Geoffrey.

"Silence, you fool!" the doctor yelled back. Then, summoning all of his powers, he commanded, "Charlotte–SPEAK–IT–NOW!"

"Leave her alone!"

"NOW!"

"STOP IT!"

"SPEAK!"

"LEAVE HER ALONE!! I'LL TELL YOU—"

"NO, DAD—" Charlotte reached for her father's arm.

"NOW!"

"SHE DIDN'T TELL ME BECAUSE SHE DIDN'T NEED TO. I WAS IN THE CAR WITH HER… THE WHOLE TIME!!"

THE SILVER SHOES

With Geoffrey's words came silence, leaving everyone stranded, unsure of what to think or say or do. Laura, whether she consciously meant to or not, pulled away from him.

"I was… in the car with her… the whole time. I watched my wife beat my daughter…"

"Dad, you…" Charlotte said, crying. "It doesn't matter."

"Of course, it matters. Your doctor's right. We have to talk about it, all of it. No matter what…"

Geoffrey swallowed hard then glanced toward Dr. Elder.

"Please continue," replied the doctor.

Geoffrey nodded. "I, I was home when Charlotte's school called… that day. I remember Victoria was, well, *angry* that she had to drop everything to go get her. She had so many things she needed to do, I guess. I don't know. Anyway, I offered to go but I remember she said 'No!' like it was the stupidest idea she'd ever heard of. She did that a lot. And then she said something like, 'But you could at least offer to drive me,' like she was angry that I hadn't offered."

"So, just like Charlotte said, her knee was all scraped up. We put her in the backseat and Victoria sat back there with her. Charlotte could see her mother was *not happy* and was very apologetic. Growing up, it seemed like Charlotte was always apologizing for something or another, even things that clearly weren't her fault, things that had nothing to do with her, so I thought she was just once again being overly concerned about her mother's feelings and was trying to please her." To Charlotte, he added, "I never knew about Mom threatening you with boarding school. We never talked about that." He shook his head, his eyes glassy. He drifted off for a moment and in almost a whisper, he muttered, "How could we have so much and have so little?" And then, silence.

"Mr. Zukor?" Dr. Elder said, trying to get him back on track.

"Right. Anyway, the more Charlotte tried to make everything okay, the more it annoyed her mother. And the more it annoyed her mother, the more Charlotte tried to make everything okay, until, just like she said, all hell broke loose. When Victoria started hitting her, I tried to reach back and stop her. Then I heard Charlotte yell the light was green, for me to go, so I went and…" Geoffrey raised his hands into the air, his left palm shaking.

"Charlotte was taken by ambulance to the hospital. I was so worried about her, and just sick about everything. Victoria though never really seemed to feel guilty or remorseful about any of it. It was so weird. Right after the accident, I can even remember her angrily asking me how I could have just gone? 'You didn't see that car coming right for us? Weren't you even looking? It was an SUV for Christ's sake!' It was like she was saying it was all my fault, that if we hadn't gotten in the accident, none of this would have happened. I don't know."

"So, what was I supposed to do? Just like Charlotte said, I, I loved Victoria. I don't know why. Was it her beauty?" He shrugged. "But I really loved her. I would have done anything to try and make her happy. God, I tried. I thought about confronting her and demand that she gets some counseling or anger management therapy or something. I thought about it and thought about it. But every time I thought it through, I don't know, no matter what I thought I might say to her, I could never imagine her ever acknowledging what she'd done — not because of anything I said to her anyway. No matter how I imagined bringing it up, she was always so angry, so disgusted at me for having the gall to even suggest such a thing to her. Her response wasn't really so much a denial as it was a reprimand for my misguided loyalty and my daring to think I had the authority to criticize her. 'How dare you?' I would always hear her say, as if she were like above reproach and governed by laws that I couldn't understand. 'How dare you?' I don't know if she really would have reacted like that, but I couldn't imagine her saying anything else." And then with a shrug added, "I don't know, maybe I was just afraid."

"Afraid of what?" asked the doctor.

He shook his head. "I don't know. I've asked myself that question a million times. Was I afraid of… her? Or of losing her? Both? I don't know. Afraid of losing everything we had? Even though she was this whirlwind of anger, and I was nowhere near her match, I always felt I needed to take care of her. It's so preposterous. I don't know."

"Love is complicated," replied the doctor.

"Yeah," said Geoffrey. "Of course I thought about calling the police or Child Services and reporting her but…" Geoffrey shook his head, shrugged again. "It just seemed so… I don't know, I thought if I did anything like that, I would lose her. I didn't know what to do, and so I… I didn't do anything at all. Nothing."

Geoffrey stood silent, alone with his long-held feelings of guilt and inadequacy now exposed for all to see; feelings so personal, so raw, as to make even breathing difficult for those who looked on.

None of them moved, the pain of the moment impenetrable. And that's how things stayed for a good long while.

But then, but then it was Laura, without a word, who stepped back to him and placed her hand on his. Looking on, Dr. Elder thought of all the surprising little acts of love he had witnessed throughout his life and nodded. *The reason God has not forsaken us is because we have not forsaken each other.*

"For what it's worth, I have always been ashamed, really ashamed of how I handled it. I guess that's why I rarely tried to bring it up. But we should have talked about all this a long time ago, Charlotte. I really let you down. I'm so sorry I—" He buried his face in his hands and cried.

"Dad, you—"

"Charlotte," Dr. Elder interjected, "I know this is difficult to hear, but let's let your father speak." His eyes shifted back to Geoffrey. "Please go on, Mr. Zukor. I admire your honesty. I admire it a great deal."

Geoffrey shrugged. "There isn't much more to say. I felt like I was being forced to choose between my wife and my daughter. Like I said, I didn't know what to do so I didn't do anything. I never called the police. I never call Child Services. I never even mentioned it to Victoria, or anyone else. The only thing I knew for certain was I could never let it happen again, which meant I had to make sure that Charlotte was never left alone with Victoria, not ever, not for a single second. Charlotte and I had always been so close anyway, and we always did so many things together, just the two of us, it wouldn't really be that much of a change. I thought if I could keep her safe and still keep us all together, that had to be at least some benefit to Charlotte. I don't know but that's what I told myself."

"But then I'd take a step back and think what I was doing was wrong, that I was just putting myself before my daughter. It worried me then and it has worried me ever since. What kind of man was I? What kind of message was I sending to her? Did I handle it all wrong? Yeah, probably. I probably did. I don't know, but I probably did."

Dr. Elder was looking up toward the far corner of the room and nodding, but there was a frown on his face. Something was still bothering him. "She said, 'shut up?'"

They were all surprised by the question. He tried to explain.

"When your mother was hitting you, you said she yelled, 'Shut up! Shut up!' Are you certain those were her exact words?"

Father and daughter looked at each other, thought about it for a moment. Charlotte shrugged. Geoffrey looked toward the doctor and nodded, saying, "It was something like that. It might have been, 'Stop it!' now that I think about it." Charlotte seemed to agree.

"Sometimes she would say, 'Stop it' in her sleep. I thought I was tossing and turning too much, or snoring, or dreaming wrong— doing something wrong anyway."

Dr. Elder nodded. "Right," he said pensively to no one in particular. Then he turned to Charlotte and asked, "Was there ever a repeat of the incident with your mother, in any form or circumstance? Perhaps even something your father doesn't know about?"

"No."

"Did she ever lay a hand on you after that, even as a method of disciple, like a spanking or grabbing your arm or shaking you? Anything like that?"

"No. I never had much to do with my mother after that. It was like we lived in two separate worlds."

"When you went home after the hospital, did you feel safe? Did you ever worry that your mother might beat you again?"

"No."

"You never worried? What about if you disappointed her, or angered her for some reason? You weren't worried she might lash out?"

"No. I don't know why, but I never was."

"It would be normal and certainly understandable if you had dreams afterward where your mother was hitting you, perhaps a reenactment of what happened in the car or maybe in a different setting. I'll bet your father had dreams about what happened. How often did you have dreams like that?"

"Never. I can't remember a single one," Charlotte answered.

"How about dreams of being attacked by a bear or a shark, monsters, or even an inanimate object, like a car or a house? Anything like that?

"No."

"Any dreams relating to the incident with your mother at all?"

"I can think of one, for sure. I am on a playground at school and some kids would pull off my hairpiece and I'd be completely bald. I've dreamt that a lot, even recently."

"Always children, never adults pulling it off? Never teachers?"

"No, it's always kids, sometimes a lot of them, a big group. One of them would pull it off and then they'd all start laughing at me. Sometimes they'd play keep-away with it and I'd have to chase them, but they never give it back. Sometimes they threw it in the mud, or a puddle of dirty water and I'd have to go get it. I'd put it on and muddy water would run down my face. Sometimes the kids would run away. Sometimes some would stay and laugh at me."

Dr. Elder nodded, turned to Geoffrey. "Shame, but no pronounced fear. Hard to be completely emphatic about it but in my professional opinion, for what that's worth to you, your unorthodox choice might have been precisely the right thing for Charlotte. You see, I believe she has probably struggled with clinical depression her whole life and that might have worked in your favor in a strange way. When she returned home from the hospital, she didn't fear her mother, in part because you made her feel safe, but also because at that point I imagine she didn't really care what happened to her. She was resigned. Over time, by your allowing Victoria to remain in the house, you demystified her and her brutality, which may have gone a long way to prevent further psychological scarring."

"Also, I don't think your wife said, 'Shut up!' when she was hitting your daughter. If she had, I think I'd feel quite differently. I would certainly feel differently if the attack was sexual in nature, but it clearly wasn't. No, I believe your wife was reacting to something else entirely. Perhaps something from her past. I'd like to think about it further, but given your circumstance, the way you chose to handled things may have actually been the wisest choice of all, for everyone concerned. One thing is certain — she's a very lucky girl to have had you for a father. Very lucky indeed. Without you, I think we'd be looking at a very different Charlotte today."

Then he rose from his chair and walked to side of her bed. "It has been my great pleasure meeting you, Charlotte, something I'll not forget. You're a very strong young lady, stronger than you realize even now, perhaps far, far stronger. You have a very good heart, and a very good brain, and certainly all the courage you will ever need. But should you ever come to doubt that, even for a single moment, you be sure to look me up. My door will always open to you, little one."

The doctor then looked into her eyes and beyond, as if they were portals through which he could divine her destiny. After a good long moment, he nodded with a genuine smile. Charlotte wondered what he saw that seemed to interest him so; whatever it was, she found it reassuring, exciting even. His last words to her were whispered. "The vine of brutal soil produces the most miraculous fruit of all." And with nary a word more, Dr. Isaac Elder excused himself, bidding all a good night.

Donn walked Laura back to her office to retrieve a few things and lock up for the evening, leaving Geoffrey at Charlotte's bedside.

"I still feel like I let you down." Geoffrey said, softly.

"Not for one minute, Dad."

"I don't know."

"Not for one single minute of my entire life. I don't know where I would be without you."

Geoffrey smiled at her, a tear falling from his cheek.

"But there is something I've always wanted to ask you. I remember one night when I was still in the hospital. I remember waking up and everything was hazy, but I saw you standing over me and you were glowing like an angel. And you touched my cheek with your hand and there were big tears in your eyes. And you whispered, *I promise I'll never let her hurt you again.* I must have fallen back to sleep because that's all I remember. Was that a dream or did that really happen?"

Geoffrey leaned over and smiled as tears filled his eyes. He gently touched her cheek exactly as she remembered him doing so long ago. Then he nodded and whispered, "I love you, my little angel. I always have and I always, always will."

THE "PRADA INTIFADA" RETURNS!

Special to *The Los Angeles Times*
As reported by Frieda Volipanocha, Associated Press

(Rome, Italy) It was a robbery attempt like few others, stealing not from a bank or a Fendi-laden tourist, but from the nation's most needy and vulnerable.

For nearly 400 years, the Francisco de Christo Orphanage has been Italy's largest caretaker of orphaned and abandoned children, housing 625 boys and girls ranging from newborn to 18 years of age. This venerable institution is famed for taking these young, discarded souls and molding them into many of Italy's most powerful and significant citizens, producing individuals of renowned in nearly every walk of life, be it politics, entertainment, fashion, science, architecture, or finance.

It has been widely publicized that the Francisco de Christo Orphanage receives patronage from some of the wealthiest and most celebrated people in the world. What is lesser known is that over half of its annual budget comes from a most unusual source — one of Italy's most loved attractions, the Trevi Fountain.

Trevi Fountain, designed by poet/architect Nicola Salvi (1697-1751), was constructed over a 34-year span from 1732 to 1766. The fountain features a festival of sumptuous statues and bas-reliefs. Three Popes (Lawrence VII, Morris XIV, and Curlios-Joseph VI) were committed to the completion of the work and, as a tribute, their names are prominently inscribed along the arch supports of the center rotunda. Upon completion, the Trevi became the largest fountain in all of Rome and has remained so to this day.

Depending on whom you ask, it may or may not be the most beautiful fountain in Rome, but it is unquestionably her most famous. Trevi Fountain even served as the focal point of the 1954 film, *Three Coins in a Fountain* featuring the Oscar winning Jule Styne/Sammy Cahn title song of the same name, first popularized by Frank Sinatra. In addition to being a banquet for the eyes, Trevi Fountain, which is fed by a two-thousand-year-old aqueduct constructed during the rule of the Rome's first emperor, Augustus Caesar, is championed by cognoscenti throughout the world for its excellent drinking water, a particular treat for those who love money soaked in their water before drinking.

So famous is the attraction, it plays a central role in the popular legend that states whoever throws a coin into the fountain, will be assured of returning to Rome one day. As a result, busloads of tourists under Rome's spell happily throw thousands upon thousands of coins a day into the large pool of water that forms its base. It was by decree of Pope Shempo II in 1789, successor to Curlios-Joseph VI, that all coins thrown into the fountain become the dominion of the Francisco de Christo Orphanage, in exchange for their upkeep of the masterwork.

The fountain is swept of currency twice a day, except on Good Friday, Easter, and Christmas. Afterward, the coins are carted to the orphanage for processing. First, they are sorted and tallied by nation of origin and then closely filtered by a highly skilled team of experts for their numismatic value. It is rumored that the orphanage's culling of collectable coins accounts for nearly twice as much as the face value of all currency retrieved from the fountain. Once the collectable coins have been carefully restored, they are sold through the orphanage's private network of coin dealers. Although repeatedly queried, officials at the Francisco de Christo Orphanage refused to disclose any information about their dealer network.

Just after 2 a.m. on Sunday, January 14, three children from the orphanage began performing their nightly duties at the Trevi as two French tourists looked on from a table at the Restaurante Trevi Fountain across the piazza. (Those familiar with the recent history of the area will recall that the site where the Restaurante Trevi Fountain now stands was originally the home of Italy's first Kentucky Fried Chicken franchise, the smell of which still remaining quite pronounced despite massive clean-up efforts over extended periods using nuclear-grade solvents.)

As the children completed their work, the French tourists saw four masked young men perhaps in their

20's, arrive on Vespas. The tallest of the lot unsheathed what appeared to be a large, steel hunting knife and demanded the five wet sacks of coins that had just been loaded into the orphanage's wooden cart.

Long had the children been taught that the coins they gathered here were to be honored, revered almost, for it was the fruit of this fountain that kept food in their stomach and clothes on their backs, for themselves and their brothers and sisters, staples that many had not always been accustomed. This kind of indoctrination made simply giving the money to the thieves and running away, impossible.

But before they could figure out what to do, one of the thieves snuck behind and delivered a vicious two-fisted sucker-punch to the back of one of the children's heads. It must have been the way the twelve-year-old girl crumbled into unconsciousness that fueled such a hearty round of laughter and self-congratulations among her attackers.

One of the other children, seeing her older sister hurt, began to scream and cry. The third, a boy of 14, grabbed the cart, yanked it around, and yelled *"Run!"* as he tried to make off in the direction of the orphanage. He didn't get far. One of the assailants took three large steps and then leapt into the air. With a *"Hiyaaa!"* he scissored his left foot down while raising his right, thrusting the heel of his boot deep into the boy's back and sending him forward with such force as to flip him over onto the cart alongside the bags of coin. Bruce Lee would have been so proud, as were the thief's compatriots, who joined in a second round of laughter and high-fives.

"Two down, one to go," the man with the knife said to the young girl hunkered down and crying next her unconscious sister. In response, she scrambled to her feet and backed away, screaming even more hysterically, which succeeded only in motivating her attacker all the more. Not only did he find her crying terribly annoying, he knew it was also far too loud. Someone would hear. How dare she try to screw up his plans...

"You little bitch," he said, and without a second thought plunged his knife into what he hoped would soon be her bloody silence. Surprisingly though, the girl dodged his attack, folding forward as her hips retreated backward, moving like a pulsating squid. The knife missed its mark, succeeding only in catching the tip of her chin. It all happened so quickly. The young girl found herself being spun around, back and away, like a square dance at an ADHD clinic. And then suddenly in her place stood a masked woman wearing a tight, pink one-piece jumpsuit with soft orange trims, tailored perfectly to her athletic form and exposing just enough of her breasts to make thinking about anything else almost impossible. She stood with her feet spread shoulder width apart, her fisted hands placed symmetrically atop each hip. Her posture and proportions were so perfect as to give her the illusion of being much taller than her natural 5-foot, 3-inch frame. Or maybe it was those matching ever-so-provocative pumps. In any case, one thing was clear: *The Prada Intifada had returned!*

She took immediate action, moving so fast the French tourists reported hearing a "*Swoosh!*" as she charged the knife-totting thief. She grabbed his fist with her left hand and seeing the young girl's blood on his blade, whispered a disapproving, "Now that wasn't very gentlemanly of you, was it?" Without waiting for a reply, she rammed her right hand upward into the bottom of his upper bicep, landing with such force that his arm dislocated from his shoulder socket. Letting out a nauseating yelp, he fell to his knees, his forehead pressing hard against the ancient cobblestones. His dislocated arm lay motionless beside him, trailing off in a distinctly unnatural direction.

Standing over him like a conquering hero, the Prada Intifada asked, "Oh, you want something to cry about? I'll give you something to cry about." She took aim and stomped on the back of his calf, shattering both his tibia and fibula.

For some reason, the remaining robbers must have decided on an abrupt career change, as one of them scurried off to the right while the two others fled to the left.

Looking each way, the Prada Intifada released a barely audible, *"Shit!"* In a blur, she was at the wooden cart, grabbed a large bag of coins, and began to spin like a juiced Al Oerter. At precisely the right moment, she released the bag, the centrifugal force sending the bundled coins arching high into the air.

"Hey," she shouted. "You forgot your bag of money!" The robber running right turned, and in that instant his face was reacquainted with that for which he came. No Brooks Robinson he, his nose was forced to do that which his hands could not. Those watching were divided on which hurt more, the speeding bag of coins hitting his head or his speeding head hitting the cobblestone street. He skidded several more meters across the piazza before smacking into a stone gutter.

The two remaining bandits had disappeared toward the Spanish Steps, precisely the direction from which Rome's finest were now arriving in squad cars with their blue lights flashing and sirens blaring.

The Prada Intifada quickly huddled the children together and said, "Meet me back here at 5:30 in the morning, that's just a few hours from now, and I'll have a surprise for you. But promise, not a word to anyone." And then she disappeared in the direction of the orphanage in the blink of a child's tearing eye.

What seemed like a grand idea at 2:15 a.m. had lost most of its luster when 5:20 in the morning rolled around, but still the three children all met near the orphanage gate and silently slipped out toward the fountain. They had done just as they were instructed but were met with only a thick, pre-dawn fog and the sounds of scavenging pigeons. Fifteen minutes passed, as did most of their hope, before the mist began to give way to first light. And then, there it was — their gift.

In shock, they lowered their heads and repeatedly crossed themselves, all the while fervently muttering something or another. But then, one by one, they looked up, sheepishly at first, just to make sure they weren't dreaming; no, they certainly were not dreaming.

Two young men, once thieves in the night, were now facing them, having been duct-taped to each side of mighty Neptune himself, the centerpiece of Trevi Fountain, as water spouted from the mouths of stone fish onto their shivering naked bodies. The robber on the left had the word "WE'RE" painted in red across his chest, while his counterpart to the right finished the sentence with a similarly painted "SORRY."

Screaming with laughter, the orphans hugged and danced, spending the morning telling their tale and celebrating like those with so little, rarely get a chance to do.

THE SILVER SHOES

The room had grown dark, illuminated only by the distant lights of Los Angeles filtered through the evening haze. Charlotte sat just as she had for hours in a crushed chenille chair, running the mirrored maze of her past. A cautiously opened envelope boasting an oversized stamp and addressed in familiar script lay abandoned on an adjacent end table. Its contents, pages of linen stationary, dangled from her hand. It was from her mother.

Dear Charlotte,

I don't know how to write this letter, I only know I must. And so it is finally started, from a balcony at the Hassler, overlooking the City of Rome.

Something has happened here, Charlotte, something I am struggling to understand. I don't know how or why, but something has happened to me.

I arrived tired, so tired of living the empty life I made for myself and for everyone around me, tired of trying to contol the uncontrollable, and most of all I think, tired of running, running from who or what I really am and all the horrors that I've created. I have so much to say to you, my daughter, so much to ask and so much to share, things I have never shared with anyone before. But with you, I must. With you, more than anyone. There is so much you don't know about me, so much I need to explain.

I grew up living in fear, every day, every night— especially the night. For that's what life is like, living in the shadow of a monster — a monster whose name I will never speak. As I grew older, that fear became anger — brooding, black and vicious. How it raged in me, a rage that knew no mercy. I stopped the monster. I will not say how, only know that what I did was utterly inhuman. And never for a single moment have I ever regretted it.

But the cost of my vengence was high. I had lived with a monster but once the monster was no more, I had something far, far worse to fear; the monster in me. The monster was me. Charlotte, the monster is me.

I was so traumatized by what I did, I've lived in fear of my feelings ever since. I pushed them away, but they were always there. I tried to detach myself from who I really was — what I really was. And that was how I lived, angry for being trapped, imprisioned, locked away from myself, my feelings, from everything really important in life — and worst of all, from you. I was lost, all was lost, lost for so very long.

I know I have failed you so completely, my daughter, my perfect, beautiful daughter, your life so cruelly marred by my inadequacies. So frequent and ugly they were, so glaring and humiliating, I was powerless in their presence. But I am powerless no more.

Every kindness you showed me was met, at best, with cool indifference, and at worst, with brutality. Brutality. There, I've said it. My brutality... My God, what have I done? I hit my daughter. No, that isn't the full of it, is it? I beat you. I beat you. It is a shame I will never live down. How could I have ever done that to you? I'm so sorry, my little girl, I am so sorry. What kind of monster have I been? What kind of monster am I still?

And that was not the worst of it. I knew how unhappy you were. And I knew you needed me. I knew. I knew. I always knew. It was all I saw when I looked at you — and so I couldn't look. I couldn't face you without facing myself. And so I pushed you away. What kind of mother pushes their daughter away, a daughter that needs her so much? And you'd come back, over and over again, each time with ever more hopeful and desperate eyes, your fragile, beating heart in your hands as your offering, and needing only a hug in return — and instead, instead I beat you. What have I done, my Charlotte? What have I done to you?

I drown in questions, in regret, in shame. I am a monster. I am now that which I have always feared I was.

My only hope is that you know how sorry I am for my unspeakably shameful behavior and my consistant failure to give you all you so rightfully needed and deserved. I hope you truly know how beautiful, strong, and perfect you are today and have always been. Perfect. And lastly, I hope you know how much I love you, my daughter, my lost treasure.

I pray my deeds from this day forward will prove these things to you as often as you will let me. I have learned much in my new life here and long to share it with you, long to finally make things right, right for both of us, whatever that means, whatever that takes. Will you let me try? Please let me try.

I am flying home, my Charlotte, I am coming home.

Love,

Victoria

— a woman who does not deserve the honor of calling herself a mother, let alone the mother of someone as special as you.

The Ballad of Rosie and Rae
A Love Story
Part Five

(310) 278-4329 to (310) 278-7822

"Rae?"

"Rae? It's Rose."

"Rae? I can barely hear you. Are you okay? What? Are you alright? Have you fallen down or something? I can barely hear you. Can you speak up? Do you need me to come over? Rae, answer me! ARE YOU ALRIGHT? SHOULD I CALL 411?"

Then it came to her. "RAE, ARE YOU HOLDING THE PHONE UPSIDE DOWN AGAIN?"

And just like that, as clear as day, Rae said, "Hello, this is Rae. How can I help you?"

"You were holding the phone upside down again, weren't you?"

"Me?"

"No, the other Rae I'm talking to right now. You were holding it upside down again, weren't you?"

"Oh, and that's supposed to be my fault? I'm not the Einstein that made this thing look exactly the same on both ends. I'll tell you, ever since my son got me this cockamamie cordless phone, it's been hit and miss."

"Rae, maybe it's time you got yourself some help in the house. You know, someone to look after you a bit."

"Oh please, don't start. If I wanted to live with a complete stranger, I'd move in with my son. Anyway, I don't need anyone to look after me. I am doing perfectly fine on my own."

"Rae, you are not doing so perfectly fine, and you know it. Remember last week when I came by with bagels? The phone rang and you couldn't find it, so you looked in the bedroom. Then you picked up your vibrator and said, 'Hello?' Remember that? You nearly chipped your tooth."

"I told you, that was not my vibrator! Someone must have left it there by mistake."

"Oh, sure they did. I hate when that happens. I had the girls over for pan last week, and three of them left their vibrators. In the old days, it would have been sunglasses or car keys. Today, it's vibrators."

"Yeah, well, I don't know how it got there. And if you tell anyone that I have a vibrator, I'll tell everyone about your sex tape."

"Rae, I told you before, *How Harry Met Sally* is not a sex tape."

"Really? Then why is it when Sally comes to deliver the pizza, Harry answers the door with nothing on except some Saran Wrap crinkled around his *schmeckel*?"

"Rae, that's not Saran Wrap."

"Spare me the details, Dr. Ruth."

"Listen, I didn't call to argue. If I wanted to argue, I would have called my daughter."

"So why did you call? Are you working as a telemarketer now, just dialing numbers to bother people?"

"Well, look who woke up on the grouchy side of the bed."

"Rose, what am I going to do? I think you're the only person in the world that really cares about me, you know that?"

"What are you talking about? *Everyone* loves you."

Rae shook her head. "Just because you say it, doesn't make it true. My daughter-in-law, Miss Sour Punnim of 1963, she gets one of those new digital cameras for Hanukkah. So, when she brings the boys by last week, which I think was the first time I've seen them since their *Bris*, she's starts taking all these pictures. You think I don't know what's going on? Please. Mark my words, if I died tomorrow, God forbid, my things would be splattered all over eBay by *Shabbat*."

"Rachael, why do you say such things? You're always so hard on the poor girl."

"Oh, maybe you're right. I should at least give her the benefit of the doubt. She's probably just a nice girl who's developed this sudden desire to become the Ansel Adams of dinette photography. Yeah, that's probably it."

"Very funny, Rae."

"Trust me, if you see her crying while she's sitting *shivah*, you'll know the reason why — my bids didn't come in high enough!"

"Rae, please, let's talk of better things. I've got some good news. Marcy called."

"Marcy? From Florida?"

"Yeah, from Florida. She called to invite us both down for a little vacation. She said we could stay by her."

"In Florida?"

"No, at her old house on Crescent Heights. We'll just tell the new owners Marcy said it would be okay if we stayed by them for a couple of weeks. Yeah, of course, in Florida! At her condo in Miami."

"You expect me to leave Los Angeles to go to Florida? Please. That would be like leaving Paul Newman to run away with Rabbi Berg."

"Rae, there is so much to do in Florida."

"Buying matzo-flavored Geritol at the Piggly-Wiggly is not my idea of a good time."

"I told her maybe we would come next week. She's lonely, Rae, now that Herschel's gone."

"Oy, Herschel, may he rest in pieces. What a piece of work that one was. So now you want me to go all the way to Florida just to listen to Marcy talk about how much she misses that *nogoodnik* husband of hers? Forget it. She never had one nice thing to say about the louse when he was living but now that he's gone, all of a sudden he's Pope Herschel the Perfect."

"I know. It's just like the rabbi says, 'You don't know what you've got until they're not around to aggravate the crap out of you all the time.' And there's something else I want you to think about, too. When we get back, maybe, I don't know but maybe I would give up my apartment and come stay by you, you know, if you wanted me to. I'm a bit lonely here living by myself, and I don't know, but maybe you are too? So, I was thinking we could be like, like roommates."

"Are you kidding? I could never. People might think we're lesbians."

"I'm serious, Rachel. It could be great for both of us."

"Oh sure, just great. When the phone rings, we could have races to see who answers my vibrator first!"

THE SILVER SHOES

Victoria walked down Via G. Relinto toward Banc Paltarese Benedetto with the upward carriage of a top runway model half her age. Her gait, her form, her perfect proportions were noticed by many she passed that day, even attracting the attention of a black limousine that slowed beside her, tracking her progress, and then turned right, stopping at the entrance of a piazza, blocking Victoria's path. A tall, slender Italian wearing a black suit of sumptuous cloth over a released wing-collared shirt, opened the rear passenger door and stood, moving with an effortless charm.

"Madam?"

"Yes?"

"American, just as I thought," he said with a smile. "Please forgive my boldness. I mean you no disrespect. You somehow caught my eye and I had to stop to tell you how fortunate I am to see such a thing of beauty on this day."

Victoria said nothing, just stared at the handsomest man she had ever seen. But it wasn't just that; it was something more, something much more.

"I know, I am a fool, a silly fool. Buena sera, my beauty." The gentleman began his retreat back into the limousine's dark hold and as he did, to Victoria's surprise, it felt like he were taking a part of her with him. The rear door started to close, but then stopped. Two eyes peeked out boyishly from just above the window frame. And as he stood, those eyes, a vibrant mix of blues and browns, returned to her with a directness, a presence, that seemed not only to block out the rest of the world, but redefine the pull of gravity in his direction. Those eyes, so kind, so real, so full of life. There was something very special about those eyes. "My name is—."

"I know," she found herself saying.

He smiled. "I wanted to say hello." He extended his hand.

"Hello," she heard herself say. Her hand found his to be of the finest fabric, conveying a tenderness, a warmth. "I'm cold," she added, as if to explain the temperature of her own, but in the air it sounded more like a private confession.

"No," he replied, still smiling. His eyes caressed her as he whispered. "You are perfect. And you always have been." And there was silence.

They shared this moment, this intimacy, this brief intoxicated melding of their souls. And in it, his skin became her skin, his body her body, his heart her heart as the two united around a core of glorious warmth. And in their joining, her past was sealed away, forgiven by a wash of morning light.

"Thank you, thank you," she said softly and then noticed the tear flowing down her cheek. "Oh, look at me, I'm a mess." She lightly brushed off her dress, to catch her bearings as much as anything else. "I, I have to go. I'm leaving today… for Los Angeles. I miss my daughter."

He smiled in recognition of the truth. "This is hello, not good-bye." He handed her a small, white card. "I will see you again?" he said, half question, half statement.

"Yes."

"What is it you say… pinky promise?" A knowing yet mischievous smile crossed his lips.

She wanted to step back, to understand how all this was possible, how any of this was possible, but staring into his eyes she found no reason to; it was okay. It was all okay. No matter what happened, it would all be okay. "I do," she replied, and then embarrassed her response sounded too much like a marriage vow, she quickly added, "I mean, I, I will."

He raised his hand to which hers was immediately drawn. As their fingers intertwined, he moved into her, close, kissing her cheek, a warm summer breeze after a long, cold winter. And then he whispered, "I do too, my Bella. The perfect one…"

Stepping back, his eyes smiled into hers, imprinting deep and unmistakably. At long last, the world was right again.

As Victoria cornered the red marble columns at the entrance to Banc Paltarese Benedetto, she turned, not so much expecting to see him again but rather to gaze at the spot where they met, where they stood. And though he was gone, the street shimmered with a light, a sparkle, she had never seen before. It was no small thing. It was like she was seeing the world with new eyes.

THE SILVER SHOES

Victoria pushed past the bank's revolving brass doors before nearly tripping over an oak desk, behind which sat a rather odd-looking security guard. The branch manager had moved the desk out of the way on countless occasions only to find it always returned to spot where it was, nearly blocking the bank's entrance. The culprit he knew was sitting at the desk with his trademark scowl firmly affixed to his face, not exactly a welcoming sight for arriving customers. His name was Baobar Benedetto and he sat there perfectly still with only his eyes cranking left and right scouring the scene, ready to pounce on any wrongdoers he might surveil. He was wearing his dress military uniform in dark blue with a matching tie that was knotted precisely around his thick neck and heavily starched white collar. Neither his outfit nor his assumed title, Commander-in-Chief of Security at Banc Paltarese

Benedetto, were bank issue; no, these were all his doing and excused only because his grandfather was the founder of the venerable institution back in 1948. Baobar had come to the bank after a career in the Italian military, which he often referred to as, "his finest days." In truth, his military *career* spanned barely two years, its sole distinction being its utter lack of distinction. Considering his family's influence and connections, had he possessed even the slightest suggestion of ability, he could have easily risen to the rank of Captain. But the only trait Baobar displayed was consistency — and it wasn't the good kind of consistency either. The exact phrased used by an evaluating officer was, "I have marveled, truly marveled, at the consistency of his mind-boggling ineptitude. In short, the man's a boob. And not the good of boob either!"

But being a fool just made Baobar human. What separated him from the rest of us was he was such an obnoxious, insufferable fool. Baobar Benedetto, you see, had an opinion about everything and it seemed the less he knew about something, the stronger his opinions were; suffice it to say, he was a man of *very* strong opinions. A subsequent commander reported him as being, "...an encyclopedia of trivial and incorrect information, delivered in a manner totally devoid of charm or social skill." He went on to add, "And the only thing more offensive than his personality is his body odor. Among the men, he has acquired the nickname, Roquefort." And those were his *finest* days.

After the military, Baobar joined the family business, where his career path resembled that of a pachinko ball hurdling precipitously downward, bouncing from one department to another until finally landing with a dull thud in Security. And even that he could barely handle, his frequent missteps keeping him in a near constant state of reprimand since the day he arrived. Unfortunately, strict instructions from corporate made firing him impossible as was treating him disrespectfully, "...however warranted that most certainly will be." Had it not been for his family, there would be a long list of individuals so sick of him they would have paid handsomely to be the lucky soul graced with the pleasure of giving him the big black boot out of the building, not the least of which being his long-embattled supervisor, Rinaldo Gochi.

Mr. Gochi, once a highly regarded rising star within the institution, had been transferred to Baobar's branch to shore up its sagging performance, an assignment that was rumored to be nothing more than a brief pit-stop before being kicked upstairs to corporate where he would assume a far more prestigious range of responsibilities. Little did he know this "brief pit-stop" would end up not only costing him further advancement and repute, but most of his hair as well. For despite its swanky Via G. Relinto address, which easily made it the best-located branch in the bank's system, Mr. Gochi had been completely ineffective in turning around the underperforming asset. Months and months of exhaustive research developing new marketing strategies amounted to nothing more than a string of crushing failures with his name on it, his every effort undermined by a certain unnamed individual who possessed the seemingly supernatural ability to utterly destroy the goodwill of every single customer he encountered. And so it was that every quarter for the last five years, Mr. Gochi was faced with the dismal task of reporting to the Board of Director the lowest volume of walk-in traffic of any outlet in their network. The look on their faces said it all; he had failed. Mr. Gochi had been asked to tackle a *"specific problem"* but instead had allowed that *"specific problem"* to tackle him. And Gochi knew it, too.

What made dealing with Baobar and his blunders so incredibly aggravating was his intractable conviction that not only had he done nothing wrong, he had actually exercised great wisdom in doing precisely what it was he did, wisdom far beyond the grasp of any "feeble-minded ignoramus" tasked with reprimanding him. His harebrained explanations didn't help either. For instance, he had been rebuked on a number of occasions for his rank castigation of bank customers who failed to appreciate the supreme importance of standing in a laser-straight line while waiting for a teller, once going so far as to strike a "crooked line-stander" with a nightstick he had smuggled in from home. The injured party, now communicating with the bank exclusively through his lawyer, was not at all pleased. And neither was Rinaldo Gochi who was once again charged with resolving a *slight misunderstanding* between Baobar and a long-standing customer of the bank. Most would find it unnecessary to explain why bank employees should not strike one of their customers with a stick, but such was not the case with Baobar, who just sat there across the desk from Rinaldo like he had so many times before, completely unbothered by the stern rebuke he was receiving.

"Oh, please!" Baobar scoffed. "Don't make me laugh. It was nothing! A slight poke to the ribcage and nothing more. I've hit my great grandmamma harder. And on a lot more occasions too! A lot more! Oh sure, Great Grandmamma might have moped around, whimpering for a while but she got over it, pretty much, and I'm sure this whiner will too."

"In fact, that guy should thank me for what I did. I taught him a lesson he should have learned a long time ago. God knows, I did. My grandfather, the founder of this institution, made sure of it. Sure, there were those who thought the reason he was always *accidentally* leaving matches around our house was because he was angry with me for always sneaking up behind his mother and whacking her with a rolling pin, but no, that wasn't it at all. He was simply teaching me the same lesson that I taught that good-for-nothing, line-slacker of yours: If you're going to play with fire, you're going to get burned! Burned! Or at least have a big chunk of your hair singed off the side of your head. A big chunk! You can still smell it in this area around here if you get real close. Go on, smell right along here—" Baobar leaned across the table and thrust the top of his head right into his supervisor's face.

"Oh God, please! Please!" Rinaldo cried, gagging while furiously fanning the air in front of him. "I just ate!"

"Go on, have your fill," Baobar said, this time going so far as to grab his supervisor's shoulders and then mush the top of his head right up into his supervisor's nose with such intensity it would have appeared to a passerby that Boabar was actually attempting to climb up into one of his nostrils. "That burnt hair smell there, that came right from the old man himself."

While leaning over, Baobar noticed that huge waxy flakes of his scalp were floating down, dusting his supervisor's desktop like the first snow of winter. "Oh geez, sorry. Sorry. Let me get that."

Before Rinaldo could stop him, Baobar inhaled and with one impetuous puff blew the dandruff right off his supervisor's desk… and right onto his supervisor and his supervisor's brand-new suit. One particularly large piece of dandruff came to rest on Rinaldo's right eyelash, and then fluttered up and down as he sat there, too horrified to do much more than blink.

"See? Good as new," Baobar said, polishing Rinaldo's desktop with the sleeve of his coat. "But oh, look at you! *Uuuhhhgghh!* You're disgusting! No wonder our loan volume is way off. You've not only lost all your hair, Ri-*bald*-o, but now you're losing all of your scalp too! You know, you really should think about changing shampoos. It's like I always say, good hygiene is the bedrock of a good first impression. And you can quote me on that, too. I mean if there's anything I know all about, it's making a good first impression!"

Rinaldo Gochi couldn't help but smile. He was daydreaming about running Baobar over with his car. And then backing up and running over him again. And then backing up and running over him again. And then again. And again.

And then going home and getting his wife's car and running over him a few times with that. Okay, maybe more than a few times.

And then hijacking a big, yellow school bus full of really fat kids and running him over with that for an hour or two.

And then maybe a tank… Yeah, he borrows a big ol' tank from the base outside of town and…

"Anyway," Baobar barked, "I can't sit around all day giving you advice, as much as you need it, Rinaldo *Career-stalled-o!* At the rate things are going around here, you'll be lucky if they keep you on as my assistant, which, I'll have you know, I've made a few inquiries about upstairs, believing that under my tutelage you might just be salvageable. Oh sure, it's going to take a while for me to impart all of my accumulated my wisdom on the proper way to…"

Rinaldo nearly barfed in his mouth. *Me? Baobar's assistant?!? Oh God, no! Nooo! Nooooo!!* He suddenly felt faint…

THE SILVER SHOES

When Rinaldo Gochi came to, he wasn't sure where he was or how long he'd been there; he only knew he was awoken by the most horrifying sound he had ever heard—the sound of Baobar Benedetto rambling on about something or another, as he was apt to do.

"But I didn't always feel that way. No, there was a time I used to think my grandfather, our beloved founder, made the biggest mistake of his life when he didn't select me to succeed him as president when he retired. I did. And Mother was very angry about it too. *Very* angry. She told me I needed to get in there and prove myself, show the old man how capable I was and how much I wanted it. So, I'd get up bright and early and go to his office to plead my case. Oh, I tried persuading him. I tried insisting, even demanding. I even begged and pleaded for him to let me be president. I'd get so worked up, I'd make myself sick. Actually sick!

But I did it so the old man could see just how much I cared. He could also see what I had for breakfast — 'cause it was usually right there, splattered all over his carpet. But no matter what I did, the man never changed his mind. Never! Oh, he changed his carpet a couple of times, sure. He even changed his office and his phone number, and no one would tell me where his new one was or how I could reach him, but he never changed his mind."

"But because he and I were so much alike, it didn't take me long to realize just how right my grandfather was. Oh sure, I would have made a fine president. Everyone in the bank knows that. They even told me so at one of our Christmas parties. I'll never forget that night, no siree. I remember I had just informed the old man that I was so angry for being passed over for president, that I was quitting, effective immediately, to pursue other, more prestigious opportunities elsewhere, perhaps even with a competitor! Well, before I could say another word, grandfather popped up, grabbed a microphone, and told everyone to quiet down because he had major announcement to make. I remember the tears streaming down his face when he announced that I was leaving the bank and that I promised never to return!"

"Well, everyone cheered. They were shouting and cheering and even dancing on tables, they were so happy for me. It was wild! Every single person there told me what a great decision I'd made. They even put me on a chair and picked me up and carried me around the room. Boy, it was something. You know, it's very tricky to stay on those chairs when they're way up like that. It kept bobbing up and down and every once in a while, I'd slip off and land right on my shoulder or my back, which really did kind of hurt. But they were all so great. They'd run right over and pick me up and put me back on the chair. And then they'd yell, "One, two, three!" and I'd fly off further and further, and everyone would cheer and cheer for me. I've never forgotten it. Once they shot me so high in the air, I hit the chandelier! It kind of knocked me backwards, I think. I can't remember exactly because I blacked out when I hit the ground but I'm pretty sure I ended up landing like right on my face in the middle of the dance floor because for the longest time I had this parquet pattern imprinted across my forehead. Let me tell you, that one *really* hurt. But even that didn't damper their enthusiasm, not a single bit! When I came to, they all cheered and high-five'd each other and put me right back up on that chair again. Boy, I was flying all over that room. And everywhere I landed people were cheering and cheering for me — except my mother who was yelling for them to stop, but they weren't really listening to her. Well, not until she really started screaming and hitting them with a candlestick she picked up from one of the tables. Then they finally stopped, which was a good thing I guess because my grandfather was getting a little carried away and started yelling, 'Out the window! Out the window!' and we were on the top of this building. He was such a joker, that guy. What a sense of humor!"

"Yeah, that night was really something. You can't imagine how touching it was to look around and see all those really blurry people so happy for me. I mean I always knew I was very popular among the employees, but I never knew I was *that* popular! The outpouring of love was so touching, I was crying like a baby. Well, I was also crying because they threw me off that chair so many times, I had these shooting pains running down my spine and my back was spasming and then after a while my entire left side went numb, like completely numb. I mean, I couldn't really stand or move my arm or anything after that. And my head, oh my head was— You see, once I landed right on one of those serving carts and a soup ladle jabbed me right in the eye. Take my word for it, pea soup stings like a motherfucker! Whoa, what a night! I'll never forget it!"

Baobar continued on, as he was apt to do. "And how could I? I mean, after such a show of love and support, what was I supposed to do, just up and leave? Could I really be so selfish and think only of my own success and glory? No, I could not! Afterall, I am a Benedetto! I realized then and there that this is where I belonged! And this is where I shall stay forever and ever! And trust me, Gochi, you've never seen anything like the look on my grandfather's face when I told him of my decision. He was so relieved, he started crying too, the old softy. In fact, he cried so much, he completely dehydrated himself! Doctors said they never saw anything like it! They had to take him to some kind of special hospital where he stayed for a very long time."

"But now I can clearly see the genius of my grandfather's decision. I mean, what do presidents really do anyway? Make a few decisions, have some drinks, play 'Guess How Many Fingers That Is?' with the secretary. That's about it, right? But my grandfather knew that as Commander-in-Chief of Security, I'd be down here, right on the front lines where the *real* work gets done, always on hand to save this bank's ass whenever the need arises. And let me tell ya', by whacking that line slacker of yours, that was exactly what I did!"

Baobar stood, grabbed his pants and shimmied his belt up to just under his armpits. "So, goatshit, why don't you just concentrate on doing your job right for once and let me do mine. Okay, Mr. Rinaldo *Always-So-Appalled-o?*"

THE SILVER SHOES

Once past Baobar's desk and into the bank's lobby, a small brass sign directed Victoria along a swoop of red velvet rope where she was eventually stopped by the all too familiar smile of young girl at the end of a teller cue. She startled Victoria, the girl's round face and bright blue eyes shining under a raggedy mop of loose blonde curls, lassoed back with a twilight blue bow. She was dressed in a clean white cotton blouse, trimmed with a simple Dutch-boy collar, over which hung a solid twilight-blue vest bearing an embroidered crest on the left chest plate. Her shirt was knee length, pleated in blue and white Scottish plaid and hovered above knee-high white socks that flowed down into a pair of rounded toe, matte-white Buster Browns. In her arms, she held an equally blonde and mopped-topped Cairn terrier, whose round black eyes were filled with a humanity few non dog lovers ever take the time to notice.

"Well, hello," Victoria said in reply to the girl's stare. "My, what big, beautiful eyes you have." The girl, suddenly shy, ducked behind her mother's skirt, only to reappear seconds later, eyes bigger than ever. "You know something, you look a lot like my daughter when she was your age. She was very beautiful, too. *Very* beautiful..." The young girl disappeared again, leaving Victoria to drift off into the past where she found young Charlotte dutifully waiting, sitting in the passenger seat of her car, looking innocent and perfect, with her big eyes staring back up at her—a mere mortal on Mt. Olympus, standing before the Gods. As Victoria reached to touch her face, a thin line of blood began running from corner of her eye, and then another—tears of blood. Then another sprang from her Charlotte's scalp. And then from her nose. Charlotte reached out for her as more and more blood began to stream down her face.

"Momma! Momma!!" she cried.

Oh my God... Oh my... Victoria stepped back, nearly toppling over the velvet rope.

"Madame? Madame?" asked the woman standing with the young girl.

"Oh, yes, I, I..." Victoria struggled to wipe the image away. "I'm, I'm okay, thank you. I'm fine." She tried to regain her focus on the present as much for herself as to ease the look of concern on the woman's face. "She looks just like my daughter." And then, so softly that only she could hear, "...only happier."

From her friendly but confused reaction, Victoria could tell the woman probably spoke little English.

"My daughter... Mi fanciulla."

The woman frowned, still not quite understanding, but then offered, "Somiglia a sua figlia? …Come si dice? Same face your daughter?"

"Yes, yes." This brought smiles to both women's faces.

"This, my Lita. Beautiful face, beautiful heart."

"Yes. A beautiful face and a beautiful heart."

THE SILVER SHOES

Baobar never saw it coming. The back of his head flattened against a considerable blow. Whatever pain had registered from the initial impact was nothing compared to the blinding shock-wave that rippled through him when his nose led his face into the top of his desk. He heard cartilage and bones disintegrating in an explosion of white, rendering him unconscious.

"SILENCIO!"

"SILENCIO!"

"SILENCIO!"

Three times the word rang out, each from a different corner of the large domed lobby, followed by startled screams.

"SILENCIO!! This is a bank robbery. Cooperate and you will live. If you do not, you will die. So, which of you wants to die today? Is it you? Is it you?" asked a tall, ugly, unshaven man dressed in a black hoodie, his face so in shadow as to make distinguishing his features impossible. He moved with a limp out from behind Baobar's desk toward the teller cue.

His two accomplices, also dressed in black and positioned on opposite ends of the teller windows, hopped the short walls separating the customers from the operations side of the bank. One of them swiftly corralled the employees and hustled them away into a back office while the other began moving from drawer to drawer, filling a black canvas duffle with fists of cash. The tallest of the three herded the ten or so waiting customers to the far end of the lobby, which was lined with molasses-stained writing desks used for the computation of deposit receipts, bank notes, and the like. He ordered them to the floor, face down, hands extended over their heads. The young girl, Lita, buried herself in her mother's skirt and started to cry.

"*Shhh!*" Victoria whispered, kneeling as she softly brushed away her tears. "Look at me. You mustn't cry. Nothing will happen to you. I promise." The girl found something reassuring in her eyes.

"Now!" their captor yelled to the three of them. As Lita's mother reached for the floor, he placed the heel boot on her backside and sent her skidding forward and down, hard onto the veined marble floor.

"Momma!" Lita cried in panic, scrambling to her mother's side.

"DOWN! NOW!!" He screamed with such anger and force everyone fell immediately to the floor. He scanned the bank, then checked his watch. "Dom, hurry!"

"Keep your panties on, Patricia" Dominic replied, looting the last drawer.

How he hated when his brother called him that, such a cocky little asshole. His eyes returned to his flock of the frightened as he removed a large black handgun from his jacket pocket, pointed it in the air and ran his right palm along its bridge, first forward, then back. Even those who had never been in the presence of a firearm before recognized the sound of a bullet being loaded into the chamber. "I SAID, PUT YOUR HANDS ABOVE YOUR HEAD!! NOW!!!"

Quivering palms quickly complied. As Lita arms stretched outward, her dog twisted and escaped her grasp.

With instincts buried deep in his DNA, instincts honed during the breed's thousand-year survival in the wild, they suddenly returned anew, rushing through him with every beat of his heart and promptly turning what had been a gentle and affectionate pooch back into an undomesticated killing machine. With fury and abandon, the dog charged the gunman. He intuitively sensed his target's most vulnerable area, leapt into the air, and then, with all of his might viciously bit down, embedding his teeth deeply, deeply, ever so deeply. Unfortunately, all that ever so deep embedding was not into the robber, but into the robber's flapping pant leg. That small miscalculation seemed of little import to the four-and-a-half-pound Cairn terrier who must have thought he had his enemy by the juggler as he proudly and with great machismo thrashed his head from side to side. Surely, he sensed victory was at hand.

I gotcha! Oh, yes I do! So give it up, sucka, 'cause you is goin' down! thought the pooch. *I sure hope they're getting all this on video, cause I gotcha now, big boy!*

But then seemingly out of nowhere, a giant hand swooped down, grabbed him by his light blue collar, and yanked him high into the air.

I gotcha! I — Aiyee, aiyee, aiyee, you gotch me! You gotch me! All right already, you gotch me! I give! I give already! So much for the deeply buried instincts of the Cairn terrier.

As the dog yelped, horror-struck by his sudden inability to breath, Lita sprang to his rescue. Victoria had been waiting for the right time to strike but it had not arrived, too many guns, too many people. But now she could wait no longer. She had to move.

In one fluid movement, Victoria rolled onto her back and then kicked both of her heels into the air as she undulated her body, bucking herself like a fallen bronco rider in reverse right back up onto her feet. Her plan was not to take out the gunman but rather she would grab Lita, wrap her in her arms, and then fall back to the floor; hopefully that would placate him. Then, with the girl safe, she would do what she could to save the dog. Victoria took two quick steps, leaned, and began to unfurl her long arms, a la Elasto-Girl.

Almost... almost...

But the girl's mother also began to move to her daughter's rescue, her rising body tripping Victoria and sending them both tumbling over onto the marble floor.

"Nooo! Mio cane! Mio cane!" little Lita screamed, trying to jump high enough into the air to grab him.

Victoria scrambled back to her feet, but again she was not alone. From her left came a barreling, if shaky, "HALT!!!"

To everyone's surprise, Baobar stood teetering a few feet in front of his desk, blood flowing from his nose, across his lips and chin, and soaking a portion of shirt. His right arm was fully extended and in his trembling hand he held what looked like a German Lugar. The bank robber responded by dropping the dog and then scooping up Lita in his left arm for cover. With his right, he locked the sights of his handgun on Baobar.

Victoria watched as Baobar's eyes widened in reaction to being the final resting place of a soon to be incoming bullet. His facial muscles began to wince, telegraphing his next move. Victoria shouted, *"NNNOOOOOOOO!"* but knew it was useless. And then to life, to God, and to her fate now revealed, she repeated, "No.... no..."

As Baobar eyes narrowed to nothing, he pulled the trigger. By then, Victoria was already airborne, diving toward Lita. With all of her strength, she pushed the young girl into her captor, sending them both tumbling backwards.

THE SILVER SHOES

The first police unit arrived minutes later, finding a confused mob in the street in front of the bank. The sound of ringing alarms echoed between buildings. Early reports were that shots had been fired inside. As the policemen scrambled to assess the situation, Lita's mother burst through the crowd, screaming, "She's hurt! Hurry!! HURRY!!"

One of the officers blared something into a microphone strapped to his shirt as he followed her though the bank's revolving doors.

"There! There!"

THE SILVER SHOES

Victoria knew these were her last moments, her last words. She looked into the face of the young girl beside her mother, both of them kneeing over her. She could think only of her daughter. Blood pooled on the floor beneath her.

"Beautiful face, beautiful heart. My daughter...I was going home to her after being away... for so long... forever...

She blinked tears from her eyes. "...tell her that I always loved her... always... my little girl... I didn't... I didn't... sorry... I'm so sorry... I'm so sorry." She let out an anguished scream.

But then, in the young girl's eyes, she saw another. She saw the eyes of the man she met on the street. Or was she confused? No, no she didn't think so. They seemed so much like his eyes. His eyes... She felt like she was falling into them... The world grew pale, thin. There was no air.

She spoke, her voice a whisper, "I never... I never held my daughter... never held her..."

Her last words, "I never told her that I love her..."

Her confession a cry, a pitched, nearly silent cry, a cry that silenced everything....

It was that cry, that confession, more than anything else, that killed her.

THE SILVER SHOES

A spring, sometime in the future.
Cedars-Sinai Medical Center
Maternity Ward, Room 594

With red, watery eyes all around, Geoffrey Zukor gazed with wonder over Donn's shoulder as he held a newborn, tightly wrapped in a white flannel blanket, striped in pink and blue, the bulk of which taking on all the appearances of an overstuffed #3 from Pepe's House of Burritos. The infant was crowned with a pink knit cap, the word LOVE embroidered across the brim, a hand-made gift from Cedars-Sinai's Woman's Guild.

"Isn't she the most beautiful thing you've ever seen?" Donn asked.

"B'ruch Ashem," Geoffrey whispered, thanking Gd.

Donn kissed her softly on the cheek. "You know, instead of new car smell, car washes should offer new baby smell."

"Maybe we should pass that along to P-Dawg?" Geoffrey asked.

Laura shook her head. "You're terrible."

"My turn," Geoffrey said, taking the baby from Donn, holding her, staring at her. "She's perfect, isn't she?"

"As perfect as her mother," Charlotte added with a squeeze of Laura's hand. "Can I get you anything?"

"Bring me my baby, would you? With those two baby hogs around, I've barely gotten a chance to see her."

Charlotte smiled and walked to the far side of the bed. "Boys, do you think it would be okay if mom got a chance to hold her for a minute?"

"A whole minute?" asked Donn.

"You know, Laura's been through so much today, maybe she should rest for a while. Donn and I can handle things here." Geoffrey kissed the baby and nuzzled his nose gently across her cheek.

"Come on, cough her up."

Geoffrey looked at Donn. "We could make a run for it?"

"Not with Charlotte around. Have you ever seen her run? The girl's fast! I'm not kidding. I've never seen anyone run as fast as she can. And she's not even winded afterward. It's amazing."

"Really?" Geoffrey looked at Charlotte.

"Really," answered Donn. "She's not just fast. She's like weird fast."

"She probably gets it from me," Geoffrey replied. "You know I'm weird fast. Really. I can eat a glazed donut in 3.2 seconds. Even faster when I'm depressed."

"Wow, you are fast. I had no idea."

"Yeah. I can also really wolf them down when I'm angry. Or I'm frustrated. Or when I'm—"

"Dad, don't start."

"You know, one of Charlotte's uncles owns a donut shop right in Westwood. Why don't you tell him about it, Charlotte?" Geoffrey went back to nuzzling his baby.

"Very funny, *Zook*. Now quit your stalling and give her to me."

"Stalling? Who's stalling?" asked Donn.

"Beats me. Neither of us are stalling," said Geoffrey. And then to Charlotte, he added, "She's really something, isn't she? Look."

Charlotte looked down at her new baby sister, instantly captivated.

"Hey, isn't it my turn to hold her now?" asked Donn.

"You just gave her to me."

"What are you talking about? That was like twenty minutes ago."

"No way. That was like a minute and a half ago."

"Come on. My turn." But then Donn added, "She likes it if you kind of rock back and forth."

"Like this?"

"Yeah, that's perfect. See. See how she's kind of smiling?"

"She is kind of smiling, isn't she?

"Okay, my turn." Donn took the baby back into his arms.

"She likes it when you rock her," Geoffrey told Donn. "But not too much. We don't want her getting seasick."

"Right. How's this?"

"Perfect. Look at her. She's really smiling!"

"She *is* smiling," Charlotte said, surprised. Then she leaned toward her father and whispered, "Am I completely crazy or does she look exactly like mom?"

"Victoria?" Geoffrey whispered back.

Charlotte nodded.

Geoffrey glanced toward Laura, who lay resting with her eyes closed. The coast was clear. "I've been thinking the exact same thing! She looks just like your mom's baby picture, the one in your room in the porcelain frame. It's the weirdest thing I've ever seen in my life! And look at this..." He opened the baby's blanket. "These are your mother's hands. Exactly. Look at the long fingers. See how perfect they are. And her toes, too. Same thing. Exactly like your mother's."

"That is so weird!" Charlotte said.

"I know," Geoffrey nodded. Then he leaned in toward the baby. "Victoria, is that you?"

Baby Zukor's hand shot up and smacked Geoffrey's cheek so hard it nearly knocked him over.

"What was that?" Laura asked, awakened by the sound of the slap.

"Nothing," said Geoffrey.

"No, nothing," agreed Charlotte.

But then Geoffrey and Charlotte looked at each other and in unison mouthed the words, *Oh—my—God!*

THE END

AFTERWORD

A few things have happened since our story ended…

A month after returning from Florida, Rae moved in with Rose, two best friends since childhood, now roommates. Sophie, Rose's daughter, came to visit that afternoon, finding them in the kitchen.

"Who put this on your front door, Ma?" Sophie held up a piece of paper printed with the words, "We're Lesbians!" Rose did a slow take to Rae, a stern look on her face.

"What?" said Rae. "I thought I'd give the neighbors a little something to talk about!"

After another arrest, a very short stint at AA, then a brutal bar fight that resulted in a 9-day hospitalization and months of rehabilitation, and then finally, a more committed return to AA, P-Dawg was back on top, marketing his patented *"New Baby Smell"* to carwashes and consumers nationwide.

"Yes, finally *your* car can smell as fresh as the day *you* were born!"

Donn Olson was eventually cleared to return to work where he was named Employee of the Year and selected to run Southwest's Emergency Operations Training Center. He is still dating Charlotte, who has never been happier.

They sometimes return to that lone cypress tree on Old Algiers Point.

And then there are times when Donn returns there alone.

And speaking of Charlotte, at Dr. Sheinman's invitation, she accepted a full-time position at Cedars-Sinai as Laura's assistant before eventually becoming the youngest — and certainly least shy — Director of Public Relations the hospital has ever had.

And perhaps most importantly of all, there's the matter of a recent *Los Angeles Times* article about a mysterious, masked, twenty-something year old woman clad in a provocative Prada jumpsuit who single-handedly saved…

(Although no one knows for certain except the Governors of the Given, the emergence of this mysterious, young crime fighter on the L.A. scene might just have been the reason they intervened in Geoffrey's life in the first place.)

As for Dr. Sheinman, Dr. Alacombre, and Dr. Elder, well, they continue doing what our Gods have intended all of us to do: to spend our lives taking good care of each other.

They seem to instinctually know that by changing *JUST ONE LIFE,* they might just change the world.

◈   ◈   ◈

The author welcomes comments at

www.ECintheOC.com
ec@ecintheoc.com

Made in the USA
Las Vegas, NV
15 December 2023

82906860R00260